They closed the case.

And hoped the killer was dead.

Years later it's up to Harry Bosch
to make them right.

THE
NARROWS

more...

THE
NARROWS

ALSO BY MICHAEL CONNELLY

THE NARROWS

MICHAEL CONNELLY

WARNER BOOKS

NEW YORK   BOSTON

Copyright © 2004 by Hieronymus, Inc.
All rights reserved. No part of this book may be reproduced in any form or by any electronic or mechanical means, including information storage and retrieval systems, without permission in writing from the publisher, except by a reviewer who may quote brief passages in a review.

Warner Vision is a registered trademark of Warner Books.

Warner Books

Time Warner Book Group
1271 Avenue of the Americas, New York, NY 10020
Visit our Web site at www.twbookmark.com

Printed in the United States of America

Originally published in hardcover by Little, Brown and Company
First International Paperback Printing: September 2004
First United States Paperback Printing: March 2005

10 9 8 7 6

ATTENTION CORPORATIONS AND ORGANIZATIONS:
Most WARNER books are available at quantity discounts with bulk purchase for educational, business, or sales promotional use. For information, please call or write: Special Markets Department, Warner Books, Inc. 135 W. 50th Street, New York, NY 10020-1393.
Telephone: 1-800-222-6747 Fax: 1-800-477-5925.

In memory of Mary McEvoy Connelly Lavelle,
who kept six of us out of the narrows

All they did was trade one monster for another. Instead of a dragon they now have a snake. A giant snake that sleeps in the narrows and bides its time until the moment is right and it can open its jaws and swallow someone down.

— JOHN KINSEY, *father of a boy lost in the narrows,* Los Angeles Times, *July 21, 1956*

THE
NARROWS

I THINK MAYBE I only know one thing in this world. One thing for sure. And that is that the truth does not set you free. Not like I have heard it said and not like I have said it myself the countless times I sat in small rooms and jail cells and urged ragged men to confess their sins to me. I lied to them, tricked them. The truth does not salvage you or make you whole again. It does not allow you to rise above the burden of lies and secrets and wounds to the heart. The truths I have learned hold me down like chains in a dark room, an underworld of ghosts and victims that slither around me like snakes. It is a place where the truth is not something to look at or behold. It is the place where evil waits. Where it blows its breath, every breath, into your mouth and nose until you cannot escape from it. This is what I know. The only thing.

I knew this going in on the day I took the case that would lead me into the narrows. I knew that my life's mission would always take me to the places where evil waits, to the places where the truth that I might find would be an ugly and horrible thing. And still I went without pause. And still I went, not being ready for the moment when evil would come from its waiting place. When it would grab at me like an animal and take me down into the black water.

I

SHE WAS IN DARKNESS, floating on a black sea, a starless sky above. She could hear nothing and see nothing. It was a perfect black moment but then Rachel Walling opened her eyes from the dream.

She stared up at the ceiling. She listened to the wind outside and heard the branches of the azaleas scratching against the window. She wondered if it was the scratching on glass or some other noise from within the house that had awakened her. Then her cell phone rang. She wasn't startled. She calmly reached to the bed table. She brought the phone to her ear and was fully alert when she answered, her voice showing no indication of sleep.

"Agent Walling," she said.

"Rachel? It's Cherie Dei."

Rachel knew right away that this would not be a Rez call. Cherie Dei meant Quantico. It had been four years since the last time. Rachel had been waiting.

"Where are you, Rachel?"

"I'm at home. Where do you think I'd be?"

"I know you cover a lot of territory now. I thought maybe you—"

"I'm in Rapid City, Cherie. What is it?"

She answered after a long moment of silence.

"He's resurfaced. He's back."

Rachel felt an invisible fist punch into her chest and then hold there. Her mind conjured memories and images. Bad ones. She closed her eyes. Cherie Dei didn't have to use a name. Rachel knew it was Backus. The Poet had resurfaced. Just as they knew he would. Like a virulent infection that moves through the body, hidden from the outside for years, then breaking the skin as a reminder of its ugliness.

"Tell me."

"Three days ago we got something in Quantico. A package in the mail. It contained—"

"Three days? You sat on it for three—"

"We didn't sit on anything. We took our time with it. It was addressed to you. At Behavioral Sciences. The mail room brought it down to us and we had it X-rayed and then we opened it. Carefully."

"What was in it?"

"A GPS reader."

A global positioning system reader. Longitude and latitude coordinates. Rachel had encountered one on a case the previous year. An abduction out in the Badlands where the missing camper had marked her trail with a handheld GPS. They found it in her pack and traced her steps back to a camp where she had encountered a man and he had followed her. They got there too late to save her but they would have never gotten there at all if it hadn't been for the GPS.

"What was on it?"

Rachel sat up and swung her legs over the side of the bed. She brought her free hand to her stomach and closed it like a dead flower. She waited and soon Cherie Dei continued. Rachel remembered her as once being so green, just an observer and learner on the go team, assigned to her under the bureau's mentoring program. Ten years later and the cases, all the cases, had etched deep grooves into her voice. Cherie Dei wasn't green anymore and she needed no mentor.

"It had one waypoint in its record. The Mojave. Just inside the California border at Nevada. We flew out yesterday and we went to the marker. We've been using thermal imaging and gas probes. Late yesterday we found the first body, Rachel."

"Who is it?"

"We don't know yet. It's old. It had been there a long time. We're just starting with it. The excavation work is slow."

"You said the *first* body. How many more are there?"

"As of when I left the scene last we were up to four. We think there's more."

"Cause of death?"

"Too early."

Rachel was silent as she thought about this. The first questions that ran through her filters were why there and why now.

"Rachel, I'm not calling just to tell you. The point is the Poet is back in play and we want you out here."

Rachel nodded. It was a given that she would go there.

"Cherie?"

"What?"

"Why do you think he was the one who sent the package?"

"We don't think it. We know it. We got a match a little while ago on a fingerprint from the GPS. He replaced the batteries on it and we got a thumb off of one of them. Robert Backus. It's him. He's back."

Rachel slowly opened her fist and studied her hand. It was as still as a statue's. The dread she had felt just a moment before was changing. She could admit it to herself but no one else. She could feel the juice begin moving in her blood again, turning it a darker red. Almost black. She had been waiting for this call. She slept every night with the cell phone near her ear. Yes, it was part of the job. The call outs. But this was the only call she had truly been waiting for.

"You can name the waypoints," Dei said in the silence. "On the GPS. Up to twelve characters and spaces. He named this point 'Hello Rachel.' An exact fit. I guess he still has something for you. It's like he's calling you out, has some sort of plan."

Rachel's memory dredged up an image of a man falling backward through glass and into darkness. Disappearing into the dark void below.

"I'm on my way," she said.

"We're running it out of the Vegas field office. It will be easier to keep a blanket on it from there. Just be careful, Rachel. We don't know what he has in mind with this, you know? Watch your back."

"I will. I always do."

"Call me with the details and I'll pick you up."

"I will," she repeated.

Then she pushed the button that disconnected the call. She reached to the bed table and turned on the light. For a moment she remembered the dream, the stillness of the black water and the sky above, like black mirrors facing each other. And her in the middle, just floating.

2

GRACIELA MCCALEB WAS WAITING by her car outside my house in Los Angeles when I got there. She had been on time for our appointment but I had not. I quickly parked in the carport and jumped out to greet her. She didn't seem upset with me. She seemed to take it in stride.

"Graciela, I am so sorry I'm late. I got backed up on the ten with all the morning traffic."

"It's okay. I was kind of enjoying it. It's so quiet up here."

I used my key to unlock the door. When I pushed it open it wedged against some of the mail that was on the floor inside. I had to bend down and reach around the door to pull the envelopes free and get the door open.

Standing and turning back to Graciela I extended my hand into the house. She passed by me and entered. I didn't smile under the circumstances. The last time I had seen her was at the funeral. She looked only marginally better this time, the grief still holding in her eyes and at the corners of her mouth.

As she moved past me in the tight entry hall I smelled a sweet orange fragrance. I remembered that from the funeral, from when I had clasped her hands with both of mine, said how sorry I was for her loss and offered my help if she needed it in any way. She was wearing black then. This day she was wearing a flowery summer dress that went better with the fragrance. I pointed her to the living room and told her to have a seat on the couch. I asked if she wanted something to drink, even though I knew I had nothing in the house to respond with but probably a couple bottles of beer in the box and water from the tap.

"I'm fine, Mr. Bosch. No thank you."

"Please, call me Harry. Nobody calls me Mr. Bosch."

Now I tried a smile but it didn't work on her. And I didn't know why I expected it would. She'd been through a lot in her life. I'd seen the movie. And now this latest tragedy. I sat down in the chair across from the couch and waited. She cleared her throat before speaking.

"I guess you must be wondering why I needed to talk to you. I was not very forthcoming on the phone."

"That's all right," I said. "But it did make me curious. Is something wrong? What can I do for you?"

She nodded and looked down at her hands, which held a small black-beaded purse on her lap. It looked like something she might have bought for the funeral.

"Something is very wrong and I don't know who to turn to. I know enough about things from Terry—I mean how they work—to know I can't go to the police. Not yet. Besides, they'll be coming to me. Soon, I suppose.

But until then, I need someone I can trust, who will help me. I can pay you."

Leaning forward I put my elbows on my knees and my hands together. I had only met her that one other time—at the funeral. Her husband and I had once been close but not in the last few years and now it was too late. I didn't know where the trust she spoke of came from.

"What did Terry tell you about me that would make you want to trust me? To choose me. You and I don't really even know each other, Graciela."

She nodded like that was a fair question and assessment.

"At one time in our marriage Terry told me everything about everything. He told me about the last case you two worked together. He told me what happened and how you saved each other's life. On the boat. So that makes me think I can trust you."

I nodded.

"He one time told me something about you that I always remembered," she added. "He told me there were things about you he didn't like and that he didn't agree with. I think he meant the way you do things. But he said at the end of the day, after all the cops and agents he had known and worked with, if he had to pick somebody to work a murder case with, that it would be you. Hands down. He said he would pick you because you wouldn't give up."

I felt a tightness around my eyes. It was almost like I could hear Terry McCaleb saying it. I asked a question, already knowing the answer.

"What is it you want me to do for you?"

"I want you to investigate his death."

3

EVEN THOUGH I KNEW it was going to be what she would ask me, Graciela McCaleb's request gave me pause. Terry McCaleb had died on his boat a month earlier. I had read about it in the *Las Vegas Sun*. It had made the papers because of the movie. FBI agent gets heart transplant and then tracks down his donor's killer. It was a story that had Hollywood written all over it and Clint Eastwood played the part, even though he had a couple decades on Terry. The film was a modest success at best, but it still gave Terry the kind of notoriety that guaranteed an obituary notice in papers across the country. I had just gotten back to my apartment near the strip one morning and picked up the *Sun*. Terry's death was a short story in the back of the A section.

A deep tremor rolled through me when I read it. I was surprised but not that surprised. Terry had always seemed to be a man on borrowed time. But there was nothing suspicious in what I had read or what I had then heard when I went out to Catalina for the funeral service. It had been his heart—his new heart—that had failed. It had given him six good years, better than the national average for a heart transplant patient, but then it had succumbed to the same factors that destroyed the original.

"I don't understand," I said to Graciela. "He was on the boat, a charter, and he collapsed. They said . . . his heart."

"Yes, it was his heart," she said. "But something new has come up. I want you to look into it. I know you're retired from the police, but Terry and I watched on the news last year what happened here."

Her eyes moved around the room and she gestured with her hands. She was talking about what had happened in my house a year earlier when my first post-retirement investigation had ended so badly and with so much blood.

"I know you still look into things," she said. "You're like Terry was. He couldn't leave it behind. Some of you are like that. When we saw on the news what happened here, that's when Terry said he would want you if he had to pick someone. I think what he was telling me was that if anything ever happened to him, I should go to you."

I nodded and looked at the floor.

"Tell me what has come up and I will tell you what I can do."

"You have a bond with him, you know?"

I nodded again.

"Tell me."

She cleared her throat. She moved to the edge of the couch and began to tell it.

"I'm a nurse. I don't know if you saw the movie but they made me a waitress in the movie. That's not right.

I'm a nurse. I know about medicine. I know about hospitals, all of it."

I nodded and didn't say anything to stop her.

"The coroner's office conducted an autopsy on Terry. There were no signs of anything unusual but they decided to go ahead with the autopsy at the request of Dr. Hansen—Terry's cardio doctor—because he wanted to see if they could find out what went wrong."

"Okay," I said. "What did they find?"

"Nothing. I mean, nothing criminal. The heart simply stopped beating . . . and he died. It happens. The autopsy showed that the muscles of the heart's walls were thinning, getting narrow. Cardiomyopathy. The body was rejecting the heart. They took the normal blood samples and that was it. They released him to me. His body. Terry didn't want to be buried—he always told me that. So he was cremated at Griffin and Reeves and after the funeral service Buddy took the children and me out on the boat and we did what Terry asked. We let him go then. Into the water. It was very private. It was nice."

"Who is Buddy?"

"Oh, he is the man Terry worked with on the charter business. His partner."

"Right. I remember."

I nodded and tried to retrack her story, looking for the opening, the reason she had come to see me.

"The blood scan from the autopsy," I said. "What did they find in it?"

She shook her head.

"No, it's what they didn't find."

"What?"

"You have to remember that Terry took a ton of meds.

Every day, pill after pill, liquid after liquid. It kept him alive—I mean, until the end. So the blood scan was like a page and a half long."

"They sent it to you?"

"No, Dr. Hansen got it. He told me about it. And he was calling because there were things missing from the scan that should have been there but weren't. CellCept and Prograf. They weren't in his blood when he died."

"And they're important."

She nodded.

"Exactly. He took seven capsules of Prograf every day. CellCept twice a day. These were his key meds. They kept his heart safe."

"And without them he would die?"

"Three or four days would be all it would take. Congestive heart failure would come up quickly. And that is exactly what happened."

"Why did he stop taking them?"

"He didn't and that is why I need you. Someone tampered with his meds and killed him."

I pushed all of her information through the grinder again.

"First, how do you know he was taking his medicine?"

"Because I saw him and Buddy saw him and even their charter, the man they were with on the last trip, said he saw him taking his meds. I asked them. Look, I told you, I'm a nurse. If he wasn't taking his meds I would've noticed."

"Okay, so you are saying he was taking his pills but they weren't really his pills. Somebody tampered with them. What makes you say that?"

Her body language indicated frustration. I wasn't making the logic jumps she thought I should be making.

"Let me back up," she said. "A week after the funeral, before I knew anything about all of this, I started to try to get things back to normal and I cleared out the closet where Terry kept all his meds. You see, the meds are very, very expensive. I didn't want them to go to waste. There are people who can barely afford them. *We* could barely afford them. Terry's insurance had run out and we needed Medi-Cal and Medicaid just to pay for his medicine."

"So you donated the meds?"

"Yes, it's a tradition with transplants. When somebody . . ."

She looked down at her hands.

"I understand," I said. "You give everything back."

"Yes. To help the others. Everything is so expensive. And Terry had at least a nine-week supply. It would be worth thousands to somebody."

"Okay."

"So, I took everything across on the ferry and up to the hospital. Everybody thanked me and I thought that was that. I have two children, Mr. Bosch. As hard as it was, I had to move on. For their sake."

I thought about the daughter. I had never seen her but Terry had told me about her. He'd told me her name and why he had named her. I wondered if Graciela knew that story.

"Did you tell Dr. Hansen this?" I asked. "If somebody tampered with them you have to warn them that—"

She shook her head.

"There's an integrity procedure. All the containers are examined. You know, the seals on bottles are checked, expiration dates checked, lot numbers checked against recall and so on. Nothing came up. Nothing had been tampered with. Nothing I had given them, at least."

"Then what?"

She moved closer to the edge of the couch. Now she would get to it.

"On the boat. The open containers I didn't donate because they don't take them. Hospital protocol."

"You found tampering."

"There was one more day's dosage of Prograf and two more days of CellCept in the bottles. I put them in a plastic bag and took them to the Avalon clinic. I used to work there. I made up a story. I told them a friend of mine found the capsules in her son's pocket while doing the laundry. She wanted to know what he was using. They ran tests and the capsules—all of them—were dummies. They were filled with a white powder. Powdered shark cartilage, actually. They sell it in specialty shops and over the Internet. It's supposed to be some sort of homeopathic cancer treatment. It's easily digestible and gentle. Contained in a capsule, it would have tasted the same to Terry. He would not have known the difference."

From her small purse she pulled out a folded envelope and handed it to me. It contained two capsules. Both white with small pink printing running along the side.

"Are these from the last dosage?"

"Yes. I saved those two and gave four to my friend at the clinic."

Using the envelope to catch its contents I used my fingers to pull one of the capsules open. It came apart freely without damaging the two pieces of the casing. The white powder it had held poured into the envelope. I knew then that it would not be a difficult process to pour the intended content of the capsules out and to replace it with a useless powder.

"What you are telling me, Graciela, is that when Terry was on that last charter he was taking pills he thought were keeping him alive but they weren't doing a thing for him. In a way, they were actually killing him."

"Exactly."

"Where did those pills come from?"

"The bottles came from the hospital pharmacy. But they could have been tampered with anywhere."

She stopped and allowed time for this to register with me.

"What is Dr. Hansen going to do?" I asked.

"He said he has no choice. If tampering took place in the hospital, then he has to know. Other patients could be in danger."

"That's not likely. You said two different medicines had been tampered with. That means it likely happened out of the hospital. It happened after they were in Terry's possession."

"I know. He said that. He told me he is going to refer it to the authorities. He has to. But I don't know who that will be or what they will do. The hospital is in L.A. and Terry died on his boat about twenty-five miles off the coast of San Diego. I don't know who would—"

"It would probably go to the Coast Guard first and then it will be referred to the FBI. Eventually. But that will take several days. You could move it along if you called the bureau right now. I don't understand why you are talking to me instead of them."

"I can't. Not yet anyway."

"Why not? Of course you can. You shouldn't be coming to me. Go to the bureau with this. Tell the people he worked with. They'll go right at this, Graciela. I know they will."

She stood up and went to the sliding door and looked out across the pass. It was one of those days when the smog was so thick it looked like it could catch on fire.

"You were a detective. Think about it. Someone killed Terry. It could not have been random tampering—not with two different meds from two different bottles. It was intentional. So, the next question is, who had access to his meds? Who had motive? They are going to look at me first and they may not look any further. I have two children. I can't risk that."

She turned and looked back at me.

"And I didn't do it."

"What motive?"

"Money, for one thing. There's a life insurance policy from when he was with the bureau."

"For one thing? Does that mean there is a second thing?"

She looked down at the floor.

"I loved my husband. But we were having trouble. He was sleeping on the boat those last few weeks. It's probably why he agreed to take that long charter. Most of the time he just did day trips."

"What was the trouble, Graciela? If I'm going to do this, then I have to know."

She shrugged as if she didn't know the answer but then answered it.

"We lived on an island and I no longer liked it. I don't think it was a big secret that I wanted us to move back to the mainland. The problem was, his job with the bureau had left him afraid for our children. Afraid of the world. He wanted to shelter the children from the world. I didn't. I wanted them to see the world and be ready for it."

"And that was it?"

"There were other things. I wasn't happy that he was still working cases."

I stood up and joined her next to the door. I slid it open to let some of the stuffiness out. I realized I should have opened it as soon as we got inside. The place smelled sour. I'd been gone two weeks.

"What cases?"

"He was like you. Haunted by the ones that got away. He had files, boxes of files, down on that boat."

I had been in the boat a long time ago. There was a stateroom in the bow McCaleb had converted into an office. I remembered seeing the file boxes on the top bunk.

"For a long time he tried to keep it from me but it became obvious and we dropped the pretext. In the last few months he was going over to the mainland a lot. When he didn't have charters. We argued about it and he just said it was something he couldn't let go of."

"Was it one case or more than one?"

"I don't know. He never told me what exactly he was working on and I never asked. I didn't care. I just wanted him to stop. I wanted him to spend time with his children. Not those people."

"Those people?"

"The people he was so fascinated by, the killers and their victims. Their families. He was obsessed. Sometimes I think they were more important to him than we were."

She stared out across the pass as she said this. Opening the door had let the traffic noise in. The freeway down below sounded like a distant ovation in some sort of arena where the games never ended. I opened the door all the way and stepped out onto the deck. I looked down into the brush and thought about the life-and-death struggle that had taken place there the year before. I had survived to find out that, like Terry McCaleb, I was a father. In the months since, I had learned to find in my daughter's eyes what Terry had once told me he had already found in his daughter's. I knew to look for it because he had told me. I owed him something for that.

Graciela came out behind me.

"Will you do this for me? I believe what my husband said about you. I believe you can help me and help him."

And maybe help myself, I thought but didn't say. Instead I looked down at the freeway and saw the sun reflected on the windshields of the cars moving through the pass. It was like a thousand bright, silver eyes were watching me.

"Yes," I said, "I will do it."

4

MY FIRST INTERVIEW WAS on the docks at the Cabrillo Marina in San Pedro. I always liked coming down this way but rarely did. I didn't know why. It was one of those things you forget about until you do it again and then you remember that you like it. The first time I arrived I was a sixteen-year-old runaway. I made my way down to the Pedro docks and spent my days getting tattooed and watching the tuna boats come in. I spent my nights sleeping in an unlocked towboat called *Rosebud*. Until a harbormaster caught me and I was sent back to the foster home, the words *Hold Fast* tattooed across my knuckles.

Cabrillo Marina was newer than that memory. These weren't the working docks where I had ended up so many years before. Cabrillo Marina provided dockage for pleasure craft. The masts of a hundred sailboats poked up behind its locked gates like a forest after a wildfire. Beyond these were rows of power yachts, many in the millions of dollars in value.

Some not. Buddy Lockridge's boat was not a floating castle. Lockridge, who Graciela McCaleb told me was her husband's charter partner and closest friend at the end, lived on a thirty-two-foot sailboat that looked like it had the contents of a sixty-footer on its deck. It was a junker, not by virtue of the boat itself but by how it was cared for. If Lockridge had lived in a house it would've had cars on blocks in the yard and walls of stacked newspapers inside.

He had buzzed me in at the gate and emerged from the cabin wearing shorts, sandals and a T-shirt worn and washed so many times the inscription across the chest was unreadable. Graciela had called him ahead of time. He knew I wanted to talk to him but not the exact reason why.

"So," he said as he stepped off the boat onto the dock. "Graciela said you are looking into Terry's death. Is this like an insurance thing or something?"

"Yes, you could say that."

"You like a private eye or something?"

"Something like that, yeah."

He asked for identification and I showed him the laminated wallet copy of my license that had been sent to me from Sacramento. He raised a quizzical eyebrow at my formal first name.

"Hieronymus Bosch. Like that crazy painter, huh?"

It was rare that someone recognized the name. That told me something about Buddy Lockridge.

"Some say he was crazy. Some think he accurately foretold the future."

The license seemed to appease him and he said we could talk in his boat or we could walk over to the chandlery to get a cup of coffee. I wanted to get a look inside his home and boat—it was basic investigative strategy —but didn't want to be obvious about it so I told him I could use some caffeine.

The chandlery was a ship's store that was a five-minute walk down the dock. We small-talked as we walked over and I mostly listened to Buddy complain about his portrayal in the movie that had been inspired by McCaleb's heart transplant and his search for his donor's killer.

"They paid you, didn't they?" I asked when he was finished.

"Yes, but that's not the point."

"Yes it is. Put your money in the bank and forget about the rest. It's just a movie."

There were some tables and benches outside the chandlery and we took our coffees there. Lockridge started asking questions before I got the chance. I let him run his line out a little bit. My view was that he was a very important piece of my investigation, since he knew Terry McCaleb and was one of two witnesses to his death. I wanted him to feel comfortable with me so I let him ask away.

"So what's your pedigree?" he asked. "Were you a cop?"

"Almost thirty years. With the LAPD. Half of the time I worked homicides."

"Murders, huh? Did you know Terror?"

"What?"

"I mean, Terry. I called him Terror."

"How come?"

"I don't know. I just did. I give everyone nicknames.

Terry had seen firsthand the terror of the world, you know what I mean? I called him Terror."

"What about me? What's my nickname going to be?"

"You . . ."

He looked at me like a sculptor sizing up a block of granite.

"Um, you are Suitcase Harry."

"How come?"

"Because you're sort of rumpled, like you live out of a suitcase."

I nodded.

"Pretty good."

"So, did you know Terry?"

"Yes, I knew him. We worked a few cases together when he was with the bureau. Then one more after he got the new heart."

He snapped his fingers and pointed at me.

"Now I remember, you were the cop. You were the one who was here that night on his boat when those two goons showed up to do him in. You saved him and then he turned around and saved you."

I nodded.

"That's right. Now can I ask some questions, Buddy?"

He spread his hands wide, indicating he was available and had nothing to hide.

"Oh, sure, man, I didn't mean to be hogging the microphone, you know?"

I took out my notebook and put it on the table.

"Thanks. Let's start with that last charter. Tell me about it."

"Well, what do you want to know?"

"Everything."

Lockridge expelled his breath.

"That's a tall order," he said.

But he began to tell me the story. What he initially told me matched the minimal accounts I had read in the Las Vegas papers and what I had then heard when I attended McCaleb's funeral. McCaleb and Lockridge had been on a four-day, three-night charter, taking a party of one into waters off Baja California to fish for marlin. While returning to Avalon Harbor on Catalina on the fourth day McCaleb collapsed at the boat's topside helm station. They were 22 miles off the coast, midway between San Diego and Los Angeles. A help call was radioed to the U.S. Coast Guard and a rescue chopper was dispatched. McCaleb was airlifted to a hospital in Long Beach, where he was pronounced dead on arrival.

When he was finished telling it I nodded like it had matched everything I had already heard.

"Did you actually see him collapse?"

"No, not really. I felt it, though."

"How do you mean?"

"Well, he was up on top at the wheel. I was in the pit with the charter party. We were headed north, going home. The party'd had enough fishing by then so we weren't even trolling. Terry had it flat out, probably doing twenty-five knots. So me and Otto—he's the party—we were in the cockpit and the boat suddenly made a ninety-degree turn to the west. Out to sea, man. I knew that wasn't in the plan so I climbed up the ladder to poke my head up there and I see Terry sort of hunched over the wheel. He'd collapsed. I got to him and he was alive but, man, he was out of it."

"What did you do?"

"I was a lifeguard once. Venice Beach. I still know my CPR. I called Otto up on top and I went to work on Terry while Otto got control of the boat and got on the radio to call the Coast Guard. I was never able to bring Terry around but I kept putting air into him until that helicopter showed up. Took them long enough, too."

I wrote a note in my notebook. Not because it was important but because I wanted Lockridge to know I took him seriously and that whatever he thought was important was also important to me.

"How long did they take?"

"Twenty, twenty-five minutes. I'm not sure how long but it seemed like an eternity when you're trying to keep somebody breathing."

"Yeah. Everybody I talked to said you did your best. So you're saying he never said a word. He just collapsed at the wheel."

"Exactly."

"Then what was the last thing he said to you?"

Lockridge started chewing the nail on one of his thumbs as he tried to recall this.

"That's a good question. I guess it was when he came back to the railing that looks down into the cockpit and he yelled down that we'd be home by sunset."

"And how long was this before he collapsed?"

"Maybe a half hour, maybe a little longer."

"He seemed fine then?"

"Yeah, he seemed like the regular Terror, you know? Nobody could've guessed what was going to happen."

"By now you men had been on the boat for four straight days, right?"

"That's right. Pretty close quarters because the party

got the stateroom. Me and Terry bunked it in the forward cabin."

"During that time did you see Terry take his meds every day? You know, all the pills he had to take."

Lockridge nodded emphatically.

"Oh, yeah, he was popping his pills right and left. Every morning and every night. We'd been out on a lot of charters together. It was his ritual—he set his watch by it. He never missed. And he didn't on this trip either."

I made a few more notes just to keep silent so that Lockridge might keep talking. But he didn't.

"Did he say anything about them tasting different, or him feeling different after taking them?"

"Is that what this is about? You people are trying to say Terry took the wrong pills and then not have to pay the insurance? If I had known that, I would've never agreed to talk to you."

He started to get up from his bench. I reached over and gripped his arm.

"Sit down, Buddy. That's not what this is about. I don't work for the insurance company."

He dropped heavily back onto the bench and looked at his arm where I had gripped it.

"Then what is it about?"

"You already know what it's about. I'm just making sure Terry's death was what it was supposed to be."

"Supposed to be?"

I realized that I had used an unfortunate choice of words.

"What I'm trying to say is that I want to make sure he didn't have any help."

Lockridge studied me for a long moment and slowly nodded.

"You mean like the pills were tainted or messed with?"

"Maybe."

Lockridge set his jaw tightly with resolve. It looked genuine to me.

"You need any help?"

"I might need some, yeah. I'm going over to Catalina tomorrow morning. I'm going to look at the boat. Can you meet me there?"

"Absolutely."

He seemed excited and I knew I would eventually drop a rock on that but for now I wanted his full cooperation.

"Good. Now let me ask a few more questions. Tell me about the charter party. Did you know this guy Otto beforehand?"

"Oh, yeah, we take Otto out a couple times a year. He lives over there on the island, that's the only reason why we got the multiday charter. See, that was the problem with the business but Terror never cared. He just was happy to sit there in that little harbor and wait on half days."

"Slow down a second, Buddy. What are you talking about?"

"I'm talking about Terry keeping the boat over there on that island. What we got over there were people who are visiting Catalina and want to go fishing for a few hours. We didn't get the big charters. The three-, four-, five-day jobs where you make the good money. Otto was the exception because he lives over there and he wanted to go fishing off Mexico a couple times a year and get his ashes hauled in the process."

Lockridge was giving me more information and avenues of questioning than I could handle at once. I stayed on McCaleb but would definitely come back to Otto, their charter client.

"You're saying that Terry was content to sort of be small-time."

"Exactly. I kept telling him, 'Move the charter over here to the mainland, put out some ads and get some serious work.' But he didn't want to."

"Did you ever ask him why?"

"Sure, he wanted to stay on the island. He didn't want to be away from the family all the time. And he wanted time to work on his files."

"You mean his old cases?"

"Yeah, that and some new ones."

"What new ones?"

"I don't know. He was always clipping articles out of the newspaper and sticking them in files, making phone calls, things like that."

"On the boat?"

"Yeah, on the boat. Graciela wouldn't allow it in the house. He told me that, that she didn't like him doing it. Sometimes it got to the point he was sleeping on the boat at night. At the end. I think it was because of the files. He'd get obsessed with something and she'd end up telling him to stay on the boat until he got over it."

"He told you that?"

"He didn't have to."

"Any case or file you remember he was interested in lately?"

"No, he no longer included me in that stuff. I helped

him work on his heart case and then he sort of shut me out of that stuff."

"Did that bother you?"

"Not really. I mean, I was willing to help. Chasing bad guys is more interesting than chasing fish, but I knew that was his world and not mine."

It sounded too much like a stock answer, like he was repeating an explanation McCaleb had once given to him. I decided to leave it at that but I knew this was a subject I would come back to with him.

"Okay, let's go back to Otto. You fished with him how many times?"

"This was our third—no, fourth—trip."

"Always down to Mexico?"

"Pretty much."

"What does he do for a living that he can afford to do this?"

"He's retired. Thinks he's Zane Grey and wants to go sportfishing, catch a black marlin and put it up on his wall. He can afford it. He told me he was a salesman, but I never asked what he sold."

"Retired? How old is he?"

"I don't know, midsixties."

"Retired from where?"

"Just across the water. Long Beach, I think."

"What did you mean a minute ago when you said he liked to go fishing and get his ashes hauled?"

"I meant exactly that. We took him fishing and when we'd stop off in Cabo, he always had something on the side."

"So each night on this last trip, you guys brought the boat into port, always to Cabo."

"The first two nights in Cabo and then the third night we made it to San Diego."

"Who chose those places?"

"Well, Otto wanted to go to Cabo, and San Diego was just the halfway point on the trip back. We always take it slow going back."

"What happened in Cabo with Otto?"

"I told you, he had a little something on the side down there. Both nights he got cleaned up and went into town. I think he was meeting a senorita there. He had made some calls on his cell phone."

"Is he married?"

"Far as I know. I think that's why he liked the four-day charters. His wife thought he was out there fishing. She probably didn't know about stopping in Cabo for a Margarita—and I'm not talking about the drink."

"What about Terry, did he go into town?"

He answered without hesitation.

"Nope, Terry had nothing going in that department and he would never leave the boat. He'd never even step on the dock."

"How come?"

"I don't know. He just said he didn't need to. I think he was superstitious about it."

"How so?"

"You know, the captain stays with the vessel, that sort of thing."

"What about you?"

"Most of the time I hung with Terry and the boat. Every now and then I'd go to town to one of the bars or something."

"What about on that last trip?"

"No, I stayed with the boat. I was a little short of bread."

"So on that last trip, Terry never got off the boat?"

"That's right."

"And nobody besides you, Otto and him were ever on the boat, right?"

"That's—well, not exactly."

"What do you mean? Who was on the boat?"

"On the second night going into Cabo we got stopped by the *federales*. The Mexican Coast Guard. Two guys came on board and looked around for a few minutes."

"Why?"

"It's sort of a routine. Every now and then they stop you, make you pay a little tariff, then they let you go."

"A bribe?"

"A bribe, a payoff, a bite, whatever you want to call it."

"And that happened this time."

"Yeah, Terry gave them fifty bucks when they were in the salon and then they split. It was all pretty fast."

"Did they search the boat? Did they look at Terry's medicine?"

"No, it didn't get to that. That's what the payoff is for, to avoid all of that."

I realized I hadn't been taking notes. A lot of this information was new and worth exploring further but I sensed that I had enough for the moment. I would digest what I had and come back to it. I had a feeling that Buddy Lockridge would give me whatever time I needed, as long as I made him feel like a player in the investigation. I asked him for the exact names and locations of the marinas where they had docked overnight on the trip with Otto and I did write this information in my notebook. I then reconfirmed our appointment on McCaleb's boat for the next morning. I told him I was taking the first ferry across and he told me he'd be on it as well. I left him there because he said he wanted to go back into the chandlery to pick up some supplies.

As we dumped our coffee cups into the trash can, he wished me luck with the investigation.

"I don't know what you're going to find. I don't know if there is anything to find, but if Terry had help with this, I want you to get whoever it was who helped him. You know what I am saying?"

"Yes, Buddy, I think I know what you are saying. I'll see you tomorrow."

"I'll be there."

5

O N THE PHONE THAT night from Las Vegas my daughter asked me to tell her a story. Just five years old, she was always wanting me to sing to her or tell her stories. I had more stories than songs in me. She had a scruffy black cat she called No Name and Maddie liked me to make up stories involving great peril and bravery that ended with No Name winning the day by solving the mystery or finding the lost pet or the lost child or teaching a bad man a lesson.

I told her a quick story about No Name finding a lost cat named Cielo Azul. She liked it and asked me for another but I said it was late and I had to go. Then, out of the blue, she asked me if the Burger King and the Dairy Queen were married. I smiled and marveled at how her mind worked. I told her they were married and she asked me if they were happy.

You can become unhinged and cut loose from the world. You can believe you are a permanent outsider. But the innocence of a child will bring you back and give you the shield of joy with which to protect yourself. I have learned this late in life but not too late. It's never too late. It hurt me to think about the things she would learn about the world. All I knew was that I didn't want to teach her anything. I felt tainted by the paths I had taken in my life and the things I knew. I had nothing from it I wanted her to have. I just wanted her to teach me.

So I told her, yes, the Burger King and the Dairy Queen were happy and that they had a wonderful life together. I wanted her to have her stories and her fairy tales while she could still believe them. For soon enough, I knew, they would be taken away.

Saying good night to my daughter on the phone felt lonely and out of place. I had just come off of a two-week trip out there and Maddie had gotten used to seeing me and I had gotten used to seeing her. I picked her up at school, I watched her swim, I made dinner for her a few times in the small efficiency apartment I had rented near the airport. At night when her mother played poker in the casinos I took her home and put her to bed, leaving her under the watch of the live-in nanny.

I was a new thing in her life. For her first four years she had never heard of me and I had never heard of her. That was the beauty and difficulty of the relationship. I was struck with sudden fatherhood and reveled in it and did my best. Maddie suddenly had another protector who floated in and out of her life. An extra hug and kiss on the top of the head. But she also knew that this man who had suddenly entered her world was causing her mother a lot of pain and tears. Eleanor and I had tried to keep our discussions and sometimes harsh words away from our daughter but sometimes the walls are thin and kids, I was learning, are the best detectives. They are masterful interpreters of the human vibe.

Eleanor Wish had withheld the ultimate secret from me. A daughter. On the day she finally presented Maddie to me, I thought that everything was right in the world. My world, at least. I saw my salvation in my daughter's dark eyes, my own eyes. But what I didn't see that day were the fissures. The cracks below the surface. And they were deep. The happiest day of my life would lead to some of the ugliest days. Days in which I could not get past the secret and what had been kept from me for so many years. Whereas in one moment I thought I had everything I could possibly want from life, I soon learned I was too weak a man to hold it, to carry the betrayal hidden in it in exchange for what I had been given.

Other, better men could do it. I could not. I left the home of Eleanor and Maddie. My Las Vegas home is a one-room efficiency across the parking lot from the place where millionaire and billionaire gamblers park their private jets and head by whispery limos to the casinos. I have one foot in Las Vegas and one remains here in Los Angeles, a place I know I can never leave permanently, not without dying.

After saying good night my daughter handed the phone to her mother, who was on a rare night at home. Our relationship was more strained than it had ever been. We were at odds over our daughter. I didn't want her to grow up with a mother who worked nights in the casinos. I didn't want her eating at Burger King for dinner. And I didn't want her to learn about life in a city that wore its sins on its sleeve.

But I was in no position to change things. I know that I run the risk of seeming ridiculous because I live in a place where the randomness of crime and chaos is always near and poison literally hangs in the air, but I don't like the idea of my daughter growing up where she is. I see it as the subtle difference between hope and desire. Los Angeles is a place that operates on hope and there is still something pure about that. It helps one see through the dirty air. Vegas is different. To me it operates on desire and on that road is ultimate heartbreak. I don't want that for my daughter. I don't even want it for her mother. I am willing to wait, but not that long. As I spend time with my daughter and know her better and love her more, my willingness frays at the middle like a rope bridge crossing a deep chasm.

When Maddie handed the phone back to her mother neither of us had much to say, so we didn't. I just said I would check in with Maddie the next time I could and we hung up. I put the phone down, feeling an ache inside I was not used to. It wasn't the ache of loneliness or emptiness. I knew those pains and had learned how to live with them. It was the pain that came with a fear for what the future holds for someone so precious, someone you would lay your own life down for without hesitation.

6

THE FIRST FERRY GOT me to Catalina at 9:30 the next morning. I had called Graciela McCaleb on my cell while I was crossing, so she was waiting for me at the pier. The day was sunny and crisp and I could taste the difference in the smogless air. Graciela smiled at me as I approached the gate where people waited for travelers from the boats.

"Good morning. Thanks for coming."

"No problem. Thanks for meeting me."

I had half expected Buddy Lockridge to be with her. I had not seen him on the ferry and figured that maybe he had gone across the night before.

"No Buddy yet?"

"No. Is he coming?"

"I wanted to go over things on the boat with him. He said he would be on the first boat but he didn't show."

"Well, they're running two ferries. The next will be here in forty-five minutes. He's probably on that. What would you like to do first?"

"I want to go to the boat, start there."

We walked over to the tenders dock and took a Zodiac with a little one-horsepower engine on it out into the basin where the yachts were lined in rows, tied up to floating mooring balls and moving with the current in a synchronized fashion. Terry's boat, *The Following Sea*, was second from the end of the second row. An ominous feeling came over me as we approached and then bumped up against the fantail. On this vessel Terry had died. My friend and Graciela's husband. It used to be one of the tricks of the trade for me to find or manufacture an emotional connection to a case. It helped stoke the fire and gave me that needed edge to go where I had to go, do what I had to do. I knew I would not need to look for that in this case. No manufacturing necessary. It was already part of the deal. The largest part.

I looked at the boat's name, painted in black letters across the stern, and remembered how Terry had explained it to me once. He had told me that the following sea was the wave you had to watch out for. It came up in your blind spot, hit you from behind. A good philosophy. I had to wonder now why Terry hadn't seen what and who had come up behind him.

Unsteadily I stepped off the inflatable and onto the boat's fantail. I reached back for the rope to tie it up. But Graciela stopped me.

"I'm not going on board," she said.

She shook her head as if to ward off any coercing from me and handed a set of keys toward me. I took them and nodded my head.

"I just don't want to be on there," she said. "The one time I went to collect his meds was enough."

"I understand."

"This way the Zodiac will be back at the dock for Buddy to use if he shows up."

"If?"

"He isn't always that reliable. At least that is what Terry said."

"And if he doesn't show up, what do I do?"

"Oh, just flag down a water taxi. They come by about every fifteen minutes. You won't have a problem. You can just bill me. Which reminds me, we haven't talked about what I'll be paying you."

It was something she had to bring up to make sure, but she knew and I knew that this wasn't a job for pay.

"That won't be necessary," I said. "If I do this, there is only one thing I'd like in return."

"What's that?"

"Terry once told me about your daughter. He said you two named her Cielo Azul."

"That's right. He picked the name."

"Did he ever tell you why?"

"He just said he liked it. He said he knew a girl named Cielo Azul once."

I nodded.

"What I would like for payment for doing this is to meet her someday—when this is all over, I mean."

That gave Graciela a moment of pause. Then she nodded her agreement.

"She's a sweetheart. You'll like meeting her."

"I'm sure I will."

"Harry, did you know her? The girl Terry named our daughter after?"

I looked at her a moment and nodded.

"Yes, you could say I knew her. Someday if you'd like I'll tell you about her."

She nodded and started to push the Zodiac off the fantail. I helped with my foot.

"The little key opens the salon door," she said. "The rest you should be able to figure out. I hope you find something that helps."

I nodded and held up the keys as if they would open every door I would ever encounter. I watched her head back to the dock and then I climbed over the stern and into the cockpit.

Some sort of sense of duty made me climb the ladder to the upper helm before I went inside the boat. I pulled the canvas cover off the control station and stood for a moment next to the wheel and the seat and envisioned the story Buddy Lockridge had told me of Terry collapsing here. It somehow seemed appropriate for him to collapse at the wheel, yet with what I now knew, it also seemed so wrong. I put my hand on the top of the chair as if resting it on someone's shoulder. I decided that I would find the answers to all of the questions before I finished here.

The small chrome key on the ring Graciela had given me opened the mirrored sliding door that led inside the boat. I left it open to air out the interior. There was a briny, funky smell inside. I traced it to the rods and reels stored on ceiling racks, artificial baits still in place. I guessed that they had not been washed off and properly cared for after the last charter. There had not been time. There had not been a reason.

I wanted to go down the steps to the stateroom in the bow where I knew Terry kept all his investigative files. But I decided to leave that place for last. I decided to begin in the salon and work my way down.

The salon had a functional layout with a couch, chair and coffee table on the right side leading to a chart desk built behind the seat of the interior helm. On the opposite side was a restaurant-style booth with red leather padding. A television was locked down in a partition that separated the booth from the galley and then there was a short stairway I knew led down to the forward staterooms and a bathroom.

The salon was neat and clean. I stood in the middle of the space and just observed it for a half minute before going to the chart station and opening drawers. McCaleb had kept the charter business files here. I found listings of customers and a calendar for charter reservations. There were also records dealing with his collection from Visa and MasterCard, which he evidently accepted from customers as payment. The charter business had a bank account and there was a checkbook in the drawer, too. I checked the register and saw that just about everything that came in went back out again to cover fuel and mooring charges as well as fishing and other charter supplies. There was no record of cash deposits so I concluded that if the business was profitable it was in the unrecorded cash payments from customers, depending on how many of these there were.

In the bottom drawer there was a bad-check file. There were only a few and they were spread out over time, none so large that they could seriously damage the business.

I noticed that in the checkbook and with most of the business records either Buddy Lockridge's or Graciela's name was listed as the operator of the charter business. I knew this was because, as Graciela had told me, Terry was seriously limited in what he could earn as official income. If he made over a certain level—which was shockingly low—he was not eligible to receive state and federal medical assistance. If he lost that, he would then end up paying medical expenses himself—a quick route to personal bankruptcy for a transplant recipient.

In the bad-check file I also found a copy of a sheriff's report unrelated to bad paper. It was a two-month-old incident report stemming from an apparent burglary of *The Following Sea*. The complainant was Buddy Lockridge and the summary indicated that only one thing was taken from the boat, a handheld global positioning system reader. Its value was placed at $300 and the model was listed as a Gulliver 100. An added note said that the complainant could not provide the serial number of the missing device because he had won it in a poker game from a person he could not identify and he had never bothered to write the tracking number down.

Once I had made a quick check through all of the drawers in the chart station I went back to the client files and started going through them more thoroughly, looking carefully at each customer McCaleb and Lockridge had taken on board in the six weeks before Terry's death. None of the names struck me as curious or suspicious and there were no notations by Terry or Buddy in the file that raised any of those feelings either. Nevertheless, I took a notebook from the back pocket of my blue jeans and wrote a list that showed the name of each client, the number in the party and the date of the charter. Once I had this I was able to see that the charters were by no means regular. A good week for the business was three or four half-day charters. There was one week in which there were no charters at all and another in which there was only one. I was beginning to see Buddy's point about the need to move the business to the mainland in order to increase the frequency and length of charter bookings. McCaleb was running the charter business as a hobby and that wasn't the way to make it thrive.

Of course, I knew why he was running it that way. He had another hobby—if you want to call it that—and he needed time to devote to that as well. I was putting the records back into the chart station drawer, with the intention of heading down to the bow to explore Terry's other hobby, when I heard the salon door roll open behind me.

It was Buddy Lockridge. He had come up on the boat without my hearing the Zodiac's little engine or feeling its nudge against the fantail. I also hadn't felt Buddy's considerable weight as he climbed onto the boat.

"Morning," he said. "Sorry I'm late."

"That's okay. I've got a lot to look through here."

"Find anything interesting yet?"

"Not really. I'm about to go below, check out his files."

"Cool. I'll help."

"Actually, Buddy, where you can help is if maybe you called the man who was the last charter."

I looked at the last name written on the page in my notebook.

"Otto Woodall. Could you call him and vouch for me and see if I could come by this afternoon to see him?"

"That's it? You wanted me to come all the way over to make a phone call?"

"No, I have questions for you. I need you here. I just don't think you should be going through the files down there. Not yet, at least."

I had a feeling that Buddy Lockridge had probably already perused every file in the bow. But I was playing him this way on purpose. I had to keep him close but distant at the same time. Until I had cleared him to my satisfaction. Yes, he was McCaleb's partner and had received credit for his efforts to save his fallen friend, but I had seen stranger things in my time. At the moment I had no suspects and that meant I had to suspect everybody.

"Make the call and then come downstairs to see me."

I left him there and headed down the short set of steps to the lower part of the boat. I had been here before and knew the layout. The two doors on the left side of the hallway led to the head and a storage closet. Straight ahead was a door to the small stateroom in the bow. The door on the right led to the master stateroom, the place where I would have been killed four years before if Terry McCaleb had not leveled a gun and fired on a man about to ambush me. This had occurred moments after I had saved McCaleb from a similar end.

I checked the paneling in the hallway where I remembered two of McCaleb's shots had splintered the wood. The surface was heavily varnished but I could tell it was newer wood.

The shelves in the storage closet were empty and the bathroom was clean, the overhead vent popped open on the forward deck above. I opened the master stateroom door and looked in but decided to leave it for later. I went to the forward room and had to use a key from the ring Graciela had given me to open the door.

The room was as I had remembered it. Two sets of V-bunks on each side, following the line of the bow. The bunks on the left still functioned as sleeping compartments, their thin mattresses rolled up and held by bungee cords. But on the right the lower bunk had no mattress and had been converted into a desk. The bunk above was where four long cardboard file boxes sat side by side.

McCaleb's cases. I looked at them for a long and solemn moment. If someone had murdered him, I believed I would find the suspect in there.

"Anytime today."

I almost jumped. It was Lockridge standing behind me. Once again I had not heard or felt his approach. He was smiling because he liked sneaking up on me.

"Good," I said. "Maybe after lunch we can head over there. I'll need a break from this by then anyway."

I looked down at the desk and saw the white laptop with the recognizable symbol of an apple with a bite out of it in silhouette. I reached down and opened it, unsure of how to proceed.

"Last time I was here, he had a different one."

"Yeah," Lockridge said. "He got that one on account of the graphics. He was getting into digital photography and stuff."

Without my bidding or approval Lockridge reached over and depressed a white button on the computer. It started to hum and then the black screen filled with light.

"What kind of photography?" I asked.

"Oh, you know, amateur stuff mostly. His kids and

sunsets and shit. It started with the clients. We started taking their pictures with their trophy fish, you know? And Terry could just come down here and print out eight-by-ten glossies on the spot. There's a box of cheap-ass frames in here someplace. The client catches a fish, he gets a framed photo. Part of the deal. It worked pretty good. Our gratuities went way up with that."

The computer finished booting up. The screen was a sky of light blue that made me think of McCaleb's daughter. Several icons were spread across the field. Right away I noticed one that was a miniature file folder. Underneath it the word PROFILES was printed. I knew that was a folder I wanted to open. Scanning across the bottom of the screen I saw an icon that looked like a camera set in front of a photo of a palm tree. Since the subject had just been photography I pointed to it.

"Is that where the photos are?"

"Yup," Lockridge said.

Again he moved without my request. He moved his finger on a small square in front of the keyboard, which in turn moved the arrow on the screen to the camera icon. He used his thumb to depress a button below the square and the screen quickly took on a new image. Lockridge seemed at ease with the computer and it begged the questions why and how. Did Terry McCaleb allow him access to the computer—after all, they were in business together—or was this something Lockridge became efficient at without his partner's knowledge?

On the screen a frame opened under the heading iPhoto. There were several folders listed. Most were listed by dates, usually a few weeks or a month. There was one folder simply titled MAIL CALL.

"Here we go," Lockridge said. "You want to see some of this stuff? It's clients and fish."

"Yeah, show me the most recent photos."

Lockridge clicked on a folder that was labeled with dates ending just a week before McCaleb's death. The folder opened and there were several dozen photos listed by individual date. Lockridge clicked on the most recent date. A few seconds went by and a photo opened on the screen. It showed a man and woman, both badly sunburned and smiling as they held up a horribly ugly brown fish.

"Santa Monica Bay halibut," Buddy said. "That was a good one."

"Who are they?"

"Um, they were from . . . Minnesota, I think. Yeah, St. Paul. And I don't think they were married. I mean, they were married but just not to each other. They were staying on the island. Shacking up. They were the last charter before the trip down to Baja. Pictures from that trip are probably still on the camera."

"Where is the camera?"

"It should be here. If not, then Graciela probably has it."

He clicked on a left arrow above the photo. Soon another photo appeared, the same couple and same fish. Lockridge kept clicking and eventually he came to a new customer and his trophy fish, a pinkish white creature about fourteen inches long.

"White sea bass," Lockridge said. "Nice fish."

He kept clicking, showing me a procession of fishermen and their catches. Everybody seemed happy, some even had the obvious glaze of alcohol in their eyes.

Lockridge named all the fish but not all the clients. He didn't remember them all by name. Some of them he simply classified as good or bad tippers and that was it.

Eventually, he came to a man with a delighted smile on his face as he held up a small white sea bass. Lockridge cursed.

"What's wrong?" I asked.

"He's the prick who walked off with my goddamn fish box."

"What fish box?"

"My GPS. He's the guy who took it."

7

BACKUS STAYED AT LEAST a hundred feet behind her. Even in the crowded Chicago airport he knew she would be on what they always called "Six Alert" when he had been with the bureau. Watching her back—her six—and always checking for a trailer. It had been tricky enough traveling with her so far. The plane from South Dakota had been small and fewer than forty people had been on board. The random assignment of seats had put him only two rows from her. So close he thought he could actually smell her scent—the one beneath the perfume and the makeup. The one the dogs could pick up.

It was intoxicating to be so close and still such a long distance apart. He wanted the whole time to turn and look back at her, maybe catch a glimpse of her face between the seats, see what she was doing. But he didn't dare. He had to bide his time. He knew that good things come to those who plan carefully and then wait. That was the thing, the secret. Darkness waits. All things come to the dark.

He followed her through half of the American Airlines terminal until she took a seat at gate K9. It was empty. No travelers were waiting here. No American employees were behind the gate counter waiting and ready to work the computers and check tickets. But Backus knew that this was only because she was early. They both were early. The flight to Las Vegas would not leave from gate K9 for another two hours. He knew this because he was on the Vegas flight as well. In a way he was Rachel Walling's guardian angel, a silent escort who would be with her until she reached her final destination.

He walked on by the gate, careful not to be obvious about glancing at her but curious to see how she was going to pass the time waiting for the next flight. He hooked the strap of his large cowhide carry-on bag over his right shoulder so that if she happened to look up, her eyes might be drawn to it instead of his face. He wasn't worried about her recognizing him for who he was. All the pain and the surgeries had taken care of that. But she might recognize him from the flight from Rapid City. And he didn't want that. He didn't want her to get suspicious.

His heart jumped in his chest like a baby kicking under a blanket as he made the one furtive glance while passing by. She had her head down and was reading a book. It was old and worn from many readings. There was a profusion of yellow Post-its poking out from its pages. But he recognized the cover design and the title. *The Poet*. She was reading about him!

He hurried on by before she could sense she had a

watcher and look up. He went down two more gates and into the restroom. He went into a stall and carefully locked the door. He hung his bag on the door hook and quickly went to work. Off came the cowboy hat and the vest. He sat down on the toilet and took off the boots, too.

In five minutes Backus transformed himself from a South Dakota cowboy to a Las Vegas gambler. He put on the silk clothes. He put on the gold. He put on the earring and the shades. He clipped the gaudy chrome cell phone to his belt, even though there was no one who would call him and no one he would call. From the bag he took out another bag, much smaller and with the figure of the MGM lion emblazoned on it.

The components of his first skin were pushed into the new bag and he stepped out of the stall, the strap of the MGM bag over his shoulder.

Backus went to the sink to wash his hands. He admired himself for the preparation he had taken. It was the planning and attention to the small details like that that made him who he was, that made him a success at his craft.

For a moment he thought about what was waiting. He was going to take Rachel Walling on a tour. By the end of it she would know the depths of darkness. His darkness. She would pay for what she had done to him.

He felt himself getting an erection. He left the sink and stepped back into one of the stalls. He tried to change his thoughts. He listened to the fellow travelers coming and going in the restroom, relieving themselves, washing themselves. One man spoke on a cell phone while defecating in the next stall. The whole place smelled horrible. But that was okay. It smelled like the tunnel where he was reborn in blood and darkness so long ago. If they only knew who was in their presence here.

He momentarily caught a vision of a dark, starless sky. He was falling backward, his arms flailing, the featherless and useless wings of a baby bird pushed out of the nest.

But he had survived and had learned to fly.

He started to laugh and used his foot to flush the toilet and cover his sound.

"Fuck you all," he whispered.

He waited for his erection to subside, pondering its cause and smiling. He knew his own profile so well. In the end it was always about the same thing. There was only a nanometer of difference between power and sex and fulfillment when it came to the narrow spaces between the synapses in the gray folds of the mind. In those narrows it all came down to the same thing.

When he was ready he flushed the toilet again, careful to use his shoe, and stepped out of the stall. He washed his hands again and checked his look in the mirror. He smiled. He was a new man. Rachel would not recognize him. Nobody would. Feeling confident, he unzipped the MGM bag and checked on his digital camera. It was there and ready to go. He decided he would take the risk and shoot some photos of Rachel. Just some keepsakes, a few secret shots he could admire and enjoy after everything was all over.

8

THE FISH BOX. BUDDY'S mention of it reminded me of the sheriff's report up in the chart station drawer.

"I meant to ask you about that. You say this guy took the GPS?"

"Phony bastard, I'm sure it was him. He went out with us, the next thing we know my GPS is gone and he starts a charter over on the isthmus. Put two and two together and you get asshole. I've been meaning to go over there and pay him a little visit."

I was having trouble following the line of his story. I asked him to explain it to me in English, as if I didn't know a fish charter from a fish chowder.

"This is the deal," he said. "That little black box had all our best spots on it. Our fishing holes, man. Not only that, it had the points marked by the guy I won it from. I won it in a poker game from another fish guide. The value assigned was not for the box but what was on it. The guy was putting his best twelve spots on the table and I won 'em with a full fucking house."

"All right," I said. "I get it now. Its value was in the co-ordinates of the fishing spots recorded on it, not the device itself."

"Exactly. Those things cost a couple hundred bucks. But the fishing spots, those come from years of work and skill, fishing experience."

I pointed at the photo on the computer screen.

"And this guy comes along and takes it and then he starts out his charter business ahead of the game. Using your experience as well as the guide's you won it from."

"Way ahead. Like I said, I'm going to go pay him a visit one of these days."

"Where is the isthmus?"

"On the other side, where the island pinches together like a figure eight."

"Did you tell the sheriff's department you thought he stole it?"

"Not at first because we didn't know, you know? The thing turned up missing and we thought maybe some kids came onto the boat or something at night and grabbed whatever they saw. It gets pretty fucking boring growing up on the island, from what I hear. Just ask Graciela about Raymond—the kid's going stir crazy. So anyway we made a report and that was that. Then a couple weeks later I see this ad in *Fish Tales* and it's announcing this new charter out of the isthmus and there's a picture of the guy and I say, 'Hey, I know that guy' and I put it together. He *stole* my fish box."

"Did you call the sheriff then?"

"Yeah, I called and told them he was the guy. They didn't act too excited. I called back the next week and they said they talked to the guy—by phone. They didn't even bother to go out there for a face-to-face. He denied it like of course he would and that was that as far as they were concerned."

"What's this guy's name?"

"Robert Finder. His operation is called Isthmus Charters. In the ad he calls himself Robert 'Fish' Finder. My ass. More like 'Fish Stealer.'"

I looked down at the photo on the screen and wondered if this meant anything at all to my investigation. Could the missing GPS box be at the center of Terry McCaleb's death? It seemed unlikely. The idea that someone would steal a competitor's fishing spots was understandable. But then to engage in a complicated plot to also kill the competitor seemed on the far limit of belief. It would require a hell of a plan and execution on Finder's part, that was for sure. It would require a hell of a plan on anyone's part.

Lockridge seemed to read my thoughts.

"Hey, you think this bastard could've had something to do with Terror going down?"

I looked up at him for a long moment, realizing that the idea of Lockridge being involved in McCaleb's death as a means of gaining control and location of the charter business and *The Following Sea* was a more believable theory.

"I don't know," I said. "But I'll probably be checking it out."

"Let me know if you want somebody to go with you."

"Sure. But listen, I noticed on the sheriff's report that the GPS was the only thing reported stolen. Did that hold up? Nothing else ever turned up missing?"

"That was it. That's why me and Terry thought it was so strange at first. Until we figured out it was Finder."

"Terry thought that, too, that it was him?"

"He was coming around to it. I mean, come on, who else could it have been?"

It was a worthy question, but not one I thought I needed to put front and center at the moment. I pointed at the laptop screen and told Lockridge to keep moving back through the photos. He did so and the procession of happy anglers continued.

We came across one more curiosity in the photo series. Lockridge backed up to a set of six photos that depicted a man whose face was not shown clearly at first. In the three initial shots he was posed holding a brilliantly colored fish up to the camera. But in each shot he held the fish up too high, obscuring most of his face. In each of these shots his dark glasses peeked over the ridge of the fish's dorsal fin. The fish appeared to be the same in each of these three shots, which led me to assume that the photographer was repeatedly trying to get a photo that included the fisherman's face. But to no avail.

"Who took these?"

"Terror. I wasn't there on that one."

Something about the man or maybe the way he had avoided the camera in the trophy photo had made McCaleb suspicious. That seemed obvious. The next three photos in the series were shots of the man taken without his knowledge. The first two were taken from inside the salon, shooting out into the cockpit where the fisherman leaned against the right gunwale. Because the glass on the salon door had reflective film on it, the man would not have seen or known that McCaleb had taken photos of him.

The first of these two photos was in profile. The next a

full-on face shot. Take away the setting and McCaleb had instinctively gotten mug shot poses, another confirmation of his suspicion. Even with these photos the man was still obscured. He had a full beard of brownish gray hair and wore dark sunglasses with large lenses and a blue L.A. Dodgers hat. What little could be seen of the man's hair appeared to be close cropped and matching the colorations of his beard. He had a gold hoop earring in his right ear.

In the profile shot his eyes were crinkled and hooded, naturally hidden even with the dark sunglasses. He wore blue jeans and a plain white T-shirt beneath a Levi's jacket.

The sixth photo, the last in the sequence, was taken after the charter had ended. It was a long shot of the man walking on the Avalon pier, apparently after leaving *The Following Sea*. His face was turned slightly toward the camera, though it still wasn't much more than a profile. But I wondered if the man had continued to turn after the shot and perhaps had then seen McCaleb and his camera.

"So what about this guy?" I asked. "Tell me about him."

"Can't," Lockridge said. "I told you, I wasn't there. That was one Terry picked up on the fly. No reservation. The guy just showed up on the water taxi while Terry was on the boat and asked to go out. He paid for a half a day, the minimum charter. He wanted to go out right away and I was over on the mainland. Terry couldn't wait on me, so he took him out without me. Alone, which is a pain in the ass. But they got a nice Spanish mack out there. Not bad."

"Did he talk about the guy after?"

"No, not really. He only said that the guy didn't take

the full half. He wanted to pack it in after just a couple hours. So they did."

"Terry had an alert on. He took six photos, three while the guy wasn't looking. You sure he didn't say anything about that?"

"Like I said, not to me. But Terry kept a lot of stuff to himself."

"Do you know this guy's name?"

"No, but I'm sure Terry put something in the charter book. You want me to go get it?"

"Yes. And I'd also like to know the exact date and how he paid. But first, can you print out these photos?"

"All six of them? It will take a while."

"Actually, all six and give me one of Finder while we're at it. I have the time."

"I don't suppose you want them framed, too."

"No, Buddy, that won't be necessary. Just the photos."

I stepped back while Buddy sat down on the cushioned stool in front of the computer. He turned on a nearby printer, loaded in photo-quality paper, and expertly went through the commands that sent the seven pictures to the printer. Again I noted his ease with the equipment. I had the feeling that there wasn't any content on the laptop that he was not familiar with. Probably nothing in the file boxes on the bunk above us either.

"Okay," he said as he got up. "Takes about a minute for each one. They come out a bit sticky, too. Might want to spread 'em out till they dry all the way. I'll go up and see what the charter book says about your mystery man."

After he was gone I sat down on the stool. I had watched how Lockridge worked the photo files and was a quick learner. I went back to the main listing and double-clicked on the photo folder labeled MAIL CALL. A frame opened containing 36 small photos in a grid. I clicked on the first one and the photo enlarged. It showed Graciela pushing a stroller with a little girl sleeping in it. Cielo Azul. Terry's daughter. The setting appeared to be a shopping mall. The photo was similar to Terry's photos of the mystery man in that it appeared that Graciela did not know she was being photographed.

I turned around and looked back through the doorway toward the steps to the salon. There was no sign of Lockridge. I got up and moved quietly into the hallway. I slipped through the open door of the bathroom. I pressed myself against the wall and waited. Soon enough Lockridge moved across the opening in the hall, carrying the logbook. He was moving very quietly so as to make no noise. I let him pass and then moved into the hallway behind him. I watched as he went through the door of the forward stateroom, ready to startle me with his sudden appearance again.

But it was Lockridge who was startled when he realized I wasn't in the room. When he turned I was right behind him.

"You like sneaking up on people, don't you, Buddy?"

"Uh, no, not really. I was just—"

"Don't do it with me, okay? What's it say in the book?"

His face took on a pink hue beneath the permanent fisherman's tan. But I had given him an out and he quickly took it.

"Terry put his name down in the book but nothing else. It says 'Jordan Shandy, half day.' That's it."

He opened the book and turned it to show me the entry.

"What about his method of payment? How much is half a day anyway?"

"Three bills for a half, five for a full. I checked the credit-card log and there was nothing there. Also the checking deposits. Nothing. That means he paid cash."

"When was this? I assume it is logged by date."

"Yeah. They went out on February thirteenth—hey, that was Friday the thirteenth. Think that was intentional?"

"Who knows? Was that before or after the charter with Finder?"

Lockridge put the logbook down on the desk so we could both look at it. He ran his finger down the list of clients and stopped it at Finder.

"He came a week after. He went out February nineteenth."

"And what's the date on the sheriff's report on the boat burglary?"

"Shit, I have to go back up."

He left and I heard him bound up the stairs. I took the first photo out of the printer and put it on the desk. It was the shot of Jordan Shandy hiding his face with sunglasses and the Spanish mackerel. I stared at it until Lockridge came back into the room. He didn't try to sneak up on me this time.

"We made the burglary report February twenty-second."

I nodded. Five weeks before McCaleb's death. I wrote all the dates we had been talking about down in my notebook. I wasn't sure if there was significance to any of it.

"Okay," I said. "You want to do one more thing for me now, Buddy?"

"Sure. What?"

"Go on up and take those rods down off the ceiling and go out and wash them down. I don't think anybody did it after that last trip. They're making this place smell sour and I think I'm going to be hanging out here for a couple days. It would help me a lot."

"You want me to go up and wash off the rods."

He said it like a statement, a treatise of insult and disappointment. I looked from the photo to his face.

"Yes, that's right. It would help me a lot. I'll finish up with the photos and then we can go visit Otto Woodall."

"Whatever."

He left the room dejected and I heard him trudge up the steps, equally as loud as he had been silent before. I took the second photo out of the printer and placed it down next to the first. I took a black marker out of a coffee mug on the desk and wrote in the white border beneath the photo the name Jordan Shandy.

Back on the stool I turned my attention once again to the computer and the photo of Graciela and her daughter. I clicked on the forward arrow and the next photo came up. Again it was a photo from inside a mall. This one was taken from a further distance and there was a grainy quality to it. Also in this picture was a boy trailing behind Graciela. The son, I concluded. The adopted son.

Everyone in the family was in the photo but Terry. Was he the photographer? If so, why at such a distance? I clicked the arrow again and then continued through the photos. Almost all of them were from inside the mall and all were taken from a distance. In not one photo was any family member looking at or acknowledging the camera. After twenty-eight similar shots the venue changed and the family was now on the ferry to Catalina. They were heading home and the photographer was there along with them.

There were only four photos in this sequence. In each of these Graciela sat in the middle rear of the ferry's main cabin, the boy and girl on either side of her. The photographer had been positioned near the front of the cabin, shooting across several rows of seats. If Graciela had noticed, she probably would not have realized that she was the center of the camera's focus and would have dismissed the photographer as just another tourist going to Catalina.

The last two photos of the thirty-six seemed out of place with the others, as if they were part of a completely different project. The first was of a green highway sign. I enlarged it and saw that it had been shot through the windshield of a car. I could see the frame of the windshield, part of the dashboard and some sort of sticker in the corner of the glass. Part of the photographer's hand, resting on the steering wheel at eleven o'clock, was also in the picture.

The highway sign stood against a barren desert landscape. It said

ZZYZX ROAD

I MILE

I knew the road. Or, more accurately, I knew the sign. Anybody from L.A. who made the road trip to and from Las Vegas as often as I had in the last year would have known it. At just about the halfway point on the 15 freeway was the Zzyzx Road exit, recognizable by its unique name if nothing else. It was in the Mojave and it appeared to be a road to nowhere. No gas station, no rest stop. At the end of the alphabet at the end of the world.

The last photo was equally puzzling. I enlarged it and saw that it was a strange still life. At center in the frame was an old boat—the rivets of its wooden planks sprung and its yellowed paint peeling back under the blistering sun. It sat on the rocky terrain of the desert, seemingly miles from any water on which to float. A boat adrift on a sea of sand. If there was any specific meaning at all to it, I did not readily see it.

Following the procedure I had watched Lockridge use, I printed the two desert photos and then went back to review the other photos to choose a sampling of shots to print. I sent two photos from the ferry and two photos from the mall to the printer. While I waited I enlarged several of the mall shots on the screen in hopes of seeing something in the background that would identify what mall Graciela and the children were in. I knew I could simply ask her. But I wasn't sure I wanted to.

In the photos I was able to identify bags carried by various shoppers as coming from Nordstrom, Saks Fifth Avenue and Barnes & Noble. In one of the photos the family walked through a food court that included the concessions Cinnabon and Hot Dog on a Stick. I wrote all of these down in my notebook and knew that with these five locations I would probably be able to determine in which mall the photos had been taken, if I decided it was necessary to know this information and I did not want to ask Graciela about it. That was still an open question. I did not want to alarm her if it was not necessary. Telling her she may have been stalked while with her family—and possibly by someone with a strange connection to her husband—might not be the best avenue to take. At least at first.

That connection turned stranger and more alarming when the printer finally spit out one of the photos I had chosen from the mall sequence. In the picture the family was walking in front of the Barnes & Noble bookstore. The shot had been taken from the other side of the mall but the angle was almost perpendicular to the storefront. The front display window of the bookstore caught a dim reflection of the photographer. I had not seen it on the computer screen but there it was in the print.

The image of the photographer was too small and too whispery against the display behind the window—a full-size stand-up photo of a man in a kilt that was surrounded by stacks of books and a sign that said IAN RANKIN HERE TONIGHT! I realized then that I could use the display to place the exact day that the photos of Graciela and her children were taken. All I had to do was call the store and find out when Ian Rankin had been there. But the display also helped hide the photographer from me.

I went back to the computer and found the photo among the miniatures and enlarged it. I stared at it, realizing I didn't know what to do.

Buddy was in the cockpit using a hose attached to a gunwale faucet to spray the eight rods and reels leaning against the stern. I told him to turn the water off and to come back down to the office. He did so without a word. When we were back in the office I signaled him to the stool and then leaned over him and outlined the area of the photographer's reflection on the screen.

"Can this be enlarged here? I want to see this area better."

"It can be enlarged but you lose a lot of definition. It's digital, you know? You get what you get."

I didn't know what he was talking about. I just told him to do it. He played with some of the square buttons that ran along the top of the frame and started enlarging the photograph and then repositioning it so the area of the reflection stayed on the screen. Soon he said that he had maximized the enlargement. I leaned in close. The image was even murkier. Not even the lines on the author's kilt were crisp.

"You can't tighten it up any?"

"You mean make it smaller again. Sure, I—"

"No, I mean like bring it more into focus."

"No, man, that is it. What you see is what you get."

"Okay, print it. It came out better before when I printed it. Maybe this will, too."

Lockridge put in the commands and I spent an uneasy minute waiting.

"What is this, anyway?" Buddy asked.

"A reflection of the photographer."

"Oh. You mean it wasn't Terry?"

"No, I don't think so. I think somebody took pictures of his family and sent them to him. It was some sort of message. Did he ever mention this?"

"No."

I took a shot at seeing if Buddy might let something slip.

"When did you first notice this file on the computer?"

"I don't know. It must've been . . . actually, I just saw them for the first time with you here."

"Buddy, don't bullshit me. This could be important. I've watched you work this thing like it was yours since high school. I know you went into that machine when Terry wasn't around. He probably knew, too. He didn't care and neither do I. Just tell me, when did you first see this file?"

He let a few moments pass while he thought about it.

"I first saw them about a month before he died. But if your real question is when did Terry see them, then all you have to do is look at the file archive and see when it was created."

"Then do it, Buddy."

Lockridge took over the keyboard again and went into the photo file's history. In a few seconds he had the answer.

"February twenty-seventh," he said. "That was when that file was created."

"Okay, good," I said. "Now, assuming that Terry didn't take these, how would they end up on his computer?"

"Well, there's a few ways. One is that he got them in an e-mail and downloaded them. Another is that somebody borrowed his camera and shot them. He then found them and downloaded them. The third way is maybe somebody just sent him a photo chip right out of the camera or a CD with the pictures already on it. That would probably be the most untraceable way."

"Could Terry do e-mail from here?"

"No, up at the house. There is no hard line on the boat. I told him he ought to get one of those cellular modems, go wireless like that commercial where the guy's sitting at his desk in the middle of a field. But he never got around to it."

The printer kicked out the photo and I grabbed it ahead of Buddy's reach. But then I placed it down on the desk so we could both view it. The reflection was blurred and dim but still more recognizable on the print than it was on the computer screen. I could now see that the photographer was holding the camera in front of his face, obscuring it completely. But then I was able to identify the overlapping L and A configuration of the Los Angeles Dodgers logo. The photographer was wearing a baseball cap.

On any given day there might be fifty thousand people wearing Dodgers caps in this city. I don't know for sure. But what I do know is that I don't believe in coincidences. I never have and I never will. I looked at the murky reflection of the photographer and my sudden guess was that it was the mystery man. Jordan Shandy.

Lockridge saw it, too.

"Goddamn," he said. "That's the guy, right? I think that's the charter. Shandy."

"Yeah," I said. "Me, too."

I put the print of Shandy holding up the Spanish mackerel next to the enlargement. There was no way to make a match but there was nothing that made me think the other way. There was no way to be sure but I was sure. I knew that the same man who had showed up unannounced for a private charter with Terry McCaleb had also stalked and photographed his family.

What I didn't know was where McCaleb had gotten these photos and whether he had made the same jump as I had just made.

I started stacking all of the photos I had printed. All the time I was trying to put something together, some connection of logic. But it wasn't there. I didn't have enough of the picture. Only a few pieces. My instincts told me that McCaleb had been baited in some way. Photos of his family came to him in the form of an e-mail or a photo chip or a CD. And the last two photos were the key. The first thirty-four were the bait. The last two were the hook hidden inside that bait.

I believed the message was obvious. The photographer wanted to draw McCaleb out to the desert. Out to Zzyzx Road.

9

RACHEL WALLING RODE THE escalator down into the cavernous baggage pickup area at McCarran International. She had carried her luggage during the journey from South Dakota but the airport was designed so that every passenger had to go this way. The escalator landing area was crowded with people waiting. Limo drivers held signs with the names of their clients, others just held up signs that announced the names of hotels or casinos or tour companies. The cacophony rising from the room assaulted her as she descended. It was nothing like the airport where she had started her travels that morning.

Cherie Dei was going to meet her. Rachel had not seen the fellow FBI agent in four years and that was only a brief interaction in Amsterdam. It had been eight years since she had really spent any kind of time with her and she wasn't sure she would recognize her or that she would be recognized herself.

It didn't matter. As she searched the sea of faces and signs it was a sign that caught her eye.

BOB BACKUS

The woman holding it was smiling at her. Her idea of a joke. Rachel approached, without returning the smile.

Cherie Dei had reddish brown hair pulled back into a ponytail. She was attractive and trim with a good smile, her eyes still with a lot of light in them. Rachel thought she looked more like the mother of a couple of Catholic school kids than a serial killer hunter.

Dei extended her hand. They shook and Dei proffered the sign.

"I know, bad joke, but I knew it would get your attention."

"Yes, it did."

"Did you have a long layover in Chicago?"

"A few hours. Not much choice flying out of Rapid City. Denver or Chicago. I like the food better at O'Hare."

"Do you have bags?"

"No, just this. We can go."

Rachel was carrying one bag—a midsize duffel. She had packed only a few changes of clothing. Dei pointed toward one of the banks of glass doors and they headed that way.

"We got you in at the Embassy Suites where the rest of us are staying. We almost didn't but they had a cancellation. The town is crowded because of the fight."

"What fight?"

"I don't know. Some super heavyweight or junior middleweight boxing match at one of the casinos. I didn't pay attention. I just know it's the reason this place gets so crowded."

Rachel knew that Cherie was talking because she was nervous. She didn't know the reason for this, whether anything had happened or it was simply because Rachel had to be handled carefully in this situation.

"If you want we can go to the hotel, get you settled in there. You could even take some time to rest if you want. There's a meeting later at the FO. You could start there if—"

"No. I'd like to go to the scene."

They stepped through the automatic glass doors and Rachel felt the dry Nevada air. It wasn't at all as hot as she'd expected and packed for. It was cool and crisp, even in the direct sun. She took out her sunglasses and decided the jacket she had worn to the airport in South Dakota would be needed here. It was stuffed into her bag.

"Rachel, the scene is two hours from here. Are you sure you—"

"Yes. Take me there. I'd like to start there."

"Start what?"

"I don't know. Whatever it is that he wants me to start."

This seemed to give Dei pause. She didn't respond. They walked into the parking garage and found her car—a government Crown Vic so dirty that it looked like it was in desert camouflage.

Once they were driving, Dei took out a cell phone and made a call. Rachel heard her tell someone—probably her boss or partner or the scene supervisor—that she had picked up the package and would be taking it to the scene. There was a long pause as the person she'd called responded at length. Then she said good-bye and hung up.

"You are cleared to the scene, Rachel, but you have to step back. You're here as an observer, okay?"

"What are you talking about? I'm an FBI agent, same as you."

"But you're not in Behavioral anymore. This is not your case."

"You're saying I am here because Backus wants me here, not you people."

"Rachel, let's try to get off to a better start than we did in Am—"

"Anything new come up so far today?"

"We're up to ten bodies now. They think that's going to be it. At least for this location."

"IDs?"

"They're getting there. What they have is tentative but they're putting it all together."

"Is Brass Doran at the scene?"

"No, she is in Quantico. She's work—"

"She should be here. Don't you people know what you've got here? She—"

"Whoa, Rachel, slow down, okay? Let's get something straight here. I'm the case agent on this, okay? You are not running this investigation. This is not going to work if you confuse that."

"But Backus is talking to me. He called me out."

"And that's why you are here. But you aren't calling the shots, Rachel. You have to stand to the side and watch. And I have to tell you I don't like how this is starting out. This isn't Driving Miss Rachel. You mentored me but that was ten years ago. I've now been in Behavioral longer than you ever were and I've booked more cases than you ever did. So don't talk down to me and don't act like my mentor or my mother."

Rachel didn't respond at first and then she simply asked Dei to pull over so she could get her jacket out of her bag, which was in the trunk. Dei pulled into the Travel America on Blue Diamond Road and popped the trunk.

When Rachel got back into the car she was wearing a baggy black all-weather coat that looked like it might have been designed for a man. Dei didn't say anything about it.

"Thanks," Rachel said. "And you're right. I apologize. I guess you get like me when it turns out your boss—your mentor—is the same evil thing you've been hunting all your life. And they punish *you* for it."

"I understand that, Rachel. But it wasn't just Backus. It was a lot of things. The reporter, some of the choices you made. Some people say you were lucky you still had a job at the end of it."

Rachel's face grew hot. She was being reminded that she was one of the bureau's embarrassments. Even within the ranks. Even with the agent she had mentored. She had slept with a reporter working on her case. That was the shorthand version. It didn't matter that it was a reporter who was actually a part of the case, who was working with Rachel side by side and hour by hour. The shorthand version would always be the story that agents heard and whispered about. A reporter. Was there a lower breach in agent behavior and etiquette? Maybe a mobster or a spy, but nothing else.

"Five years in North Dakota followed by a promotion to South Dakota," she said weakly. "Yeah, I was lucky all right."

"Look, I know you paid the price. My point is that you have to know your place here. Use some finesse. A lot of people are watching this case. If you play it right it could be your ticket back in."

"Got it."

"Good."

Rachel reached down to the side of her seat and adjusted it so she could lean back.

"How long did you say?" she asked.

"About two hours. We've been using choppers from Nellis mostly, saves a lot of time."

"Hasn't drawn attention?"

She was asking about the media, whether news of the investigation in the desert had leaked yet.

"We've had a few fires to put out but so far it is holding up. The scene is in California and we're working it out of Nevada. I think that has somehow kept the lid on. To be honest, there are some people worried about you now."

Rachel thought about Jack McEvoy, the reporter, for a moment.

"Nobody has to worry," she said. "I don't even know where he is."

"Well, if this thing finally hits the radar, you can expect to see him. He wrote a bestselling book on the first go-round. I guarantee he'll be back for the sequel."

Rachel thought about the book she had been reading on the plane and that was now in her bag. She wasn't sure whether it was the subject or the author that had drawn her to read it so many times.

"Probably."

She left it at that and pulled her jacket around her

shoulders and folded her arms. She was tired, not having slept since getting the call from Dei.

She leaned her head against the side window and pretty soon she was out. Her dream of darkness returned. But this time she was not alone. She could not see anyone because she could only see blackness. But she sensed another presence. Someone close but not necessarily someone with her. She moved and turned in the darkness, trying to see who it was. She reached out but her hands touched nothing.

She heard a moaning sound and then realized it was her own voice from deep in her throat. Then she was grabbed. Something had her and shook her very hard.

Rachel opened her eyes. She saw the freeway rushing at her through the windshield. Cherie Dei let go of her jacket.

"You all right? This is the exit."

Rachel looked up at a passing green freeway sign.

ZZYZX ROAD

I MILE

She straightened up in the seat. She checked her watch and realized she had slept for over ninety minutes. Her neck was stiff and painful on the right side from leaning so long against the window. She started working it with her fingers, digging deeply into the muscle.

"You all right?" Dei asked again. "Sounded like you were having a bad one."

"I'm fine. What did I say?"

"Nothing. You just sort of moaned. I think you were running from something or something had you."

Dei hit the blinker and turned into the exit lane. Zzyzx Road appeared to be in the middle of nowhere. At the top of the exit there was nothing, not even a gas station or even an abandoned structure. There was no visible reason for the exit or the road.

"We're over here."

Dei turned left and took the overpass across the freeway. Once off the overpass the road disintegrated into an unpaved trail that wound south and down into the flat basin of the Mojave. The landscape was stark. The white soda on the surface of the flats looked like snow in the distance. Joshua trees reached their bony fingers toward the sky and smaller plants wedged themselves between the rocks. It was a still life. Rachel had no idea what sort of animal might be able to subsist in such a barren place.

They passed a sign that said they were headed toward Soda Springs and then the road curved and Rachel could suddenly see the white tents and RVs and vans and other vehicles ahead. She could see a military green helicopter, its blades still, parked to the left of the encampment. Further past the encampment there was a complex of small buildings set at the base of the hills. It looked like a roadside motel but there were no signs and no road.

"What is this place?" Rachel asked.

"This is Zzyzx," Dei said, pronouncing it *zie-zix*. "As far as I can tell, it is the asshole of the universe. Some radio preacher named it and built it sixty years ago. He got control of the land by promising the government he would be prospecting. He paid winos from skid row in L.A. to do that while he went on the radio and called on the faithful to come here to bathe in the spring waters and guzzle the mineral waters he bottled. It took the Bureau of Land Management twenty-five years to get rid of him. The place was then turned over to the state university system for desert studies."

"Why here? Why did Backus bury them here?"

"Far as we can guess is because it is federal land. He wanted to make sure we—meaning you, probably—worked the case. If that's what he wanted, he got it. It's a major excavation. We've had to bring in our own power, shelter, food, water, everything."

Rachel said nothing. She was studying everything, from the crime scene to the distant horizon of gray mountain ridges that enclosed the basin. She didn't agree with Dei's take on the place. She had heard the coastline of Ireland described as a terrible beauty. She thought that the desert with its barren lunar landscape was in its own way beautiful, too. There was a harsh beauty to it. A dangerous beauty. She had never spent much time in the desert, but her years in the Dakotas had given her an appreciation for harsh places, the empty landscapes where people were the intruders. That was her secret. She had what the bureau called a "hardship posting." It was designed to wear her down and make her quit. But she had beaten them at this game. She could last forever there. She would not quit.

Dei slowed as they approached a checkpoint set up about a hundred yards before the tents. A man in a blue jumpsuit with the white letters FBI on the breast pocket stood beneath a beach-type tent with open sides. The desert winds were threatening to tear it from its moorings, just as they had already played havoc with the agent's hair.

Dei lowered the window. She didn't bother to give her own name or identification. She was a given. She gave the man Rachel's name and identified her as a "visiting agent," whatever that meant.

"Is she cleared with Agent Alpert?" he asked, his voice as dry and flat as the desert basin behind him.

"Yes, she's cleared."

"Okay, then. I just need her credentials."

Rachel handed over her ID wallet. The agent wrote down her serial number and handed it back.

"From Quantico?"

"No, South Dakota."

He gave her a look, the kind that said he knew she was a fuckup.

"Have fun," he said as he turned to go back to his tent.

Dei moved the car forward, raising her window, leaving the agent in a cloud of dust.

"He's from the Vegas FO," she said. "They're not too happy about things, playing second string."

"So what's new?"

"Exactly."

"Is Alpert the SAC?"

"That's him."

"What's he like?"

"Well, remember your theory about agents being either morphs or empaths?"

"Yes."

"He's a morph."

Rachel nodded.

They came to a little cardboard sign taped to a branch

of a Joshua tree. It said VEHICLES and had an arrow pointing to the right. Dei turned and they parked last in a row of four equally dirty Crown Vics.

"What about you?" Rachel asked. "Which did you turn out to be?"

Dei didn't answer.

"You ready for this?" she asked Rachel instead.

"Absolutely. I've been waiting four years for another shot at him. This is where it starts."

She cracked the door and stepped out into the bright desert sun. She felt at home.

10

BACKUS FOLLOWED THEM DOWN the exit ramp. He was a safe distance behind. He crossed over the freeway and put on his blinker to get back on in the opposite direction. If they were watching him in the mirror he would simply look like someone turning around to head back to Vegas.

Before turning back onto the freeway he watched the FBI car go off the paved road and head across the desert to the site. His site. A white cloud of dust kicked up behind the car. He could see the white tents in the distance. He felt an overwhelming sense of accomplishment. The crime scene was a city he had built. A city of bones. The agents were like ants between pieces of glass. They lived and worked in the world of his creation, unknowingly doing his bidding.

He wished he could get closer to that glass, to take it all in and see the horror he etched on their faces, but he knew the risk was too great.

And he had other things to do. He pushed his foot

down hard on the accelerator and headed back toward the city of sin. He had to make sure everything was ready and things were set.

As he drove he felt a slight sense of melancholy slide in beneath his ribs. He guessed that this came with the letdown of leaving Rachel behind in the desert. He took a deep breath and tried to exorcize the feeling. He knew it would not be long before he was close to her again.

After a moment he smiled at the memory of seeing his name on the sign held by the woman who had met Rachel at the airport. An inside joke between agents. Backus recognized the greeter. Agent Cherie Dei. Rachel had mentored her just as he had mentored Rachel. That meant some of his special insights had been passed on through Rachel to this new generation. He liked that. He wondered what Cherie Dei's reaction would have been if he had stepped up to her and her stupid sign at the bottom of the escalator and said, "Thanks for meeting me."

He looked out through the car's windows at the flat, barren plain of the desert floor. He believed it was truly beautiful, made even more so by the things he had planted in the sand and rock out there.

He thought about that and soon the pressure in his chest eased and he felt wonderful again. He checked the rearview for trailers and saw nothing that was suspicious. He checked himself then and admired the surgeon's work once more. He smiled at himself.

II

As they got close to the tents Rachel Walling began to smell the scene. The unmistakable odor of decaying flesh was carried on the wind as it worked through the encampment, billowed the tents and moved out again. She switched her breathing to her mouth, haunted by knowledge she wished she didn't have, that the sensation of smell occurred when tiny particles struck sensory receptors in the nasal passages. It meant if you smelled decaying flesh that was because you were breathing decaying flesh.

There were three small square tents in the approach to the site. These were not the kind for camping. They were field command tents with straight sides to eight feet. Behind these three was a larger rectangular tent. Rachel noticed that all of the tents had open vent flaps on top. She knew that there were body excavations taking place in each. The vents were to let some of the heat and stink escape.

Overlapping everything was the noise. There were at

least two gasoline-powered generators providing electricity to the scene. There were also two full-size RVs parked to the left of the tents and their rooftop air handlers were rumbling.

"Let's go in here first," Cherie Dei said, pointing to one of the RVs. "Randal is usually in here."

The RV looked like any supercamper Rachel had seen on the freeway. This one was called the "Open Road" and it had an Arizona plate on the back. Dei knocked on the door and then pulled it open without waiting for a response. They stepped up and in. The vehicle wasn't set up on the inside for camping on the open road. Partitions and the comforts of home had been removed. It was one long room set up with four folding tables and many chairs. Along the rear wall was a counter with all the usual office machinery—computer, fax, copier and coffeemaker. Two of the tables were covered with paperwork. On the third, incongruous to the purpose and setting, was a large bowl of fruit. The lunch table, Rachel guessed. Even at a mass burial site you have to have lunch. At the fourth table was a man on a cell phone, an open laptop computer in front of him.

"Have a seat," Dei said. "I'll introduce you as soon as he is off."

Rachel sat at the lunch table and took a precautionary sniff of the air. The RV's air handler was on recycle. The odor from the excavation wasn't noticeable. No wonder the man in charge stayed in here. She looked at the bowl of fruit and thought about taking a handful of grapes, just to keep her energy up, but decided not to.

"You want some fruit, go ahead," Dei said.

"No, thanks, I'm fine."

"Suit yourself."

Dei reached over and picked off some grapes and Rachel felt foolish because she had painted herself into a corner with the fruit. The man on the cell, who she assumed was Agent Alpert, was talking too low to be heard—probably by the person he was talking to as well. Rachel noticed that the long wall along the left side of the RV was covered with photographs of the excavations. She looked away. She didn't want to study the photographs until after she had been in the tents. She turned and looked out the window next to the table. This RV had the premiere view of the desert. She could see down into the basin and the entire ridgeline. She wondered for a moment if the view meant anything. If Backus had chosen the spot because of the view and if so, what was the significance of it.

When Dei turned her back Rachel grabbed some grapes and put three in her mouth at once. At the same moment, the man snapped his phone closed and got up from his table and approached her with his hand out.

"Randal Alpert, special agent in charge. We're glad you are here."

Rachel shook his hand but had to wait to get the grapes down before speaking.

"Nice to meet you. Not such nice circumstances."

"Yeah, but look at that view. Sure beats the brick wall I've got back in Quantico. And at least we're out here the end of April and not August. That would have been a killer."

He was the new Bob Backus. Running the shop at Quantico, coming out on the big ones and of course this was a big one. Rachel decided she didn't like him and that Cherie Dei was right about him being a morph.

Rachel had always found that agents in Behavioral were of two kinds. The first type she called "morphs." These agents were much like the men and women they hunted. Able to keep it all from getting to them. They could move on like a serial killer from case to case without being dragged down by all the horror and guilt and knowledge of the true nature of evil. Rachel called them morphs because these agents could take that burden and somehow morph it into something else. The site of a multiple body excavation became a beautiful view better than anything at Quantico.

The second type Rachel called "empaths" because they took all the horror in and kept it in. It became the campfire they warmed themselves by. They used it to connect and motivate, to get the job done. To Rachel, these were the better agents because they would go to the limit and beyond to catch the bad guy and solve the case.

It was certainly healthier to be a morph. To be able to move on without any baggage. The halls of Behavioral were haunted by the ghosts of the empaths, the agents who couldn't go the distance, for whom the burden became too much. Agents like Janet Newcomb, who put her gun in her mouth, and Jon Fenton, who drove into a bridge abutment, and Terry McCaleb, who literally gave his heart to the job. Rachel remembered them all and above all she remembered Bob Backus, the ultimate morph, the agent who was both hunter and prey.

"That was Brass Doran on the phone," Alpert said. "She said to say hello."

"She's back at Quantico?"

"Yes, she's agoraphobic about that place. Never wants to leave. She's heading up things on that end for us. Now, Agent Walling, I know you know the score. We've got a delicate situation here. We're glad you are here but you are here strictly as an observer and possibly a witness."

She didn't like him being so formal with her. It was a way of keeping her outside the circle.

"A witness?" she asked.

"You might be able to give us some ideas. You knew this guy. Most of us were on the street chasing bank robbers when the whole thing with Backus went down. I came into the unit right after your thing went down. After OPR went through the place. Cherie here is one of the few still around from then."

"My thing?"

"You know what I mean. You and Backus going at it."

"Can I go look at the excavation now? I'd like to see what you've got."

"Well, Cherie will take you out in a second. We don't have a lot to look at but today's carcass."

Spoken like a true morph, Rachel thought. She glanced at Dei and their eyes met in confirmation.

"But there is something I want to talk about first."

Rachel knew what was coming but let Alpert have his say. He moved toward the front of the RV and pointed through the windshield out into the desert. Rachel followed his line but couldn't see anything but the mountain ridge.

"Well, you can't really see it from this angle," Alpert

said, "but out there lying on the ground we've got a great big sign. It says in big letters, FILMING — NO FLY-OVERS, NO NOISE. That's for anybody up there who might get curious about all these tents and vehicles. Pretty good idea, huh? They think it's a movie set. Helps keep them away from us."

"And your point?"

"My point? My point is we have thrown a real thick blanket over all of this. Nobody knows and we want to keep it that way."

"And you are suggesting I am a media leak?"

"No, I am not suggesting that. I am giving you the same talk I give everybody that comes out here. I don't want this in the media. I want to control it this time. Is that understood?"

More like bureau command or the Office of Professional Responsibility wants to control it this time, she thought. The Backus revelations almost decimated the ranks and reputation of the Behavioral Sciences unit last time, not to mention the colossal public relations fiasco it was for the bureau as a whole. Now with the failings of 9/11 and the bureau's competition with Homeland Security for budget dollars as well as headlines, media focus on a mad killer agent was not what bureau command or the OPR had in mind. Especially when the general public had been led to believe that the mad killer agent was long since dead.

"I understand," Rachel said coolly. "You won't have to worry about me. Can I go out now?"

"One other thing."

He hesitated for a moment. Whatever it was, it was delicate.

"Not everyone involved in this investigation is aware of the connection to Robert Backus. It's 'need to know' and I want to keep it that way."

"What do you mean? The people working out there don't know it was Backus who did this? They should be—"

"Agent Walling, this is not your investigation. Don't try to make it yours. You were brought here to observe and help, leave it at that. We don't know for sure it was Backus and until we do—"

"Right. His fingerprints were only all over the GPS and his MO all over everything else."

Alpert glanced at Dei, throwing her a look of annoyance.

"Cherie should not have told you about the prints and as far as the MO goes, there is nothing known about that for sure."

"Just because she shouldn't have told me doesn't mean it isn't true. You're not going to be able to cover this up, Agent Alpert."

Alpert laughed in frustration.

"Who said anything about a cover-up? Look, all we're doing right now is controlling information. There is a right time for revealing data. That is all I am telling you. Your presence alone here will be revealing enough, okay? I just don't want you deciding what to reveal and who to reveal it to. That's my job. Understood?"

Rachel nodded without conviction. She glanced at Dei as she did so.

"Perfectly."

"Good. Then, Cherie, take her away. Take her sight-seeing."

They left the RV and Dei led her toward the first small tent.

"You certainly ingratiated yourself with him," she said to Rachel as they went.

"It's funny. Some things just never change. I think it might be impossible for a bureaucracy to evolve, to learn anything from its mistakes. Anyway, never mind. What do we have here?"

"So far we have eight bags and gas on another two. We just haven't gotten to them yet. Classic inverted pyramid."

Rachel knew the shorthand. She had invented some of it. Dei was saying eight bodies had been recovered and readings from gas probes indicated there were another two bodies still interred and waiting for excavation. Tragic history created data from which models of similar behavior were formed. It had been seen before, a killer who returns with victims to the same burial spot follows a pattern, the newer burials radiating out from the original in an inverted pyramid or V pattern. So was the case here, with Backus either unintentionally or consciously following a pattern based on data he helped accumulate as an agent.

"Let me ask you one thing," Rachel said. "He was talking to Brass Doran on the phone in there. She's got to know about the Backus connection, right?"

"Yes, she knows. She found the prints on the package."

Rachel nodded. At least she had one confederate she could trust and who was in the know.

They reached the tent and Dei pulled back the entry flap. Rachel went in first. Because the overhead venting flap was open it was not dark in the tent. It was only dim.

Rachel's eyes adjusted immediately and she saw a large rectangular hole in the center of the tent. There was no fill pile. She assumed the dirt and rock and sand removed from the grave had been shipped to Quantico or the field office lab for sifting and analysis.

"This first site is where the anomalies are," Dei said. "The others are straight burials. Very clean."

"What are the anomalies?"

"The reading on the GPS came back to this spot. Sitting here when they got here was a boat. It was—"

"A boat? Here in the desert?"

"You remember that preacher I told you started this place? He dug a canal for the spring water to fill. We figure the boat came from back then. It had been sitting here for decades. Anyway, we moved it, sank a probe and started digging. Anomaly number two is that the grave contained the first two victims. All the other graves are individual."

"These first two, were they buried at the same time?"

"Yes. One on top of the other. But one was wrapped in plastic and he had been dead a lot longer than the other. Seven months longer, we think."

"So he sat on one body for a while. Wrapped it for safekeeping. And when he had the second he realized he had to do something and so he came out to the desert to bury them. He used the boat as a marker. As a sort of gravestone and for himself because he knew he'd be back with more."

"Maybe. But why'd he need the boat if he had the GPS?"

Rachel nodded and felt a little buzz of adrenaline

start to tick in her blood. The brainstorming had always been the best part of the job.

"The GPS came later. Recently. That was just for us."

"Us?"

"You. The bureau. Me."

Rachel moved to the edge and looked down into the hole. It had not been deep, especially for two bodies. She stopped breathing through her mouth and took the fetid air in through her nose. She wanted to remember this.

"IDs yet?"

"Nothing official. No contact with kin yet. But we know who some of them were. Five of them at least. The first one was three years ago. The second seven months after that."

"Have you built a cycle?"

"Yes, we have it. About an eight percent reduction. We think the last two will bring us up to November."

Meaning that the intervals between the killings were decreasing by eight percent from the initial seven-month period between killings one and two. Again, it was familiar. The decreasing interval was common in case history, a symptom of the killer's diminishing control of his urges at the same time his belief in his invincibility grows. You get away with the first one and the second comes easier and sooner. And so on.

"I guess that makes him overdue," Rachel said.

"Supposedly."

"Supposedly?"

"Come on, Rachel, it's Backus. He knows what we know. He's just playing with us. It's like Amsterdam. He's gone before we even recognize it is him. Same here. He's moved on. I mean, why send us the GPS if he hasn't? He's split already. He's not overdue and he's not coming back here. He's somewhere laughing at us, watching us follow our models and routines, knowing that we won't get any closer to him than we did the last time."

Rachel nodded. She knew Dei was right but decided to be optimistic.

"He's got to make a mistake somewhere. What about the GPS? Anything on that?"

"We're working it, obviously. Brass is on that."

"What else is there?"

"There is you, Rachel."

Rachel didn't say anything. Again Cherie Dei was right. Backus had something in play. His obscure but direct message to Rachel seemed to make this obvious. He wanted her here, wanted her to be part of the play. But what was it? What did the Poet want?

Like Rachel had mentored Dei, Backus had mentored Rachel. He was a good teacher. In retrospect, better than she or anyone could have imagined. She was mentored by both agent and killer, hunter and prey, a unique combination in the annals of crime and punishment. Rachel always remembered a throwaway line Backus had spoken one night when they were walking up the stairs from the basement at Quantico, leaving the unit behind for the day.

"In the long run I think it is all bullshit. We can't predict how these people act. We can only react. And at the end of the day, that means we're largely useless. We make good headlines and Hollywood makes good movies about us, but that's about it."

Rachel was a rookie in the unit at the time. She was

full of ideals and plans and faith. She spent the next thirty minutes trying to talk Backus out of such a belief. Now she was embarrassed by the memory of the effort and the things she had said to a man she would later realize was a killer.

"Can I go into the other tents now?" Rachel asked.

"Sure," Dei said. "Whatever you want."

12

I T WAS LATE AND the batteries on the boat were beginning to run low. The lights in the forward berth
were steadily dimming. Or at least it seemed so to me.
Maybe it was my eyes that were dimming. I had spent
seven hours reading through files pulled out of the boxes
on the top bunk. I had filled my notebook to the last page
and then flipped it over and started back to front.

The afternoon interview had been uneventful if not
unhelpful. Terry McCaleb's last charter was a man
named Otto Woodall who lived in a luxury condo behind the fabled Avalon Casino building. I talked to him
for an hour, getting much the same story I had already
gotten from Buddy Lockridge. Woodall, who was sixty-
six years old, confirmed all aspects of the trip that were
of interest to me. He said he did leave the boat during
their dockage in Mexico and spent time with women he
knew there. He was unembarrassed and unashamed. His
wife was over on the mainland shopping for the day and
he apparently didn't mind opening up. He told me he

was retired from his job but not from life. He said he still had a man's needs. I let that line of questioning go at that point and focused on the last moments of McCaleb's life.

Woodall's observations and recollections mirrored Buddy's in all important details. Woodall also confirmed that on at least two specific instances during the trip he saw McCaleb take his meds, downing the pills and liquids with orange juice each time.

I took notes but knew they wouldn't be needed. After an hour I thanked Woodall for his time and left him to his view of the Santa Monica Bay and the bloom of smog that rose beyond it on the mainland.

Buddy Lockridge was waiting for me out front in a golf cart I had rented. He was still brooding over my last-minute decision to interview Woodall without him. He'd accused me of using him to get the interview with Woodall. He was right about that but his complaints and concerns weren't even on my radar.

We drove silently back to the pier and I turned in the cart. I told Buddy he could head home because I was going to be busy reading files the rest of the day and into the night. He meekly offered to help but I told him he already had helped enough. I watched him walk off toward the ferry docks with his head down. I still wasn't sure about Buddy Lockridge. I knew I had some thinking to do about him.

Not wanting to fool around with the Zodiac I took a water taxi back to *The Following Sea*. I conducted a quick search of the master stateroom—finding nothing of note—and moved into the forward cabin.

I noticed that Terry had a compact disc player in the

converted office. His small collection of music was mostly blues and 1970s rock and roll. I plugged in a more recent Lucinda Williams CD called *World Without Tears* and liked it so much I ended up letting it play over and over during the next six hours. The woman had long journeys in her voice and I liked that. By the time the power started faltering on the boat and I turned the music off I had unconsciously memorized the lyrics to at least three songs I could sing to my daughter the next time I put her to bed.

Back in McCaleb's converted office, the first thing I did was go back to his computer and open the folder marked PROFILES.

It gave me a listing of six different files, all titled by dates in the previous two years. One by one I called them up in chronological order and found each to be a forensic suspect profile of a murder case. Written in the unadorned and clinical language of the professional, each profile drew conclusions about a killer based on specific crime scene details. It was clear from these details that McCaleb had done more than simply read newspaper articles. It was obvious he had full access to the crime scenes—either in person or more likely by photos and tapes and investigators' notes. It was very clear to me that these were not practice runs worked up by a profiler who missed the job and wanted to keep in tune. These were the work of an invited guest. The cases were all from the jurisdictions of small police departments in the west. My guess was that McCaleb had heard of each case through news reports or other means and simply volunteered his help to the police department struggling with the case. Offer accepted, he was probably sent the crime scene information and he then set to work analyzing and drawing up the profile. I wondered if his notoriety helped or hindered him when he offered his talents. How many times was he turned down to be accepted these six times?

When accepted, he probably worked each case from the desk where I was sitting, without ever leaving the boat. Or thinking his wife knew in detail what he was doing.

But I could tell each profile had taken a good amount of his time and attention. I was beginning to understand more and more what Graciela had said had become a problem in their marriage. Terry couldn't draw a line. He couldn't let it go. This profile work was a testament not only to his dedication to his mission as an investigator but also to his blind spot as a husband and father.

The six profiles came from cases in Scottsdale, Arizona; Henderson, Nevada; and the four California cities of La Jolla, Laguna Beach, Salinas and San Mateo. Two were child murders and the other four were sex slayings involving three women and one male victim. McCaleb drew no links between them. It was clear they were simply separate cases that had drawn his attention in the last two years. There was no indication in any of the files that Terry's work had been helpful or if any of the cases had been cleared. I wrote down the basics from each in my notebook with the idea that I would follow up with the departments to check the status of each investigation. It was a long shot but it was still possible that one of these profiles could have triggered McCaleb's death. It wasn't a priority but I would need to check it out.

Finished with the computer for the time being, I directed my attention to the file boxes stored on the top bunk. One by one I pulled them down until there was no room on the floor of the forward room. I found that they contained a mix of files from both solved and unsolved cases. I spent the first hour just sorting them and pulling out the open-unsolveds, thinking that it was more likely than not that if Terry's death was related to a case, then it was one with a suspect still at large. There was no reason for him to be working or reworking a closed case.

The reading was fascinating. Many of the files were on cases I was familiar with or had even had a part in. They were not files that had gathered dust. I got the distinct impression that the open cases were in endless rotation. From time to time McCaleb pulled them out and rethought the investigations, the suspects, the crime scenes, the possibilities. He made calls to investigators and lab people and even witnesses. All of this was clear because McCaleb's practice was to use the inside front flap of the file to write notes on the moves he made, meticulously dating these entries as well.

From these dates I could tell that McCaleb had been working many cases at once. And it was clear he still had a pipeline into the FBI and the Behavioral Sciences unit at Quantico. I spent a whole hour reading the fat file he had accumulated on the Poet, one of the more notorious if not embarrassing serial killer cases in the FBI annals. The Poet was a killer later revealed to be the FBI agent who had been heading the squad essentially hunting for himself. It was a scandal that had rocked the bureau and its vaunted Behavioral Sciences Section eight years before. The agent, Robert Backus, chose homicide detectives as his victims. He staged the killing scenes as suicides, leaving behind suicide notes containing verses from the poems of Edgar Allan Poe. He killed eight men across the country in a period of three years before a reporter discovered the false suicides and the manhunt began. Backus was revealed and shot by another agent in Los Angeles. At the time he was supposedly targeting a detective from the homicide table in the LAPD's Hollywood Division. That was my table. The target, Ed Thomas, was my colleague and that was my connection. I remember taking a very high personal interest in the Poet.

Now I was reading the inside story. Officially the case was closed by the bureau. But the unofficial word had always been that Backus had gotten away. After being shot Backus initially escaped into the storm-water tunnel system that ranged beneath Los Angeles. Six weeks later a body was found with a bullet hole in the right place but decomposition made a physical identification and fingerprint comparison impossible. Foraging animals—it was reported—had made off with parts of the body, including the lower mandible and the only teeth that could have been used for identification through dental records. Backus had also conveniently disappeared without leaving DNA exemplars behind. So they had the body with the bullet hole but nothing to compare it to. Or so they said. The bureau quickly announced that Backus was presumed dead and the file was closed, if only to bring a speedy end to the agency's humiliation at the hands of one of its own.

But the records McCaleb had accumulated since then confirmed that the folklore was true. Backus was still alive and out there. Somewhere. Four years earlier he had surfaced in Holland. According to confidential FBI bulletins provided by bureau sources to McCaleb, a killer took the lives of five men over a two-year period in Amsterdam. All the victims were foreign visitors who had disappeared after venturing into the city's red-light district. Each man was found strangled and floating in the Amstel River. What connected the killings to Backus were notes sent to local authorities in which the writer took credit for the killings and asked that the FBI be called into the case. The writer, according to the confidential reports, asked specifically for Agent Rachel Walling, the agent who had shot Robert Backus four years earlier. The police in Holland invited the FBI to take an unofficial look at the case. The sender had signed each letter as simply "The Poet." FBI handwriting analysis of the letter indicated—not conclusively—that the writer was not a killer trying to ride the notorious coattails of Robert Backus, but Backus himself.

Of course, by the time the bureau, local authorities and even Rachel Walling mobilized in Amsterdam, the killer was long gone. And Robert Backus had not been heard from again—at least as far as Terry McCaleb's sources knew.

I replaced the thick file in one of the boxes and moved on. I soon learned that McCaleb was not just working old cases. In fact, anything that caught his attention was subject to his focus and skills. There were dozens of files that contained only a single newspaper story and some notes jotted on the file flap. Some cases were high profile, others obscure. He put together a file of newspaper clips on the Laci Peterson case, the disappearance of a pregnant woman from Central California on Christmas Eve two years before. The case had garnered long-term media and public attention, particularly after her dismembered body was found in the bay where her husband had earlier told investigators he had been fishing when she disappeared. An entry on the file flap dated before the woman's body was found said, "Definitely Dead—in the water." Another note dated before her husband's arrest said, "There's another woman."

There was also a file with seemingly prescient notes on Elizabeth Smart, a child kidnapped in Utah who was found and returned after nearly a year. He correctly wrote "alive" under one of the newspaper photos of the young girl.

McCaleb also made an unofficial study of the Robert Blake case. The former film and television star was accused of murdering his wife in another headlining case. The notes in the file were intuitive and on point, ultimately borne out as correct as the case entered the courts.

I had to ask myself if it was possible that McCaleb had entered the notes in his files and predated them, using information from media accounts and making it appear that he was predicting case aspects or suspect traits from his own work when he wasn't. While anything was possible, it seemed entirely unrealistic to me to think McCaleb had done this. I could see no reason for him to commit such a quiet and self-defeating crime. I believed the work was real and was his.

One file that I found contained newspaper stories on the LAPD's new cold case squad. Noted on the flap were the names and cell numbers of four detectives assigned to the unit. Terry had obviously been able to cross the gulf between the LAPD and the FBI if he had their cell numbers. I knew detectives' cell numbers were not handed out to just anyone.

One of the four detectives I knew. Tim Marcia had spent time in Hollywood Division, including the homicide table. I knew it was late but cops expect to get late calls. I knew Marcia wouldn't mind. I took out my cell and called the number McCaleb had written next to his name on the file. Marcia answered immediately. I identified myself, got through the long-time-no-see pleasantries and explained that I was calling about Terry McCaleb. I didn't lie but I didn't say I was working a murder investigation. I said I was sorting through his files for his wife and came across Marcia's name and number. I was simply curious about what their relationship had been.

"Harry, you worked some cold cases in your time, right? That thing up at your house last year came out of a cold case, didn't it?"

"Right."

"Then you know how it goes. Sometimes you grasp at straws, you take any help you can get. Terry called me up one day and offered his services. Not on a specific case. I think he had seen a story in the *Times* about the unit and he basically said if I ever needed him to work a profile he was there for me. He was one of the good ones. I was really sorry to hear what happened. I wanted to get over to Catalina for the service but things sort of came up."

"Like they always do. Did you ever take him up on the offer to do a profile?"

"Yeah, sort of. I know I did and a couple other of the guys here did, too. You know how it is. The department has no profiling to speak of and sometimes waiting on the bureau and Quantico can take months. Here was this guy who knew what he was doing and he didn't want anything back. He just wanted to work. So we used him. We bounced a few things off him."

"And how did he do?"

"He did good. We're working this one case now that's interesting. When the new chief put the squad together we started going back through the open-unsolveds. We linked six cases—body dumps up in the Valley. They had some similar aspects but were never connected before. We copied the files to Terry and he confirmed. He connected them through what he called 'psychological commonalities.' We're still working it but at least we know what we have now. We're on the track is what I mean. I'm not sure we would be where we are if Terry hadn't helped us out."

"Good, I'm glad to hear he helped with it. I'll tell his wife and I'm sure it will help her to know that."

"Good. So, Harry, you coming back in?"

I was expecting him to ask what I was really doing with McCaleb's files, not whether I was coming back to the department.

"What are you talking about?"

"You heard about the three-year ticket the chief instituted?"

"No, what's that?"

"He knows we lost a lot of talent in recent years. All the scandals and whatnot, good people saying, what the hell, I'm out of here. So he's opening the door for people to come back. If you reapply within three years of retirement and are accepted you can get back in without having to go to the academy. That's perfect for old guys like you."

I heard the smile in his voice.

"Three years, huh?"

"Yeah. What's it been for you, two and a half?"

"Just about."

"Well, there you go. Think about it. We could use you here in cold cases. We've got seven thousand open-unsolveds. Take your pick, man."

I didn't say anything. Out of the blue, I was struck with the idea of going back. In that moment I was blind to the negatives. I only thought about what it would be like to carry the badge again.

"Then again, maybe you're having too much fun being retired. You need anything else, Harry?"

"Uh, no, that was it. Thanks, man, I appreciate it."

"Anytime. And think about the three-year plan. We could sure use you, whether it's here or back in Hollywood or wherever."

"Yeah, thanks. Maybe I will. I'm going to think about it."

I closed the phone and sat there surrounded by another man's obsessions but thinking about my own. I thought about going back. I thought about seven thousand unanswered voices from the grave. That was more than the number of stars you see when you look up into the sky at night.

My phone buzzed while it was still in my hand. It pulled me out of the reverie and I opened it, expecting it to be Tim Marcia calling back and saying that three-year thing had just been a gag. But it was Graciela calling.

"I can see lights on in the boat," she said. "Are you still there?"

"Yeah, I'm here."

"Why so late, Harry? You missed the last ferry."

"I wasn't going to go back tonight. I was going to stay over and finish up here. Maybe head back tomorrow. I might want to come up and talk to you, too."

"That's fine. I'm not working tomorrow. I'll be here packing."

"Packing?"

"We're going to move back to the mainland. We'll live in Northridge. I got my old job back in the ER at Holy Cross."

"Is Raymond one of the reasons you're moving back?"

"Raymond? What do you mean?"

"I was wondering if there were any troubles with the boy. I heard he didn't like living on the island."

"Raymond doesn't have a lot of friends. He doesn't fit in so well. But the move is not just because of Raymond. I want to go back. I wanted to before Terry was gone. I told you that."

"Yes, I know."

She changed the subject.

"Is there anything you need? Did you get something to eat?"

"I found some stuff in the boat's kitchen. I'm fine."

She groaned in disgust.

"That all must be old. Check the expiration dates before you eat anything else."

"I will."

She hesitated and then asked the question she had called to ask.

"Have you found anything yet?"

"Well, I've found some things I am curious about. But nothing that particularly stands out yet."

I thought about the man in the Dodgers cap. He certainly stood out for me but I didn't want to bring him up yet with Graciela. I wanted to know more before talking to her about him.

"Okay," she said. "But keep me informed about things, okay?"

"That's the deal."

"Okay, Harry, I'll talk to you tomorrow. Are you staying in a hotel or on the boat?"

"The boat, I think. If that's all right with you."

"It's fine with me. Do what you want to."

"Okay. Can I ask you something?"

"Sure, what?"

"You were talking about packing and I'm just curious about something. How often do you go over to the mainland? You know, to go to the mall or restaurants or see family."

"Usually about once a month. Unless something specific comes up and I need to go."

"You take the kids?"

"Usually. I want them to be used to it. You grow up on an island where they have golf carts instead of cars and everybody knows everybody . . . it can be strange to suddenly move to the mainland. I'm trying to get them ready for it."

"I guess that's smart. What mall is closest to the ferry docks?"

"I don't know what one is closest, but I always go up to the Promenade on Pico. I just shoot up the four-oh-five from the harbor. I know there are closer malls—Fox Hills, for example—but I like the Promenade. I like the stores there and it's easy. Sometimes I meet friends from the Valley and it is a good halfway point for all of us."

And easy to be followed to, I thought but didn't say.

"Good," I said, not sure what I was saying was good. "One other thing. I'm running out of light here. The batteries, I guess. Is there a switch or something I should hit to recharge or how do you do that?"

"You didn't ask Buddy?"

"No, I didn't know I was going to run out of light when I was with Buddy."

"Oh, Harry, I'm not sure. There's a generator that has to run. I'm not sure even where it is."

"Okay, well, don't worry about it. I can call Buddy. I'll let you go, Graciela. I ought to get back to work while I still have some light."

I hung up and wrote the name of the mall down in my notebook, then left the room and went around the boat turning off all the lights but the one on the desk in the forward berth in an effort to conserve power. I called Buddy on the cell after that and he answered in a groggy voice.

"Hey, Buddy, wake up. It's Harry Bosch."

"Who? Oh. What do you want?"

"I need your help. Is there like a generator or something on this boat that will give me some light? The batteries are dying on me."

"Man, don't let those things drain all the way down. You'll kill them."

"Then what do I do?"

"You've got to crank the Volvos, man, and then turn

on the generator. The thing is it's near midnight. Those folks sleeping on their boats in line with you aren't going to take so kindly to hearing that."

"All right, forget it. But in the morning I should do it, so what do I do, use a key?"

"Yeah, just like a car. Go to the helm in the salon, put in the keys and turn them to the ON position. Then above each key is the ignition toggle. Flip it up and she should start right up—unless you've used all the juice up and there's no charge."

"Okay, I'll do it. You got any flashlights on this thing?"

"Yeah, there's one in the galley, one over the chart table and one in the master in the built-in drawer to the left of the bed. There's also a lantern in the lower cabinet of the galley. But you don't want to use that down in the front room. The kerosene smell will build up in there and you might croak yourself. Then there'd be another mystery to solve."

He said the last line with a note of contempt in his voice. I let it go.

"Thanks, Buddy. I'll talk to you."

"Yeah. Good night."

I hung up and went looking for the flashlights, coming back to the forward berth with a small one from the master stateroom and a large table light from the galley. I put the large light on the desk and turned it on. I then killed the berth's lights. The table light's glow hit the small room's low ceiling and spread. It wasn't bad. Between that and the handheld light I would still be able to get some work done.

I was down to less than half a box of files to go and

wanted to finish before figuring out where I was going to sleep. These were all thin files, the most recent additions to McCaleb's collection, and I could tell most of them contained little more than a newspaper clip and maybe a few notes on the flap.

I reached in and picked one out at random. I should have been in Vegas throwing dice. Because the file I picked turned out to be a long-shot winner. It was the file that gave my investigation focus. It put me on the road.

13

THE FILE TAB SIMPLY said 6 MISSING. It contained a single clipping from the *Los Angeles Times* and several dated notes and names and phone numbers handwritten on the inside flap, as was McCaleb's routine. I sensed that the file was important before I even read the story or understood the meaning of some of the notes. It was the dating on the flap that triggered this response. McCaleb had jotted his thoughts down on the file four different times, beginning on January 7 and ending on February 28 of this year. He would be dead a month later on March 31. Those notes and those dates were the most recent found in any of the files I had reviewed. I knew I was looking at what might have been Terry's last work. His last case and obsession. There were still files to look at but this one gave me the vibe and I went with it.

A reporter I knew wrote the story. Keisha Russell had been working the cop beat at the *Times* at least ten years and was good at it. She was also accurate and fair. She had lived up to every deal I had ever made with her in the years I was on the job, and she had gone out of her way to play fair with me the year before, when I was no longer on the job and things turned bad on my first private case.

The bottom line was that I felt comfortable taking anything she wrote as fact. I started to read.

SEARCH FOR A MISSING LINK

ARE NEVADA DISAPPEARANCES OF 2 L.A. MEN, 4 OTHERS CONNECTED?

by Keisha Russell
Times Staff Writer

The mysterious disappearances of at least six men, including two from Los Angeles, from gambling centers in Nevada have got investigators searching for a missing link among the men.

Detectives with the Las Vegas Metro Police said Tuesday that while the men did not know each other and came from widely disparate hometowns and backgrounds, there still may be a commonality among them that could be the key to the mystery.

The men, ranging in age from 29 to 61, were reported missing by their families during the past three years. Four were last known to be in Las Vegas, where police are heading the investigation, and two disappeared while on trips to Laughlin and Primm. None of the men left any indication in their hotel rooms or vehicles or homes as to where they were going or what became of them.

"At this point it is a stone-cold mystery," said

Detective Todd Ritz of Vegas Metro's Missing Persons unit. "People disappear from here or any-where all the time. But they usually show up later, dead or alive. And there's usually an explanation. With these guys there's nothing. It's a thin air case."

But Ritz and other detectives are sure there is an explanation and they are enlisting the public's help in finding it. Last week detectives from Las Vegas, Laughlin and Primm gathered at the Vegas Metro offices to compare notes and set an investigative strategy. They also went public with the case, hop-ing photographs of the men and their stories would spark new information from the public. On Tuesday, a week later, Ritz reported that not much in the way of usable information had come in.

"There has got to be someone who knows some-thing or saw something or heard something," said Ritz in a telephone interview. "Six guys just don't get up and disappear without somebody knowing something. We need that somebody to come for-ward."

As Ritz said, missing persons cases are numer-ous. The fact that these six men came to Nevada for business or pleasure and never went home is what makes this case different.

The publicity comes at a time Las Vegas is once again redefining its image. Gone is the marketing strategy that billed the neon city as a family desti-nation. Sin is back in. In the past three years nu-merous clubs featuring nude or partially nude dancers have been licensed, and many of the casinos on the fabled strip have produced shows featuring nudity and strictly adult subject matter. Billboards featuring nudity in their advertisements have been erected and drawn the ire of some community activists. It has all helped change the complexion of the city. Once again it is being marketed as a leave-the-kids-at-home adult playground.

As the recent billboard skirmishes suggest, the change hasn't played well with everyone and many speculate that the disappearances of these six travelers may in some indirect way be linked to the region's return to an anything-goes atmosphere.

"Let's face it," said Ernie Gelson, a columnist for the Las Vegas Sun, "they tried the family fun thing and it didn't play. The town is going back to what plays. And what plays is what pays. Now, is that the missing link that connects these six guys? I don't know. Maybe we never will."

Still, Gelson is uneasy about jumping to any conclusions that would link the missing men to the changing image of Las Vegas.

"First of all, remember, they didn't all disappear from Las Vegas," he said. "And second to that, there are not enough facts to substantiate any theory at the moment. I think we have to sit back and let the mystery resolve itself before we jump on any bandwagons."

The missing men are:

—Gordon Stansley, 41, of Los Angeles, missing since May 17, 2001. He checked into the Mandalay Bay Resort and Casino in Las Vegas but his bed was never slept in and his suitcase never unpacked. He is married and has two children.

—John Edward Dunn, 39, of Ottawa, Canada, who was driving from his home to Los Angeles on a vacation. He never made it to his intended destination, his brother's home in Granada Hills. Dunn's 30-foot recreational vehicle was found Dec. 29, 2001, at an RV park in Laughlin. That was 20 days after his expected arrival in Granada Hills.

—Lloyd Rockland, 61, disappeared from Las Vegas on June 17, 2002. His plane from Atlanta arrived at 11 a.m. at McCarran International Airport. He picked up a Hertz rental car, but he never checked in to the MGM Grand, where he had a reservation. His car was returned to the Hertz rental car center at the airport at 2 p.m. the next day but nobody seems to remember the father of four and grandfather of three being the one who returned it.

—Fenton Weeks, 29, of Dallas, TX, was reported missing Jan. 25, 2003, after he did not return from a business trip to Las Vegas. Police determined he had checked in to the Golden Nugget in downtown Las Vegas and attended the first day of an electronics exposition held at the Las Vegas Convention Center but was not in attendance on the second and third days. His wife reported him missing. He has no children.

—Joseph O'Leary, 55, of Berwyn, PA, disappeared May 15 of last year from the Bellagio where he was staying with his wife. Alice O'Leary left her husband in the casino playing blackjack while she went to spend the day at the resort's spa. Several hours later her husband failed to return to their suite. O'Leary, a stockbroker, was reported missing the next day.

—Rogers Eberle, 40, of Los Angeles, disappeared Nov. 1 while on a day off from his work as a graphic designer at the Disney Studios in Burbank. His car was found parked in the lot outside the Buffalo Bill's Casino in Primm, NV, just across the California border on the Interstate 15 freeway.

Investigators say there are few leads in the investigation. They point to Rockland's rental car as possibly being the best clue they have. The car was returned 27 hours after it was picked up by Rockland. It had been driven 328 miles during that period, according to Hertz records. Whoever returned it to the Hertz airport center dropped it off without waiting for a receipt or to speak to a Hertz clerk.

"They just pulled in, got out of the car and walked away," Ritz said. "Nobody remembers anything. They process about a thousand cars a day in that center. There are no cameras and there is no record but the rental record."

And it is those 328 miles that Ritz and the other detectives wonder about.

"That is a lot of miles," said Detective Peter Echerd, Ritz's partner. "That car could have gone a lot of places. You figure a hundred and sixty-four out and a hundred and sixty-four back in and you've got a hell of a big circle to cover."

Nevertheless, the investigators are trying to do

just that, hoping their efforts will uncover a clue that makes the circle smaller and possibly leads to the answers to the six missing family men.

"It's tough," said Ritz. "These guys all have families and we're doing our best for them. But at the moment we have lots of questions and not any answers."

The article was nicely drawn with the *Times*'s signature method of finding larger significance to a story than the story itself. In this case it was the theorizing that the disappearance of these men was symptomatic of the newest permutation of Las Vegas as an adult playground. It reminded me of a time I was working a case in which a man who owned an auto garage cut the hydraulic lines on a lift and a seven-thousand-pound Cadillac came down and crushed his longtime partner beneath it. A *Times* reporter called me up for the details for a story and then asked if the killing was symptomatic of the tightening economy in which money woes turned partners against partners. I said, no, I thought it was symptomatic of one guy not liking his partner screwing his wife.

Larger implications aside, the story was a plant. I could tell that. I had done the same thing with the same reporter in my time. Ritz was trolling for information. Since half the missing men were either from or going to Los Angeles, why not call the *Times,* plant a story with the cop reporter and see who and what pops up?

One person who popped up was Terry McCaleb. He obviously read the story on January 7, the day it was published, because his first set of notes on the file flap was dated as such. The notes were short and cryptic. At the top of the flap the name Ritz and a phone number with a 702 area code had been jotted down. Beneath this, McCaleb had written:

1/7—
    44 avg.
    41—39—40
    find intersection
    cycle disruption—there are more
    car—328
    triangle theory?
        1 point gives 3
    DD—check desert

1/9—
    call back—png

2/2
    Hinton—702 259-4050
    n/c story?

2/28
    Zzyzx—possible? how?
    miles

Written along the side border of the file were two more phone numbers with 702 area codes. These were followed with the name William Bing.

I reread the notes and looked at the clipping again. I

noticed for the first time that McCaleb had circled two things on the newspaper article, the mention of the 328 miles found to have been put on the rental car and the word *circle* in Echerd's comment about the circle of the investigation being 164 miles in any direction. I didn't know why he had circled these two things but I did know what most of the notes on the flap meant. I had spent more than seven hours reading through McCaleb's files. I had seen notation after notation in file after file. The ex-agent used a shorthand of his own invention but one that was decipherable because in some files he spelled out what he chose to abbreviate in others.

Immediately recognizable to me was what he meant by the use of "DD." It meant "definitely dead," a classification and conclusion McCaleb made on the wide majority of the missing cases he reviewed. Also easy to decipher was "png," which meant *persona non grata*, meaning McCaleb's offer to help with the investigation was not received well or not received at all.

McCaleb had also found some significance in the age of the missing men. He wrote down an average age and then pulled out three of the victims' ages because they were within two years of each other and very close to the average. This appeared to me to be notes relating to a victim profile but there wasn't one in the file and I didn't know if McCaleb ever proceeded past the notes stage.

The "find intersection" reference seemed to also be part of this profile. McCaleb was referring to a geographic or lifestyle intersection of the six missing men. Just as the Metro detective had put forth in the *Times* article, McCaleb was operating under the belief that there had to be a connection between these men. Yes, they were from as far apart as Ottawa and Los Angeles and did not know one another, but there had to be a point where they came together in some way.

"Cycle disruption—there are more" I suspected was a reference to the frequency of the disappearances. If someone was abducting and killing these men, as McCaleb believed, there would usually be a recognizable time cycle. Serial killers operate this way in most cases, with violent psychosexual urges building and then subsiding after a kill. McCaleb had apparently worked out the cycle and found holes in it—missing victims. He believed there were more than six men missing.

What puzzled me most about the notes was the reference to "triangle theory" and the phrase "1 point gives 3" below it. This was something I had not seen come up in the previous files and I did not know what was meant by it. It was noted in conjunction with references to the car and the 328 miles that had been put on it. But the more I played with it, the more puzzled I became by it. It was code or shorthand for something I didn't know. It bothered me but there was nothing I could do about it with what I currently knew.

The January 9 reference was to a call back from Ritz. McCaleb had probably called and left a message and the Vegas detective had called back, listened to his pitch and maybe his profile, and had said not interested. This was not surprising. The FBI was often unwanted by the locals. The clash of egos between feds and locals was a routine part of the job. A retired bureau man would likely be treated no differently. Terry McCaleb was persona non grata.

That might have been it for this file and this case but

then came the February 2 notation. A name and a number. I opened my cell phone and called the number, not caring about how late it was. Or early, depending on how you looked at it. I got a recording of a female voice.

"This is Cindy Hinton at the *Las Vegas Sun*. I can't take your call right now but it is important to me. Please leave your name and number and I will call you back as soon as I can. Thank you."

There was a beep and I hesitated, not sure I wanted to make contact yet. But I went ahead anyway.

"Uh, yes, hello, my name is Harry Bosch. I'm an investigator from Los Angeles and would like to talk to you about Terry McCaleb."

I left my cell phone number and closed the phone, still not sure I had made the right move but thinking that leaving it short and cryptic was the best way to go. It might get her to call me back.

The last reference in the notes was the most intriguing of all. McCaleb had written "Zzyzx" and then asked if it was possible and if so, how. This had to be a reference to Zzyzx Road. This was a leap. A giant leap. McCaleb had received photos from someone who had watched and photographed his family. That same person had taken photographs at Zzyzx Road near the California-Nevada border. Somehow McCaleb saw a possible link and was asking himself if one mystery could be related to the other. Could he have set something in motion by calling Vegas Metro and offering to help with the missing men case? To be able to make the leap to such questions was impossible. It meant I was missing something. I was missing the bridge, the piece of information that made the jump possible. McCaleb had to have known something that wasn't noted in the file but that made the possibility of a link seem real to him.

The last notations to check were the two Las Vegas phone numbers written on the border of the file along with the name William Bing. I opened my cell again and called the first number. The call was picked up by a recorded voice announcing that I had reached the Mandalay Bay Resort and Casino. I hung up as the voice began to list a number of options I could choose from.

The second number was followed by the name. I punched it into the phone, prepared to awaken William Bing and ask him what his connection to Terry McCaleb was. But the call was answered after several rings by a woman who said, "Las Vegas Memorial Medical Center, how would you like me to direct your call?"

I wasn't expecting that. To gain some time while I thought about what to do I asked her for the hospital's location. By the time she was finished giving me the address on Blue Diamond Road I had come up with a valid question.

"Do you have a doctor on staff named William Bing?"

After a moment the answer came back negative.

"Do you have any employee named William Bing?"

"No, we don't, sir."

"How about a patient?"

There was another pause as she consulted a computer.

"Not currently, no."

"Did you formerly have a patient there named William Bing?"

"I don't have access to that kind of information, sir."

I thanked her and closed the phone.

I thought about the last two numbers in McCaleb's

notes for a long moment. My conclusions were simple. Terry McCaleb was a heart transplant recipient. If he were to travel to another city he would need to know where to go and who to ask for if there was an emergency or any medical problem. My guess was that McCaleb had called information to get the two numbers noted on the file. He then made a reservation at the Mandalay Bay and checked in with a local hospital as a precaution. The fact that there was no William Bing on staff at Las Vegas Memorial Medical Center did not preclude that he might be a cardio specialist who handled patients there.

I opened the phone, checked the time on the display screen and called Graciela anyway. She answered quickly, her voice alert, though I could tell she had been sleeping.

"Graciela, sorry to call so late. I have a few more questions."

"Can I answer them tomorrow?"

"Just tell me, did Terry go to Las Vegas within the month before he died?"

"Las Vegas? I don't know. Why?"

"What do you mean you don't know? He was your husband."

"I told you, we had . . . separated. He was staying on the boat. I know he went over to the mainland a few times but if he went to Vegas from there I wouldn't have any way of knowing unless he told me, and he didn't tell me."

"What about credit-card bills and cell phone records, ATM withdrawals, things like that?"

"I paid them but I don't remember anything like that, like a hotel or anything."

"Do you have those records still?"

"Of course. I have them here at the house somewhere. They're probably packed already."

"Find them and I'll come for them in the morning."

"I'm already in bed."

"Then find them in the morning. First thing. It's important, Graciela."

"Okay, I will. And look, the one thing I can tell you is that usually if Terry was going to the mainland, he took the boat across so he had a place to stay while he was there. If he was going across but wasn't going to be in L.A. or was going to be staying at Cedars for tests or something, he would take a ferry because otherwise it would cost too much in boat fuel."

"Okay."

"Well, there was one trip in that last month. I think he was gone for like three days. Yes, three days, two nights. He took the ferry. So that meant he was either going across and then somewhere else or to the hospital. And I'm pretty sure it wasn't the hospital. I think he would have told me and I know everybody in cardio at Cedars anyway. They would have let me know he was there and what was going on. I had that place wired."

"Okay, Graciela, that's good. That helps. Do you remember exactly when that was?"

"Not exactly. It was the end of February, I think. Maybe the first couple days of March. I remember it was bill time. I called him on his cell to talk about money and he said he was on the mainland. He didn't say where. He just said he was over there and he'd be back in a couple days. I could tell he was driving when we talked. And I knew he hadn't taken the boat because I was on the balcony looking at it in the harbor when we talked."

"Why were you calling him, do you remember?"

"Yes, we had bills to pay and I didn't know what if anything he had taken in on the boat in February. The credit-card payouts were sent directly here but Terry had a bad habit of walking around with personal checks and cash from customers in his wallet. When he died and I got his wallet back, there were three checks in there for nine hundred dollars that he'd had in there for two weeks. He wasn't very good at business."

She said it as though it was one of her husband's endearing and humorous qualities, though I was pretty sure that during his life she didn't smile at these oversights.

"A couple more things," I said. "Do you know if it would be his routine to check in with a hospital in a city he was going to? In other words, if he was going to Las Vegas would he set things up at a local hospital in case he needed anything?"

There was a pause before she answered.

"No, that doesn't sound like anything he would do. Are you saying he did that?"

"I don't know. I found a phone number in one of the files. And a name. The number was for Vegas Memorial and I'm trying to figure out why he would call there."

"Vegas Memorial has a transplant program, I know that. But I don't know why he would call there."

"What about the name William Bing, does that mean anything? Could it be a doctor he was recommended to?"

"I don't know that . . . something about that name is familiar but I can't place it. It could be a doctor. Maybe that's where I heard it."

I waited a moment to see if it came to her but it didn't. I pressed on.

"Okay, one last thing, where is Terry's car?"

"It should be over there at Cabrillo, at the marina. It's an old Jeep Cherokee. There's a key on the ring I gave you. Buddy also has a key because he uses it sometimes. He basically takes care of it for us. I mean, me now."

"Okay, I'm going to check that out in the morning, so I'll need to keep the key. Do you know when the first ferry goes back across?"

"Not till nine-fifteen."

"Then can we meet at seven-thirty or eight at your house? I want to get those records and also show you a few things. It won't take too long and then I'll grab the first ferry."

"Um, can we make it eight? I should be back by then. I usually walk Raymond to school and take CiCi to day care."

"No problem. I'll see you at eight."

We ended the conversation and I immediately called Buddy Lockridge again, one more time rousing him from sleep.

"Buddy, it's me again."

He groaned.

"Did Terry go to Las Vegas the month before he died? Like maybe around March first?"

"I don't know, man," he said in a tired, annoyed voice. "How would I know that? I can't remember what *I* did March first."

"Think, Buddy. He made a road trip around then. He didn't bring the boat across. Where did he go? Did he tell you anything about it?"

"He didn't tell me jack. But I remember that trip now because the Jeep came back dirtier than shit. Had salt or some shit all over it. And I was the one who was left to wash it."

"Did you ask him about it?"

"Yeah, I said, 'Where have you been, out off-roading?' and he said, 'Yeah, something like that.'"

"And that was it?"

"That's all he said. I washed the car."

"What about the inside? Did you clean that out?"

"No, I'm just talking about the outside. I took it over to the drive-through in Pedro and power-sprayed the thing. That's all I did."

I nodded as I concluded I had gotten everything I needed from Lockridge. For the time being.

"You going to be around tomorrow?"

"Yup, I'm always around these days. Got nowhere to go."

"All right. I'll see you then."

After ending the conversation I made one more call, punching in the number McCaleb had written at the top of the file flap after the name of Ritz, the detective quoted in the *Times* article.

The call was picked up by a tape announcing that the Vegas Metro's Missing Persons unit was open from 8 a.m. to 4 p.m. Monday through Friday. The message advised anyone with an emergency to hang up and dial 911.

I closed the phone. It was late and I had an early start in the morning but I knew I wasn't going to sleep any time soon. I had the wire in the blood now and knew from long experience that sleep was not an option. Not yet.

I was marooned on a boat with two flashlights to see by, but there was still work to be done. I opened my notebook and started constructing a chronological record of the dates and times of events in the weeks and months before Terry McCaleb's death. I put everything on the page, the important and not important, the real connections and imagined connections. Just as experience had taught me about sleep and the ability to go long stretches without it, I knew the details were important. The answer is always in the details. What is seemingly not important now is all-important later. What is cryptic and unconnected now becomes the magnifying glass through which things become clear later.

14

YOU CAN ALWAYS TELL who the locals are. They're the ones who sit inside and work crossword puzzles while the ferry makes the ninety-minute crossing. The tourists are usually up top or lining the bow or stern with their cameras and last glimpses of the island as it shrinks in the mist behind them. On the first boat out the next morning I was inside with the locals. But I was working a puzzle of a different kind. I sat with the file in which Terry McCaleb had made his case notations open on my lap. I also had the chronology I had worked up the night before. I studied it, hoping to commit as much of it as I could to memory. An instant command of case details is required for the successful completion of an investigation.

Jan. 7—McC reads about missing men in Nevada, calls Vegas Metro
Jan. 9—Vegas Metro not interested
Feb. 2—Hinton, Vegas Sun. Who called who?

Feb. 13—half-day charter with Jordan Shandy
Feb. 19—charter with Finder
Feb. 22—GPS stolen/sheriff's report
Feb. 27—McC creates photo file
March 1?—McC on mainland for three-day period
March 28—Last charter. McC on The Following Sea
 with meds
March 31—McC dies

I now added what I had learned an hour earlier from Graciela. The same credit-card records I had asked her to gather in regard to her husband's movements contained her purchases as well. There was a Visa charge attributed to a Nordstrom department store on February 21. When I asked about it she said she had made the purchase at the Promenade. I asked if she had been back since then and she said no.

As I added the date into the chronology I noted that it was the day before the GPS device was reported stolen from *The Following Sea*. This meant it was likely the same day it was stolen. The photo stalker had been on the ferry with Graciela on the way back to the island. Could he have been the one who snuck onboard *The Following Sea* that night and took the GPS device? If so, why? And if so, could this also have been the night that Terry McCaleb's medicine was tampered with, real capsules exchanged for dummies?

I circled the letters GPS on the chronology. What was the significance of this device and this theft? I wondered if I was putting too much emphasis on this. Perhaps Buddy Lockridge's theory was the correct one, the device had simply been stolen by Finder, a competitor. Perhaps that was all it was, but the proximity to the mall stalking of Graciela made me think otherwise. My instincts told me there was a connection. I just didn't have it yet.

Despite that, I felt as though I was getting close to something. The chronology was very helpful in allowing me to see connections and the timeliness of things. There was more still to add and I remembered I had intended to follow up with phone calls to Las Vegas this morning. I opened my cell phone and checked the battery. I had been unable to recharge it on *The Following Sea*. Now I was running out of juice. I had maybe one last call on it before it died. I punched in the number for the Missing Persons unit at Vegas Metro. The call went through and I asked for Detective Ritz. I was put on hold for nearly three minutes, during which time the phone started to beep every minute, warning me it was running low on power.

"This is Detective Ritz, how can I help you?"

"Detective, my name is Bosch. I'm LAPD retired. Homicide mostly. I'm doing a favor for a friend. Her husband passed away last month and I'm sort of putting his things in order. I came across a file of his that had your name and number in it and a newspaper article about one of your cases."

"What case?"

"The six missing men."

"And what was your friend's husband's name?"

"Terry McCaleb. He was FBI retired. He worked—"

"Oh, him."

"You knew him?"

"I talked to him on the phone once. That doesn't qualify as knowing him."

"You talked about the missing men?"

"Look, what did you say your name is?"

"Harry Bosch."

"Well, listen, Harry Bosch, I don't know you and I don't know what you are doing, but it's usually not my practice to talk about open cases over the phone with strangers."

"I could come see you."

"That wouldn't change things."

"You know he's dead, don't you?"

"McCaleb? I heard he had a heart attack and he was out on his boat and nobody could get to him in time. It sounded stupid. What's a guy with a heart transplant doing twenty-five miles out in the middle of nowhere?"

"Making a living, I guess. Look, some things have come up about that and I'm checking into what Terry was into at the time. To sort of see if he might've drawn somebody's eye, if you know what I mean. All I want—"

"Actually, I don't know what you mean. You talking voodoo? Somebody put the hex on him and gave him a heart attack? I'm kind of busy here, Bosch. Too busy for that bullshit. You retired guys think us working stiffs have all the time in the world for you and your long-shot voodoo theories. Well, guess what, we don't."

"Is that what you said to him when he called? You didn't want to listen to his theory or his profile of the case? You called it voodoo?"

"Look, man, what good is a profile? Those things don't narrow down shit. They're bullshit and that's what I told him and that was—"

His last word was cut off by my phone's warning beep.

"What was that?" he asked. "Are you recording this?"

"No, it's my phone's low-battery warning. Terry didn't come over there to talk to you about this?"

"Nope. I think he ran to the newspaper with it instead. Typical fed move."

"There was a story about his take on this in the *Sun*?"

"I wouldn't call it that. I think they pretty much thought he was full of shit, too."

That line revealed an untruth. If Ritz thought McCaleb and his theory were full of shit, he had to have listened to it in order to make such a determination. I believed that it revealed that Ritz had discussed the case with McCaleb, possibly at length.

"Let me ask you one last thing and then I'll leave you alone. Did Terry mention something about a triangle theory? Something about one point giving three? Does any of that make sense?"

The laugh I heard over the phone wasn't pleasant. It wasn't even good-natured.

"That was three questions, Bosch. Three questions, three sides of a triangle and three strikes and you're—"

The phone went dead, its battery drained.

"Out," I said, completing Ritz's line.

I knew it meant he was not going to answer my question. I closed the phone and dropped it back into my pocket. I had a charger in my car. I'd have the phone back up and running as soon as we got across the Santa Monica Bay. There was still the reporter at the *Sun* to talk to but I doubted I'd be having further conversations with Ritz.

I got up and walked out onto the stern to have the cool morning air refresh me. Catalina was far in the distance, just a jagged gray rock sticking up in the mist. We were more than halfway across. I heard a little girl exclaim, "There!" very loudly to her mother and I followed her pointed finger out to the water where a school of porpoises were breaking the surface in the boat's wake. There must have been twenty of them and soon the stern became crowded with people and their cameras. I think maybe some of the locals even came out to look. The porpoises were beautiful, their gray skin shining like plastic in the morning light. I wondered if they were just having fun or had mistaken the ferry for a fishing boat and were hoping to feed on the debris of the day's catch.

Soon the show wasn't enough to hold everyone's attention and the passengers returned to their former positions. The little girl who first sounded the alert stayed at the gunwale and watched, and so did I, until the porpoises finally dropped off the wake and disappeared in the blue-black sea.

I went inside and took up McCaleb's file again. I reread everything he and I had written. No new ideas came up. I then looked at all the photos I had printed out the night before. I had shown the photos of the man named Jordan Shandy to Graciela but she didn't recognize him and hit me with more questions than answers about him, questions I didn't want to try to answer just yet.

Next in the review were the credit-card and phone records. I had already looked at these in Graciela's presence but wanted to check them more thoroughly. I paid closest attention to the end of February and the beginning of March, when Graciela was sure her husband had been on the mainland. But there was no purchase with a credit card nor phone call made on his cell that gave any indication of where he was, let alone in Los Angeles or maybe Las Vegas. It was almost as if he wanted to leave no trail.

A half hour later the boat pulled into the Los Angeles Harbor and docked next to the *Queen Mary*, a permanently moored cruise ship that had been turned into a hotel and convention center. As I was walking through the parking lot to my car I heard a shriek and turned around to see a woman bouncing and swaying upside down from the end of a bungee cord extending down from a jumping platform at the stern of the *Queen Mary*. She had her arms clamped to the sides of her torso and I realized that the reason she had screamed was not because of the fear and adrenaline rush of the free fall, but because her T-shirt had apparently threatened to fall down over her shoulders and head, exposing her to the crowd that lined the railing of the cruise ship.

I turned away and headed on to my car. I drive a Mercedes-Benz sport utility vehicle, the kind some people think helps keep terrorists in business. I don't get involved in such debates but I do know that the people who go on talk shows to argue such things usually pull up in stretch limos. As soon as I got into the car and cranked it, I plugged my phone into the charger and waited for it to come back to life. When it did I saw I had gotten two messages in the forty-five minutes the phone had been out of commission.

The first was from my old partner Kizmin Rider, who now handled administrative and planning duties in the chief of police's office. She left no message other than a request for me to call her. This was curious because we hadn't talked in nearly a year and that conversation had not been the most pleasant. Her usual Christmas card to me had carried her signature only and not the usual cordial note and promise to get together soon. I wrote her direct number down—at least I still rated that—and saved the message.

The next message was from Cindy Hinton, the *Sun* reporter. She was simply returning my call. I started the Benz and headed toward the freeway so I could loop over to San Pedro and the Cabrillo Marina, where Terry McCaleb's Jeep was waiting for me. I called Hinton back on the way and she answered immediately.

"Yes, I was calling about Terry McCaleb," I said. "I'm sort of re-creating his movements in the last couple months of his life. I assume you had heard he passed away. I remember that the *Sun* carried an obituary."

"Yes, I knew. You said on your message last night that you are an investigator. An investigator for what agency?"

"Actually, I'm a state-licensed private detective. But I was a cop for almost thirty years."

"Is this related to the missing persons case?"

"In what way?"

"I don't know. You called me. I don't understand what it is you want."

"Well, let me ask you a question. First of all, I know from Detective Ritz over at Metro that Terry had taken an interest in the missing persons case. He studied the facts that were available to him and called on Detective Ritz, offering his time and expertise to work on the case or provide investigative theories. You with me so far?"

"Yes. I know all of this."

"Okay, good. Terry's offer to Ritz and Vegas Metro was rejected. What my question is is what happened next? Did he call you? Did you call him? Did you write a story that said he was investigating this case?"

"And why is it that you want to know these things?"

"Sorry, hold on a second."

I had realized I should not have made the call while driving. I should have expected Hinton to be cagey with me and should have known the call would need my undivided attention. I glanced at the mirrors and cut across two lanes to go down an exit. I didn't even see the sign and didn't know where I was going. I found myself in an industrial area where trucking depots and warehouses lined the street. I pulled to a stop behind a tractor-trailer parked in front of the open garage doors of a warehouse.

"Okay, sorry, I'm back. You asked why I wanted to know the answers to these questions. Well, Terry McCaleb was my friend. And I'm picking up some of the things he was working on. I want to finish his work."

"There sounds like there is something else, something you're not telling me."

I thought for a moment of how to handle this. Giving a reporter information, especially a reporter you didn't know, was risky business. It could snap back on you in bad ways. I had to figure out a way to give her what she needed in order to help me, but then I needed to take it all back.

"Hello? Are you still there?"

"Uh, yeah. Tell you what, can we go off the record here?"

"Off the record? We're not even talking about anything here."

"I know. I am going to tell you something if I can tell it to you off the record. Meaning, you can't use it."

"Sure, fine, whatever, we're off the record. Could you please get to the point or whatever this important information is because I need to write a story this morning?"

"Terry McCaleb was murdered."

"Uh, no, actually he wasn't. I read the story. He had a heart attack. He had a heart transplant like six years before. He—"

"I know what was put out in the press and I'm telling you it is wrong. And it will come out that it is wrong. And I'm trying to find out who killed him. Now can you tell me whether or not you put out a story that had his name in it?"

She seemed exasperated when she answered.

"Yes, I wrote one story that he was in. For like a paragraph or two. Okay?"

"Just a paragraph? What did it say?"

"It was a follow-up to my story on the missing men. I did a follow-up to see what had come in. You know, what new leads, if any. McCaleb was mentioned, that's all. I said he came forward and offered his help and a theory but Metro said no thanks. It was worth throwing in because the story was dry as a bone and he was sort of famous because of the movie and Clint Eastwood and all of that. Does that answer your question?"

"So he didn't call you?"

"Technically, yes, he did. I got his number from Ritz and called him. I left a message and he called me back.

So technically he called me, if that's how you want it. What is it you think happened to him anyway?"

"Did he tell you what his theory was? The one Ritz wasn't interested in?"

"No, he said he didn't want to comment at all and he asked me to keep his name out of the paper. I talked to my editor and we decided to keep it in. Like I said, he was famous."

"Did Terry know you put his name in the story?"

"I don't know. I never spoke to him again."

"In that one conversation you had, did he say anything about the triangle theory?"

"Triangle theory? No, he didn't. Now I answered your questions, you answer mine. Who says he was murdered? Is that official?"

Now it was time to back out. I needed to stop her in her tracks, make sure she wouldn't hang up and immediately start making calls to check me or my story out.

"Well, not really."

"Not really? Are you—well, what exactly makes you say this?"

"Well, because he was in perfect shape and he had a young person's heart in him."

"So, what about organ rejection and infection? A thousand different things could have—do you have any official finding about this or confirmation? Is there an official investigation?"

"No. That would be like asking the CIA to investigate the Kennedy assassination. The third one. It would just be a cover-up."

"What are you talking about? The third what?"

"The third Kennedy. The son. John-John. You think

his plane just dove into the water like they said? There were three witnesses in New Jersey who saw men carrying their bodies onto that plane *before* it took off. The witnesses have disappeared, too. It was part of the triangle theory and then—"

"Okay, mister, thanks a lot for your call. But I'm on deadline right now and need to—"

She hung up before finishing her own sentence. I smiled. I thought I was safe and was particularly proud of my creativity. I reached over to the passenger seat and lifted the file. I opened it and looked at the chronology. Terry had noted the conversation with Hinton on February 2. The story probably ran in the next day or two. As soon as I got to a library with a computer I would be able to look the story up and get the exact date and read what had been written in the one reference to McCaleb.

For the time being I listed it on the chronology on February 3. I studied what I had for a few moments and started putting my own case theory into form:

McCaleb sees the January 7 *Los Angeles Times* story on the missing men. He gets interested. He sees something in the story that the cops may have missed or misinterpreted. He works up a theory and his thoughts and calls Ritz at Metro two days later. Ritz gives him the cold shoulder but happens to mention the call to Hinton when she does a follow-up. After all, it serves Ritz to keep the story circulating in the press and dropping a "celebrity" investigator's name might help do so.

Hinton's follow-up story with the mention of McCaleb runs in the *Sun* the first week of February. Less than two weeks later—February 13—McCaleb is alone on his boat when Jordan Shandy shows up on a water taxi and asks for a half-day charter. McCaleb grows suspicious of the man while they are fishing and surreptitiously takes photos of him. A week later Shandy is at the Promenade mall stalking McCaleb's family and surreptitiously taking photographs—the same thing McCaleb had done to him. That same night someone takes the GPS device from *The Following Sea* and possibly tampers with McCaleb's medicine.

By February 27 McCaleb has received the photos of his family at the mall. The origin or method of delivery of the photos is unknown but this date is documented by the creation record of the photo file on his computer. Just two days after putting the photos into his computer he leaves Catalina for the mainland. His destination is unknown but his car is returned in dirty condition, as if he had been off-road with it. There is also a record of him having phone numbers for a hospital in Las Vegas and the Mandalay Bay Resort, one of the last known locations of one of the missing men.

Possibilities and interpretations abounded. My guess was that everything turned on the photos. I believed that it was seeing those photos that drew McCaleb across to the mainland. I believed that his car came back dirty after three days because he had gone into the desert at Zzyzx Road. He had taken the bait, whether knowingly or not, and gone to the desert.

I looked at my chronology again and concluded that the mention of McCaleb in the follow-up story in the *Sun* had drawn a response. Shandy was somehow involved in the disappearances. If so, he would probably keep an eye on the media for any updates on the investigation. When he saw McCaleb's name in the follow-up, he came to Catalina to check him out. On the boat that morning during the four-hour charter he could have seen McCaleb taking his medicine, seen the capsules, and hatched a plan to eliminate the threat.

That left the question of the GPS device and why it was taken during the February 21 boat break-in. I now believed it was simply taken as cover. Shandy could not be sure his entry to the boat to change Terry's meds would go unnoticed. So he took the device so McCaleb wouldn't wonder further about the intentions of the intruder if he discovered there had been a break-in.

The larger question was why McCaleb was seen as a threat if his triangle theory was not revealed in the *Sun* story. I didn't know. I thought there was a possibility that he wasn't seen as a threat at all, that he was just a celebrity whom Shandy liked outwitting by killing. It was one of the unknowns.

It was also one of the contradictions. My theory certainly had contradictions. If the first six men disappeared without a trace, why was McCaleb killed in such a way that there were witnesses and a body that could possibly reveal the truth? This was incongruous. My only answer was that if McCaleb simply disappeared, then it would spark an investigation and perhaps a second look at his view and theory of the missing men case. This could not be allowed by Shandy, so McCaleb was eliminated in a way that would hopefully seem natural or accidental and below the radar of suspicion.

My theory was built on speculation and this made me uncomfortable. When I carried a badge, relying on speculation was like putting sand in your gas tank. It was the road to ruin. I felt ill at ease at how easily I had slipped into building theories upon interpretation and speculation instead of the bedrock of fact. I decided then to put theories aside and go back to concentrating on facts. I knew that Zzyzx Road and the desert were real and part of the chain of facts. I had the pictures to prove it. I didn't know if Terry McCaleb had actually gone there or what he might have found if he had. But I now knew I was going there. And that, too, was a fact.

15

BUDDY LOCKRIDGE WAS WAITING in the parking
lot at Cabrillo Marina when I got there. I had called
him and told him I was on the move and in a hurry. My
plan to hook up with him for further discussion would
be delayed. I told him I just wanted to quickly go
through McCaleb's Cherokee and then move on. I knew
what my destination was, whether or not I found anything in the car that pointed me toward the desert and
Las Vegas.

"What's all the hurry?" he asked as I pulled up and
got out.

"Velocity," I told him. "Main thing about an investigation is to keep your velocity up. You slow down . . .
and you slow down. I don't want that."

Before returning the boat keys to Graciela I had taken
the Cherokee's key off the ring. I now used it to unlock
the driver's door. I leaned in and began a general obser-
vation of the car before getting in.

"Where are you headed?" Lockridge said from behind me.

"San Francisco," I lied, just to see if I'd get a reaction.

"San Francisco? What's up there?"

"I don't know. But I think that's where he went on that last trip."

"Must've taken the dirt road way."

"Maybe."

There was nothing readily apparent in the Cherokee that gave me a second thought. The car was in clean condition. There was a faintly sour odor. It smelled like the windows had been left open during a rainstorm at some point. I opened the compartment between the two front seats and found two pairs of sunglasses, a pack of breath-freshening gum and a small, plastic action figure toy. I handed it out the door behind me to Lockridge.

"You left your superhero in here, Buddy."

He didn't take it.

"Funny. That's from McDonald's. There ain't one over there on the island, so the first thing they do when they get over here is take the kids to Mickey D's. It's like crack, man. They get the kids hooked on those French fries and shit early and then they're hooked for life."

"There are worse things."

I put the plastic hero back into the compartment and closed it. I leaned further in so I could reach across to open the glove box.

"Hey, you want me to come with you? Maybe I could help."

"No, that's okay, Buddy. I'm leaving right from here."

"Hell, I could be ready in five minutes. I mean, I'll just put some clothes in a bag."

The glove box contained another plastic figure and operating manuals for the car. There was also a box containing a book on tape called *The Tin Collectors*. There was nothing else. This stop was turning into a bust. All I was getting out of it was Buddy pushing to be my partner. I pulled back out of the car and straightened up. I looked at Lockridge.

"No, thanks, Buddy. I'm working this alone."

"Hey, I helped Terry, man. It wasn't like in the movie where I was made out to be the creep who—"

"Yeah, yeah, I know, Buddy. You told me all of that. This has got nothing to do with that. I just work alone. Even with the cops. That's the way I was, that's the way I am."

I thought of something and leaned back into the car, checking the windshield on the passenger side for a sticker like the one seen in the photo of the Zzyzx Road sign on McCaleb's computer. There was no sticker or anything else in the lower corner of the windshield. It was another confirmation that McCaleb had not taken the photo.

I backed out of the car, walked around and opened the rear hatch. The storage compartment was empty except for a pillow shaped like a cartoon character named SpongeBob SquarePants. I recognized it because my daughter was a SpongeBob fan and I, too, enjoyed watching the show with her. I guessed he was a favorite in the McCaleb home, too.

I then went to one of the rear doors and looked into the passenger compartment. Clean again, but I noticed in the pocket behind the front passenger seat there was a map book that could be reached from the driver's seat. I pulled it out and paged through it, careful not to let Buddy see what I was looking at.

On the page for southern Nevada I noticed that the map included parts of contiguous states. In California, near the southwest corner of Nevada, someone had drawn a circle around the Mojave Preservation Area. And on the right border of the map someone had jotted down several numbers in ink, one above the other, and then added them together. The sum was 86. Below this was written "Actual—92."

"What is it?" Lockridge asked, looking through the car at me from the other passenger door.

I closed the map book and dropped it on the car seat.

"Nothing. It looks like he wrote down some directions for one of his trips or something."

I leaned into the car and then down so that I could look under the front passenger seat. I saw more McDonald's toys and some old food wrappers and other debris. Nothing that looked worthwhile. I got out and came around the other side, asking Buddy to step back so I could do the same thing with the driver's seat.

Beneath the driver's seat there was more debris but I noticed several small crumpled balls of paper. I reached under and swept these out so I could see them. I opened one up and smoothed it out and saw that it was a credit-card receipt for a purchase of gas in Long Beach. It was dated almost a year earlier.

"You don't check under the seats when you clean the car, do you, Buddy?"

"They never asked me to," he said defensively. "Besides, I really just take care of the outside."

"Oh, I see."

I started unraveling the rest of the paper balls. I didn't expect anything that would help me. I had already reviewed the credit-card receipts and knew there were no purchases I could use to pinpoint McCaleb's location on his three-day trip. But the rule was always to be thorough.

There were a variety of receipts for local purchases. This included food items from Safeway and fishing equipment from a San Pedro tackle store. There was a receipt for ginseng extract from a health food store called BetterFit, and a receipt from a Westwood bookstore for a book on tape called *Looking for Chet Baker.* I never heard of the book but knew who Chet Baker was. I decided I would check into it later when I had time to read or listen to a book.

The rule paid off on the fifth paper ball. I unraveled a cash receipt from a Travel America truck stop in Las Vegas. It was located on Blue Diamond Road, the same street as Vegas Memorial. The date of the purchase was March 2. The purchase was for sixteen gallons of gasoline, a half-liter of Gatorade and the book on tape edition of *The Tin Collectors.*

The receipt placed McCaleb in Las Vegas during his three-day trip. It was another confirmation of what I thought I already knew. Nevertheless my adrenaline kicked in another notch. I wanted to get moving again, keep that case velocity going.

"You find something?" Lockridge asked.

I crumpled the receipt and threw it down onto the floor of the car with the others.

"Not really," I said. "Turns out Terry was a big books-on-tape guy. Didn't know that."

"Yeah, he listened to a lot of them. Out on the boat when he was up on the helm. He usually had the earphones on."

I reached back into the car and took the map book off the seat.

"I'm going to borrow this," I said. "I don't think Graciela's going anywhere where she'll need it."

I didn't wait for Buddy's approval. I closed the passenger door, hoping that he was buying my act. I then closed the driver's door and locked the vehicle.

"That's it, Buddy. I'm out of here. You going to be near your phone if anything comes up and I need you?"

"'Course, man, I'm around. It's a mobile, anyway."

"All right then, you take care."

I shook his hand and headed to my black Benz, half expecting to find him following me. But he let me go. As I drove out of the lot, I checked the mirror and saw him still standing next to the Cherokee, watching me go.

I took the 710 up to the 10 and rode that out to the 15 freeway. After that it would be a straight shot out of the smog and into the Mojave and then on to Las Vegas. I had been making this trip two or three times a month for the past year. I always enjoyed the drive. I liked the starkness of the desert. Maybe I drew from it what Terry McCaleb drew from living on an island. A sense of distance from all the nastiness. As I drove it I felt the constrictions lift, as if the molecules of my body expanded and got a little more space between each other. Maybe it was no more than a nanometer but that little narrow space was enough to make a difference.

But this time I felt different. I felt as though this time the nastiness was ahead of me, that it was waiting for me in the desert.

I was settling into the drive, letting the case facts rotate in my mind, when my cell buzzed. My guess was that it would be Buddy Lockridge making a final plea to be included but it was Kiz Rider. I had forgotten to call her back.

"So, Harry, I guess I don't even rate a call back from you?"

"Sorry, Kiz, I was going to call you. I had a busy morning and sort of forgot."

"Busy morning? You're supposed to be retired. You're not running around on another case, are you?"

"Actually, I'm driving to Vegas. And I'm probably about to lose my signal in the dead zone. What's going on?"

"Well, I saw Tim Marcia this morning when I was getting my coffee. He told me you two had talked recently."

"Yeah, yesterday. Is this about that three-year deal he told me about?"

"It certainly is, Harry. Have you thought about it?"

"I just heard about it yesterday. I haven't had time to think about it."

"I think you should, Harry. We need you back here."

"That's nice to hear, especially from you, Kiz. I thought I was PNG with you."

"What does that mean?"

"Persona non grata."

"Come on now. It was nothing a cooling-off period couldn't cure. Seriously, though, we could use you back here. You could probably work with Tim's unit if you wanted."

"If I wanted? Kiz, you make it sound like all I have to do is waltz in there and sign on the dotted line. What do you think, everybody in that building is going to be there to welcome me back? Are they going to be lined up in the hallway on the sixth floor, throwing rice or something while I walk to the chief's office?"

"You talking about Irving? Irving got downsized. He's running the department of future planning. I'm calling to tell you, Harry, that if you want to come back, then you are back. It's that simple. After I talked to Tim I went up to six and had my usual nine a.m. with the chief. He knows of you. He knows your work."

"I wonder how that could be, since I was gone before he was brought over from New York or Boston or wherever it was they got him from."

"He knows because I told him, Harry. Look, let's not get into an argument over this. Okay? Everything is cool. All I'm saying is that you should think about it. The clock is ticking on it and you ought to think about it. You could help us and the city and maybe even help yourself, depending on where you're at in the world."

That last part raised a good question. Where was I in the world? I thought about it for a long moment before speaking.

"Yeah, okay. Kiz, I appreciate it. And thanks for putting in the word with the man. Tell me something, when did Irving get dumped? I hadn't heard about that."

"That happened a few months ago. I think the chief thought he had his finger in too many pies. He put him to the side."

I couldn't help but smile. Not because Deputy Chief Irvin Irving had always had me under his heel, but because I knew a man like Irving wouldn't let anyone put him to the side, as Kiz had said.

"The man carries all the secrets," I said.

"I know. We're waiting for his move. We'll be ready."

"Then good luck to you."

"Thanks. So what's it going to be, Harry?"

"What, you want my answer now? I thought you just told me to think about it."

"A guy like you, I already think you know the answer."

I smiled again but didn't answer. She was wasting her time in administration. She should be back in homicide. She knew how to read people better than anyone I had ever worked with.

"Harry, you remember the thing you told me when I first got assigned as your partner?"

"Um, chew your food, brush after every meal?"

"I'm serious."

"I don't know, what?"

"Everybody counts or nobody counts."

I nodded and was quiet for a moment.

"Do you remember?"

"Yeah. I remember."

"Words to live by."

"I guess so."

"Well, think about that while you're thinking about coming back."

"If I come back, I'm going to need a partner."

"What, Harry? You're breaking up."

"I'm going to need a partner."

There was a pause and I think now she was smiling, too.

"That's a possibility. You—"

She cut out on me. I think I knew what she was going to say.

"I bet you miss it as much as me."

"Harry, you're going into the dead zone. Call me back when . . . don't take too long."

"Okay, Kiz, I'll let you know."

I was still smiling after closing the phone. There is nothing like being wanted or being welcomed. Being valued.

But also the idea of having a badge again in order to do what I had to do. I thought about Ritz at Metro and how he had treated me. How I had to fight just to get the attention and help of some people. I knew a lot of that would go away with the badge again. In the last two years I had learned that the badge didn't necessarily make the man, but it sure as hell made the man's job easier. And for me it was more than a job. I knew that badge or no badge, there was one thing on this earth I could and should be doing. I had a mission in this life, just as Terry McCaleb had. Spending the day before in his floating shop of horrors, studying his cases and his dedication to his mission, made me realize what was important and what I had to do. In his dying my silent partner may have saved me.

After forty minutes of mulling over my future and considering my choices, I came to the sign I had seen in the photo on Terry's computer.

ZZYZX ROAD
I MILE

It was not the exact sign. I could tell by the horizon behind it. The photo had been taken from the other side, by someone heading to L.A. from Vegas. Nevertheless, I felt a deep tug of anticipation. Everything I had seen or read or heard since Graciela McCaleb had called me led to this place. I put on the blinker and took the exit off the freeway.

16

MIDMORNING ON THE DAY after Rachel Walling's arrival the agents assigned to what had been labeled the "Zzyzx Road case" gathered in person and by phone in the squad room on the third floor of the John Lawrence Bailey Building in Las Vegas. The room was windowless and poorly ventilated. A photograph of Bailey, an agent killed during a bank robbery twenty years earlier, looked upon the proceedings.

The agents in attendance sat at tables lined in rows, facing the front of the room. At the front was Randal Alpert and a two-way television that was connected by phone and camera to a squad room in Quantico, Virginia. On the screen was Agent Brasilia Doran, waiting to provide her report. Rachel was at the second row of tables, sitting off by herself. She knew her place here and outwardly tried to show it.

Alpert convened the meeting by graciously introducing those present. Rachel thought that this was a nicety allowed for her but soon realized that not everyone in attendance in person or by audiovisual hookup knew everyone else.

Alpert first identified Doran, also known as Brass, on the line from Quantico, where she was handling the collating of information and acting as liaison to the national lab. He then asked each person seated in the room to identify themselves and their specialty or position. First was Cherie Dei, who said she was the case agent. Next to her was her partner, Tom Zigo. Next was John Cates, a representative agent from the local FO and the only nonwhite person in attendance.

The next four people were from the science side and Rachel had seen and met two of them at the site the day before. They included a forensic anthropologist named Greta Coxe, who was in charge of the excavations, two medical examiners named Harvey Richards and Douglas Sundeen, and a crime scene specialist named Mary Pond. Ed Gunning, another agent from Behavioral Sciences in Quantico, brought the introductions around to Rachel, who was last.

"Agent Rachel Walling," she said. "Rapid City field office. Formerly with Behavioral. I have some . . . familiarity with a case like this."

"Okay, thanks, Rachel," Alpert said quickly, as though he thought Rachel was going to mention Robert Backus by name.

This told Rachel that there were people in the room who had not been informed of the major fact of the case. She guessed that would be Cates, the token agent from the FO. She wondered if some of the science team, or all of it, was in the dark as well.

"Let's start with the science side," Alpert continued. "First of all, Brass? Anything from out there?"

"Not on science. I think your crime scene people have all of that. Hello, Rachel. Long time."

"Hello, Brass," Rachel said quietly. "Too long."

She looked at the screen and their eyes met. Rachel realized that it had probably been eight years since she had actually seen Doran. She looked weary, her mouth and eyes drawn down, her hair short in a cut that suggested she didn't spend much time with it. She was an empath, Rachel knew, and the years were taking their toll.

"You look good," Doran said. "I guess all that fresh air and open country agrees with you."

Alpert stepped in and saved Rachel from delivering a false compliment in return.

"Greta, Harvey, who wants to go first?" he asked, stepping all over the electronic reunion.

"I guess I will since everything starts with the dig," Greta Coxe said. "As of seven p.m. yesterday we have fully excavated eight bodies and they are at Nellis. This afternoon when we get back there, we will begin with number nine. What we saw with the first excavations is holding true with the latter. The plastic bags in each incidence and the—"

"Greta, we have a tape going here," Alpert interrupted. "Let's be fully descriptive. As if speaking to an uninformed audience. Don't hold back."

Except when it comes to mentioning Robert Backus, Rachel thought.

"Okay, sure," Coxe said. "Um, all eight bodies excavated and exhumed so far have been fully clothed.

Decomposition is extensive. Hands and feet bound by tape. All have plastic bags over the head, which in turn have been taped around the neck. There is no variation on this methodology, even between victims one and two. Which is unusual."

Late the day before Rachel had seen the photos. She had gone back into the command RV and looked at the wall of photos. It seemed clear to her that the men had all been suffocated. The plastic bags had not been clear plastic but even in their opaqueness she could see the features of the faces and the mouths wide open and searching for air that wasn't going to come. They reminded her of photos of wartime atrocities, disinterred bodies from mass graves in Yugoslavia or Iraq.

"Why is that unusual?" Alpert asked.

"Because what we most often see is that the killing plan evolves. For lack of a better way of describing it, the killing gets better. The unsub learns from victim to victim how to do it better. That is usually seen in the data we have."

Rachel noted that Coxe had used the word *unsub*. Short for unknown subject. It most likely meant she was out of the loop and didn't know that the subject was very much known to the FBI.

"Okay, so the methodology was set from day one," Alpert said. "Anything else, Greta?"

"Just that we will probably be finished with the excavations the day after tomorrow. Unless we get another hit with the probes."

"Are we still probing?"

"Yes, when we have the time. But we've gone sixty feet past the last hit with the probes and haven't gotten anything. We also got another flyover from Nellis last night. There was nothing new from thermal imaging. So we feel pretty comfortable at this time that we've got them all."

"And thank God for that. Harvey? What have you got for us?"

Richards cleared his throat and leaned forward so that his voice would be heard by the electronic pickups, wherever they were.

"Greta's right, we have all eight excavated so far in the morgue at Nellis. So far the veil of secrecy is holding up. I think people there think we're bringing in aliens off a crashed saucer in the desert. This is how urban legends start, people."

Only Alpert cracked a smile. Richards continued.

"We've conducted full autopsies on four so far and initial exams of the others. Similar to what Greta said, we're not finding a hell of a lot of difference from body to body. This guy is a robot. No variation on theme. It's almost like the killings themselves are of no import. Perhaps it is the hunt that juices this guy. Or perhaps the killings are just part of a larger plan we don't know about yet."

Rachel stared pointedly at Alpert. She hated that people working so closely on the case were still working in the dark. But she knew if she said anything she would quickly be on the outside looking in. She didn't want that.

"You have a question, Rachel?"

He'd caught her off guard. She hesitated.

"Why are the bodies being taken to Nellis instead of here or L.A.?"

She knew the answer before asking the question but needed to say something to escape the moment.

"It's easier to keep a lid on things this way. The military knows how to keep a secret."

His tone suggested an unspoken final line: *Do you?* He swung his view back to Richards.

"Doctor, go on."

Rachel picked up on the subtle difference. Alpert had called Richards Doctor, whereas he had simply addressed Greta Coxe by her first name. It was a character trait. Alpert either had trouble with women in positions of power and knowledge or he didn't respect the science of anthropology. She guessed it was the former.

"Well, we're looking at suffocation as the cause on these," Richards said. "It's pretty obvious from what we've got. There is not a lot left to work with on most of them but with what we've got we're not seeing other injuries. The unsub overpowers in some way, tapes wrists and ankles and then puts the bag in place over the head. The taping around the neck we think is significant. That is indicative of a slow death. In other words the unsub was not holding the bag in place. He took his time, pulled it over the head, taped it and then could step back to watch."

"Doctor?" Rachel asked. "Was the tape applied from the front or back?"

"The ends are at the back of the neck, indicating to me that the bag may have been pulled over from behind, possibly when the victim was in a sitting position, and then taped in place."

"So he—the, uh, unsub—may have been ashamed or afraid to face his victims when he did this."

"Quite possibly."

"How are we doing on identification?" Alpert asked.

Richards looked at Sundeen and he took over.

"Still just the five that were included in the Las Vegas investigation. We assume the sixth from their group will be one of the final two excavations. The others we have nothing on so far. We've got no useable prints. We've forwarded the clothing—what's left of it—to Quantico and perhaps Brass has an update on that. Meantime, we—"

"No, no update," Doran said from the television screen.

"Okay," Sundeen said. "We have the dental data just going into the computer today. So maybe we'll get a hit there. Other than that we're just waiting for something to happen."

He nodded at the completion of his report. Alpert took back the lead.

"I want to go to Brass last, so let's hear about the soil."

Mary Pond took it from there.

"We've sifted all of the sites and it's all come up clean except for one piece we got yesterday that is exciting. In excavation seven we found a wad of gum in a wrapper. Juicy Fruit, according to the wrapper. It was between twenty-four and thirty inches down in a three-foot grave. So we really feel it is related and could be a good break for us."

"Dental?" Alpert asked.

"Yes, we have dental. I can't tell you what yet but it looked like three good impressions. I boxed it and sent it to Brass."

"Yes, it is here," Doran said from the television. "Came in this morning. I put it in motion but I don't have anything on it yet either. Maybe late today. I agree, though. From what I saw we'll get at least three teeth out of it. Maybe even DNA."

"Could be all we need," Alpert added excitedly.

Even though she distinctly remembered that Bob Backus had a habit of chewing Juicy Fruit gum, Rachel was not excited. The gum in the grave was too good to be true. She thought there was no way that Backus would allow himself to leave such important evidence behind. He was too good as both a killer and agent for that. She could not properly express this doubt in the meeting, however, because of her agreement with Alpert not to bring up Backus in front of other agents.

"It's got to be a plant," she said.

Alpert looked at her a moment, weighing the risk of asking her why.

"A plant. Why do you say that, Rachel?"

"Because I can't see why this guy who is burying a body in the middle of nowhere, probably in the middle of the night, would take the time to put his shovel down, take the gum out of his mouth, wrap it in its foil, which he had to take out of his pocket, and then drop it. I think if he'd been chewing gum he would have just spit it out. But I don't think he was chewing gum. I think he picked that little wad up somewhere, brought it to the grave and dropped it in so we would spin our wheels with it when he decided to lead us to the bodies with his GPS trick."

She glanced around the room. She had their eyes but she could tell she was more of a curiosity to them than a respected colleague. The silence was broken by the television.

"I think Rachel is probably right," Doran said. "We

have been manipulated from day one on this. Why not with the gum? It does seem like an incredible mistake for such a well-planned action."

Rachel noticed Doran wink at her.

"One piece of gum, one mistake, in eight graves?" said Gunning, one of the agents from Quantico. "I don't think that is such a long shot. We all know nobody's ever committed the perfect crime. Yes, people get away but they all make mistakes."

"Well," Alpert said, "let's wait and see what we get with this before we jump to any conclusions one way or the other. Mary, anything else?"

"Not at this time."

"Then let's go to Agent Cates to see how the locals are doing with the IDs."

Cates opened a leather-bound folder on the table in front of him. It contained a legal pad with notes on it. That he had such a nice and expensive holder for a basic legal pad told Rachel that he was very proud of his work and what he did. Either that or the person who gave him the folder had those feelings. Either way, it made Rachel like him right away. It also made her feel like she was missing something. She no longer carried that kind of pride in the bureau or what she did.

"Okay, we started sniffing around Vegas Metro on their missing persons case. We're handicapped by the need for secrecy. So we're not going in there like gangbusters. We've just made contact and said we're interested because of the state line thing—victims from multiple states and even one other country. That gives us an in but we don't want to show our hand by blasting in there. So we're supposed to have a sitdown with them later today. Once we reach the beach, so to speak, we'll start back tracing these individuals and looking for the common denominator. Keep in mind these guys have been on this for several weeks and as far as we know don't have shit."

"Agent Cates," Alpert said. "The tape."

"Oh, excuse my language there. They don't have anything is what I meant to say."

"Very good, Agent Cates. Keep me informed."

And only silence followed. Alpert continued to smile warmly at Cates until the local agent got the message.

"Oh, um, you want me to leave?"

"I want you out there working on those victims," Alpert said. "No sense wasting time in here listening to us hash things around to no end."

"Okay, then."

Cates got up. If he had been a white man the embarrassment would have been more recognizable on his face.

"Thank you, Agent Cates," Alpert said to his back as he went through the door.

Alpert then turned his attention back to the table.

"I think Mary, Greta, Harvey and Doug can all be excused as well. We need you guys back in the trenches, I'm afraid. No pun intended."

There was that administrative smile again.

"Actually," Mary Pond said, "I'd like to stay and hear what Brass has to say. It might help me in the field."

Alpert lost his smile at the challenge.

"No," he said firmly, "that won't be necessary."

An uneasy silence engulfed the room until it was finally punctuated by the sounds of the science team's chairs being pushed back from their tables. The four of them got up and left the room without speaking. It was painful for Rachel to watch. The unchecked arrogance of command staff was endemic in the bureau. It was never going to change.

"Now, where were we?" Alpert said, easily morphing past what he had just done to five good people. "Brass, your turn now. I have you down here for the boat, the tape and bags, the clothes, the GPS device, and now you have the gum, which we all know will lead nowhere, thank you very much, Agent Walling."

He said the word *agent* like it was synonymous with *idiot*. Rachel raised her hands in surrender.

"Sorry, I didn't know half the field team is in the dark on the suspect. Funny, but when I was in Behavioral we never did it that way. We pooled information and knowledge. We didn't hide it from one another."

"You mean when you were working for the man we are looking for right now?"

"Look, Agent Alpert, if you are trying to taint me with that brush, then you—"

"This is a classified case, Agent Walling. That is all I am trying to get across to you. As I told you before, it is 'need to know.'"

"Obviously."

Alpert turned away from her as if dismissing her from memory and looked at the television screen.

"Brass, can you begin please?"

Alpert made sure he stood between Rachel and the screen, to further underline her position as outsider on the case.

"Okay," Doran said, "I have something significant and . . . well, strange, to begin with. I told you about the boat yesterday. The initial fingerprint analysis of manageable surfaces came back negative. It had been out there in the elements for who knows how long. So we took it another step. Agent Alpert approved disassembly of the evidence and that was done in the hangar at Nellis last night. On the boat there are grip locations—handholds for moving the boat. This at one time was a navy lifeboat, built in the late thirties and probably sold off as military surplus after World War Two."

As Doran continued Dei opened a file and pulled out a photo of the boat. She held it for Rachel to see, since Rachel had never actually seen the boat. It was already at Nellis by the time she had gotten to the excavation site. She thought it was amazing and typical that the bureau could amass so much information about a boat set adrift in the desert but so little about the crime it was attached to.

"We could not get into the interior of the grip holes with our first analysis. When we disassembled the piece we were able to get in there. This is where we got lucky because this little hollow was protected from the elements for the most part."

"And?" Alpert asked impatiently. He obviously wasn't interested in the journey. He just wanted the destination.

"And we got two prints out of the port side grip on the bow. This morning we ran them through the data banks and got a hit almost right away. This is going to sound strange but the prints came from Terry McCaleb."

"How can that be?" asked Dei.

Alpert didn't say anything. His eyes stared down at the table in front of him. Rachel sat quiet as well, her mind racing to catch up with and understand this latest piece of information.

"At some point he put his hand into the grip hole on the boat, that's the only way it can be," Doran said.

"But he's dead," Alpert said.

"What?" Rachel exclaimed.

Everyone in the room turned and looked at her. Dei slowly nodded.

"He died about a month ago. Heart attack. I guess the news didn't get to South Dakota."

Doran's voice came from the speaker.

"Rachel, I am so sorry. I should have gotten word to you. But I was too upset about it and went out to California right away. I'm sorry. I should have told you."

Rachel looked down at her hands. Terry McCaleb had been her friend and colleague. He was one of the empaths. She felt a sudden and deep sense of loss, despite the fact that she had not spoken to him in years. Their shared experiences had left them bonded for life and now that life, for him, was gone.

"Okay, people, let's take a break here," Alpert said. "Fifteen minutes and then back in here. Brass, can you call back?"

"I will. I've got more to report."

"Talk to you then."

They all filed out to get coffee or use the restrooms. To leave Rachel alone.

"Are you all right, Agent Walling?" Alpert asked.

She looked up at him. The last thing she would take would be comfort from him.

"I'm fine," she said, moving her eyes back to the blank TV screen.

17

RACHEL REMAINED IN THE conference room by herself. Her initial shock gave way to a wave of guilt coming up behind her like a following sea. Terry McCaleb had attempted to contact her over the years. She had gotten the messages but had never responded. She had sent him a card and a note when he was in the hospital recovering from the transplant. That had been five or six years ago. She couldn't remember. She did remember specifically deciding not to put a personal return address on the envelope. At the time she told herself it was because she wasn't going to be stuck in Minot for very long. But she knew then as she knew now that the real reason was she didn't want the connection. She didn't want the questions about the choices she had made. She didn't want that link to the past.

Now she didn't have to worry, the link was forever gone.

The door opened and Cherie Dei looked in.

"Rachel, do you want a bottle of water?"

"Sure, that would be nice. Thank you."

"Tissues?"

"No, that's all right, I'm not crying."

"Be right back."

Dei closed the door.

"I don't cry," Rachel said to no one.

She put her elbows on the table and held her hands over her face. In the darkness she saw a memory. She and Terry on a case. They weren't partners but Backus had put them together on this one. It was a crime scene analysis. A bad one. A mother and daughter tied up and thrown into the water, the girl squeezing so hard on a crucifix it left its full impression on her hand. The mark was still there when the bodies were found. Terry was working with the photos and Rachel went to the cafeteria to get coffee. When she came back she could tell he had been crying. That was when she knew he was an empath, that he was her kind.

Dei came back into the room and put a bottle of spring water and a plastic cup down in front her.

"You okay?"

"Yes, fine. Thanks for the water."

"It was quite a shock. I didn't really know him and it bowled me over when the word spread."

Rachel just nodded. She didn't want to talk about it. The speakerphone rang and Rachel reached for it ahead of Dei. She picked up the handset rather than push the teleconference button. This way she could speak privately at first to Doran—at least, Doran's side of it would not be overheard.

"Brass?"

"Rachel, hi, I am so sorry I didn't—"

"It's all right. It isn't your job to keep me informed of everything."

"I know but this I should have told you about."

"It was probably in one of the bulletins and I just missed it. It's just strange finding out about it this way."

"I know. I'm sorry."

"So you went to the funeral?"

"The service, yes. It was out on the island where he lived. Catalina. It was really beautiful there and really sad."

"Were there many agents?"

"No, not too many. It was kind of hard to get to. You have to take a ferry. But there were a few and there were some cops and family and friends. Clint Eastwood was there. I think he took his own helicopter out."

The door opened and Alpert came in. He seemed renewed, as if he had been sucking on pure oxygen during the break. The other two agents, Zigo and Gunning, followed him in and sat down.

"We're ready to start," Rachel said to Doran. "I've got to put you on the screen now."

"Okay, Rachel. We'll talk later."

Rachel handed the phone to Alpert, who set up the teleconference. Doran appeared on the screen, looking more tired than before.

"Okay," Alpert said. "We ready to continue?"

After no one said a word he continued.

"All right then, what do these prints on the boat mean?"

"It means we've got to find out when and why McCaleb was out in the desert before he died," Dei said.

"And it means we've got to go over to L.A. and take a

look at his death," Gunning said. "Just to be sure a heart attack was a heart attack."

"I agree with that but there is a problem," Doran said. "He was cremated."

"That sucks," said Gunning.

"Was there an autopsy?" Alpert asked. "Blood and tissue taken?"

"I don't know about that," Doran said. "All I know is that he was cremated. I flew out for the service. The family let his ashes go over the side of his boat."

Alpert looked at the faces around the room and stopped at Gunning's.

"Ed, you're on it. Go over there and see what you can come up with. Do it quick. I'll call the FO over there and tell them to give you the people you need. And for God's sake keep it out of the press. McCaleb was a minor celebrity because of the movie thing. If the press gets a whiff of this they'll be on us like the jacket on a book."

"Got it."

"Other ideas? Suggestions?"

Nobody said anything at first. Then Rachel cleared her throat and spoke quietly.

"You know, Backus was Terry's mentor, too."

There was a pause of silence and then Doran said, "That's right."

"When they started the mentoring program Terry was the first one Backus picked. I was next after that."

"And what is the significance of that to us now?" Alpert asked.

Rachel shrugged.

"Who knows? But Backus called me out with the GPS. Maybe he called Terry out before me."

Everybody paused for a moment to think about that.

"I mean, why am I here? Why did he send the package to me when he knows I'm not in Behavioral anymore? There's a reason. Backus has some kind of plan. Maybe Terry was the first part of it."

Alpert slowly nodded his head.

"I think it is an angle we need to be aware of."

"He could be watching Rachel," Doran said.

"Well, let's not jump ahead of ourselves here," Alpert said. "Let's stay with the facts. Agent Walling, I want you to exercise all caution of course. But let's check out the McCaleb situation and see what we've got before we start jumping. Meantime, Brass, what else have you got?"

They waited as Doran looked down and off camera at some paperwork and apparently shifted gears from McCaleb back to the rest of the evidence.

"We've got something that might tie in with McCaleb. But let me go down my list and get this other stuff out of the way first. Uh, first, we're just starting now with the tape and the bags recovered with the bodies. Give us another day on that and I'll have a report. Let's see, on the clothes, they're probably going to be in the drying room another week before they're ready for analysis. So nothing there. The gum we already talked about. We'll put the dental profile into the bite mark database by the end of the day. Which leaves the GPS."

Rachel noticed that everyone in the room was staring intently at the television screen. It was as if Doran was in the room with them.

"We're making some good progress here. We traced

the serial number to a Big Five Sporting Goods store in Long Beach, California. Agents from the Los Angeles FO went to the store yesterday and obtained a store sales record showing the purchase of this Gulliver one hundred model by a man named Aubrey Snow. Turns out Mr. Snow is a fishing guide and was out on the water yesterday. Last night, when he finally returned to dock he was questioned at length about his Gulliver. He told us that he lost the device about eleven months ago in a poker game with several other guides. It was valuable because at the time it had several waypoints corresponding to his favorite or most productive fishing spots along the coast of Southern California and Mexico."

"Did he give us the guy who won it?" Alpert asked quickly.

"Unfortunately, no. It was an impromptu game. There was bad weather at the time and business was slow. A lot of guides were stuck in dock and they were getting together to play poker almost every night. Different nights, different players. A lot of drinking. Mr. Snow could not remember a name or much else about the man who won the GPS. He didn't think he was from the marina where Mr. Snow keeps his boat because he hasn't seen the man since. The FO was supposed to get together with Snow and an artist today so they can try to come up with a picture of this guy. But even if they get a good drawing, that area has marinas and fishing charters all over the place. I was already told that the FO has only two agents to spare on this."

"I'll make a call and change that," Alpert said. "When I call to get Ed set up on the McCaleb thing,

I'll get more bodies on this. I'll go right to Rusty Havershaw."

Rachel knew the name. Havershaw was the special agent in charge of the Los Angeles field office.

"That'll be a help," Doran said.

"You said this connects to McCaleb. How so?"

"Well, did you see the movie?"

"Actually, no, I didn't get around to it."

"Well, McCaleb was running a fishing charter out of Catalina. I don't know how plugged in he was to that community but there is a possibility that he knew some of the guides in those poker games."

"I see. It's a stretch but it is there. Ed, keep that in mind."

"Got it."

There was a knock on the door but Alpert ignored it. Cherie Dei got up and answered it. Rachel could see it was Agent Cates. He whispered something to Dei.

"Anything else, Brass?" Alpert asked.

"Not at the moment. I think we need to shift emphasis to L.A. and find—"

"Excuse me," Dei said, bringing Cates back into the room. "Listen to this."

Cates flicked his hands up like he was signaling that this was no big deal.

"Uh, I just got a call from the checkpoint out at the site. They're holding a man there who just drove up. He's a private detective from L.A. His name is Huhromibus Bosch. He—"

"You mean Hieronymus Bosch?" Rachel asked. "Like the painter?"

"Yeah, that's it. I don't know about any painter but

that is how my guy said it. Anyway, this is the deal. They put him in one of the RVs and took a look in his car without him knowing. He had a file on the front seat. There are notes and stuff but there also are photos. One of the photos is of the boat."

"You mean the boat from out there?" Alpert asked.

"Yeah, the one that marked the first grave. There also was a news article on the six missing men."

Alpert looked at the others in the room for a moment before speaking.

"Cherie and Tom, call Nellis and have them get ready with a chopper," he finally said. "Get out there and get going. And take Agent Walling with you."

18

THEY PUT ME IN an RV and told me to make myself at home. There was a kitchen and a table and a sitting area. There was a window but the view was of the side of another RV. The air-conditioning was on and that kept the smell out for the most part. When I asked questions they hadn't answered them. They told me that other agents were coming soon to speak to me.

An hour went by and it gave me time to think about what I had stumbled into. There was no doubt that this was a body recovery site. The smell, that unmistakable smell, was in the air. Besides that, I had seen two unmarked vans with no windows on the sides or back. That told me something right there. Body movers. And there was more than one body to be moved.

At the ninety-minute mark I was sitting on the couch reading a month-old FBI *Bulletin* I had picked up off the coffee table. I heard a helicopter fly over the RV and then its turbines rev down and quit after it landed. Five minutes later the RV's door opened and the agents I had been waiting for came in. Two women and a man. One of the women I recognized right off but I couldn't place from where. She was late thirties, tall and pretty with dark hair. There was a deadness in her eyes that I had seen before, too. She was an agent and that meant there could have been a lot of places where our paths had crossed.

"Mr. Bosch?" said the other woman, the one in charge. "I'm Special Agent Cherie Dei. This is my partner, Tom Zigo, and this is Agent Walling. Thank you for waiting for us."

"Oh, I had a choice? I didn't realize that."

"Of course. I hope they didn't tell you that you had to stay."

She smiled disingenuously. I decided not to argue the point and get things off to a bad start.

"Do you mind if we move into the kitchen and sit at the table?" Dei asked. "I think it will be best to talk there."

I shrugged like it didn't matter but I knew it did. They were going to sit me down and then corner me, one sitting across from me and then one on either side. I got up and took the seat I knew they'd want me in, the one where my back would be to the wall.

"So," Dei said after sitting down across the table from me. "What brings you out to the desert, Mr. Bosch?"

I made the shrug again. I was getting good practice at it.

"I was just on my way to Vegas and pulled off to look for a place to take care of some business."

"What kind of business?"

I smiled.

"I had to take a leak, Agent Dei."

Now she smiled.

"Oh, and then you just happened to stumble onto our little outpost here."

"Something like that."

"Something like that."

"It is hard to miss. How many bodies you got out there?"

"What makes you ask that? Who said anything about bodies?"

I smiled and shook my head. She was going to play it hard all the way.

"Do you mind if we take a look inside your car, Mr. Bosch?" she asked.

"I think you probably already have."

"And what makes you think that?"

"I was a cop in L.A. I worked with the FBI before."

"And so you know it all."

"Put it this way, I know what a body dig smells like and I know you've looked in my car. You just want to get my permission now to cover your ass. I'm not giving it to you. Stay out of my car."

I looked at Zigo and then over at Walling. It was then that I placed her and a whole profusion of questions came up out of the depths.

"I remember you now," I said. "It's Rachel, right?"

"Excuse me?" Walling asked.

"We actually met once. A long time ago in L.A. In Hollywood Division. You were out from Quantico. You were chasing the Poet and you thought one of the guys on the table was the next target. All the time you were right there with the Poet."

"You worked homicides?"

"That's right."

"How is Ed Thomas?"

"Like me, he retired. But Ed went and opened a bookstore down in Orange. Sells mystery novels, if you can believe it."

"I can."

"You're the one who shot Backus, right? In the house on the hill."

She didn't answer. Her eyes went from mine to Agent Dei's. There was something I didn't get. Walling was playing the lesser role here, but she obviously should have had seniority on Dei and her partner, Zigo. Then I put it together. She had probably been knocked down a notch or two in the scandal that came in the aftermath of the Poet investigation.

That leap led to another. I took a shot in the dark.

"That was a long time ago," I said. "Even before Amsterdam."

Walling's eyes flared for a split second and I knew I had hit something solid.

"How do you know about Amsterdam?" Dei asked quickly.

I looked back over at her. I pulled out the shrug again and gave it to her.

"I just know, I guess. Is that what this is about? Is that the Poet's work out there? He's back, isn't he?"

Dei looked at Zigo and signaled him to the door. He got up and left the RV. Dei then leaned forward so that I would not misunderstand the severity of the situation and her words.

"We want to know what you are doing here, Mr. Bosch. And you are not going anywhere until we get what we want."

I mirrored her posture by leaning forward. Our faces were two feet apart.

"Your guy at the checkpoint took my license. I'm sure you took a look at it and know what I do. I'm working a case. And it's confidential."

Zigo came back in. He was short and squat, must've just made it in over bureau regs. His hair was cut short like a military man's. He carried Terry McCaleb's file on the missing men in his hand. I knew inside it were the photos I had printed from Terry's computer. Zigo put the file down in front of Dei and she opened it. The photo of the old boat was on top. She lifted it and slid it across to me.

"Where did you get this?"

"That's confidential."

"Who are you working for?"

"That's confidential."

She flipped through the photos and came to the surreptitious shot Terry had taken of Shandy. She held it up to me.

"Who is this?"

"I don't know for sure but I'm thinking it's the long lost Robert Backus."

"What?" Walling exclaimed.

She reached over and **grabb**ed the photo out of Dei's hands. I watched her eyes flick back and forth as she studied it.

"Jesus Christ!" she whispered.

She got up and walked with the photo over to the kitchen counter. She put it down and studied it some more.

"Rachel?" Dei asked. "Don't say anything else."

Dei turned back to the file. She spread the other photos of Shandy out on the table. She then looked back up at me. There was fire in her eyes now.

"Where did you take these photos?"

"I didn't."

"Who did? And don't say it's confidential again, Bosch, or you are going to find yourself in a deep dark hole until it becomes *un*-confidential. This is your last chance."

I had been in one of the FBI's deep dark holes before. I knew if I had to I could take her best shot. But the truth was I wanted to help. I knew I should help. I had to balance that desire with what would be the best move for Graciela McCaleb. I had a client and I had to protect her.

"Tell you what," I said. "I want to help. And I want you to help me. Let me make a phone call and see if I can't get released from confidentiality. How does that sound?"

"You need a phone?"

"I have one. I just don't know if it works out here."

"It will. We put up a repeater."

"That's nice. You guys think of everything."

"Make your call."

"I need to do it in private."

"Then we'll leave you here. Five minutes, Mr. Bosch."

I was back to Mr. Bosch with her. That was an improvement.

"Actually, I would rather you wait here while I took a walk out in the desert. More private that way."

"Suit yourself. Just do it."

I left Rachel standing at the counter staring at the photo and Dei at the table looking at the file. I was escorted out of the RV and out to the open desert near the makeshift helicopter landing pad. Zigo stopped and let me walk on out by myself. He lit a smoke and kept his eyes on me. I pulled out my phone and checked the screen showing my last ten calls. I chose Buddy Lockridge's number and called it. I knew I had a good shot at reaching him because his phone was a cell.

"Yeah?"

It didn't sound like him.

"Buddy?"

"Yeah, who is this?"

"It's Bosch, where are you?"

"I'm in bed, man. You always call me in bed."

I looked at my watch. It was past noon.

"Well, get up. I'm putting you to work."

His voice immediately took on an alertness.

"I'm up. What do you want me to do?"

I tried to quickly put together a plan. On the one hand I was annoyed with myself for not bringing McCaleb's computer with me, but on the other hand I knew that if I had brought it, then it would be in the bureau's hands now and not much use to me.

"I need you to get to *The Following Sea* as fast as you can. In fact, take a helicopter and I'll pay you back. Just get over there and get on the boat."

"Not a problem. Then what?"

"Go on Terry's computer and into the photos. Print out the front and side shots of Shandy. Can you do that?"

"Yeah, but I thought you already printed—"

"I know, Buddy, I need you to do it again. Print those out, then go up into the file boxes on top. I forget which box but one of them has a file on a guy named Robert Backus. It's a—"

"The Poet—yeah, I know which one."

Of course you do, I almost said.

"Okay, good. Take the file and the photos and bring them to Las Vegas."

"Vegas? I thought you were in San Francisco."

For a moment that confused me but then I remembered how I had lied to him to throw him off my track.

"Changed my mind. Bring it all to Las Vegas, check into a hotel and wait for my call. Make sure your phone is charged. But don't call me, I'll call you."

"How come I can't call you when I get in?"

"Because in another twenty minutes I may not have this phone. Get moving now, Buddy."

"You're going to pay for all of this, right?"

"I'll pay. I'll also pay you for your time. You're on the clock, Buddy, so get moving."

"All right, I'm on it. You know, there's a ferry in twenty minutes. I could take that and save you a bunch of money, you know."

"Take a chopper. You'll beat the ferry by an hour. I need that hour."

"Okay, man, I'm gone."

"And Buddy? Don't tell anybody where you're going and what you're doing."

"Right."

He hung up and I checked Zigo before disconnecting. The agent had on dark glasses now but it appeared he was watching me. I faked like I had lost the signal and yelled *hello* a few times into the phone. I then closed it and reopened it and called Graciela's number. My luck was holding. She was home and answered.

"Graciela, it's Harry. Some things are happening and I need your permission to talk with the FBI about Terry's death and my investigation."

"The FBI? Harry, I told you I couldn't go to them first. Not until I—"

"I didn't go to them. They came to me. I'm out in the middle of the desert, Graciela. Things I found in Terry's office led me out here and the FBI was already here. I think it is safe to talk. I think the person they are looking for here is the one who hurt Terry. I don't think this is going to come back on you now. I think I should talk to them, tell them what I've got. It might help catch this guy."

"Who is it?"

"Robert Backus. Do you know the name? Did Terry mention it?"

There was silence while she thought about it.

"I don't think so. Who is it?"

"A guy he used to work with."

"An agent?"

"Yes. He was the one they called the Poet. Did you ever hear Terry talk about the Poet?"

"Yes, a long time ago. I mean, three or four years. I remember he was upset because I think he was supposed to be dead but it looked like he wasn't. Something like that."

It must have been around the time that Backus had

supposedly resurfaced in Amsterdam. Terry had probably just gotten the internal files on the investigation.

"Nothing since then?"

"No, I can't remember anything."

"Okay, Graciela. So what do you think? I cannot talk to them unless you allow it. I think it is okay."

"Then go ahead if you think it will help."

"It means they'll be coming out there soon. FBI agents. They'll probably take *The Following Sea* back to the mainland to go over it."

"What for?"

"Evidence. This guy was on the boat. First as a charter and then he came back and snuck on. That was when he changed the meds."

"Oh."

"And they'll also come to the house. They'll want to talk to you. Just be honest, Graciela. Tell them everything. Don't hold anything back and it will be all right."

"Are you sure, Harry?"

"Yes, I'm sure. So you're all right with this?"

"I'm all right."

We said good-bye and disconnected. As I was walking back toward Zigo I opened my phone again and called my home number. I then disconnected and repeated the process nine more times, wiping out any record on my phone of the calls to Buddy Lockridge and Graciela McCaleb. If things went wrong in the RV and Dei wanted to know who I called, it wouldn't be easy for her. She'd get nothing off my phone. She'd have to go to the phone company with a warrant.

As I approached, Zigo saw what I was doing. He smiled and shook his head.

"You know, Bosch, if we wanted your phone numbers, we would've picked them out of the air."

"Is that right?"

"That's right, if we wanted to."

"Wow, you guys are really rather special, aren't you?"

Zigo looked at me over his sunglasses.

"Don't be an asshole, Bosch. It gets tiring after a while."

"You should know."

19

ZIGO ESCORTED ME BACK in without another word. Agent Dei was waiting at the table. Rachel Walling still stood by the counter. I calmly sat down and looked at Dei.

"How'd it go?" she asked in a pleasant tone.

"It went fine. My client says I can talk to you. But it's not going to be a one-way street. We trade. I answer your questions, you answer mine."

She shook her head.

"Uh-uh, that's not how it works. This is an FBI investigation. We don't trade information with amateurs."

"You're saying I'm an amateur? I bring you a photo of the long-lost Robert Backus and I'm the amateur?"

I saw movement and looked over to Rachel. She had brought her hand up to her face to hide a smile. When she saw me looking at her she turned toward the counter and acted like she was studying the photo of Backus again.

"We don't even know if that *is* Backus," Dei said.

"You've got a guy with a beard, a hat and dark glasses. It could be anybody."

"And it could be the guy that is supposedly dead but somehow managed to kill five men in Amsterdam a few years ago and now, what, six men here. Or is it more than the six listed in that newspaper story?"

Dei gave me a tight, unpleasant smile.

"Look, you may be impressing yourself with all of this, but we're still not impressed. It still comes down to one thing: you want to get out of here, then start talking to us. Now you have your client's permission. I suggest you start by telling us who this client is."

I leaned back. She was a fortress I didn't think I could break through. But if nothing else, I had gotten that smile from Rachel Walling. That told me I might have a shot at climbing over the FBI barricade with her later.

"My client is Graciela McCaleb. Terry McCaleb's wife. Widow, I mean."

Dei blinked, then quickly recovered from the surprise. Or possibly it wasn't surprise. Possibly it was a confirmation of some sort.

"And why did she hire you?"

"Because somebody switched out her husband's medicine and killed him."

That brought a momentary silence. Rachel slowly stepped away from the counter and came back to her chair. With few questions or any direction from Dei I told them the story of how I had come to be called by Graciela, the details of her husband's tainted medications, and my investigation up until the point I reached the desert. I began to believe I was not surprising them with anything. Rather, it seemed more like I was confirming something or at least telling a story they already knew parts of. When I was finished Dei hit me with a few clarifying questions related to my movements. Zigo and Walling asked nothing.

"So," Dei said after the story was finished. "That's an interesting story. A lot of information. Why don't you put it into context for us now. What does it all mean to you?"

"You're asking me that? I thought that's what Quantico does, puts it all into the blender and pours out a case profile and all of the answers."

"Don't worry, we will. But I'd like your view of it."

"Well," I said, but then didn't continue. I was trying to put it all together and into my own blender, adding Robert Backus in as the newest ingredient.

"Well, what?"

"Sorry, I was just trying to put it together."

"Just tell us what you are thinking."

"Did anybody here know Terry McCaleb?"

"We all did. What does that have to do with—"

"I mean really know him."

"I did once," Rachel said. "We worked cases. But I hadn't been in touch. I didn't even know he was dead until today."

"Well, you should know, and will know once you go over there and check his house and his boat and everything else, that he was still working cases. He couldn't let it go. He worked some of his own old unsolveds and he worked new cases. He read the papers and watched TV. He made calls to cops on cases that interested him and offered to help out."

"And this got him killed?" Dei asked.

I nodded.

"Eventually. I think so. In January the *L.A. Times* ran that story in the file you have there. Terry read it and got interested. He called over to Vegas Metro to offer his services. They shined him on, not interested. But they weren't above dropping his name in the local paper when it ran a follow-up story on the missing men."

"When was that?"

"Beginning of February. I'm sure you can check. Anyway, that story, his name in that story, drew the Poet to him."

"Look, we're not confirming anything about the Poet. Do you understand that?"

"Sure, whatever you want. You can take this whole thing as a hypothetical if you want."

"Go on with it."

"Somebody was abducting those men—and we now know burying them in the desert. Like all good serial killers he kept his eye on the media, to see if anybody was putting two and two together and getting close. He sees the follow-up story and he sees McCaleb's name. It's an old colleague. My guess is he knew McCaleb back in the day. At Quantico, before Terry came out to set up the Behavioral Sciences outpost in L.A. Before he went down with the bad heart."

"Actually, Terry was the first agent Backus mentored in the unit," Walling said.

Dei looked at her like she had betrayed some trust. Walling ignored her and I liked that about her.

"There you go," I said. "They had that connection. Backus sees the name in the paper and one of two things happened. He took it as a challenge or he knew McCaleb was relentless and was going to keep coming, despite the apparent lack of interest in him from Metro."

"So he went after McCaleb," Dei said.

"Right."

"And he had to eliminate him in a way that would not raise questions," Rachel added.

"Right."

I looked at Zigo. It was time for him to chime in but he said nothing.

"So he went over there and checked him out," I continued. "He had the beard, the hat, the glasses, probably a little plastic surgery to go with it. He hired Terry to take him fishing."

"And Terry didn't know it was him," Rachel said.

"Terry got suspicious of something but I'm not sure of what. Those photos were part of a series. Terry knew something was up with the guy and took extra photos. But I think that if he knew then that the guy was Backus he would've done something about it. He didn't, and that makes me think he wasn't sure what he had or who the guy was."

I looked at Rachel.

"You looked at the photo. Can you tell, is it him? I mean, in a hypothetical sort of way."

"I can't say, hypothetically or not. I can't see his eyes or enough of his face. If it's him he was cut. His nose is different. So are his cheeks."

"Easily changeable," I said. "Come to L.A. sometime. I'll take you to a guy I know in Hollywood who does work for the escort trade. He's got some before and after photos that will make you praise the wonders of medical science."

"I'm sure," Dei said, even though I was talking to Rachel. "Then what? When's he switch McCaleb's meds?"

I wanted to consult my chronology but my notebook was in my coat pocket. They hadn't searched me yet, so I wanted to keep the notebook out of it, maybe get out of there with it.

"Um, about two weeks after the charter Terry's boat was broken into. Whoever it was took a GPS device but I think that was just as a cover in case Terry realized somebody had—what is it?"

I had watched their reactions. The GPS meant something.

"What kind of GPS was it?" Rachel asked.

"Rachel," Dei cut in quickly. "You're an observer, remember?"

"A Gulliver," I said. "I don't remember the exact model. The sheriff's report is on the boat. It actually wasn't Terry's. It was his partner's."

"Do you know the partner's name?" Dei asked.

"Yeah, Buddy Lockridge. Don't you remember him from the movie?"

"I didn't see it. Do you know anything more about the history of this GPS device?"

"Buddy told me he won it in a poker game. It had a lot of good fishing spots marked on it. He was pissed off when it got stolen, thought it was another fishing guide who took it."

I could tell by their reactions that I was hitting every pitch. The GPS was important. It had not been taken simply as a cover. I was wrong about that. It took me a minute but then I put it together.

"I get it," I said. "That's how you found this place, isn't it? Backus sent you people the GPS with this place marked. He led you here like he did with Terry."

"This is not about us," Dei said. "It's about you."

But I glanced at Rachel and saw the confirmation in her eyes. I took the next jump and figured it had been sent to her. That was why she was here as an observer. Backus called her out, just as he had called out Terry.

"You said Terry was the first agent Backus mentored in the unit. Who was the second?"

"Let's move on," Dei said.

Rachel didn't answer but she gave me that slight smile that looked so sad with those dead eyes. She was telling me I had it right. She came after Terry McCaleb in the mentoring program.

"I hope you are taking appropriate precautions," I said quietly.

Dei opened the file on the table.

"That's actually no business of yours," she said. "Now, there are some things in your notes here I want to ask you about. First of all, who is William Bing?"

I looked at Dei. She thought that it was my file and my notes.

"I don't know. Just a name I came across."

"Where?"

"I think Terry had written it down. I haven't figured out who it is yet."

"And this reference to the triangle theory, what does it mean?"

"What does it mean to you?"

"Mr. Bosch, don't annoy me. Don't play cute."

"Cherie?" Rachel asked.

"What?"

"I think those are probably Terry's notes."

Dei looked down at the file and realized Rachel was right. I looked at Rachel like I was hurt that she had ratted me out. Dei closed the file abruptly.

"Right. Of course."

She looked up at me.

"You know what that means?"

"No, but I think you'll tell me."

"It means we'll take it from here. You can head on back to L.A. now."

"I'm not going to L.A. I'm going to Las Vegas. I have a place there."

"You can go wherever you want but stay away from this investigation. We are officially taking it over."

"You know I don't work for any police department, Agent Dei. You can't take anything over from me unless I want you to. I'm a private operator."

She nodded like she was understanding of my situation.

"That's fine, Mr. Bosch, we'll be speaking to your employer later today and you'll be unemployed before sunset."

"I'm just trying to make a living."

"I'm just trying to catch a killer. So understand me, your services are no longer required. Stay away from it. You're out. You're finished. Can I be any clearer?"

"Think maybe you could put it in writing, too?"

"You know what, I think you should get out of here and go home while you still can. Tom, would you get Mr. Bosch his license and keys and escort him to his car?"

"Gladly," Zigo said, his first word uttered in the motor home.

I reached for the file but she snatched it away from my grasp.

"And we'll be keeping this."

"Sure. Happy hunting, Agent Dei."

"Thank you."

I followed Zigo toward the door. I glanced back and nodded to Rachel and she did the same to me. I think I saw a trace of light enter her eyes.

20

THE THREE AGENTS WERE still talking about Bosch when the helicopter lifted off the desert floor and they began the forty-minute journey back to Las Vegas. The three agents wore headphones so they could communicate with each other despite the noise of the rotor wash. Dei clearly remained annoyed with the private detective and Rachel thought that maybe Cherie felt that somehow Bosch had gotten something over on her. Rachel remained amused. She knew they hadn't seen the last of Bosch. He had seen-it-all-twice eyes, and that nod at the end told her he wasn't going to just fold up his tent and go home.

"What about the triangle theory?" Dei said.

Rachel waited for Zigo to go first but as usual he said nothing.

"I think Terry was probably onto something," she said. "Somebody should go to work on it."

"At the moment I don't know if we have the bodies to chase all of this stuff. I'll ask Brass if she's got anybody.

And this William Bing—that name hasn't come up before."

"My guess is that he is a doctor. Terry was coming over here and probably wanted to have a name in case something went wrong."

"Rachel, when we get back, can you just run that down? I know what Alpert said, you're an observer and all, but if that's just a loose end, then it will be good to nail it down."

"No problem. I can do it from my hotel room if you don't want him seeing me working a phone."

"No, stay in the FO. If Alpert doesn't see you he'll start wondering what you're up to."

Dei, who was in the front passenger seat, turned and looked back at Rachel, who was behind the pilot's seat.

"What was with you two, anyway?"

"What do you mean?"

"You know what I mean. You and Bosch. All the looks, the smiles. 'I hope you are taking appropriate precautions.' What's going on with that, Rachel?"

"Look, he's outnumbered here, okay? It's natural that he'd pick one of us to play to. It's covered in the manual on interview techniques and tendencies. Check it out sometime."

"And what about you? Are you playing to him? Is that in the manual, too?"

Rachel shook her head as if to dismiss the whole discussion.

"I just like his style. He acts like he still has the badge, you know? He didn't stand down to us and I think that's sort of cool."

"You've been out in the boonies too long, Rachel, or

you wouldn't say that. We don't like people who won't stand down to us."

"Maybe I have."

"So does that mean you think he's going to be a problem?"

"Definitely," said Zigo.

"Probably," added Rachel.

Dei shook her head.

"I don't have the people for all of this. I can't spend my time watching this guy."

"You want me to keep tabs on him?" Rachel asked.

"You volunteering?"

"I'm looking for something to do. So, yeah, I'm volunteering."

"You know, before nine-eleven and Homeland Security, we used to get whatever we needed. Bagging serials were the best headlines the bureau got. Now it's terrorists twenty-four-seven and we can't even get overtime."

Rachel noted how Dei pointedly did not say whether she wanted her to check up on Bosch or not. A nice way to have deniability if something went wrong. She decided that once back at the field office she would get Dei alone and get her to run a check on whether Bosch really had a home in Las Vegas. She'd try to find out what he was up to and keep a loose watch on him.

She looked out her window and down at the black asphalt ribbon that cut through the desert. They were following it back to the city. At that same moment she saw a black Mercedes-Benz SUV heading in the same direction. It was dirty from off-roading in the desert. She knew it was Bosch making his way to Vegas. Then she noticed the drawing on the roof of the Mercedes. He had used a rag or something to draw a happy face in the white dust on the roof. The drawing made her smile, too.

Dei's voice came in through the earphones.

"What is it, Rachel? What are you smiling at?"

"Nothing. I'm just thinking about something."

"Yeah, I wish I could smile knowing that there might be a psycho-agent out there waiting to put a plastic bag over my head."

Rachel looked at Dei, annoyed by such a snide and brutal remark. Dei apparently saw something in her eyes.

"Sorry. I just think you better start taking this more seriously."

Rachel looked at her until Dei had to look away.

"You really think I'm not serious about this?"

"I know you are. I shouldn't have said anything."

Rachel looked back down at the I-15 freeway. They were long past the black Mercedes. Bosch was gone, far behind them.

She studied the terrain for a while. It was all so different yet all the same. A moonscape carpet of rock and sand. She knew it was full of life but all life was hidden. The predators were underground, waiting to come out at night.

"Ladies and gentlemen?" the pilot's voice said in her ear. "Switch to channel three. You've got an incoming call."

Rachel had to take her headset off to figure out how to change the frequency. She thought that the headset had a stupid design. When she put the set back on she heard Brass Doran's voice. She was talking rapid-fire the way Rachel remembered she always did whenever something big came up.

"—cent integrity. It definitely came from him."

"What?" Rachel said. "I didn't hear any of that."

"Brass," Dei said, "start again."

"I said we got a match from the bite mark database. With the gum. It's got ninety-five percent integrity, which is one of the highest matches I've ever seen."

"Who?" Rachel asked.

"Rach, you are going to love this. Ted Bundy. That gum was chewed by Ted Bundy."

"That's impossible," Dei said. "First of all, Bundy's been dead for years, long before any of these men went missing. And he was never known to have gotten to Nevada or California or to have targeted men. Something's wrong with the data, Brass. It's a bad read or—"

"We ran it twice. Both times it came up Bundy."

"No," Rachel said. "It's right."

Dei turned and looked back at her. Rachel was thinking about Bundy. The ultimate serial killer. Handsome, smart and vicious. He was a biter, too. He had been the only one to really give her the creeps. The others she just felt a loathing and disgust for.

"How do you know it's right, Rachel?"

"I just know. Twenty-five years ago Backus helped set up the VICAP database. Brass remembers. Over the next eight years the data was collected. Agents from the unit were sent out to interview every serial killer and rapist who was incarcerated in the country. That was before I was there but even later, when I was there, we kept doing interviews and adding to the base. Bundy was interviewed several times, mostly by Bob. Right before his execution he called Bob down to Raiford and Bob took me with him. We spent three days interviewing him. I remember that Ted kept borrowing gum from Bob. It was Juicy Fruit. That's what Bob chewed."

"Then what, he'd spit it back into Bob's hand?" Zigo asked incredulously.

"No, he'd throw it in the trash can. We interviewed him in the death house captain's office. There was a trash can. When we were done each day, Bundy was led out. There were many points when Bob was alone in that office. He could have just taken the gum out of the can."

"So you're saying Bob more or less went Dumpster diving for Ted Bundy's gum and then held on to it so he could put it in a grave all these years later?"

"I'm saying he took the gum out of that prison, knowing it had Bundy's teeth marks in it. Maybe it was just a souvenir then. But it became something else later. Something maybe to taunt us with."

"And where'd he been keeping it, in the fridge?"

"Maybe. That's where I'd keep it."

Dei turned back around in her seat.

"What do you think, Brass?" she asked.

"I think I should've thought of it myself. I think Rachel is onto something. I think Bob and Ted actually got along. He went down there several times to talk to him. Sometimes alone. He could have gotten the gum any one of those times."

Rachel watched Dei nod her head in agreement.

Zigo cleared his throat and spoke.

"So this was just another way of him coming out and

telling us he did this and how smart he was about it. To taunt us. First the GPS with the prints and now the gum."

"That's what I would say," Doran agreed.

It wasn't that simple, Rachel knew. She unconsciously shook her head and Zigo, sitting next to her, picked up on it.

"You disagree, Agent Walling?"

She noted that Zigo must have attended the Randal Alpert school of building relations among fellow colleagues.

"I just don't think it is as simple as that. You are looking at it from the wrong angle. Remember, the GPS and his prints came to us first but that gum was in that grave first. He might have intended for the gum to be found first. Before there was any direct connection to him."

"If that was the case, what was he doing?" Dei asked.

"I don't know. I don't have the answer. I'm just saying, don't assume at this point we know what the plan or even the sequence was supposed to be."

"Rachel, you know we always keep an open mind on things. We take things as they come and never stop looking from all angles."

That sounded like a line taped to the wall in the public information office in Quantico, where agents always had pithy policy and procedure statements to deliver over the phone to reporters. Rachel decided to step back from tangling with Dei on this. She had to be careful not to outstay her welcome and she sensed she was nearing that point with her former student.

"Yes, I know," she said.

"Okay, Brass, anything else new?" Dei asked.

"That was it. That was enough."

"Okay. Then we'll talk to you at the next one."

Meaning the next conference room case session. Doran said good-bye and broke off and then the onboard communication link remained silent as the helicopter crossed the dividing line between the harsh undeveloped landscape and the beginning of the sprawl of Las Vegas. As Rachel looked down she knew it was merely a trading of one form of a desert for another. Down there, beneath all the barrel tile and gravel roofs, predators still waited to come out at night. To find their victims.

21

THE EXECUTIVE EXTENDED STAY motel was off the south end of the strip. It had no neon lights flashing in front of it. It had no casino and no floor show. In fact, no executives stayed there. It was a place populated by the fringe dwellers of Vegas society. The addicted gamblers, the take-off men, the sex trade workers, the kind of people who can't leave the place but at the same time can't put down permanent roots either.

People like me. Often when you meet a fellow tenant at the Double X, as the longtimers call the place, they'll ask you how long you've been there and how long you're staying, as if you're working off jail time. I believe that many of the tenants of the motel have had the real experience of jail time and I chose such a place for two reasons. One was that I still carried a mortgage in Los Angeles and could not afford to stay over time at a place like the Bellagio or the Mandalay Bay or even the Riviera. And two was that I didn't want to get comfortable in Las Vegas. I didn't want things to feel right there. Because I knew when it was time for me to go, I just wanted to turn in the key and leave.

I got to Vegas by three and knew my daughter would be home from day care and I could go to my ex-wife's home to see her. I wanted to but I also wanted to wait. I had Buddy Lockridge coming in and I had things to do. The FBI had let me out of the RV with my notebook still in my pocket and Terry McCaleb's map book still in my car. I wanted to put them to good use before Agent Dei maybe realized her mistake and came back to me. I wanted to see if I could make the next step in the case before she did.

I pulled into the Double X and parked in my usual spot near the fence that separated the motel from the private jet stalls on the McCarran tarmac. I noticed that a Gulfstream 9 that was parked there when I left Vegas three mornings earlier was still in place. There was also a smaller but sleeker-looking black jet parked next to it. I didn't know what kind of jet it was, only that it looked like money. I got out and walked up the steps to my one-bedroom efficiency on the second floor. It was neat and functional and I tried to spend as little time there as I had to. The best thing about it was the small balcony off the living room. In the brochures they offered in the rental office it was called a smoking balcony. It was too small a space to actually fit a chair. But I could stand out there and lean on the extra-high railing and watch the billionaires' jets come in. And I found myself doing that often. I found myself standing there and even wishing that I still smoked. Oftentimes one of the tenants from the apartment on either side of my unit would be standing on their balcony smoking when I was out there. On one side was a card counter—or an "advantage player," as he called it—and on the other a woman of indeterminate means of income. My conversations with them were perfunctory. Nobody wanted to ask or answer too many questions at this place.

The last two days' editions of the *Sun* were on the worn rubber mat outside my door. I hadn't canceled it because I knew the woman who lived next door liked to sneak over and read the paper, after which she would re-fold it and put it back in its plastic bag. She didn't know that I knew this.

Inside I dropped the newspapers on the floor and put McCaleb's map book down on the dinette table. I took the notebook out of my pocket and put that down, too. I went over to the sliding door and opened it to let some of the stuffiness out. Whoever had the place before me didn't use the smoking balcony and the place seemed to have a permanent nicotine funk.

After plugging my phone's charger into the wall below the dinette I called Buddy Lockridge's number but the call rang through to voice mail. I disconnected before leaving a message. I next called Graciela McCaleb's number and asked if the FBI had shown up yet.

"They just left," she said. "They went through a lot of stuff here and they just went down to the boat. You were right, they're going to take the boat with them. I don't know when I'll get it back."

"Have you seen Buddy around today?"

"Buddy? No, was he supposed to come by?"

"No, I was just wondering."

"Are you still with the FBI?"

"No, they let me go a couple hours ago. I'm at my place in Vegas. I'm going to keep working on the case, Graciela."

"Why? It seems—the agents told me it was a priority investigation now. They think that agent changed his meds. Backus."

What she was asking was what it was I could do that the august powers of the Federal Bureau of Investigation couldn't do. The answer of course was nothing. But I remembered what Terry had said to Graciela about me. That he would want me on the case if anything ever happened to him. It left me unable to walk away.

"Because it's what Terry wanted," I said. "But don't worry, if I come up with anything the bureau doesn't have, I'll give it to them. Just like today. I'm not trying to compete with them. I'm just working the case, Graciela."

"Okay."

"But you know you don't have to tell them that if they ask. They might not be happy about it."

"I know."

"Thank you, Graciela. I'll call if anything comes up."

"Thank you, Harry. Good luck."

"I'll probably need it."

After disconnecting I tried Buddy Lockridge once more but got voice mail again. I guessed that maybe he was on a plane with his phone turned off. I hoped, anyway. I hoped he had gotten onto the boat and then off before the bureau agents saw him. I put the phone down and went to the refrigerator. I made a quick sandwich of processed cheese and white bread. I had both in the box in case my daughter should want a grilled cheese sandwich when she visited. It was one of her staples. I skipped the grilling and just stood at the counter and quickly ate the tasteless sandwich to fill the void in my stomach. I then sat at the table and opened my notebook to a new page. I used a couple of self-relaxation exercises I had learned years ago in hypnosis class. In my mind I saw a blank chalkboard. Pretty soon I picked up the chalk and started writing in white across the black surface of the board. As best as I could I re-created Terry McCaleb's notes from the missing men file—the notes the FBI had taken away. When I had as much as I could remember on the board, I started rewriting it all in my notebook. I thought that I got most of it, except for the phone numbers and I didn't care so much about them because I could recover them by simply dialing information.

Through the open balcony door I heard the high-pitched whine of jet engines. Another plane was parking out there. I heard the engines quit and it got peaceful again.

I opened McCaleb's map book. I checked every page and found no handwritten notations other than those on the page illustrating southern Nevada and the contiguous sections of California and Arizona. Again, I looked at what McCaleb had done. He had circled the Mojave Preservation Area, which I knew included the Zzyzx Road exit and the location of the FBI's body excavation scene. On the outside margin of the map, he had written a column of numbers and added them up to 86. Beneath this he had drawn a line and written "Actual—92."

My guess was that these numbers corresponded to miles. I looked at the map and found that it noted mile counts between distances on all significant roadways. In a matter of seconds I found numbers that matched the column McCaleb had written on the side of the page. He had added up the mileage counts between Las Vegas and a point on I-15 in the middle of the Mojave. Zzyzx Road was too small and inconsequential to be listed on the map by name. But my guess was that it was the unnamed point on the 15 from which McCaleb had started to add up the mileage.

In my notebook I wrote and added the numbers myself. McCaleb got it right—86 miles, according to the map. But then he had disagreed or charted a different route, coming up with 92 miles. My guess was that he had driven the route himself and gotten a different count from the map on his car's odometer. This conflict would have occurred because in Las Vegas he would have had a specific destination. The map's mileage counts would have used a different end point in the city.

McCaleb's destination was unknown to me. I had no idea when the markings on the map page had been made or whether they were in any way connected to the case. But I thought they were because he began his count at Zzyzx Road. That could not be a coincidence. There are no coincidences.

From the balcony I heard a cough. I knew it was the woman next door smoking on her balcony. I found her very curious and kept somewhat of a watch on her whenever I was staying at the Double X. She wasn't much of a smoker and she seemed to go out on the balcony only when a private jet was coming into a parking stall. Sure, some people like to watch planes. But I thought she was up to something and that made me all the more curious. I thought maybe she was spotting marks for the casinos or maybe other gamblers.

I got up and walked out through the door. As I stepped out I looked to my right and saw my neighbor throw something backward into her apartment. Something she didn't want me to see.

"Jane, how you doing?"

"Fine, Harry. Haven't seen you around lately."

"I've been gone a couple days. What do we have out here?"

I looked across the parking lot to the tarmac. Another sleek black jet had parked next to its twin. A matching black limo was waiting near the jet's stairs. A man wearing a suit, sunglasses and a maroon turban was coming out of the plane. I realized I was ruining Jane's surveillance if that was a camera or set of binoculars she tossed back into her place when she saw me.

"The sultan of swing," I said, just to be saying something.

"Probably," she said.

She took a drag on her cigarette and coughed again. I knew she wasn't a smoker. She smoked so it would look plausible for her to be on the balcony watching rich men and their airplanes. She also didn't have brown eyes—I had seen her on the balcony one day when she'd forgotten to put in the tinted contacts—and her hennaed black hair was probably not the real color either.

I wanted to ask her what she was up to, what the game or the con or the scheme was. But I also liked our balcony-to-balcony conversations and I wasn't a cop anymore. And the truth was that if Jane—I didn't know her last name—was in the business of separating those rich men from some of their riches, then down deep I couldn't work up a good deal of outrage over it. The whole city was built on the same principle. You roll the dice in the city of desire and you get what you deserve.

I sensed something intrinsically good about her. Damaged but good. One time when I brought my daughter to the apartment we ran into Jane on the steps and she stopped to talk to Maddie. The next morning I found a little stuffed panther on the doormat next to my paper.

"How's your daughter?" she asked, as if she knew my thoughts.

"She's good. The other night she asked me if the Burger King and the Dairy Queen were married."

Jane smiled and I saw that sadness in her eyes again. I knew it had something to do with kids. I asked her something I had been thinking about for a long time.

"You got kids?"

"One. She's a little older than yours. I'm not with her anymore. She lives in France."

That was all she said and I left it at that, feeling guilty because of what I had in my life and because I knew before I asked the question that I was tempting the grief in her. But my question prompted her to ask one she had probably been holding on to for a while, too.

"Are you a cop, Harry?"

I shook my head.

"Was. In L.A. How'd you know that?"

"Just a guess. I think it was the way I saw you walking with your daughter out to your car. Like you were ready to jump on anything that moved. Anything bad."

I shrugged. She had pegged me.

"I thought that was kind of nice," she added. "What do you do now?"

"Nothing really. I'm thinking about it, you know."

"Yes."

We were suddenly becoming more than neighbors exchanging superficial conversation.

"What about you?" I asked.

"Me? I'm just waiting on something."

So much for that. I knew that was the end of the line in that direction. I turned from her and watched another sultan or sheik start his way down the jet's steps. The limo driver was waiting with the door open. It looked to me like the driver had something under his jacket, something he could pull out if the going got tough. I looked back at Jane.

"I'll see you, Jane."

"Okay, Harry. Say hi to her for me."

"I will. You be careful."

"You, too."

Back at the dinette I tried Buddy Lockridge once more and got the same result. Nothing. I picked up the pen and drummed it impatiently on my notepad. He should've answered by now. I wasn't getting concerned. I was getting annoyed. The reports on Buddy were that he was unreliable. That was not something I had time for.

I got up and went to the kitchenette and took a beer out of the under-the-counter refrigerator. There was a bottle opener on the doorjamb. I cranked the bottle open and took a long draw. The beer cut through the desert dust and tasted good going down. I figured I deserved it.

I went back to the balcony door but didn't step out. I didn't want to spook Jane again. Staying inside, I glanced out and saw that the limousine was gone and the new jet was buttoned up tight. I leaned out and checked Jane's balcony. She was gone. I noticed that in the ashtray perched on top of the railing she had butted out her smoke after only a quarter burn. Somebody ought to tell her that was a giveaway.

A few minutes later the beer was gone and I was back at the dinette looking at my notes and McCaleb's map book. I knew I was missing something, I just couldn't touch it. It was there, it was close. But I just couldn't reach out to it yet.

My cell phone rang. Finally, it was Buddy Lockridge.

"Did you just call me?"

"Yeah, I did. But I told you not to call me at this number."

"I know but you just called me. I thought that meant it was safe."

"What if it hadn't been me?"

"I've got caller ID. I knew it was you."

"Yeah, but how did you know it was me? What if it was someone else with my phone?"

"Oh."

"Yeah, 'oh' is right, Buddy. Look, if you're going to work for me you gotta listen to what I tell you."

"All right, all right, I understand."

"Good. Where are you?"

"Vegas, man. Like you told me."

"You get the stuff off the boat?"

"Got it."

"No FBI?"

"Nah, man. Everything's cool."

"Where are you right now?"

As I was speaking I noticed something on my notes and remembered something else about the *Times* story on the missing men. Rather, I remembered the circle Terry had drawn on the newspaper clip.

"I'm at the B," Lockridge said.

"The B? Where's the B?"

"The big B, man."

"Buddy, what are you talking about? Where are you?"

He whispered his reply.

"I thought everything was on the QT, man. Like they might be listening."

"Buddy, I don't care if they're listening. Quit with the code. What is the big B?"

"The Bellagio. It's a simple code, dude."

"A simple code for a simple mind. You're telling me you checked into the Bellagio on my tab?"

"That's right."

"Well, check out."

"What do you mean? I just got here."

"I'm not paying for the Bellagio. Check out and come here and get a room where I'm at. If I could afford to put you in the Bellagio I'd be staying there myself."

"No expense account, huh?"

"None."

"All right. Where are you at?"

I gave him the name and address of the Double X and right away he knew I was in a fringe location.

"They got pay-per-view there?"

"They don't have shit. Just get over here."

"Well, look, I already checked in here. They're not going to give me my money back. They already charged my card and besides, I already crapped in the toilet.

That's like implied ownership of the room, you know. I'll stay one night here and then I'll come stay over there tomorrow."

There's only going to be one night, I thought but didn't say.

"Then everything above what this dump costs is coming out of your pay, man. I didn't tell you to check into the most expensive place on the strip."

"All right, all right, dock my pay if you want. Be that way. I don't care."

"All right, I will. You got a car?"

"No, I took a cab."

"Okay, go down the elevator and get another one and bring that stuff over here to me."

"Can I get a massage first?"

"Buddy, Jesus Christ, if you don't—"

"I'm kidding, I'm kidding! Can't you take a joke, Harry? I'm on my way."

"Good. I'm waiting."

I disconnected without saying good-bye and immediately dropped the conversation from my radar screen. I was excited. I moved on. I thought I had inexplicably solved one of the mysteries. I looked at my re-creation of McCaleb's file notes and at one line in particular.

Triangle theory?—1 point gives 3

On the newspaper story he had also circled the word *circle* in the Metro detective's quote about the mileage on the rental car of one of the missing men, giving the investigators a large circle in which to look for clues as to what happened to the missing man.

I now believed that McCaleb may have circled the word because he thought it was wrong. The search zone was not a circle. It was a triangle, meaning that the miles on the rental car formed the three sides of a triangle. Point one was the airport, the origin. The renter picked up the car and drove to point two. Point two was the place where he crossed paths with the abductor. And point three was the place where the abductor took his victim. Afterward, the car was returned to point one, completing the triangle.

When McCaleb had written his notes he didn't know about Zzyzx Road. He had one point—the airport car rental return. So he wrote, "1 point gives 3," because he knew that if one more point on the triangle was identified, it would lead to the remaining point as well.

"One more point of the triangle means we can figure out all three," I said out loud, translating McCaleb's note from shorthand.

I got up and started pacing. I was jazzed and thought I was getting close. It was true that the abductor could have made any number of stops with the rental car, thereby leaving the triangle theory worthless. But if he didn't, if he avoided distractions and single-mindedly took care of the business at hand, then the triangle theory would hold. His thoroughness might contain his weakness. That would make Zzyzx Road point three on the triangle because that would have been the last stop for the car before it was returned to the airport. And that would make point two the remaining unknown. It was the intersection. The place where predator and prey came together. Its location was not known at the moment but thanks to my silent partner I knew how to find it.

22

Backus saw Rachel pull out of the side lot of the FBI building in a dark blue Crown Victoria. She turned left onto Charleston and headed toward Las Vegas Boulevard. He hung back. He was sitting behind the wheel of a 1997 Ford Mustang with Utah plates. He had taken the car from a man named Elijah Willows, who no longer needed it. His eyes left Rachel's car and held on the street scene, watching for movement.

A Grand Am with two men in it pulled out into traffic from the office building next to the FBI building. It went in the same direction as Rachel's car.

"There's one," Backus said to himself.

He waited and then he watched a dark blue SUV with triple antennas pull out of the FBI lot and turn right onto Charleston, going in the opposite direction as Rachel. Another Grand Am pulled out behind it and followed.

"There's two and three."

Backus knew it was what was called a "sky bird" surveillance. One car to maintain a loose visual surveillance while the subject was tracked by satellite. Rachel, whether she knew it or not, had been given a car with a GPS transponder on it.

All of this was okay with Backus. He knew he could still track her. All he needed to do was follow the follow car and he would get there just the same.

He started the Mustang. Before pulling out onto Charleston to catch up to the Grand Am following Rachel, he reached over and opened the glove compartment. He was wearing rubber surgeon's gloves, size small so they would stretch across his hands and be almost unnoticeable from a distance.

Backus smiled. Sitting in the glove box was a little two-shot vest gun that would nicely complement his own remaining weapon. He knew he had sized Elijah Willows up perfectly when he had first seen him leaving the Slots-o-Fun on the down side of the strip. Yes, he was what Backus had been looking for physically—same size and build—but he had also sensed a detachment about the man. He was someone who dwelled alone and on the edge. The gun in the glove box seemed to prove that. It gave Backus confidence in his choice.

He hit the gas and pulled loudly out onto Charleston. He did this purposely. He knew that on the off chance there was a fourth car, a trailer, the car they would find the least suspicious would be the one with the driver boldly drawing attention to himself.

23

I T CAME DOWN TO basic high school geometry. I had two of the three points on a triangle and I needed the third. It was that simple and that difficult at the same time. To get that point I had the total distances of all three sides of the triangle to work with. I sat down, opened my notebook to a new page and went to work with McCaleb's map.

I recalled from the *Times* article that the mileage recorded on the rental car of one of the missing men was 328 miles. Under what I believed McCaleb's theory to be, that mileage count would equal the total of all three sides of the triangle. I knew, thanks to the notations on the map page, that one side of the triangle—Zzyzx to the airport in Vegas—was 92 miles. That left 236 miles for the remaining two sides. That number could be divided in a variety of ways, putting the missing point of the triangle in a myriad of possible positions on the map. What I needed was a charting compass to accurately plot the triangle but I made do with what I had.

According to the map's legend, one inch equaled 50 miles of terrain. I took out my wallet and removed my driver's license. Holding one of its short edges to the legend I was able to determine that the side of the license equaled 100 miles on the map. Working with that I composed a number of triangles that approximated the remaining 236 miles of roadway. I plotted points both north and south of the baseline I had drawn from Zzyzx Road to Las Vegas. I spent twenty minutes working the possibilities, my plotting taking the third possible point of the triangle down into Arizona and as far as the Grand Canyon and then north into the bombing and gunnery ranges under the command and restriction of Nellis Air Force Base. I soon grew frustrated, realizing the possibilities were endless and that I could have already identified the missing point of the triangle and not even know it.

I got up and went to the half-fridge for another beer. Still annoyed with myself I opened the cell and called Buddy Lockridge. The call went through to voice mail without being answered.

"Buddy, where the hell are you?"

I slammed the device closed. It wasn't like I needed Buddy there that moment. I just needed to yell at somebody and he was the easy target.

I stepped back out onto the balcony and checked for Jane. She wasn't there and I felt a glimmer of disappointment. She was a mystery and I liked talking to her. My eyes swept across the parking lot and the jets beyond the fence and caught on the figure of a man standing in the far corner of the lot. He had on a black baseball hat with gold lettering I couldn't read. He was clean-shaven and wore mirrored glasses and a white shirt. His lower half was hidden by the car he stood behind. He seemed to be looking right at me.

The man in the hat did not move for at least two minutes and neither did I. I was tempted to leave the apartment and go down into the lot but was afraid if I lost sight of the man for even a few seconds he would disappear.

We stood locked in our stares until the man suddenly broke from position and started walking across the lot. As he came out from behind the car I saw he wore black shorts and some sort of equipment belt. That was also when I could make out the word *Security* on his shirt and realized he apparently worked for the Double X. He walked into the passageway that separated the two buildings that made up the Double X and was gone from my sight.

I let it go. It was the first time I had seen a security man at the place in daylight but it still wasn't that suspicious. I checked the next-door balcony for Jane again— there was no sign of her—and went back inside to the dinette table.

This time I approached the geometry differently. I ignored the miles and just looked at the map. My prior exercise had given me a general idea of how far and wide the triangle could stretch on the map. I started studying the roadways and towns in this zone. Each time a location interested me I measured the distances to see if I could come up with a triangle of approximately 328 miles.

I had measured out nearly two dozen locations, failing to get even close on the approximation of mileage each time, when I came across a town on the north side of the baseline that was so small that it was denoted by only a black dot, the smallest demarcation of a population center in the map legend. It was a town called Clear. I knew of this place and I suddenly got excited. In a moment of flash thought, I knew that it fit the Poet's profile.

Using my driver's license I measured the distances. Clear was approximately 80 miles north of Las Vegas on the Blue Diamond Highway. It was then another 150 miles approximately on rural routes across the California border and down through the Sandy Valley to the 15 freeway and the third point of the triangle at Zzyzx. Adding in the baseline mileage between Zzyzx and the airport in Vegas, I had a triangle of approximately 322 miles, just 6 miles shy of the total put on the rental car belonging to one of the missing men.

My blood started to jump in my veins. Clear, Nevada. I had never been there but I knew it was a town of brothels and whatever community and outside services are spawned by such businesses. I knew of it because on more than one occasion in my career as a cop I had traced suspects through Clear, Nevada. On more than one occasion a suspect who voluntarily surrendered to me in Los Angeles reported that he had spent his last few nights of freedom with the ladies of Clear, Nevada.

It was a place where men would go privately, taking care to leave no trail that would reveal them as having dipped in such murky moral waters. Married men. Men of success or religious piety. In a strong way it was much like the red-light district in Amsterdam, a place where the Poet had previously found his victims.

So much of cop work is pursuing gut instinct and hunches. You live and die by the hard facts and evidence. There is no denying that. But it is your instinct that often brings those crucial things to you and then holds them together like glue. And I was following instinct now. I had a hunch about Clear. I knew I could sit at the dinette table and plot triangles and map points for hours if I wanted to. But the triangle I had drawn with the town of Clear at the top was the one that held me still at the same time the adrenaline was jangling in my blood. I believed I had drawn McCaleb's triangle. No, more than believed it. I *knew* it. My silent partner. Using his cryptic notes as direction, I now knew where I was going. Using my license as a straightedge I added two lines to the map, completing the triangle. I tapped each point on the map and stood up.

The clock on the wall in the kitchenette said it was almost five. I decided it was too late to go north tonight. I would arrive in near darkness and I didn't want that—that could be dangerous. I quickly put a plan in motion to leave at dawn and have almost an entire day to do what I needed to do in Clear.

I was thinking about what I would need for the trip when there was a knock on my door that startled me even though I was expecting it. I walked over to let Buddy Lockridge in.

24

H ARRY BOSCH OPENED THE door and Rachel could tell he was angry. He was about to say something when he saw it was her and checked himself. That told her he was waiting for somebody and that that somebody was late.

"Agent Walling."

"Expecting someone?"

"Uh, no, not really."

She saw his eyes flick past her and check the rear parking lot.

"Can I come in?"

"Sorry, sure, come on in."

He stepped back and held the door. She entered a sad little efficiency apartment that was sparsely furnished in depressing colors. On the left was a dinette table circa 1960s and she saw on it a bottle of beer, a notebook and a road atlas open to a map of Nevada. Bosch moved quickly to the table and closed the atlas and his notebook and stacked them one on top of the other. She then noticed his driver's license was on the table as well.

"So what brings you over here to this swell place?" he asked.

"Just wanted to see what you were up to," she said, leaving suspicion out of her voice. "I hope our little welcome wagon wasn't too difficult for you today."

"Nope. Comes with the territory."

"I'm sure it does."

"How did you find me?"

She stepped further into the room.

"You're paying for this place with a credit card."

Bosch nodded but didn't seem surprised by the speed or questionable legality of her search for him. She moved on, nodding at the map book on the dinette table.

"Planning a little vacation there? I mean, now that you're not working the case anymore."

"A road trip, yeah."

"Where to?"

"Not sure yet."

She smiled and turned toward the open balcony door. She could see an expensive-looking black jet on the tarmac beyond the motel's parking lot.

"According to your credit-card records you've been renting a place here for nearly nine months. On and off but mostly on."

"Yeah, they give me the long-term discount. Comes out to like twenty bucks a day or something."

"That's probably too much."

He turned and surveyed the place, as if for the first time. "Yeah."

They were both still standing. Rachel knew he didn't

want her to sit down or stay because of the visitor he was expecting. So she decided to push things. She sat down without being asked on the threadbare couch.

"Why have you had this place for nine months?" she asked.

He pulled a chair away from the dinette and brought it over and sat down.

"It's got nothing to do with this, if that's what you mean."

"No, I didn't think it did. I'm just curious, that's all. You don't look like a gambler to me—I mean, not with money. And this looks like a place for hard-core types."

He nodded.

"It is. That and people with other addictions. I'm here because my daughter lives out here. With her mother. I've been trying to get to know her. I guess she's my addiction."

"How old is she?"

"She'll be six soon."

"That's nice. Her mother being Eleanor Wish, the former FBI agent?"

"That's her. What can I do for you, Agent Walling?"

She smiled. She liked Bosch. He got to the point. He apparently didn't let anybody or anything intimidate him. She wondered where that came from. Was it from carrying a badge or carrying other baggage?

"You can call me Rachel for starters. But I think it's more like what can I do for you. You wanted me to contact you, didn't you?"

He laughed but not with any humor attached to it.

"What are you talking about?"

"The interview. The looks, the nods and smiles, all

that. You chose me as sort of a pen pal in there. Tried to connect. Tried to even it up, turn it from three against one to a game of two on two."

Bosch shrugged and looked out the balcony.

"That was just sort of a shot in the dark. I . . . I don't know, I just sort of thought you weren't getting a fair shake there, that's all. And I guess I know what that's like."

"It's been eight years since I got a fair shake from the bureau."

He looked back at her.

"All because of Backus?"

"That and other things. I made some mistakes and the bureau never forgets."

"I know what that is like, too."

He stood up.

"I'm having a beer," he said. "Do you want one, or is this a duty visit."

"I could use one, duty or not."

He got up and took the open beer off the dinette table and went to the small efficiency kitchen. He put the bottle in the sink and got two more out of the refrigerator. He cranked off the caps and brought them out to the seating arrangement. Rachel knew she had to be careful and alert. There was a thin line between who played whom in these situations.

"This place comes with glasses in the cabinet but I wouldn't trust them," he said, handing her a bottle.

"Bottle's fine."

She took hers and made sure she chinked it off his. She then took a short pull on the bottle. Sierra Nevada, it tasted good. She could tell he was watching to see if she was really drinking. She wiped her mouth with the back of her hand even though she didn't have to.

"That tastes right."

"Sure does. So what part of this are they giving you? Or do you have to stand around and just keep quiet—like Agent Zigo?"

Rachel gave him a short laugh.

"Yeah, I don't think I've heard him utter a full sentence yet. But then again, I've only been here a couple days. Basically, they brought me in because they didn't have much of a choice. I've got my little back story with Bob Backus and the GPS was sent to me at Quantico, even though I haven't set foot there in eight years. As you picked up on in the RV, this could be about me. Maybe, maybe not, but it cuts me in."

"And where did they bring you in from?"

"Rapid City."

Bosch grimaced.

"No, that's good," she said. "Before that it was Minot, North Dakota. A one-agent office. I think in my second year there they actually had a spring."

"Man, that hurts. In L.A. what they do if they want to get rid of you is give you what they call 'freeway therapy,' transfer you to the division furthest from where you live so you have to fight the traffic every day. Couple years of two-hour commutes and guys turn in their badges."

"Is that what happened to you?"

"No, but you probably already know what happened to me."

She didn't respond to that, moving quickly back the other way.

"In the bureau they have the whole country and then some. They don't call it freeway therapy, they call it 'hardship posting.' They send you where nobody wants to go. And there are a lot of places like that, places they can bury an agent if they want to. In Minot it was all reservation stuff and on the res they don't take so kindly to those of us of the FBI persuasion. Rapid City is only a small improvement. At least there are other agents in the office. My fellow outcasts. We actually have a good time because the pressure's off. Know what I mean?"

"Yeah. How long have you been up there?"

"Eight years altogether."

"Jeez."

She waved her free hand dismissively, as if it was all water under the bridge. She knew she was drawing him in. Revealing herself would make him trust her. She wanted his trust.

"Tell me," he said. "Was it because you were the messenger? Because you shot Backus? Or because he got away?"

"All that and other things. Consorting with the enemy, chewing gum in class, the usual stuff."

He nodded.

"Why didn't you just walk away, Rachel?"

"Well, Harry, because I didn't want them to win."

He nodded again and she could see a gleam in his eyes. She had connected on that answer. She knew it, could feel it, and it felt good.

"Can I tell you something off the record, Harry?"

"Sure."

"My assignment right now is to keep an eye on you."

"Me? Why? I don't know if you were listening in that

rolling field office today but I was kind of kicked off the case."

"Yes, and I'm sure you just packed it in and are quitting."

She turned and looked toward the table, at the map book and his notebook. She then turned back to him and spoke in a stern but even tone.

"My assignment is to watch you and to shut you down hard if you come anywhere near this investigation."

"Look, Agent Walling, I don't think—"

"Don't suddenly go formal on me here."

"Okay, Rachel, then. If this is some kind of threat, then all right, message received. I get it. But I don't think you—"

"I'm not threatening you. I'm here to tell you I don't plan to carry out my assignment."

He paused and studied her for a long moment.

"What do you mean?"

"I mean I've checked you out. You were right about that. I know about you and I know about what kind of cop you were. I know what has happened with you and the bureau in the past. I know all of that and I know you're more than meets the eye. And my guess is that you're onto something, that you told us just enough today to get out of that RV in one piece."

She stopped and waited and finally he responded.

"Hey, look, if all of that is a compliment, then I'll take it. But what's your point?"

"My point is that I have a history, too. And I'm not going to sit on the sideline while they go after Backus and leave me back in the FO making coffee. Not on this one. I want to get there first, and since this is a betting town I'm betting on you."

Bosch didn't move and he didn't say anything for a long moment. She watched his dark eyes as he churned through everything she'd said. She knew she was taking an incredible risk with him. But eight years in the Badlands had made her look at risks much differently than she had when she was in Quantico.

"Let me ask you something," he finally said. "Why is it they don't have you in a hotel room with two guards on the door? You know, in case Backus shows up. Like you said, this could be all about you. First Terry McCaleb, then you."

She shook her head, dismissing the idea.

"Because maybe they're using me. Maybe I'm bait."

"Are they?"

She shrugged.

"I don't know. I'm not privy to everything about this investigation. Either way, it doesn't matter. If he is coming at me let him come. I'm not going to hide out in a hotel room. Not when he's out there and not as long as I have my pals Sig and Glock with me."

"Oh, a two-gun agent. That's interesting. Most of the two-gun cops I knew had a little too much testosterone to go with all the extra bullets. I didn't like working with those guys."

He said it with sort of a smile in his voice. She knew he was close to being hooked.

"I don't carry them both at once. One's on the job, one's off. And you're trying to change the subject."

"Which is?"

"Your next move. Look, you know how they say it in the movies? We can do this the hard way or we can—"

"Hit you in the face with a phone book."

"Exactly. You're working alone, against the grain, but you obviously have good instincts and probably know things about this we don't know yet. Why not work together?"

"And what happens when Agent Dei and the rest of the FBI hear about this?"

"I take the risk, I take the fall. But it won't be too hard. What are they going to do to me? Send me back to Minot? Big deal."

He nodded. She watched him, tried to look through those dark eyes to see how his mind worked. Her take on Bosch was that he put case sense ahead of vanity and petty things. He would churn through it and ultimately know this was the way to go.

He finally nodded again and spoke.

"What are you doing tomorrow morning?"

"Watching you. Why?"

"Where are you staying?"

"The Embassy Suites on Paradise near Harmon."

"I'll pick you up at eight."

"And where are we going?"

"To the top of the triangle."

"What do you mean? Where?"

"I'll explain tomorrow. I'm thinking I can trust you, Rachel. But let's take it one step at a time. Are you going with me?"

"All right, Bosch, I'll go with you."

"You getting formal with me now?"

"Just a slip. I don't want to get formal with you."

She smiled and she watched him try to read it.

"All right, then I'll see you tomorrow," he said. "I have to get ready now to go see my kid."

He stood up and so did she. She took one more drink from her beer and put it down half finished on the dinette table.

"Eight o'clock tomorrow," she said. "You pick me up?"

"Right."

"You sure you don't want me to drive? Uncle Sugar pay for the gas?"

"That's all right. Can you get the photos of the missing men? I had them on the newspaper clip but Agent Dei took it from me."

"I'll see what I can do. There's probably a six-pack that won't be missed at the FO."

"And one other thing. Bring both your friends."

"What friends?"

"Sig and Glock."

She smiled and shook her head at him.

"You can't carry a weapon now, can you? Legally, anyway."

"No, I can't. I don't."

"Must feel naked."

"Yeah, you could say that."

She gave him another smile.

"Well, I'm not giving you a weapon, Harry. No way."

He shrugged.

"Had to ask."

He opened the door and she walked out. After he closed it she walked down the steps to the parking lot and looked back up at the door. She wondered if he was watching her through the peephole. She got into the

Crown Vic she had signed out of the car pool. She knew she was close to the edge of trouble. What she had revealed to Bosch and agreed to do the next day with him guaranteed the final stage of the destruction of her career if things went sideways. But she didn't care. It was a gambling town. She trusted Bosch and she trusted herself. She would not let them win.

As she backed the Crown Vic out she noticed a cab pull to a stop in the parking lot. A chubby man with sunbleached hair and a loud Hawaiian shirt got out and studied the numbers on the doors of the rooms. He was carrying a thick envelope or a file folder that looked yellowed and old. Rachel watched as he bounded up the steps and walked to number 22, Bosch's door. The door was opened before he had to knock.

Rachel backed out and drove out of the lot onto Koval. She drove around the block and parked in a spot that gave her a good view of both of the parking lot exits of Bosch's sorry motel. She was sure Bosch was up to something and she was going to find out what it was.

25

BACKUS HAD CAUGHT ONLY a glimpse of the man who answered the motel room door when Rachel Walling knocked. But he thought he recognized him from a time many years before. He felt his pulse quicken. If he was right about the man she was meeting in room 22, then the stakes had grown considerably higher.

He studied the motel and his situation. He had located the three bureau surveillance cars. The agents were hanging back. One agent had deployed and was sitting across Koval on a bus bench. He looked out of place, wearing a gray suit and supposedly waiting for a bus, but that was the FBI's style.

That left the motel clear for Backus to move about. It was L-shaped with parking on all sides. He realized that if he was on the other side of the building, he might catch another glimpse of the man Rachel was with through a rear window or balcony.

He decided not to risk moving the car from the front

parking lot to the rear. It might draw the attention of the bench warmer across the street. Instead he cracked the door and slipped out of his car. He had the interior light switched off so there was no threat of exposure. He crab-walked between two other cars and straightened up, pulling a baseball cap over his head and yanking the brim down as he emerged. The hat said UNLV on it.

Backus walked through the breezeway on the bottom floor of the two-story motel. He passed the soda and candy machines and came out on the other side and started walking through the rear parking lot as if looking for his car. He glanced up at the lighted balcony that he believed corresponded with the door to room 22, where he had seen Rachel enter. He could see the sliding door was open.

Glancing around as if looking for his lost car, Backus saw that the agent on the bench did not have a visual angle on the rear lot. No one was watching him here. He casually moved to a position directly below the balcony of room 22. He tried to listen for any verbal morsel that would spill through the open slider. He heard Rachel's voice but could not make out the words until he very clearly heard her say, "Must feel naked."

This confused and intrigued him. He was thinking about the possibility of climbing up to the second level so that he could hear the conversation in room 22. The sound of a door shutting ended that idea. He guessed Rachel had just left. Backus returned to the breezeway and hid behind a Coke machine when he heard a car's ignition fire. He waited and listened. He detected the sound of another car entering the lot. He moved from the Coke machine to the corner and glanced out. A man was getting out of a taxi and Backus recognized him, too. It was Terry McCaleb's charter partner. There was no doubt. Backus felt like he had just tripped across a treasure of intrigue and mystery. What was Rachel up to? How had she connected with the charter partner so quickly? And what was the LAPD doing here?

He looked past the taxi and saw Rachel's Crown Victoria pull out onto the street and drive away. He waited a moment and saw one of the Grand Ams stop and pick up the man on the bus bench and then take off. Backus yanked the brim of his hat down again and stepped out of the breezeway. He walked toward his car.

26

I WAS LOOKING THROUGH THE peephole, thinking about Agent Walling, and wondering how the brutal terrain of the FBI and the Dakotas had not robbed her of her fire and sense of humor. I liked her for that and sensed a connection. I was thinking that I might be able to trust her at the same time I was thinking I had just been played by a pro. I was sure she hadn't told me everything she was up to, nobody ever does, but she had told me enough. We wanted the same thing, maybe for different reasons. But I wasn't second-guessing my decision to take on the extra rider in the morning.

The view through the peephole was suddenly filled with the concave image of Buddy Lockridge. I opened the door before he could knock and quickly pulled him inside. I wondered if Walling had seen him on her way out.

"Perfect timing, Buddy. Did anybody talk to you or stop you out there?"

"Where, here?"

"Yeah, here."

"No, I just got out of the cab."

"Okay, then where have you been?"

He explained his lateness by saying there were no cabs at the Bellagio, a story I didn't believe. I saw one of the pockets of his jeans bulging when I took from him the two files he carried.

"That's bullshit, Buddy. Cabs can be hard to find in this town but not at the Bellagio. There are always cabs there."

I reached over and slapped my hand against his full pocket.

"You stopped to play, didn't you? You've got a pocket full of chips there."

"Look, I stopped to play a couple quick shots of blackjack before coming. But I got lucky, man. I couldn't lose. Look at this."

He reached into the pocket and pulled out a handful of five-dollar chips.

"I was kicking ass! And you can't walk away from good luck."

"Yeah, great. That will help you pay for that room you've got."

Buddy looked around my place, taking it in. Through the open balcony there was traffic and jetliner noise.

"Gladly," he said. "I ain't going to stay here."

I almost laughed, considering what I had seen of his boat.

"Well, you're welcome to stay wherever you want because I don't need you out here anymore. Thanks for bringing the files."

His eyes widened.

"What?"

"I've got a new partner. The FBI. So you can go back to L.A. as soon as you want or you can play blackjack until you own the Bellagio. I'll pay the airfare, like I said, and for the chopper ride to the island and forty bucks toward the room. That's the daily rate at this place."

I held up the files.

"I'll throw in a couple hundred for your time getting these and getting here."

"No way, man. I came all the way out here, man. I can still help. I've worked with the agents before, when me and Terry worked a thing."

"That was then, Buddy, this is now. Come on. I'll give you a ride back to your hotel. I hear cabs are scarce and I'm going that way anyway."

After closing the balcony door I walked him out of the apartment and locked up. I brought the files with me for reading later. As we were walking down the steps to the parking lot I looked around for the security man but didn't see him. I looked around for Rachel Walling and didn't see her either. I did see my neighbor Jane putting a shoebox into the trunk of a car, a white Monte Carlo. From my angle on the steps I could see the trunk was crowded with other, larger boxes.

"You're better off with me," Buddy said, protest still clinging to his voice. "You can't trust the bureau, man. Terry was in it and he didn't even trust them."

"I know, Buddy. I've been dealing with the bureau for thirty years."

He just shook his head. I watched Jane get in her car and back out. I wondered if it was the last time I would see her. I wondered if my telling her I had been a cop had spooked her and made her split. Maybe she had heard some of my conversation with Agent Walling through the thin walls.

Buddy's comments about the bureau reminded me of something.

"You know, when you get back there they're going to want to talk to you."

"About what?"

"About your GPS. They found it."

"Wow, great! You mean it wasn't Finder? It was Shandy?"

"Think so. But the news isn't all that great, Buddy."

"How come?"

I unlocked the Mercedes and we got in. I looked at Buddy as I was starting the engine.

"All your waypoints were wiped out. There's only one on it now and you won't catch any fish there."

"Ah, goddamnit! I should've known."

"Anyway, they're going to ask you all about it and all about Terry and that last charter. Just like I did."

"So they're running behind you, huh? Playing catch-up. You're the man, Harry."

"Not really."

I knew what was coming. Buddy turned in his seat and leaned toward me.

"Take me with you, Harry. I'm telling you I can help. I'm smart. I can figure things out."

"Put your seat belt on, Buddy."

I jumped into reverse before he got a chance and he almost went into the dashboard.

We headed over to the strip and slowly made our way down to the Bellagio. It was early evening and the side-walks were cooling off and getting crowded. I saw that the overhead trams and walkways were becoming full. The neon from every façade on the street was lighting dusk up like a brilliant sunset. Almost. Buddy continued to lobby me for a part in the investigation but I fended him off at every turn. After we pulled in around the huge front fountain and under the casino's giant entry portico I told the valet man that we were just picking somebody up and he directed me to a curb, telling me not to leave the car unattended.

"Who we picking up?" Buddy asked, new life in his voice.

"Nobody. I just said that. Tell you what, you want to work with me, Buddy? Then stay here in the car for a few minutes so they won't tow it away. I need to run in here real quick."

"What for?"

"To see if somebody's here."

"Who?"

I jumped out of the car and closed the door without answering his question because I knew with Buddy that every answer led to another question and then another and I didn't have time for that.

I knew the Bellagio like I knew the turns on Mulholland Drive. This was where Eleanor Wish, my ex-wife, made her living, and where I had watched her do so on more than one occasion. I quickly made my way through the plush casino, around the orchard of slot machines and to the poker room.

There were only two poker tables working. It was very early. I quickly scanned the thirteen players and did not see Eleanor. I checked the podium and saw the table manager was a man I knew from coming here with

Eleanor and then hanging out and watching while she played. I went over.

"Freddy, what's shaking?"

"A lot of ass shaking around here tonight."

"That's good. Gives you something to look at."

"I'm not complaining."

"Do you know, is Eleanor coming in?"

It was Eleanor's habit to let the table managers know if she intended to come in and play on a particular night. Sometimes they would save places at tables of high rollers or higher skilled players. Sometimes they would set up private games. In a way, my ex was a secret Vegas attraction. She was an attractive woman who was damn good at poker. That presented a challenge to men of a certain kind. The smart casinos knew this and played to it. Eleanor was always treated well at the Bellagio. If she needed anything—from a drink to a suite to a rude player removed from a table—she got it. No questions asked. And that was why she usually played here on the nights she played.

"Yeah, she's coming in," Freddy told me. "I don't have anything for her right now but she'll be coming along."

I waited before hitting him with another question. I had to finesse this. I leaned on the railing and casually watched the dealer at the hold'em table put down the final deal of the hand, the cards scraping on the blue felt like quiet little whispers. Five people had stayed in for the whole ride. I watched a couple of their faces when they looked at the last card. I was watching for tells but didn't see any.

Eleanor had told me once that the real players call the last card in hold'em the "river" because it gives you life or takes it away with it. If you've played the hand through to the seventh card, everything rides on it.

Three of the five players folded right away. The remaining two went back and forth to a call and one of the men I had watched took the pot with three sevens.

"What time did she say she was coming in?" I asked Freddy.

"Uh, she said the usual time. Around eight."

Despite my attempt at being casual about it I could tell Freddy was getting hesitant, realizing his allegiance should be to Eleanor and not her ex-husband. I had what I needed so I thanked him and walked away. Eleanor was planning on putting our daughter to bed and then coming in to work. Maddie would be left with the live-in nanny watching over her.

When I got back to the casino entrance my car was empty. I looked around for Buddy and spotted him talking to one of the valet men. I called to him and waved good-bye. But he came running over and caught me at the door of the Mercedes.

"You taking off?"

"Yeah, I told you. I was just going in for a couple minutes. Thanks for staying with the car like I asked."

He didn't get it.

"No problem," he said. "You find him?"

"Find who?"

"Whoever you were going in there to see."

"Yeah, Buddy, I found him. I'll see you—"

"Come on, man, let's do this thing together. Terry was my friend, too."

That gave me pause.

"Buddy, I understand. But the best thing you can do

right now if you want to do something for Terry is go back home, wait for the agents to show up and then tell them every single thing you know. Don't hold back anything."

"You mean including that you sent me over there to the boat to steal the file and get the photos?"

Now he was just trying to taunt me because he finally understood that he was out.

"I don't care if you tell them," I said. "I told you, I'm working with them. They'll know it before you even meet them. But just so you have it straight, I didn't tell you to steal anything. I'm working for Graciela. That boat and everything in it belongs to her. Including those files and those photographs."

I poked him hard in the chest.

"Got it, Buddy?"

He physically backed off.

"Yeah, I got it. I was just—"

"Good."

I then put my hand out. We shook hands but there wasn't anything very pleasant about it.

"I'll catch you later, Buddy."

He let go of my hand and I got in and closed the door. I started it up and drove away. In the mirror I watched him go in through the revolving door and knew he would lose all his money back to the casino before the night was over. He had been right. He should never have walked away from luck.

The dashboard clock told me that Eleanor would not be leaving her house for the night's work at the casino for another ninety minutes. I could head over there now but knew it would be best to wait. I wanted to see my daughter but not my ex-wife. To her everlasting credit

Eleanor had been kind enough to allow me full visiting privileges while she was working. So that would not be a problem. And I didn't care if Maddie was awake or not. I just wanted to see her, hear her breathing and touch her hair. But it seemed that every time Eleanor and I crossed paths we skidded sideways and anger from both of us ruled the moment. I knew it was best this way, to come to the house when she was not there.

I could've gone back to the Double X and spent an hour reading the Poet file but instead I drove. Paradise Road was much less congested than the strip. It always is. I took Harmon over and then turned north and almost immediately into the parking lot of the Embassy Suites. I thought maybe Rachel Walling might want a cup of coffee and a fuller explanation of the next day's excursion. I cruised through the lot looking for a bureau car that would be obvious to me because of its cheap hubcaps and government plate. But I didn't see one. I pulled out my cell, called information and got the number for the Embassy Suites. I called and asked for Rachel Walling's room and was put through. The phone rang repeatedly but was not answered. I hung up and thought for a moment. I then reopened my phone and called the cell number she had given me. She answered right away.

"Hey, it's Bosch, what are you up to?" I said as casually as I could.

"Nothing, just hanging out."

"You at the hotel?"

"Yeah, why, what's up?

"Nothing. I just thought you might want a cup of coffee or something. I'm out and about and have some time to kill. I could be at your hotel in a couple minutes."

"Oh, well, thanks but I think I'm going to stay in tonight."

Of course you can't come out, I thought. You're not even there.

"I'm kind of jet-lagged, to tell you the truth. It always hits me the second day. Plus, tomorrow we've got the early start."

"I understand."

"No, it's not that I don't want to. Maybe tomorrow, okay?"

"Okay. Are we still on for eight?"

"I'll be out front."

We hung up and I felt the first weight of doubt in my stomach. She was up to something, playing me in some way.

But then I tried to dismiss it. Her assignment was to keep tabs on me. She'd been upfront about that. Maybe I had this latest thing all wrong.

I made another circuit around the parking lot, looking for a Crown Vic or an LTD, but didn't see one. I quickly drove out of the lot then and back onto Paradise Road. At Flamingo I turned west and went back across the strip and over the freeway. I pulled into the lot of a steakhouse near the Palms, the casino favored by many of the locals because it was off the strip and it drew a lot of celebrities. The last time Eleanor and I had talked civilly she told me she was thinking of switching her allegiance from the Bellagio to the Palms. The Bellagio was still where the money went, but most of that went into baccarat and pai gow and craps. Poker was a different skill and it was the only game where you weren't playing against the house. She had heard through the local grapevine that all the celebrities and athletes that came over from L.A. to the Palms were playing poker and losing lots of cash while they learned.

In the steakhouse bar I ordered a New York strip and a baked potato. The waitress tried to talk me out of ordering the steak medium-well but I remained firm. In the places I had grown up I never got any food that was pink in the middle and I couldn't start enjoying it now. After she took the order back to the kitchen I thought about an army kitchen I once wandered into at Fort Benning. There were complete sides of beef being boiled gray through and through in a dozen huge vats. A guy with a shovel was scooping oil off the surface of one of the vats and dumping it in a bucket. That kitchen was the worst thing I had ever smelled until I went into the tunnels a few months later and one time crawled into a place where the VC hid their dead from the army statistic takers.

I opened the Poet file and was settling into a thorough read when my phone buzzed. I answered without checking the ID screen.

"Hello?"

"Harry, it's Rachel. You still want to get that coffee? I changed my mind."

My guess was that she had hurried to the Embassy Suites so she could be there and not be caught in a lie.

"Um, I just ordered dinner on the other side of town."

"Shit, I'm sorry. Well, that'll teach me. You by yourself?"

"Yeah, I've got some stuff to work on here."

"Well, I know what that's like. I pretty much eat by myself every night."

"Yeah, me too. If I eat."

"Really? What about your kid?"

I was no longer comfortable or trusting while talking to her. I didn't know what she was doing. And I didn't feel like going over my sad marital or parental history.

"Uh, listen, I'm getting a look from somebody here. I think cell phones are against the rules."

"Well, we don't want to break the rules. I'll see you tomorrow at eight then."

"Okay, Eleanor. Good-bye."

I was about to close the phone when I heard her voice.

"Harry?"

"What?"

"I'm not Eleanor."

"What?"

"You just called me Eleanor."

"Oh. That was a mistake. Sorry."

"Do I remind you of her?"

"Maybe. Sort of. Not now, but from a while back."

"Oh, well, I hope not from too far back."

She was referring to Eleanor's fall from grace in the bureau. A fall so bad that even a hardship posting in Minot was out of the question.

"I'll see you tomorrow, Rachel."

"Good night, Harry."

I closed the phone and thought about my mistake. It had shot up right out of the subconscious but now that it was out in the open it was obvious. I didn't want to think about that. I wanted to retreat into the file in front of me. I knew I would be more comfortable studying the blood and madness of some other person and time.

27

A T 8:30 I KNOCKED on the door of Eleanor Wish's house and the Salvadoran woman who lived there and took care of my daughter answered. Marisol had a kind but worn face. She was in her fifties but looked much older. Her story of surviving was devastating and whenever I thought about it I was left feeling lucky about my own story. Since day one, when I had unexpectedly shown up at this house and discovered I had a daughter, Marisol had treated me kindly. She had never viewed me as a threat and was always completely cordial and respectful of my position as both father and outsider. She stepped back and let me in.

"She sleeping," she said.

I held up the file I was carrying.

"That's okay. I have work. I just want to go sit with her for a while. How are you doing, Marisol?"

"Oh, I am fine."

"Eleanor went to the casino?"

"Yes, she go."

"And how was Maddie tonight?"

"Maddie, she a good girl. She play."

Marisol always kept her reports to a minimum. I had tried speaking to her in Spanish before, thinking the reason she spoke so little was because of her English skills. But she said little more to me in her native language, preferring to keep her reports on my daughter's life and activities to a few words in any language.

"Okay, well, thank you," I said. "If you want to go to bed I'll just let myself out later. I'll make sure the door is locked."

I had no key to the house but the front door would lock after I closed it.

"Yes, is okay."

I nodded and headed down the hallway to the left. I entered Maddie's room and closed the door. There was a night-light plugged into the far wall and it cast a blue glow across the room. I made my way to the side of her bed and turned on the bed table light. I knew from experience that Maddie would not be disturbed by the light. The five-year-old's dreams were so deep she could seemingly sleep through anything, even a Lakers play-off game on the television or a 5.0 earthquake.

The light revealed a nest of tangled dark hair on the pillow. Her face was turned away from my view. I used my hand to sweep the ringlets back off her face and I leaned down and kissed her cheek. I turned my head sideways so my ear was closer to her. I checked for the sound of breathing and was rewarded. One little moment of unfounded fear fell away from me.

I walked over to the bureau and turned off the baby monitor, the other half of which I knew was in the TV room or Marisol's bedroom. There was no need for it now. I was there.

Maddie slept in a queen-size bed with a cover spread that had all manner of cats printed on it. With her little body taking up so little space in the bed, there was plenty of room for me to prop the second pillow against the headboard and climb on next to her. I slipped my hand under the covers and placed it gently on her back. I waited without moving until I could feel the slight rise and fall of her breathing. With the other hand I opened the Poet file and started to read.

At dinner I had gotten through most of the file. This included the suspect profile authored in part by Agent Rachel Walling as well as the investigative reports and crime scene photos that accumulated while the investigation was current and the bureau was tracking the killer dubbed the Poet across the country. That was eight years earlier, when the Poet killed eight homicide detectives, traveling from east to west, before his run came to an end in Los Angeles.

Now as my daughter slept next to me I began with the reports that came after FBI Special Agent Robert Backus had been identified as the suspect. After he had been shot by Rachel Walling and then disappeared.

The summary from the autopsy of a body found by a Department of Water and Power inspector in a storm water tunnel in Laurel Canyon was included here. The body was found almost three months after Backus was shot and had fallen through a window of a cantilevered home near the canyon and disappeared into the darkness and brush below. FBI credentials and a badge belonging to Robert Backus were found on the body. The deteriorated clothing was also his—a suit hand-tailored for Backus in Italy when he'd been sent over to consult on an investigation of a serial killer in Milan.

However, scientific identification of the body was inconclusive. The remains were badly decomposed, leaving fingerprint analysis impossible. And parts of the body were even missing, initially presumed to have been taken by rats and other animals foraging in the tunnels. The entire lower mandible and upper bridge were missing, precluding a comparison to the dental records belonging to Robert Backus.

Cause of death could not be determined either, though a gunshot wound channel was found in the upper abdomen—the area Agent Walling reported seeing her bullet strike—and a rib was fractured, possibly by the force of a bullet. No bullet fragments were recovered, however, suggesting a through and through wound, and so no comparison to a bullet from Walling's weapon was possible.

No DNA comparison or identification was ever made. After the shooting—when it was thought that Backus might still be alive and on the run—agents descended on the fugitive's home and office. But they were in search of evidence to the crimes he had committed and clues as to why. They did not plan for the possibility that they might one day need to identify his putrefied remains. In a gaffe that would haunt the investigation and leave the bureau open later to charges of malfeasance and cover-up, no potential DNA receptors—hair and skin from the shower drain, saliva from the toothbrush, fingernail clippings from the waste cans, dandruff and hair from the back of the desk chair—were ever collected. And three months later, when the body was found in the storm water tunnel, it was too late. Those receptors were compromised or nonexistent. The building where Backus had owned a condo mysteriously burned to the ground three weeks after the bureau had finished with it. And Backus's office had been taken over and completely renovated and redecorated by an agent named Randal Alpert, who took his place in the Behavioral Sciences unit.

A search for a blood sample from Backus proved futile and once again embarrassing for the bureau. When Agent Walling shot Backus in the house in Los Angeles a small amount of blood had spattered the floor. A sample was collected but then inadvertently destroyed in the lab in Los Angeles when medical waste was disposed of.

A search for blood that Backus may have given during personal medical examinations or as donations to blood banks proved fruitless. Through his own cunning planning, luck, and bureaucratic malfeasance, Backus had disappeared without leaving anything of himself behind.

The search for Backus officially ended with the discovery of the body in the drainage tunnel. Even though scientific confirmation of identity was never made, the credentials, badge and Italian suit were enough for bureau command to act swiftly in announcing closure to a case that had held wide sway in the media and had severely undercut the bureau's already tarnished image.

But meantime a quiet investigation continued into the psychological backgrounding of the killer agent. These were the reports I now read. Led by the Behavioral Sciences section—the very unit in which Backus worked—this investigation seemed more concerned with the question of why he did what he did than with the question of how he was able to do it under the noses of the top experts in the killing field. This investigative direction was probably a protective measure. They looked at the suspect, not the system. The file was replete with reports of investigations into Agent Backus's early nurturing, adolescence and upbringing. Despite the number of crisply written observations, speculations and summaries, there was very little there. Just a few threads unraveled from the full fabric of personality. Backus remained an enigma, his pathology a secret. He was the case that the best and brightest ultimately couldn't crack.

I sorted through the threads. Backus was the son of a perfectionist father—a decorated FBI agent, no less—and a mother he never knew. The father was reported to have been physically brutal to the boy, possibly blaming him for the mother's abandonment of the family, and punished him severely for infractions that included bedwetting and taunting of neighborhood pets. One report came from a seventh-grade classmate who reported that Robert Backus had once confided that when he was young his father punished him for bed-wetting by handcuffing him to a towel rack in the bathroom shower enclosure. Another former classmate reported that Backus once claimed that he slept each night with a pillow and a blanket in a bathtub because he feared the punishment that wetting the bed might bring. A childhood neighbor reported suspicions that it had been Backus who had killed a pet Dachshund by cutting the dog in half and leaving its parts in a vacant lot.

As an adult Backus exhibited obsessive-compulsive tendencies. He had fixations on cleanliness and order.

Many testimonials in this regard came from fellow agents in Behavioral Sciences. Backus was well known in the unit for delaying scheduled meetings for many minutes while he was in the restroom washing his hands. No one ever saw him eat anything for lunch in the cafeteria at Quantico but a simple grilled cheese sandwich. Every day, a grilled cheese sandwich. He also compulsively chewed gum and would take great pains to make sure he was never out of the Juicy Fruit brand he liked. One agent described his chewing as measured, meaning he believed that Backus may have counted the number of times he chewed each stick of gum, and when a specific number was reached he would then remove the gum and start over with a fresh stick.

There was a report on an interview with a former fiancée. She told the reporting agent that Backus required her to shower often and extensively, particularly before and after they made love. She said that while house hunting before the nuptials he told her he would want to have his own bedroom and bathroom. She called off the marriage and ended the relationship when one time he called her a slob because she had kicked off her high heels in her own living room.

The reports were just glimpses of a damaged psyche. They weren't really clues to anything. Whatever Backus's strange habits were, they still didn't fully explain why he began killing people. Thousands of people suffer from mild to severe forms of obsessive-compulsive disorder. They don't add killing to their list of personal tics. Thousands were abused as children. They do not then all become abusers.

McCaleb had acquired far fewer reports on the

reappearance four years later of the Poet—Backus—in Amsterdam. All that was in the file was a nine-page summary report in which the facts of the killings and the forensic findings were recounted. I had skimmed this report before but now read it closely and found aspects of it tying in with the theory I was formulating about the town of Clear.

In Amsterdam the five known victims were men who were tourists traveling alone. This put them in the same profile as the victims known to be buried in Zzyzx, with the exception of one man who was in Las Vegas with his wife but away from her when she spent the day in their hotel's spa. In Amsterdam the men were last seen in the city's Rosse Buurt zone, where legalized prostitution is carried out in small rooms behind the neon-framed windows where women in provocative clothing offer themselves to passersby. In two of the incidents the Dutch investigators located prostitutes who reported being with the victims the night before their bodies were found floating in the nearby Amstel River.

Though the bodies were found in different locations in the river, the reports indicated that the point of entry into the water for all five victims was believed to have been the area around the Six House. This location was a property owned by an important family in Amsterdam history. I found this of interest, partly because Six House and Zzyzx sounded a bit alike to me. But also because of the question of whether the killer had chosen the Six House randomly or in some attempt to flaunt his crimes at authority by choosing a structure that symbolized it.

The Dutch detectives never got much further with the investigation. They never found the mechanism by which the killer got to the men, controlled them and killed them. Backus would have never even made a blip on their suspect radar if he hadn't wanted to be noticed. He sent the police the notes that asked for Rachel Walling and led to his identity. The notes, according to the summary report, contained information about the victims and crimes that seemingly only the killer would know. One note contained the passport of the last victim.

To me the connection between Amsterdam's Rosse Buurt and Clear, Nevada, was obvious. Both were places where sex was legally exchanged for money. But more important, they were places where I assumed men might go without telling others, where they might even take measures to avoid leaving a trail. In some ways this made them perfect targets for a killer and perfect victims. It added an extra degree of safety to the killer.

I finished my survey of McCaleb's file on the Poet and started through it once more, hoping that I had missed something, maybe just one detail that would bring the whole picture into focus. Sometimes it happens that way. A missed or misunderstood detail becomes the key to the whole puzzle.

But I didn't find that detail on the second go-round and soon the reports just seemed repetitive and tedious. I grew tired and somehow I ended up thinking about that kid handcuffed in the shower. I kept picturing that scene and I felt bad for the kid and angry for the father who did it and the mother who never cared to know about it.

Did this mean I felt sympathy for a killer? I didn't think so. Backus had taken his own tortures and turned them into something else and then turned it on the world. I had an understanding of that process and I felt sympathy for the boy he had been. But I felt nothing for Backus the man but a cold resolve to hunt him down and make him pay for what he did.

28

T HE PLACE SMELLED HORRIBLE but Backus knew
he could live with it. It was the flies that repulsed
him the most. They were everywhere, dead and alive.
Carrying germs and disease and dirt. As he huddled
under the blanket, his knees drawn up, he could hear
them buzzing in the darkness, flying blind, hitting the
screens and the walls, making little sounds. They were
out there, everywhere. He realized he should have
known that they would come, that they were part of the
plan.

He tried to block out their sounds. He tried to think
and concentrate on the plan. It was his last day here.
Time to move. Time to show them. He wished he could
stay to watch, to bear witness to the event. But he knew
that there was much work to do.

He stopped breathing. He could feel them now. The
flies had found him and were crawling on the blanket,
looking for a way in, a way to get to him. He had given
them life but now they wanted to get to him and eat him.

His laugh broke sharply from beneath the blanket and the flies that had alighted on it scattered. He realized he was no different from the flies. He, too, had turned against the giver of life. He laughed again and he felt something go down his throat.

"Aaaggh!"

He retched. He coughed. He tried to get it out. A fly. A fly had gone down his throat.

Backus jumped up and almost tripped as he climbed out. He ran to the door and out into the night. He shoved his finger down his throat until everything came up and came out. He dropped to his knees, gagged and spit it all out. He then pulled the flashlight from his pocket and studied his effluent with the beam. He saw the fly in the greenish yellow bile. It was still alive, its wings and legs mired in the swamp of human discharge.

Backus stood up. He stepped on the fly and then nodded to himself. He wiped the bottom of his shoe on the red dirt. He looked up at the silhouette of the rock outcropping that rose a hundred feet above him. It was blocking the moon at this hour. But that was all right. That just made the stars all the brighter.

29

I PUT THE THICK file aside and studied my daughter's face. I wondered what she could be dreaming about. She had experienced so little in her life, what inspired her dreams? I was sure there were only good things waiting for her in that secret world and I wished it would always stay that way.

I grew tired myself and soon closed my eyes to rest for a few minutes. And soon I, too, dreamed. But in my dream there were shadow figures and angry voices, there were sudden and sharp movements in the darkness. I didn't know where I was or where I was going. And then I was grabbed by unseen hands and pulled up out of it, back to the light.

"Harry, what are you doing?"

I opened my eyes and Eleanor was pulling the collar of my jacket.

"Hey . . . Eleanor . . . what is it?"

For some reason I tried to smile at her but I was still too disoriented to know why.

"What are you doing? Look at this all over the floor."

I was beginning to register that she was angry. I pulled myself forward and looked over the edge of the bed. The Poet file had slid off the bed and spilled on the floor. The crime scene photos were spread everywhere. Prominently displayed were three photos of a Denver Police detective who had been shot by Backus in a car. The back of his head was obliterated, blood and brain matter all over the seat. There were other photos of bodies floating in canals, photos of another detective whose head was taken off with a shotgun.

"Oh, shit!"

"You can't do this!" Eleanor said loudly. "What if she woke up and saw this? She'd have nightmares the rest of her life."

"She's going to wake up if you don't keep your voice down, Eleanor. I'm sorry, okay? I didn't mean to fall asleep."

I slid off the bed and knelt on the floor, quickly gathering the file together. As I did so I checked my watch and saw it was almost five a.m. I had slept for hours. No wonder I was so groggy.

Seeing the time also told me that Eleanor was home late. She usually didn't play this long. It probably meant she'd had a bad night and had tried to chase her losses, a bad gambling strategy. I quickly gathered the photos and reports and slid them back into the file, then I stood up.

"Sorry," I said again.

"Goddamnit, it's not what I need to come home and find."

I didn't say anything. I knew it was a no-win situation for me. I turned and looked back at the bed. Maddie was still sleeping, with her brown ringlets across her face again. If she could sleep through anything, then I hoped she could sleep right through the roaring silence of her parents' anger toward each other.

Eleanor walked quickly out of the room and in a few moments I followed her. I found her in the kitchen leaning against a counter with her arms folded tightly in front of her.

"Bad night?"

"Don't blame my reaction to this on what kind of night I had."

I raised my hands in surrender.

"I'm not. I blame it on me. I messed up. I just wanted to sit with her for a little while and I fell asleep."

"Maybe you shouldn't do that anymore."

"What, come visit her at night?"

"I don't know."

She moved to the refrigerator and took out a bottle of spring water. She poured a glass and then held the bottle up for me. I told her I didn't want any.

"What is that file anyway?" she asked. "Are you working a case here?"

"Yes. A murder. It started in L.A. and came over this way. I have to go up into the desert today."

"What a nice convenience for you. Along the way you get to drop in here and scare your daughter."

"Come on, Eleanor, it was stupid and I'm an idiot but at least she didn't see anything."

"She could have. Maybe she did. Maybe she woke up and saw those dreadful pictures and then went back to sleep. She's probably having a horrible nightmare."

"Look, she hasn't moved all night. I can tell. She's

been down for the count. It won't happen again, so can we just leave it at that?"

"Sure. Fine."

"Look, Eleanor, why don't you tell me about your night?"

"No, I don't want to talk about it. I just want to go to bed."

"I'll tell you something then."

"What?"

I hadn't planned on bringing this up but it all sort of snowballed and I knew I needed to tell her.

"I'm thinking about going back to my job."

"What do you mean, the case?"

"No, the cops. The LAPD has a program. Old guys like me can come back in. They're looking for experience. If I do it now I won't even have to go back to the academy."

She took a long drink of water and didn't respond.

"What do you think about that, Eleanor?"

She shrugged like she didn't care.

"Whatever you want to do, Harry. But you won't see your daughter as much. You'll get involved in cases and . . . you know how that goes."

I nodded.

"Maybe."

"And maybe it won't matter. She hasn't had you around for most of her life."

"And whose fault is that?"

"Look, let's not open that can of worms again."

"If I had known about her I would have been here. I didn't know."

"I know, I know. I'm the one. It's all my fault."

"I'm not saying that. I'm—"

"I know what you're saying. You don't even have to say it."

We were both quiet for a moment, letting the anger ebb. I looked down at the floor.

"Maybe she could come over there, too," I said.

"What are you talking about?"

"What we talked about before. About this place. About her growing up here."

She shook her head very deliberately.

"And I haven't changed my mind about that. What do you think, that you're going to raise her by yourself? You, with middle-of-the-night call outs, long hours, long investigations, guns in the house, crime scene photos spread all over the floor. Is that what you want for her? You think that's better than Vegas?"

"No. I was thinking maybe you could come over there, too."

"Forget it, Harry. I'm not talking about this again. I'm staying here and so is Madeline. You make whatever decision is best for you but you don't make it for me and Maddie."

Before I could respond Marisol stepped into the kitchen, her eyes creased with sleep. She was wearing a white bathrobe with *Bellagio* written in script on the pocket.

"Very loud," she said.

"You're right, Marisol," Eleanor said. "I'm sorry."

Marisol went to the refrigerator and got out the water bottle. She poured herself a glass and then put the bottle away. She left the kitchen without further word.

"I think you should go," Eleanor said to me. "I'm too tired to talk about this right now."

"All right. I'm just going to check on her and say good-bye."

"Don't wake her up."

"No kidding."

I went back into my daughter's bedroom. We had left the light on. I sat on the side of the bed closest to her and just watched her sleep for a few moments. Then I brushed back her hair and kissed her cheek. I smelled the scent of baby shampoo in her hair. I kissed her again and whispered good night. I turned off the light and then sat there for another couple minutes, watching and waiting. For what, I don't know. I guess maybe I was hoping Eleanor would come in and sit on the bed, too, that maybe we could watch our sleeping daughter together.

After a while I got up and turned the monitor on again. I left the room to head out. The house was quiet as I walked back through to the front. I didn't see Eleanor. She had gone off to bed, not needing to see me again. I pulled the front door closed and made sure it was locked as I went out.

The loud snap of steel on steel had a finality to it that ricocheted through me like a tumbling bullet.

30

A T 8 THAT MORNING I was in my Mercedes in front of the lobby entrance of the Embassy Suites on Paradise Road. I had two large Starbucks coffees in the cup holders and a bag of doughnuts. I was freshly showered and shaved. I had changed the clothes I slept in. I had gassed up the car and maxed out my withdrawal limit at the station's ATM. I was ready for a day in the desert but Rachel Walling did not come out through the glass doors. After waiting five minutes I was about to call her when my phone rang first. It was her.

"Give me five minutes."

"Where are you?"

"I had to go into the FO for a meeting. I'm driving back now."

"What meeting?"

"I'll tell you when I see you. I'm on Paradise now."

"All right."

I closed the phone and waited, looking at the bill-board on the back of a cab that was waiting in front of me. It was an advertisement for a floor show at the Riviera. It showed the beautifully proportioned rear ends of a dozen women standing side by side and naked. It made me think about the changing nature of Vegas and what had been mentioned in the *Times* article on the missing men. I thought about all the people who had moved here on the family ticket only to have that ticket punched with this and a thousand other billboards just like it after they got here.

A basic G-car—a Crown Victoria—pulled up next to me from the opposite direction and Rachel put down the window.

"You want me to drive?"

"I want to drive," I said, thinking it would give me a little slice of control over things.

She made no argument. She pulled the Crown Vic into a parking space and got into my car.

I didn't move the Mercedes.

"Are you going to drink both of those coffees?" she asked me.

"No, one's for you. Sugar's in the bag. They didn't have cream to go."

"I don't use it."

She lifted one of the coffees and drank from it. I looked forward, out through the windshield, then I checked the rearview. And I waited.

"Well," she finally said, "are we going?"

"I don't know. I think we need to talk first."

"About what?"

"About what is going on."

"What do you mean?"

"What were you doing at the field office so early? What's going on, Agent Walling?"

She let out her breath in annoyance.

"Look, Harry, you are forgetting something here. This investigation is of high importance to the bureau. You could say the director is directly involved."

"And?"

"And so when he wants a ten a.m. briefing, that means us agents in Quantico and out in the field get together at nine a.m. to make sure we know what we're telling him and that there's not going to be blowback on anybody."

I nodded. Now I got it.

"And nine a.m. in Quantico is six a.m. in Vegas."

"You got it."

"So what happened at the ten? What did you all tell the director?"

"That's FBI business."

I looked at her and she was waiting with a smile.

"But I will tell you because you are about to tell me all of your secrets, too. The director is going to go public. It's too risky not to. It will look like a cover-up if this comes out later in uncontrolled fashion. It's all about managing the moment, Harry."

I put the car in drive and headed toward the parking lot exit. I had already plotted my route. I'd take Flamingo to the 15 and then a quick jog over to the Blue Diamond Highway. Then it would be a straight shot north to Clear.

"What's he going to say?"

"He'll hold a press conference late this afternoon. He'll announce that Backus is apparently alive and we're out looking for him. He'll hold up the picture Terry McCaleb took of the man who called himself Shandy."

"Did they check all of that out yet?"

"Yes. There's no trace line on Shandy yet—it was probably just a name he gave Terry. But photographic analysis and comparison of the photos Terry took and photos of Backus are under way as we speak. The initial report is they're going to come in as a match. It was Backus."

"And Terry didn't recognize him."

"Well, he obviously recognized something. He took the pictures, so there was some sort of suspicion. But the guy had a beard, hat and glasses. The analyst on it said he'd also changed his nose and teeth and maybe had cheek implants. There's a lot of things he could have done, even a surgery that would have changed his voice. Look, I looked at the photos and didn't see it for sure and I worked directly with Backus for five years, much longer than Terry. Terry got moved out to L.A. to man the Behavioral Sciences outpost."

"Any idea where he got all of that done?"

"We're pretty sure we know. About six years ago the bodies of a surgeon and his wife were found in their burned-out home in Prague. The home had a surgical suite and the doctor was the subject of an Interpol intelligence file. The wife was his nurse. He was suspected of being a face man—a surgeon who would change your face for a certain price. The theory was that someone he changed murdered him and his wife to cover the trail. All records he might have kept on the faces he changed were lost in the fire. It was ruled an arson."

"What connected Backus to him?"

"Nothing for sure. But as you can imagine, everything Backus did or touched as an agent was gone over once he was revealed. His entire case history was audited as much as possible. He did a lot of consulting on cases abroad. Part of the FBI image machine. He went to places like Poland, Yugoslavia, Italy, France, you name it."

"He went to Prague?"

She nodded.

"He went to Prague on a case. To consult. Young women disappearing and ending up in the river. Prostitutes. The doctor—the face man—was questioned in the investigation because he did the breast augmentations on three of the victims. Backus was there. He helped question the doctor."

"And he could have been told about the doctor's suspected sideline."

"Exactly. We think he knew and we think he went there to change his face."

"That wouldn't have been easy. His real face was on the front of every newspaper and magazine back then."

"Look, Bob Backus is a psychopathic killer but he is a very smart psychopath. Outside of the made-up guys in books and movies, nobody's ever been smarter at this. Not even Bundy. We have to assume that he had an escape plan all along. From day one. When I put him out that window eight years ago, you better believe he already had a plan in place. I'm talking about money, IDs, whatever he would need to reinvent himself and get away. He probably carried it with him. We assume from L.A. he made his way back east first and then split to Europe."

"He burned down his condo," I said.

"Right, we give him credit for that, which puts him in Virginia three weeks after I shot him in L.A. That was a shrewd move. He torched the place and then got to Europe, where he could lie low for a while, change his face and then start again."

"Amsterdam."

She nodded.

"The first killing in Amsterdam occurred seven months after the face man burned in Prague."

I nodded. It all seemed to fit together. Then I thought of something else.

"How is the director going to announce the surprise that Backus is alive when four years ago you had Amsterdam?"

"He's got all kinds of deniability on that. First and most important, that was another director's watch. So he can lay anything he needs to off on him. That's FBI tradition. But realistically, that was another country and it wasn't an investigation we were running. And it was never absolutely confirmed. We had handwriting analysis, but that was really it and that is not in the same league as fingerprinting or DNA when it comes to confirming. So the director can simply say nothing was for sure about Backus in Amsterdam. Either way he's safe. He just has to worry about the here and the now."

"Manage the moment."

"FBI one-oh-one."

"And you people are going along with his going public?"

"No. We asked for a week. He gave us the day. The press conference is at six p.m. eastern time."

"Like anything's going to happen today."

"Yeah, we know. We're fucked."

"Backus will probably go under, change his face again and not turn up for another four years."

"Probably. But the director won't get hit with any blowback on it. He'll be safe."

We were silent for a few moments thinking about that. I could understand the director's decision but it certainly helped him more than it helped the investigation.

We were on the 15 and I was pulling into the exit lane for the Blue Diamond Highway.

"What happened at the nine a.m., before the director's meeting?"

"The usual round-robin. Updates from every agent."

"And?"

"And there's not a lot that is new. A few things. We talked about you mostly. I'm counting on you, Harry."

"For what?"

"For a new lead here. Where are we going?"

"Do they know we're riding together, or are you still supposed to be watching me as in *watching* me."

"I think they would prefer the latter—in fact, I know they would. But that would be boring and besides, like I said, what are they going to do to me if they find out I'm riding with you, send me back to Minot? BFD, I got to like that place."

"Minot might not be a big fucking deal, but maybe they'll send you someplace else. Don't they have bureau offices in Guam and places like that?"

"Yes, but it's all relative. I heard Guam isn't that bad—a lot of terrorism angles, which is all the rage. And after eight years in Minot and Rapid City, a change like that might not be bad no matter what the investigations are about."

"What was said about me at the meeting?"

"It was mostly me, since you are my assignment. I told them I ran a check through the L.A. field office and got your pedigree. I gave them that and told them you went behind the wall last year."

"What do you mean, that I retired?"

"No, Homeland Security. You ran afoul of them, went behind the wall and came back out again. That impressed Cherie Dei. Made her more willing to let you run a little."

"I had been wondering about that."

Actually, I had been wondering why Agent Dei had not simply put the clamps on me.

"What about Terry McCaleb's notes?" I asked.

"What about them?"

"Better minds than mine must have gone to work on them. What did they come up with? What was their take on the triangle theory?"

"It is an established pattern with serials that they commit what we call 'triangle crimes.' We see it often. That is, the victim can be traced through three points of a triangle. There is their point of origin or entry—their home or in this case the airport. Then there is what we call the point of prey—the place where killer and victim come into contact, where they crisscross. And then there is the point of disposal. With serials the three points are never the same because it is the best way for them to avoid detection. That is what Terry saw when he read that newspaper story. He circled it because the Metro guy was going the wrong way with it. He wasn't thinking triangle, he was thinking circle."

"So is the bureau working on the triangle now?"

"Of course they are. But some things take time. Right now there is a higher emphasis on crime scene analysis. But we've got somebody in Quantico working the triangle. The FBI is effective but sometimes slow, Harry. I am sure you know this."

"Sure."

"It's a tortoise-and-hare race. We're the tortoise, you're the hare."

"What are you talking about?"

"You're moving faster than us, Harry. Something tells me you figured out the triangle theory and are taking a shot at the missing point. The point of prey."

I nodded. Whether I was being used or not didn't matter. They were allowing me to stay in the hunt and that was what was important to me.

"You start with the airport and you end with Zzyzx. That leaves one more point—the intersection of predator and prey—and I think I've got it. We're going there."

"Then tell me."

"First tell me one more thing about McCaleb's notes."

"I think I already told you everything. They're still being analyzed."

"William Bing, who is that?"

She hesitated but only for a moment.

"That's a no-go, a dead end."

"How so?"

"William Bing is a heart transplant patient who was in Vegas Memorial getting a checkup and some tests.

We think Terry knew him and when he was over here he visited him in the hospital."

"Did you people talk to Bing yet?"

"Not yet. We're trying to track him."

"Seems odd."

"What, that he would visit a guy?"

"No, not that. I mean that he would write that on the file if it wasn't connected to the case."

"Terry wrote stuff down. It's pretty obvious from all his files and notebooks that he wrote stuff down. If he was coming over here to work on this, then maybe he wrote Bing's name and the hospital number down on the file so he wouldn't forget to visit or call him. Could be a lot of reasons."

I didn't respond. I still had trouble seeing it.

"How did he know the guy?"

"We don't know. Maybe the movie. Terry got hundreds of letters from transplant people after that movie came out. He was sort of a hero to a lot of people in the same boat as he was."

As we headed north on Blue Diamond I saw a sign for the Travel America truck stop and remembered the receipt I had found in Terry McCaleb's car. I pulled in, even though I had gassed up the Mercedes after leaving Eleanor's house that morning. I stopped the car and just looked at the travel complex.

"What is it? You need gas?"

"No, we're fine. It's just that . . . McCaleb was here."

"What is this? You getting a psychic reading or something?"

"No, I found a receipt in his car. I wonder if this means he went up to Clear."

"To clear what?"

"No, the town of Clear. That's where we're going."

"Well, we might never know unless we get up there and ask some questions."

I nodded and pulled the car back onto Blue Diamond and started north again. Along the way I told Rachel my theory of the theory. That is, my take on McCaleb's triangle and how Clear fit into it. I could tell that my telling it drew her interest. She may have even been excited about it. She agreed with my take on the victims and how and why they may have been chosen. She agreed that it appeared to mirror the victimology—her word—in Amsterdam.

We brainstormed for an hour on it and then grew quiet as we started to get close. The barren, rugged landscape was giving way to outposts of humanity and we began to see billboards advertising the brothels that waited just ahead.

"Have you ever been to one of these?" Rachel asked me.

"No."

I thought about the steam-and-cream tents in Vietnam but didn't bring them up.

"I didn't mean like as a customer. But as a cop."

"Still no. But I tracked a few people through them. And by that I mean by credit cards and other means. We're not going to find the people here overly cooperative. At least I never did by phone. And calling in a local sheriff is a joke. The state collects taxes from these joints. A big chunk of it goes back to the home county."

"I get it. So how do we handle it?"

Almost smiling because she had used the word *we*, I threw the question back at her.

"I don't know," she said. "I guess we just go in through the front door."

Meaning we play it straight and just go in and ask our questions. I wasn't sure it was the right way to go but she had a badge and I didn't.

We cleared the town of Pahrump and in another 10 miles came to an intersection where a sign with CLEAR on it and an arrow to the left was posted. I turned and the asphalt soon gave way to a crushed rock road that kicked up a flume of dust behind my car. The town of Clear could see us coming from a mile away.

That is, if it was looking for us. But the town of Clear, Nevada, turned out to be little more than a trailer park. The gravel road led us to another intersection and another sign with an arrow. We turned north again and soon came to a clearing where an old trailer sat with rust dripping from its rivets. A sign running along the top edge of the trailer said, WELCOME TO CLEAR. SPORTS BAR OPEN. ROOMS FOR RENT. There were no cars parked in the clearing in front of the bar.

I drove on past the welcome wagon, and the new road curved into a neighborhood of trailer homes baking like beer cans in the sun. Few were in better shape than the welcome wagon. Eventually, we came to a permanent structure that appeared to be a town hall as well as the location of the spring the town was named for. We kept going and were rewarded by another arrow on another sign, this one reading simply BROTHELS.

Nevada licenses over thirty brothels across the state. In these places prostitution is legal, controlled and monitored. We found three of those state-licensed businesses at the end of the road in Clear. The gravel road widened into a large turnaround where three similar looking and designed brothels sat waiting for customers. They were called Sheila's Front Porch, Tawny's High Five Ranch and Miss Delilah's House of Holies.

"Nice," Rachel said as we surveyed the scene. "Why are these places always named after women—as if women actually own them?"

"You got me. I guess Mister Dave's House of Holies wouldn't go over so well with the guys."

Rachel smiled.

"You're right. I guess it's a shrewd move. Name a place of female degradation and slavery after a female and it doesn't sound so bad, does it? It's packaging."

"Slavery? Last I heard these women were volunteers. Some of them are supposedly housewives who come up from Vegas."

"If you believe that, then you are naïve, Bosch. Just because you can come and go doesn't mean you're not a slave."

I nodded thoughtfully, not wanting to get into a debate with her about this subject because I knew it would bring me back to examining and questioning things in my own past.

Rachel apparently wanted to drop it there, too.

"So which one do you want to start with?" she asked.

I pulled the car to a stop in front of Tawny's High Five Ranch. It didn't look like much of a ranch. It was a conglomeration of three or four trailers that were connected by covered walkways. I looked to my left and saw that Sheila's Front Porch was of similar design and configuration and it had no front porch. Miss Delilah's to my right was the same and I got the distinct impression that the three seemingly separate brothels were not competitors but rather branches of the same tree.

"I don't know," I said. "Looks like eenie, meenie, minie, moe to me."

Rachel cracked her door open.

"Wait a second," I said. "I've got this."

I handed her the file of photos Buddy Lockridge had brought to Vegas the day before. Rachel opened it and saw the front and side shots of the man known as Shandy but presumed to be Robert Backus.

"I'm not going to even ask where you got these."

"Fine. But you carry them. It will have more weight coming from you, since you've got the badge."

"For the moment, at least."

"Did you bring the photos of the missing men?"

"Yes, I've got them."

"Good."

She took the file and got out of the car. I did likewise. We both walked around to the front of the car, where we stopped for a moment and surveyed the three brothels again. There were a few cars parked in front of each. There were also four flat-head Harleys lined up like a row of mean chrome in front of Miss Delilah's House of Holies. Air-brushed on the gas tank of one of the bikes was a skull smoking a joint with a smoke ring forming a halo above it.

"Let's take Delilah's last," I said. "Maybe we'll get lucky before we need to go there."

"The bikes?"

"Yeah, the bikes. They're Road Saints. I say let sleeping dogs lie."

"Good enough for me."

Leading the way, Rachel marched toward the front door of Sheila's. She didn't wait for me because she knew I would be following in her wake.

31

INSIDE SHEILA'S WE WERE greeted by the sickly sweet smell of perfume mixed with too much incense. We were also greeted by a smiling woman in a purple kimono who did not seem the least bit surprised or put out by the idea of a couple coming into the brothel. Her mouth drew into an edge as straight and sharp as a guillotine's when she saw the FBI credentials Rachel flipped open.

"That's nice," she said with a falsely pleasant note in her voice. "Now let me see the warrant."

"No warrant today," Rachel replied evenly. "We would just like to ask a few questions."

"I don't have to speak with you unless you have a court order telling me to. I run a legal and fully licensed business here."

I noticed two women dressed in a page from Victoria's Secret sitting on a couch nearby. They were watching a television soap opera and seemingly uninterested in the verbal skirmish brewing at the front door.

They were both attractive in a certain way but worn down around the eyes and mouths. The scene suddenly reminded me of my mother and some of her friends. The way they looked to me when I was a boy and I watched them getting ready to go out at night and work. I suddenly felt completely ill at ease in this place and wanted to go. I even hoped the woman in the kimono would succeed in sending us out.

"No one is doubting the legality of your operation," Rachel said. "We simply need to ask a few questions of you and . . . your staff and then we'll be gone."

"Get the court order and we'll be happy to oblige."

"Are you Sheila?"

"You can call me that. You can call me anything you want as long as you're saying good-bye when you do it."

Rachel raised the ante by going to her don't-fuck-with-me voice.

"If I go for that court order, I'm going to first call for a sheriff's unit and I will have that car sit out in front of this trailer until I get back. You might run a legal operation here, Sheila, but which one of these places are all the guys going to pick when they see the sheriff sitting on this one? I figure two hours back to Vegas, a few hours waiting to get in to see the judge and then two hours back. I'm off at five so I probably won't be back till tomorrow. That okay with you?"

Sheila came back hard and swift.

"If you call the sheriff, ask him to send out Dennis or Tommy. They know the place real well and they're also customers."

She smirked at Rachel and held firm. She'd called her bluff and Rachel had nothing left. They just stared at each other as the moments went by. I was about to step in and say something when one of the women on the couch beat me to the punch.

"She?" the one closest to us offered. "Let's just get it over with."

Sheila broke her stare from Rachel and looked at the woman on the couch. She then backed down but her anger remained barely below the surface. I'm not sure there was any other way to handle it once Sheila jumped on us like that, but it was clear to me that all the posturing and threatening was going to end up getting us nothing.

We set up in Sheila's small office and interviewed the women one by one, starting with Sheila and ending with two women who were working when we first entered the establishment. Rachel never introduced me to anyone, so the problem of my standing in the investigation never came up. Uniformly the women could not or would not identify any of the missing men who ended up in the ground in Zzyzx and the same went for the photographs of Shandy on McCaleb's boat.

At the end of a half hour we were out of there with nothing to show for it but an incense intoxication headache for me and stress fractures in Rachel's outlook.

"Disgusting," she said as we walked down the pink sidewalk toward my car.

"What?"

"That place. I don't know how anyone could do that."

"I thought you said they were slaves."

"Look, it's not your job to throw things back at me."

"Right."

"What are you so upset about? I didn't see you in there saying anything to her. You were a big help."

"That's because I wouldn't have done it that way. Two minutes into that place I knew we wouldn't get anything."

"Oh, and you would have."

"No, I'm not saying that. I told you, these places are like rocks. It's hard to get water. And bringing up the sheriff was definitely the wrong way to go. I told you, half his pay probably comes from the brothels in his territory."

"So you just want to criticize and not offer any solution."

"Look, Rachel, point your gun at somebody else. I'm not the one you're angry with, all right? If you want to try something different in this next place I'll give it a shot."

"Go right ahead."

"All right then, give me the photos and you wait in the car."

"What are you talking about? I'm going in."

"This is not the place for the pomp and circumstance, Rachel. I should've realized that when I invited you. But I didn't think you'd be shoving your badge down people's throats as soon as you walked in."

"So you're going to go in there and finesse it."

"I'm not sure I'd call it finesse. I'm just going to do it the old-fashioned way."

"Does that mean taking off your clothes?"

"No, it means taking out my wallet."

"The FBI doesn't buy information from potential witnesses."

"That's right. I'm not the FBI. If I find a witness this way, the FBI won't have to pay a thing."

I put my hand on her back and gently directed her to

the Mercedes. I opened the door for her and ushered her in. I gave her the keys.

"Turn on the air conditioner. Either way, this shouldn't take too long."

I rolled the file up with the photos and put it into my back pocket under my jacket.

The sidewalk leading to the door of Tawny's High Five was also made of pink cement and I was beginning to see the appropriateness of that. The women we had encountered in Sheila's were hard cases with pink lining. And so was Rachel. I was beginning to feel like my feet were in buckets of pink cement.

I buzzed the door and was let in by a woman who was dressed in cutoff blue jeans and a halter top that barely contained her apparently surgically enhanced breasts.

"Come on in. I'm Tammy."

"Thanks."

I stepped into the front room of the trailer, where there were two couches facing each other on opposite walls. Three women sat on the couches and looked at me with practiced smiles.

"This is Georgette and Gloria and Mecca," Tammy said. "And I'm Tammy. You can choose one of us now or wait for Tawny. She's in the back with a customer."

I looked at Tammy. She seemed the most eager. She was very small and top heavy and had short brown hair. She would be considered attractive to some men but not to me. I told her she would do just fine and she led me back through a hallway that turned to the right and into another trailer. There were three private rooms on the left and she went to the third one and used a key to open it. We went in and she closed the door but didn't lock it.

There was barely enough room to stand because a king-size bed took up most of the space.

Tammy sat down on the bed and patted the spot next to her. I sat and she reached to a shelf full of well-thumbed mystery novels and pulled down what looked like a restaurant menu and gave it to me. It was a thin folder with a caricature drawing on the front. It showed a naked woman on her hands and knees and bent over, turning to look back at and wink at the man who was entering her from the rear. The man was naked, too, except for a cowboy hat and the holstered six-shooters on his hips. One hand was up in the air and holding a lasso. The rope rose above the couple and formed the words *Tawny's High Five*.

"You can get a T-shirt with that on it," Tammy informed me. "Twenty bucks."

"Great," I said, as I opened the folder.

It turned out that it was a menu of sorts. It was personalized to Tammy. It contained a single sheet of paper with two columns on it. One listed the sexual acts she was willing to perform and the lengths of individual sessions, and the other listed the prices these services would cost the customer. After two of the listed sexual acts were asterisks. At the bottom it was explained that an asterisk denoted a personal specialty.

"So," I said, staring at the columns. "I think I might need a translator for some of these."

"I'll help you. Which ones?"

"How much is it just to talk?"

"What do you mean, like talk dirty to you? Or you talk dirty to me?"

"No, just talk. I want to ask you about a guy I'm looking for. He's from around here."

Her posture changed. She sat up straighter and in doing so put a couple inches of space between us, which was fine because her perfume was searing my already incense-burned nasal plates.

"I think you better talk to Tawny when she's finished."

"I want to talk to you, Tammy. I've got a hundred bucks for five minutes. I'll double it if you give me a line on this guy."

She hesitated as she thought about it. Two hundred bucks wouldn't even cover an hour's work, according to the menu. But I had a feeling the menu prices were negotiable and, besides, there was nobody lined up on the pink cement to get in here.

"Somebody's going to take my money here," I said. "It might as well be you."

"Okay, but it has to be quick. If Tawny finds out you ain't a paying customer she's going to kick you out and put me at the back of the line."

Now I understood. She had answered the door because she was up. I could have picked from any of the women on the couches but Tammy got the first shot at me.

I reached into my pocket for my money and gave her the hundred. I kept the rest in my hand as I pulled out the file and opened it. Rachel had made a mistake asking the women at Sheila's if they recognized any of the men in the photos. That was because she didn't have the confidence I had. I was more certain of my theory and I didn't make that mistake with Tammy.

The first photo I showed her was the front shot of Shandy on Terry McCaleb's boat.

"When was the last time you saw him around here?" I asked.

Tammy looked at the photo for a long moment. She didn't take it from me, though I would have given it to her to hold. After what seemed like an interminable moment, when I thought the door would swing open and the woman named Tawny would order me out, she finally spoke.

"I don't know . . . at least a month, maybe more. He hasn't been around."

I felt like climbing on the bed and bouncing, but I kept my cool. I wanted her to believe I knew everything she was telling me. She would feel more comfortable that way and be more forthcoming.

"Do you remember where it was you saw him?"

"Just out front. I walked a customer out and Tom was there waiting."

"Uh-huh. Did he say anything to you?"

"No, he never does. He doesn't even know me really."

"Then what happened?"

"Nothing happened. My guy got in the car and they drove away."

I was beginning to get a picture. Tom had a car. He was a driver.

"Who called him? Was it you or had the client already done that?"

"It was Tawny probably. I don't really remember."

"Because it happened all the time."

"Yeah."

"But he hasn't been around in, what, a month?"

"Yeah. Maybe more. Is that enough of a lead? I mean, what do you want?"

She was looking at the second hundred in my hand.

"Two things. You know Tom's last name?"

"No."

"Okay, how does somebody get a hold of him if they need a ride?"

"Call him, I guess."

"Can you get me the number?"

"Just go over to the sports bar, that's where we call him. I don't know the number offhand. It's up there next to the phone in front."

"The sports bar, okay."

I didn't give her the money.

"One last thing."

"You keep saying that."

"I know but I mean it this time."

I showed her the six-pack of photos Rachel had brought of the missing men. These were better and much clearer than the photos that had run with the newspaper article. These were full-color candids given to Vegas Metro by their families and then turned over as a courtesy to the FBI.

"Any of these guys your customers?"

"Look, mister, we don't talk about customers. We're very discreet and don't give out that kind of information."

"They're dead, Tammy. It doesn't matter."

Her eyes widened and then lowered to the photos in my hand. These she took and she looked through them like they made up a hand of cards. I could tell by the way her eyes flared that she'd been dealt an ace.

"What?"

"Well, this one guy looks like a guy that was here. He was with Mecca, I think. You could ask her."

I heard a horn honk twice. I knew it was from my car. Rachel was getting impatient.

"Go get Mecca and bring her back here. I'll give you the rest of the money then. Tell her I've got some money for her, too. Don't tell her what I want. Tell her I just want two girls at once."

"All right, but that's it. You pay me."

"I will."

She left the room and I sat on the bed looking around while I waited. The walls were paneled with fake cherry wood. There was one window with a frilly curtain. I leaned across the bed and pulled the curtain open. The view was of nothing but barren desert. The bed and the trailer might as well be sitting on the moon.

The door opened and I turned back, ready to give Tammy the rest of her money and to dive into my pocket for Mecca's share. But there weren't two women in the doorway. There were two men. They were big—one larger than the other—and their arms below their black T-shirts were completely carved up with jailhouse ink. On the bigger man's bulging biceps was a skull with a halo above it and that told me who they were.

"What's up, Doc?" said the bigger one.

"You must be Tawny," I said.

Without a word he reached down and grabbed two fistfuls of my jacket. He pulled me up off the bed and tossed me out into the hallway to the waiting arms of his partner. The new one shoved me down the hallway in the opposite direction I had come into the trailer from. I realized that the horn honk from Rachel had been a warning, not a sign of impatience. I was wishing I had read that right when Big and Little Steroid shoved me through a back door and onto the rocky terrain of the desert.

I went down to my hands and knees and was gathering myself and getting up when one of them put his boot on my hip and shoved me down again. I tried to get up again and this time they let me.

"I said, what's up, Doc? You got business here?"

"I was just asking questions and I was willing to pay for the answers. I didn't think that was a problem."

"Well, pal, that *is* a problem."

They were advancing on me, the big man first. He was so big I couldn't even see his little brother behind him. I was taking a step backward for every one they took forward. And I had a bad feeling that that was what they wanted. They were backing me toward something, maybe a hole in the ground out there in the sand and rock.

"Who are you, boy?"

"I'm a private detective from L.A. I'm just looking for a missing man, that's all."

"Yeah, well, people who come here don't want to be looked for."

"I understand that now. I'll just clear out of here and you won't—"

"Excuse me."

We all stopped. It was Rachel's voice. The bigger man turned back toward the trailer and his shoulder lowered a few inches. I could see Rachel coming out the back door of the trailer. Her hands were at her sides.

"What's this, you bring your mother?" Big Steroid said.

"Something like that."

While he was looking at Rachel I clasped my hands

together and swung a sledgehammer into the back of his neck. He went forward and into his partner. But the blow was nothing more than a surprise attack. He didn't go down. He wheeled on me and started coming at me, balling his fists into twin sledgehammers. I saw Rachel move her arm under her blazer and flip it back to get to her gun. But her hand caught momentarily in the material and she was late getting to her weapon.

"Hold it!" she yelled.

But the Steroid boys didn't stop. I ducked under the bigger man's first punch but when I came up behind him I was right in front of little brother. He grabbed me in a bear hug and lifted me off the ground. For some reason at this point I noticed that there were women watching from the three back windows of the rear trailer. I had drawn an audience to my own destruction.

My arms were trapped inside of my attacker's embrace and I was feeling severe pressure building on my spine at the same time the air was crushed out of my lungs. Just then Rachel finally freed her weapon and fired two shots into the air.

I was dropped to the ground and I watched as Rachel crab-walked away from the trailer to make sure no one could get up behind her.

"FBI," she shouted. "On the ground. Both of you on the ground."

The big men complied. As soon as I got some air back into my lungs I got back up. I tried to dust some of the dirt off my clothes but all that did was spread it around. I looked at Rachel and nodded. She kept her distance from the men on the ground and signaled me over with her finger.

"What happened?"

"I was interviewing one of the women and asked her to bring in another. But then these guys showed up and dragged me out here. Thanks for the warning."

"I *did* try to warn you. I honked."

"I know, Rachel. Take it easy. That's what I'm thanking you for. I just misread it."

"So what do we do?"

"I don't care about these guys. Cut 'em loose. But there are two women inside, Tammy and Mecca, we need to take them. One knows Shandy and the other I think can ID one of the missing men as being a customer."

Rachel computed this and slowly nodded.

"Good. Is Shandy a customer?"

"No, he's some sort of driver. We need to get over to the sports bar and ask around there."

"Then we can't just cut these two loose. They might just come meet us again over there. Besides there were four bikes out front. Where are the other two?"

"I don't know."

"Hey, come on!" Big Steroid yelled. "We're breathing sand over here."

Rachel approached the two men on the ground.

"Okay, get up."

She waited until they were up and staring at her with malevolent eyes. She dropped her gun down to her side and spoke calmly to them, as if this was the way she normally got to know people.

"Where are you guys from?"

"Why?"

"Why? Because I'm trying to get to know you. I'm deciding whether to arrest you."

"For what? He started it."

"Not what I saw. I saw two big men assaulting a smaller man."

"He was trespassing."

"Last I checked, trespassing was not a valid defense of assault. If you want to see if I'm wrong then keep—"

"Pahrump."

"What?"

"Pahrump."

"And do you own these three operations?"

"No, we're just security."

"I see. Well, I'll tell you what. If you two find the other two whose bikes are out front and go back to Pahrump, then we'll let bygones be bygones here."

"That's not fair. He was in there asking—"

"I'm the FBI. I'm not interested in what's fair. Take it or leave it."

After a moment the bigger man broke from his stance and started walking toward the trailer. The smaller big man followed.

"Where are you going?" Rachel barked.

"We're leaving. Like you told us."

"Good. Make sure you put on your helmets, gentlemen."

Without looking back the bigger man raised a brawny arm and shot us a bird as he walked. The smaller big man saw this and did the same.

Rachel looked at me and said, "I hope this works."

32

THE WOMEN IN THE backseat were angry but Rachel didn't care. This was the closest she had been—the closest anybody had been—to Backus since that night in Los Angeles. The night she had watched him crash backward through the glass and into the void that seemed to swallow any trace of him.

Until now. And the last thing she was going to let bother her were the protests of the two prostitutes in the backseat of Bosch's car. The only thing that bothered her was her decision to let Bosch drive. They now had two custodies and were transporting them in a private car. It was a security issue and she wasn't sure yet how they were going to handle the stop at the sports bar.

"I know what we'll do," Bosch said as he drove away from the three brothels at the end of the road.

"So do I," Rachel said. "You'll stay with them while I go in."

"No, that won't work. You'll need backup. We just proved that we shouldn't split up."

"Then what?"

"I turn on the child locks on the back doors. They won't be able to open them."

"And what's to stop them from climbing over to the front seat and getting out?"

"Look, where are they going to go? They have no choice, right, ladies?"

He looked up into the rearview mirror.

"Fuck you," answered the one named Mecca. "You can't just do this. We're not the ones who committed any crimes."

"Actually, as I explained before, we can," Rachel said in a bored tone. "You have been taken into federal custody as material witnesses in a criminal investigation. You will be formally interviewed and then released."

"Well, just do it now and get it over with."

Rachel had been surprised to learn when she looked at the woman's driver's license that her name really was Mecca. Mecca McIntyre. What a name.

"Well, Mecca, we can't. I already explained that, too."

Bosch pulled into the gravel lot in front of the sports bar. There were no other cars. He lowered all the windows a couple of inches and turned off the car.

"I'm going to put the alarm on," he said. "If you climb over and open the door it will set off the alarm. We'll then come out and chase you down. So don't bother, okay? We won't be gone long."

Rachel got out and closed the door. She checked her cell phone again and was still not getting service. She saw Bosch check his and shake his head. She decided she would commandeer the phone in the sports bar, if there was one, and call the Vegas FO to report what she had. She expected Cherie Dei to be very angry and pleased.

"By the way," Bosch said as they came to the ramp leading up to the door of the trailer, "do you carry an extra magazine for your Sig?"

"Of course."

"Where, on your belt?"

"That's right, why?"

"Nothing, I just saw back there behind the trailer that your hand sort of got caught in your jacket."

"It didn't get caught. I just—what's your point?"

"Nothing. I was just going to say that I always carried my extra in my jacket pocket. It gave it some weight, you know. So when you had to flip it back the extra weight carried it all the way back and out of the way."

"Thanks for the tip," she said evenly. "Can we concentrate on this now?"

"Sure, Rachel. You going to take the lead here?"

"If you don't mind."

"Not at all."

He followed her up the ramp. She thought she saw a smile on his face in the reflection on the glass of the trailer's door. She opened it, engaging an overhead bell that announced their arrival.

They stepped into a small and empty barroom. To their right was a pool table, its green felt faded by time and stained by drink spills. It was a small table but still did not have enough clearance in the small space. Even breaking a rack would probably require holding a cue at a forty-degree angle.

To the left of the door was a six-stool bar with three shelves of glasses and take-your-pick poison behind it.

There was no one in the bar but before Rachel or Bosch could call out a hello, a set of black curtains to the left of the bar split and a man stepped out, his eyes creased with sleep even though it was almost noon.

"Can I he'p you? Kind a' early, idn't it?"

Rachel hit him with the credentials and that seemed to crack his eyes open a little wider. He was in his early sixties, she guessed, though his unkempt bed hair and the unshaven white stubble on his cheeks may have skewed her estimate.

He nodded as though he had just solved some sort of internal mystery.

"So you're the sister, right?" he asked.

"Excuse me?"

"You're Tom's sister, right? He said you might come."

"Tom who?"

"Tom Walling. Who do you think?"

"We're looking for a man named Tom who drives customers from the brothels. Is that Tom Walling?"

"That's what I'm telling you. Tom Walling was my driver. He told me that one day his sister might come here looking for him. He never said she was no FBI agent."

Rachel nodded, trying to cover the jolt. It wasn't necessarily the surprise that buzzed her. It was the audacity and the deeper meaning, the magnitude of Backus's plan.

"What is your name, sir?"

"Billings Rett. I own this place and I'm also the mayor around here."

"The mayor of Clear."

"That's right."

Rachel felt something tap her arm and looked down to see the file containing the photos. Bosch was giving it to her but staying back. He seemed to know things had suddenly swung. This was now more about her than Terry McCaleb, or even Bosch. She took the file and removed one of the photographs McCaleb had taken of the fishing client known to him as Jordan Shandy. She showed it to Billings Rett.

"Is that the man you knew of as Tom Walling?"

Rett spent only a few seconds looking at the photo.

"That's it. Right down to that Dodgers hat. We get all the games here on the dish and Tom was Dodger blue through and through."

"He drove a car for you?"

"The only car. I'm not that big of an operation."

"And he told you his sister would come here?"

"No, he said she might. And he gave me something."

He turned and looked at the shelves behind the bar. He saw what he was looking for and reached up to the top shelf. He pulled down an envelope and handed it to Rachel. The envelope left a rectangle in the dust on the glass shelf. It had been up there awhile.

The envelope had her full name on it. She turned her body slightly as if to shield it from Bosch and started to open it.

"Rachel," Bosch said. "Should you process it first?"

"It doesn't matter. I know it's from him."

She tore the envelope open and pulled out a three-by-five card. She started to read the handwritten note on it.

Dear Rachel,
If as I hope you are the first to read this, then I
have taught you well. I hope this finds you in good
health and spirits. Most of all, I hope this means
you have survived your interment within the bureau and are back on top. I hope he who taketh
away can also giveth back. It was never my intention, Rachel, to doom you. It is my intention now,
with my last act, to save you.

Good-bye, Rachel.
R

She reread it quickly and then handed it over her
shoulder to Bosch. As he read she continued with
Billings Rett.

"When did he give you that and what exactly did
he say?"

"It was about a month ago, give or take a few days,
and it was when he told me he was leaving. He paid me
the rent, said he wanted to keep the place, and he gives
me the card and says that it's for his sister and that she
might come by looking for him. And here you are."

"I'm *not* his sister," she snapped at him. "When did
he first come to Clear?"

"Hard to remember, three or four years ago."

"Why did he come here?"

Rett shook his head.

"Beats me. Why do people go to New York City?
Everybody's got their reasons. He didn't share his particular reason with me."

"How did he end up driving for you?"

"He was in here shootin' balls one day and I asked him if he needed some work. He said he wouldn't mind and it went from there. It's not a full-time gig. Just when we get a call for somebody looking for a ride. Most people drive themselves up here."

"And back then, three or four years ago, he told you his name was Tom Walling?"

"No, he told me that when he rented the trailer from me. That was when he first got here."

"What about a month ago? Did you say he paid rent and then left?"

"Yeah, he said he'd be back and wanted to keep the place. He rented it up through August. But he went traveling and I haven't heard from him."

From outside the trailer an alarm sounded. The Mercedes. Rachel turned to Bosch but he was already heading to the door.

"I got it," he said.

He went through the door, leaving Rachel alone with Rett. She turned back to him.

"Did Tom Walling ever tell you where he came from?"

"No, he never mentioned it. He didn't talk much."

"And you never asked."

"Honey, you don't ask questions in a place like this. People that come here, they don't like answering questions. Tom, he liked to do the driving and pick up a few bucks and every now and then he'd come in and shoot a game by hisself. He didn't drink, he just chewed gum. He never messed with the whores and he was never late on a pickup. All that was fine by me. The guy I got driving now, he's always—"

"I don't care about the guy you've got now."

The bell rang behind her and she turned to see Bosch coming through. He nodded to her, telling her everything was all right.

"They tried the door. I guess the child lock doesn't work."

She nodded and turned her attention back to Rett, proud mayor of a brothel town.

"Mr. Rett?" she asked. "Where is Tom Walling's place?"

"He's got the single-wide on the ridge west of town."

Rett smiled, revealing a rotten tooth on the front lower row, and continued.

"He liked being outside of town. He told me he didn't like being so close to all the excitement around here. So I set him up out there behind Titanic Rock."

"Titanic Rock?"

"You'll know when you get there—if you saw the movie. One of these smart-ass rock climbers that comes out here marked it, too. You'll see it. Just take the road behind this place west and you'll be all right. Just look for the ship going down."

33

I WAS OUTSIDE WITH the two women in the Mercedes, running the air-conditioning and cooling them down. Rachel was still inside on the bar's phone talking to Cherie Dei and coordinating the arrival of backup. My guess was that agents would soon drop out of the sky in helicopters and descend on Clear, Nevada, in force. The trail was fresh. They were close.

I tried to talk to the two girls—it was hard to think of them as women despite what they did for a living and even though they were old enough. They probably knew everything there was to know about men but they didn't seem to know anything about the world. In my mind they were just girls who had taken wrong turns or been kidnapped and taken away from womanhood. I was beginning to understand what Rachel had said earlier.

"Did Tom Walling ever come into the trailer and hire any of the girls?" I asked.

"Not that I seen," Tammy said.

"Somebody said he was probably queer or something," Mecca added.

"Why did they say that?"

"'Cause he lived like a hermit or something," Mecca replied. "An' he never wanted no pussy even though Tawny would've thrown him some on the house like with the other drivers."

"Are there a lot of drivers?"

"He was the only one from around here," Tammy said quickly, apparently not liking Mecca in the lead. "The others come up from Vegas. Some of 'em work for the casinos."

"If there are drivers down there, how come somebody would hire Tom to go all the way down and get them?"

"They didn't," Mecca said.

"Sometimes they did," Tammy corrected.

"Well, sometimes. The dummies. But mostly we called for Tom if somebody got dropped off and stayed awhile or rented one of Old Billings's trailers and then needed a ride back 'cause his ride was long gone. The casino rides don't wait around too long. Unless you're one of those high rollers and then probably . . ."

"And then what?"

"Then you wouldn't come to Clear in the first place."

"They got prettier girls in Pahrump," Tammy said matter-of-factly, as if it was strictly a business disadvantage and not something that bothered her personally.

"An' it's a bit closer an' the pussy costs more," Mecca said. "So what we get up in Clear is your cost-conscious consumer."

Spoken like a true marketing expert. I tried to get the conversation back on track.

"So, for the most part, Tom Walling came over and drove customers back to Las Vegas or wherever they came from."

"Right."

"Right."

"And these guys—these customers—could have been totally anonymous. You don't check IDs, right? The customers could use whatever name they wanted when they came in there."

"Uh-huh. Unless they look like maybe they ain't twenty-one yet."

"Right. We check the ID of the young ones."

I could see how it could be done, how Backus could have sized up brothel customers as his victims. If it appeared they had taken measures to guard their identities and hide that they had made the trip to Clear, then they had inadvertently made themselves perfect victims. It also played into what was known about the demons that drove his killing spree. The profile work in the Poet file indicated that Backus's pathology was wrapped up in his relationship with his father, a man who on the outside held the vaunted image of FBI agent, hero and good man, but on the inside was a man who abused his wife and son to the extent that one fled the home because she could, while the one who couldn't get away was left to retreat into a world of fantasies involving the killing of his abuser.

I realized there was something missing. Lloyd Rockland, the victim who had rented a car. How did he fit in if he didn't need a driver?

I opened the file Rachel had left in the car and pulled out the photo of Rockland. I showed it to the women.

"This guy, do either of you recognize him? His name was Lloyd."

"Was?" Mecca asked.

"Yeah, that's right, was. Lloyd Rockland. He's dead. Do you recognize him?"

Neither of them did. I knew it was a long shot. Rockland disappeared in 2002. I tried to think of an explanation that would allow Rockland to fit into the theory.

"You serve alcohol in there, right?"

"If the customer wants it we can provide it," Mecca said. "We got a license."

"Okay, what happens when a guy drives all the way up from Vegas and gets too drunk to drive home?"

"He can sleep it off," she responded. "He can take a room if he pays for it."

"What if he wants to get back? What if he needs to get back?"

"He can call over here and the mayor will take care of it. The driver will take him back in his car and then the driver just catches a ride back like with one of the casino cars or something. It works out."

I nodded. It worked out for my theory as well. Rockland could have gotten drunk and had to be driven back by the driver, Backus. Only he wasn't driven back to Vegas. I knew I would have to ask Rachel to check the remains identified as Rockland's for a high alcohol level. It would be another confirmation.

"Mister, are we gonna have to stay here all day?" Mecca asked.

"I don't know," I said as I looked up at the trailer door.

RACHEL TRIED TO KEEP her voice low because Billings Rett was at the other end of the bar acting like he was doing a crossword puzzle, when she knew he was trying to listen to and understand everything she was saying and that could be heard from the phone.

"What's the ETA?" she asked.

"We'll be in the air within twenty and then another twenty to you," Cherie Dei said. "So sit tight, Rachel."

"Got it."

"And Rachel, I know you. I know what you will want to do. Stay out of the suspect's trailer until we can go in there with an ERT. Let them do their job."

Rachel almost told Dei that the fact was that she didn't know her, that she couldn't begin to understand the first thing about her. But she didn't.

"Got it," she said instead.

"What about Bosch?" Dei asked next.

"What about him?"

"I want him kept away from this."

"That will be sort of hard since he found the place. This is all because of him."

"I understand that but we would have gotten there eventually. We always do. We'll thank him but we have to brush him aside after that."

"Well, you get to tell him that."

"I will. So are we set? I've got to get over to Nellis."

"All set. See you inside the hour."

"Rachel, one last thing, why didn't you drive up there?"

"It was Bosch's hunch, he wanted to drive. What's the difference?"

"You were giving him control of the situation, that's all."

"That's second-guessing after the fact. We thought we might get a line on the missing men, not be led right to—"

"That's fine, Rachel. I shouldn't have brought it up. I have to go."

Dei hung up on her end. Rachel couldn't hang up because the phone was stretched from the back wall and over the bar. She held it up to Rett and he put down his pencil and came over. He took the phone and hung it up.

"Thank you, Mr. Rett. In about an hour a couple helicopters are going to land here. Probably right in front of this trailer. Agents will want to talk to you. More formally than I did. They will probably talk to a lot of people in your town."

"Not good for business."

"Probably not, but the faster people cooperate, the faster they'll take off and be out of here."

She didn't mention anything about the horde of media that would also probably descend on the place once it was revealed publicly that the little brothel town in the desert was where the Poet had holed up unnoticed for all of these years and had chosen his latest victims.

"If the agents ask where I am, tell them I went up to Tom Walling's trailer, okay?"

"Sounded like you were getting told *not* to go up there."

"Mr. Rett, just tell them what I asked you to tell them."

"Will do."

"By the way, have you been up there since he came in here and told you he was leaving for a while?"

"No, I haven't managed to get up there. He paid the rent on the place so I didn't think it was my business to snoop around his things. That's not the way we are here in Clear."

Rachel nodded.

"Okay, Mr. Rett, thanks for your cooperation."

He shrugged as if to say he either had no choice or his cooperation was minimal. Rachel turned from the bar and headed for the door. But just as she got there she hesitated. She reached inside her blazer and pulled the extra magazine for her Sig Sauer off her belt. She hefted its weight once in her hand and then slipped it into the pocket of her blazer. She then went out the door and got into the Mercedes next to Bosch.

"So," he said, "is Agent Dei mad?"

"Nope. We just brought in the case break, how could she be mad?"

"I don't know. Some people have the ability to be mad no matter what you bring them."

"Are we just going to sit here all day?" Mecca asked from the backseat.

Rachel turned around to look back at the two women.

"We're going over to the western ridge to check out a trailer. You can go with us and stay in the car or you can go into the bar and wait. More agents are on the way. You'll probably be able to get your interviews over with here and not have to go into Vegas."

"Thank God," Mecca said. "I'll wait here."

"Me, too," said Tammy.

Bosch let them out of the car.

"Just wait here," Rachel called to them. "If you go back to your trailer or go anywhere else you won't get far and it will just make them mad."

They didn't acknowledge this cautioning. Rachel watched them walk up the ramp and into the bar. Bosch got back in and put the car into reverse.

"You sure about this?" he asked. "My guess is that Agent Dei told you to sit still until the reinforcements got here."

"She also said one of the first things she was going to do was send you on your way. You want to wait for that or do you want to go see this trailer?"

"Don't worry, I'll go. I'm not the one with the career to worry about."

"Such as it is."

WE FOLLOWED THE DIRT road Billings Rett had directed us to, and it ranged west from the settlement of Clear and up a sloping landscape for a mile. The road then leveled off and curved behind a reddish-orange outcropping of rock that was exactly as Rett had described it. It looked like the tail-end of the great passenger ship as it drew upward out of the water at a sixty-degree angle and then plunged downward into the sea. According to the movie, anyway. The rock climber Rett mentioned had climbed to the appropriate spot at the top and had used white paint to scrawl "Titanic" across the rock surface.

We didn't stop to appraise the rock or the paintwork. I drove the Mercedes around it and we soon came to a clearing where there was a small trailer sitting on concrete blocks. There was a junked car on four flats next to it and an oil drum used to burn trash nearby. On the other side was a large fuel tank and a power generator.

To preserve possible crime scene evidence I stopped just outside the clearing and killed the engine. I noticed that the generator was silent. There was a stillness about the whole scene that seemed ominous in some way. I had a real sense that I had come to the end of the world, a place of darkness. I wondered if this was where Backus had taken his victims, if this was the end of the world for them. Probably, I concluded. It was a place of waiting evil.

Rachel broke the silence.

"Well, are we just going to look at it or are we going to check it out?"

"Just waiting on you to make the move."

She opened her door and then I opened mine. We met at the front of the car. That was when I noticed that the trailer's windows were all open, not what I would expect someone would do if they were leaving their home for a long period of time. After that recognition came the odor.

"You smell that?"

She nodded. Death was in the air. It was much worse, much stronger than at Zzyzx. I instinctively knew that what we would find here would not be the buried secrets of the killer. Not this time. There was a body in that trailer—at least one—that was open to the air and decomposing.

"With my last act," Rachel said.

"What?"

"The card. What he wrote on the card."

I nodded. She was thinking suicide.

"You think?"

"I don't know. Let's check."

We walked slowly forward, neither saying a word after that. The smell grew stronger and we both knew that whatever and whoever was dead inside the trailer had been baking in there for a long time.

I broke from her side and walked to a set of windows to the left of the trailer's door. Cupping my hands to the screen I tried to look into the darkness within. My hands hitting the screen set off an alarm of buzzing flies within the trailer. They were bouncing against the screen, looking to get out as if maybe the scene and the smell inside were too much even for them.

There was no curtain across the window but I couldn't see much from the angle I had—at least not a body or an indication of one. It looked like a small sitting area with a couch and a chair. There was a table with two stacks of hardback books on it. Behind the chair was a bookcase with its shelves full of books.

"Nothing," I said.

I stepped back from the window and looked up the length of the trailer. I saw Rachel's eyes focused on the door and then the doorknob. Something came to me then, something that didn't fit.

"Rachel, why did he leave the note for you at the bar?"

"What?"

"The note. He left it at the bar. Why there? Why not here?"

"I guess he wanted to make sure I got it."

"If he hadn't left it there you would have still come up here. You would've still found it here."

She shook her head.

"What are you saying? I don't get—"

"Don't try the door, Rachel. Let's wait."

"What are you talking about?"

"I don't like this."

"Why don't you look around the back, see if there is another window you can see in or something."

"Okay, I will. You just wait."

She didn't answer me. I walked around the left side of the trailer, stepped over the hitch and headed toward the other side. But then I stopped and walked out to the trash barrel.

The barrel was one-third full with the charred remains of burned refuse. There was a broom handle on the ground that was charred on one end. I picked it up and dug around in the ashes in the barrel, as I was sure Backus had done while the fire was burning. He had wanted to make sure everything got burned.

It appeared to be mostly paperwork and books that had been burned. There was nothing recognizable until I came across a blackened and melted credit card. There was nothing I recognized on it but I guessed that the forensics experts might be able to connect it to one of the victims. I dug around further and saw pieces of melted black plastic. Then I noticed one book that was burned beyond recognition on the outside but still had some partially intact pages on the inside. With my fingers I lifted it out and gingerly opened it. It looked like it was poetry, though it was hard to be sure, since all the pages were partially burned away. Between two of these pages I found a half-burned receipt for the book. At the top it said "Book Car" but the rest was burned away.

"Bosch? Where are you?"

It was Rachel. I was out of her sight. I placed the book back into the barrel and stuck the broom handle in as well. I headed toward the back side of the trailer. I saw another open window.

"Hold on a second."

RACHEL WAITED. SHE WAS growing impatient. She was listening for the distant sound of helicopters crossing the desert. She knew as soon as she heard them that her chance would be over. She would be pushed back, possibly even punished for how she had handled Bosch.

She looked back down at the doorknob. She thought about Backus and whether this could be his last play. Was four years here in the desert enough? Did he kill Terry McCaleb and send her the GPS only to lead her eventually to this? She thought about the note he had left, his telling her he had taught her well. An anger welled up inside her, an anger that wanted her to throw open the door and—

"We've got a body!"

It was Bosch, calling from the other side of the trailer.

"What? Where?"

"Come around. I've got a view. There's a bed and I see one body. Two, three days old. I can't see the face."

"Okay, anything else?"

She waited. He didn't say anything. She put her hand on the knob. It turned.

"The door's not locked."

"Rachel, don't open it," Bosch called. "I think . . . I think there is gas. I smell something besides the body. Something besides the obvious. Something underneath."

Rachel hesitated but then turned the knob fully and opened the door an inch.

Nothing happened.

She slowly pulled the door all the way open. Nothing happened. Flies saw the opening and buzzed by her and into the light. She waved them away from her eyes.

"Bosch, I'm going in."

She stepped up into the trailer. More flies. They were everywhere. The smell hit her fully then, invading her and tightening her stomach.

Her eyes adjusted to the dimness after the brightness outside and she saw the photos. They were stacked on tables and taped to the walls and refrigerator. Photos of the victims, alive and dead, tearful, pleading, pitiful. The table in the trailer's kitchen had been turned into a workstation. There was a laptop connected to a printer on one side and three separate stacks of photos. She picked up the largest stack and started to flip through it, again recognizing some of the men in the photos as the missing men whose photos she had carried with them to Clear. But these weren't the sort of family photos she had carried. These were shots of a killer and his victims. Men whose eyes pleaded to the camera, asking forgiveness and mercy. Rachel noticed that all of the shots were at a downward angle, with the shooter—Backus—in the dominant position, focusing down on his victims as they hoped and pleaded for their lives.

When she could look no more at them she put the photos down and took up the second stack. There were fewer photos here and these were mostly focused on a woman and two children as they moved through a shopping mall. She put them down and was about to move the camera weighing down the third stack of photos when Bosch stepped into the trailer.

"Rachel, what are we doing?"

"Don't worry. We have five, maybe ten minutes. We'll back out as soon as we hear the choppers and let the evidence recovery team take over. I just want to see if—"

"I'm not talking about beating other agents to the punch. I don't like this—the door being left open. Something's not—"

He stopped when he caught his first glimpse of the photos.

She turned back to the table and lifted the camera that rested on the last stack of photos. She looked down at a photo of herself. It took her a moment to place it but then realized where she had been photographed.

"He was with me all the way," she said.

"What are you talking about?" Bosch asked.

"This is O'Hare. My layover. Backus was there watching me."

She quickly shuffled through the photos. There were six of them, all shots of her on the day she traveled. The last shot was of Rachel and Cherie Dei greeting each other in baggage claim, Cherie holding a sign down at her side that said BOB BACKUS on it.

"He's been watching me."

"Like he watched Terry."

Bosch reached to the printer's tray and used a finger from each hand to lift a photo by its edges and without leaving a print. It apparently was the last image Backus had printed here. It showed the front of a two-story house of no particular design. In the driveway was a station wagon. An old man stood next to the driver's door and was looking at a keychain as if searching for the key to unlock the car.

Bosch proffered the photo to Rachel.

"Who is this?"

She looked at it for a long moment.

"I don't know."

"The house?"

"Never seen it before."

Bosch carefully put the photo back in the tray so that it would be found in its original position by the evidence team.

Rachel moved behind him and walked down the hallway toward a closed doorway. Before she reached it she stepped through the open door of a bathroom. It was neat except for the dead flies covering all surfaces. In the bathtub she saw two pillows and a blanket arranged as if for sleeping. She remembered the intelligence gathered on Backus and felt a physical repulsion building in her chest.

She stepped out of the bathroom and went to the closed door at the end of the hallway.

"Is this where you saw it?" she asked.

Bosch turned and watched her approach the door.

"Rachel . . ."

* * *

RACHEL DIDN'T STOP. SHE turned the knob and pulled the door open. I heard a distinct metallic *ching* sound that my mind did not associate with any door lock. Rachel stopped her movement and her posture stiffened.

"Harry?"

I started moving toward her.

"What is it?"

"Harry!"

She turned toward me in the close confines of the wood-paneled hallway. I looked past her face and saw the body on the bed. A man on his back, a black cowboy hat canted down on his head to obscure his face. A pistol in his right hand. A bullet wound to the upper left chest.

Flies were buzzing all around us. I heard a louder, hissing sound and pushed further by her and saw the fuse on the floor. I recognized it as a chemical fuse, a braiding of wires treated with chemicals that would burn anywhere under any condition, even underwater.

The fuse was burning fast. We could not stop it. There were maybe four feet of it coiled on the floor and then it disappeared under the bed. Rachel bent down and reached for it to pull it.

"No, don't! That could set it off. There's nothing— we have to get out of here."

"No! We can't lose this scene! We need—"

"Rachel, no time! Go! Run! Now!"

I pushed her back up the hallway and turned my body to block any attempt by her to return. I started moving backward, my eyes fixed on the figure on the bed. When I thought Rachel had given up I turned and she was waiting. She shoved by me.

"We need DNA!" she yelled.

I watched her move into the room and leap onto the bed. Her hand came up and grabbed the hat off the dead man's head, revealing a face that was distorted and gray with decomposition. She then backed off the bed and headed toward the doorway.

Even in the moment I admired her thinking and what she had just done. The hat brim would most definitely contain skin cells that would hold the body's DNA. She carried the hat past me and started running for the door. I looked down to see the burn point on the fuse line disappear under the bed. I started to run behind her.

"Was it him?" she yelled over her shoulder.

I knew what she meant. Was the cadaver on the bed the man who showed up on Terry McCaleb's boat? Was it Backus?

"I don't know. *Just go! Go! Go!*"

I hit the door two seconds behind Rachel. She was already on the ground heading directly away, in the direction of Titanic Rock. I followed her lead. I had taken maybe five strides when the explosion ripped through the air behind me. I was hit with the full force of the deafening concussion and knocked forward to the ground. I remembered the tuck-and-roll maneuver from basic training and it served to give me a few more yards' distance from the explosion.

Time became disjointed and slow. One moment I was running. The next I was on my hands and knees, my eyes open, trying to raise my head. Something momentarily eclipsed the sun and I managed to look up to see the shell of the trailer thirty feet in the air over me. Its walls and roof intact. It seemed to float and almost hang up there. Then it came crashing down ten yards in front of me, its splintered aluminum sides as sharp as razors. It made a sound like a five-car pile-up when it hit the ground.

I checked the sky for more incoming and saw I was clear. I turned to look back at the trailer's original location and saw intense fire and thick black smoke billowing into the sky. Nothing was recognizable on the trailer pad. Everything had been consumed by the blast and fire. The bed and the man in it were gone. Backus had planned this exit perfectly.

I got to my feet but was unsteady because my eardrums were still reacting and my equilibrium was off. It sounded as though I was walking through a tunnel with trains speeding by me on both sides. I wanted to put my hands over my ears but knew that it would do no good. The noise was reverberating from inside.

Rachel had been only a few feet from me before the blast but now I couldn't see her. I stumbled around in the smoke and started to think that maybe she was under the trailer's skin.

But finally I found her on the ground to the left of the trailer debris. She was lying still in the dirt and rocks. The black hat was on the ground next to her, like a sign of death. I moved as quickly as I could to her.

"Rachel?"

I got down on my hands and knees and first examined her without touching her. She was lying facedown and her hair had fallen forward to further hide her eyes from my view. I was suddenly reminded of my daughter as I used a hand to gently pull the hair back. As I did this I noticed blood on the back of my palm and for the first time realized I was wounded in some minor way. I decided I would worry about that later.

"Rachel?"

I couldn't tell if she was breathing or not. It seemed that my senses were working on the domino theory. With my hearing gone at least temporarily, the coordination of the other senses was gone as well. I patted her cheek lightly.

"Come on, Rachel, wake up."

I didn't want to turn her over in case there were unseen injuries that I might aggravate. I patted her cheek again, this time harder. I put my hand on her back, hoping that I would feel the rise and fall of breath as I could with my daughter.

Nothing. I put my ear to her back but this was laughable considering my condition. It was just instinct moving ahead of logic. I was thinking that I had no choice and had to turn her over when I saw the fingers of her right hand twitch and then form a fist.

Rachel suddenly lifted her head off the ground and groaned. It was loud enough that I could hear it.

"Rachel, are you all right?"

"I—I'm . . . there's evidence in the trailer. We need it."

"Rachel there is no trailer anymore. It's gone."

She struggled to turn over and sit up. Her eyes opened wide at the sight of the burning debris of what had been the trailer. I could see that her pupils were dilated. She had a concussion.

"What did you do?" she asked in an accusatory tone.

"It wasn't me. The place was rigged to go up. When you opened the bedroom door . . ."

"Oh."

She turned her head back and forth as if working a kink out of her neck. She saw the black cowboy hat on the ground next to her.

"What is this?"

"His hat. You grabbed it on the way out."

"DNA?"

"Hopefully, though I'm not sure what good it will be."

She looked back at the flaming trailer bed. We were too close. I could feel the heat of the fire. But I still wasn't sure she should be moving.

"Rachel, why don't you lie back down? I think you have a concussion. You might have other injuries."

"Yeah, I think that's a good idea."

She put her head down on the ground and just looked up at the sky. I decided that wasn't a bad position and did the same. It was like we were at the beach or something. If it had been night we could have counted the stars.

BEFORE I COULD HEAR them coming, I felt the approach of the helicopters. A deep vibration in my chest made me look to the southern sky and I saw the two air force choppers coming over the top of Titanic Rock. I weakly raised an arm and waved them in.

34

"WHAT THE HELL HAPPENED out there?"

Special Agent Randal Alpert's face was rigid and almost purple. He had been waiting for them in the hangar at Nellis when the helicopter landed. His political instincts had apparently told him not to go to the scene himself. At all costs he had to be able to distance himself from the blowback that would rise from the explosion in the desert and possibly reach all the way to Washington.

Rachel Walling and Cherie Dei stood in the huge hangar and braced for the onslaught. Rachel didn't answer his question because she thought it was only the opener on a tirade. She was reacting slowly, her head still a bit fuzzy from the blast.

"Agent Walling, I asked you a question!"

"He had rigged the trailer," Cherie Dei said. "He knew she—"

"I asked her, not you," Alpert barked. "I want Agent Walling to tell me exactly why she could not follow orders and how this whole thing has gotten completely fucked up beyond recognition."

Rachel raised her hands palms out as if to signify there was not a damn thing she could have done about what happened out there in the desert.

"We were going to wait for the ERT," she said. "As Agent Dei instructed. We were on the periphery of the location and that's when we realized it smelled like there was a body in there and then we thought maybe there could be someone alive in there. Somebody hurt."

"And how the hell did you get that idea simply because you smelled a dead body?"

"Bosch thought he heard something."

"Oh, here we go, the old cry for help routine."

"No, he did. But it was the wind, I guess. Out there it picks up. The windows were left open. It must have created a sound that he heard."

"And what about you? Did you hear it?"

"No. I didn't."

Alpert looked at Dei and then back at Rachel. She could feel his eyes burning through her. But she knew it was a good story and she wasn't going to blink. She and Bosch had worked it out. Bosch was beyond Alpert's reach. If she was acting on Bosch's alarm she could not be faulted either. Alpert could rant and rave but could do nothing more than that.

"You know what the problem with your story is? It's with your first word. We. You said *we*. There was no we. You were given an assignment of maintaining a cover on Bosch. *Not* joining him in the investigation. Not joining him in his car and driving up there. Not questioning witnesses together and entering that trailer *together*."

"I understand that, but given the circumstances I decided it was in the best interest of the investigation to pool our knowledge and resources. Quite frankly, Agent Alpert, Bosch was the one who found that place. We wouldn't have what we have right now if not for him."

"Don't kid yourself, Agent Walling. We would have gotten there."

"I know that. But velocity was a factor. You said so yourself after the morning briefing. The director was going before the cameras. I wanted to push the case so that he would have as much information as possible."

"Well, forget about that now. Now we don't know what we have. He postponed the news conference and has given us until noon tomorrow to figure out what we have out there."

Cherie Dei cleared her voice and risked intruding again.

"That's impossible," she said. "That's a well-done crispy critter out there. They're using multiple bags to get it out of there. ID and cause of death are going to take weeks, if an ID and cause of death are even possible. Luckily, it appears that Agent Walling was able to obtain a DNA sampling from the body and that would speed things but we have no comparative evidence. We—"

"Maybe you weren't listening ten seconds ago," Alpert said, "but we don't have weeks. We've got less than twenty-four hours."

He turned away from them and put his hands on his hips, striking a pose that showed the burden that weighed upon him as the only intelligent and savvy agent left on the planet.

"Then let us go back up there," Rachel said. "Maybe in the debris we'll find something that—"

"No!" Alpert yelled.

He spun back around to them.

"That won't be necessary, Agent Walling. You have done enough."

"I know Backus and I know the case. I should be out there."

"I decide who should be and shouldn't be out there. I want you to get back to the field office and start the paperwork on this fiasco. I want it on my desk by eight a.m. tomorrow. I want a detailed listing of everything you saw inside that trailer."

He waited to see if she would argue the order. Rachel remained silent and this seemed to please him.

"Now, I've got the media all over this. What do we put out that doesn't give away the store and won't upstage the director tomorrow?"

Dei shrugged.

"Nothing. Tell them the director will address it tomorrow, end of story."

"That won't work. We have to give them something."

"Don't give them Backus," Rachel said. "Tell them agents wanted to speak to a man named Thomas Walling about a missing persons case. But Walling had rigged his trailer and it exploded while agents were on the premises."

Alpert nodded. It sounded good to him.

"What about Bosch?"

"I'd leave him out of it. We don't have any control over him. If a reporter got to him he might lay the whole thing out."

"And the body. Do we say it was Walling?"

"We say we don't know because we don't. ID is forthcoming, so on and so forth. That should be enough."

"If the reporters go to the brothels they'll get the whole story."

"No, they won't. We never told anyone the whole story."

"By the way, what happened to Bosch?"

Dei answered that one.

"I took his statement and released him. Last I saw he was driving back to Vegas."

"He'll keep quiet about this?"

Dei looked at Rachel and then back at Alpert.

"Put it this way, he isn't going to be looking to talk to anybody about it. And as long as we keep his name out of it, there will be no reason for anyone to go looking for him."

Alpert nodded. He dug a hand into one of his pockets and came out with a cell phone.

"When we are finished here I have to call Washington. Gut reaction time: Was that Backus in that trailer?"

Rachel hesitated, not wanting to respond first.

"At this point there is no way to tell," Dei said. "If you are asking if you should tell the director that we got him, my answer right now is no, don't tell the director that. That could've been anybody in that trailer. For all we know it was an eleventh victim and we may never know who it was. Just somebody who went to one of the brothels and was intercepted by Backus."

Alpert looked at Rachel, expecting her take.

"The fuse," she said.

"What about it?"

"It was long. It was like he wanted me to see the body but not get too close. But he also wanted me to get out of there."

"And?"

"On the body there was a black cowboy hat. I remember there was a man on my plane from Rapid City in a black cowboy hat."

"For chrissake, you were flying from South Dakota. Doesn't everybody wear cowboy hats there?"

"But he was there, with me. I think this whole thing was a setup. The note in the bar, the long fuse, the photos in the trailer and the black hat. He wanted me to get out of there in time to tell the world he was dead."

Alpert didn't respond. He looked down at the phone in his hands.

"There's too much we don't know yet, Randal," Dei offered.

He shoved the phone back into his pocket.

"Very well. Agent Dei, is your car here?"

"Yes."

"Take Agent Walling to the field office now."

They were dismissed, but not before Alpert looked at Rachel and threw one more grimace at her.

"Remember, Agent Walling, my desk by eight."

"You got it," Rachel said.

35

E LEANOR WISH ANSWERED MY knock and that surprised me. She stepped back to let me in.

"Don't look at me that way, Harry," she said. "You have this impression that I'm never here and that I work every night and leave her with Marisol. I don't. I work three or four nights a week and that's usually it."

I raised my hands in surrender and she saw the bandage around my right palm.

"What happened to you?"

"Cut myself on a piece of metal."

"What metal?"

"It's a long story."

"That thing up in the desert today?"

I nodded.

"I should have known. Is that going to hurt you playing the saxophone?"

Bored with retirement, I had started taking lessons the year before from a retired jazzman I had come across on a case. One night, when things were good between Eleanor and me, I had brought the instrument with me and played her a tune called "Lullaby." She had liked it.

"Actually, I haven't been playing anyway."

"How come?"

I didn't want to tell her that my teacher had died and music had dropped out of my life for a while.

"My teacher wanted me to switch from alto to tenor—as in *ten or* fifteen miles away from him."

She smiled at the lame joke and we left it at that. I had followed her through the house and into the kitchen, where the table was actually a felt-covered poker table—with cereal milk stains on it thanks to Maddie. Eleanor had dealt six hands faceup for practice. She sat down and started gathering up the cards.

"Don't let me stop you," I said. "I just came by to see if I could put Maddie to bed. Where is she?"

"Marisol's giving her a bath. But I was counting on putting her to bed tonight. I've worked the last three nights."

"Oh, well, that's fine. I'll just say hello then. And good-bye. I'm driving back tonight."

"Then why don't you do it? I got a new book to read her. It's on the counter."

"No, Eleanor, I want you to do it. I just want to see her because I don't know when I'll get back."

"Are you still working a case?"

"No, that all sort of ended up there today."

"The TV news didn't have much on it when I watched. What is it?"

"It's a long story."

I didn't feel like telling it once again. I walked over to

the counter to look at the book she had bought. It was called *Billy's Big Day* and its cover showed a monkey standing on the highest step at an Olympics-style award ceremony. The gold medal was being put around his neck. A lion had received the silver and an elephant the bronze.

"Are you going back to join the department again?"

I was about to open the book but I put it down and looked at Eleanor.

"I'm still thinking about it but it's looking that way."

She nodded as though it was a done deal.

"Any further thoughts from you on it?"

"No, Harry, I want you to do what you want."

I wondered why it was that when people tell you what you want them to tell you, it always comes with suspicion and second-guessing attached. Did Eleanor really want me to do what I wanted to do? Or was her saying that a way of undermining the whole thing?

Before I could say anything my daughter came into the kitchen and stood at attention. She wore blue-and-orange-striped pajamas and her dark hair was wet and slicked back on her head.

"Presenting a little girl," she said.

Eleanor and I both broke out the smiles and simultaneously offered our opened arms for hugs. Maddie went to her mother first and that was all right with me. But it felt a little like when you hold out your hand to someone to shake and they don't see it or just plain ignore it. I lowered my arms and after a few moments Eleanor saved me.

"Go give Daddy a hug."

Maddie came to me and I lifted her up into a hug. She

was no more than forty pounds. It is an amazing thing to be able to hold everything that is important to you in one arm. She put her damp head against my chest and I didn't mind that she was getting my shirt wet. That was no problem at all.

"How are you, baby?"

"I'm fine. I drew your picture today."

"You did? Can I see it?"

"Put me down."

I did as instructed and she ran off, out of the kitchen, her bare feet slapping on the stone tiles as she headed to the playroom. I looked at Eleanor and smiled. We both knew the secret. No matter what we had or didn't have for each other, we would always have Madeline and that might be enough.

The running of tiny feet could be heard again and soon she was back in the kitchen, towing a piece of paper held high like a kite. I took it from her and studied it. It showed the figure of a man with a mustache and dark eyes. He had his hands out and in one hand was a gun. On the other side of the page was another figure. This one was drawn in reds and oranges and had eyebrows drawn in a severe black V to indicate he was a bad guy.

I crouched down to my daughter's height to look at the drawing with her.

"Is this me with the gun?"

"Yes, because you were a policeman."

I nodded. She had said it like *pleaseman.*

"And who is this mean guy?"

She pointed a tiny finger at the other figure on the drawing.

"That is Mr. Demon."

I smiled.

"Who is Mr. Demon?"

"He's a wrestler. Mommy says you wrestle with demons and he's the boss of all of them."

"I see."

I looked over her head at Eleanor and smiled. I wasn't mad about anything. I was simply in love with my daughter and how she viewed her world. The literal way in which she took it all in and took it on. I knew it wouldn't last long and so I treasured every moment I saw and heard of it.

"Can I keep this picture?"

"How come?"

"Because it is beautiful and I want to always have it. I have to go away for a while and I want to be able to look at it all the time. It will remind me of you."

"Where are you going?"

"I'm going back to the place they call the City of Angels."

She smiled.

"That's silly. You can't see angels."

"I know. But look, Mommy has a new book to read to you about a monkey named Billy. So I'm going to say good night now and I'll get back to see you as soon as I can. Is that okay, baby?"

"Okay, Daddy."

I kissed her on both cheeks and hugged her tight. Then I kissed the top of her head and let her go. I stood up with my picture and handed her the book Eleanor would read to her.

"Marisol?" Eleanor called.

Marisol appeared within a few seconds, as if she had been waiting in the nearby living room for her cue. I smiled and nodded to her as she received her instructions.

"Why don't you take Maddie in and get her set up and I'll be right in after saying good night to her father."

I watched my daughter leave with her nanny.

"I'm sorry about that," Eleanor said.

"What, the picture? Don't worry about it. I love it. It's going on my refrigerator."

"I just don't know where she picked it up. I didn't directly say to her that you fight demons. She must have overheard me on the phone or something."

Somehow I would have liked it better knowing she had said it directly to our daughter. The idea that Eleanor was talking about me in such a way to someone else—someone she didn't mention at the moment— bothered me. I tried not to show it.

"It's all right," I said. "Look at it this way, when she goes to school and kids say their dad is a lawyer or a fireman or a doctor or something, she's got the trump card. She'll tell them her daddy fights demons."

Eleanor laughed but then cut it off when she thought of something.

"I wonder what she'll say her mother does."

I couldn't answer that, so I changed the subject.

"I love how her view of the world is uncluttered by deeper meanings," I said as I looked at the picture again. "It is so innocent, you know?"

"I know. I love that, too. But I can understand if you don't want her thinking you're out there literally wrestling with demons. Why didn't you explain it to her?"

I shook my head and thought of a story.

"When I was a kid and I was still with my mother, there was this time that she had a car. A two-tone Plymouth Belvedere with push-button automatic transmission. I think her lawyer gave it to her to use or something. For a couple years. Anyway, she suddenly decided she wanted to go cross-country on a vacation. So we packed the car and just took off, her and me.

"Anyway, somewhere in the south—I don't remember where—we stopped for gas and there were two water fountains on the side of this service station. There were signs, you know. One said WHITE and the other said COLORED. And I just sort of went up to the one marked COLORED because I wanted to see what color the water was. Before I got to it my mom yanked me back and sort of explained things to me.

"I remember that and sort of wish she'd just let me see the water and didn't explain anything."

Eleanor smiled at the story.

"How old were you?"

"I don't know. About eight."

She stood up then and came over to me. She kissed me on the cheek and I let her. I put my arm loosely around her waist.

"Good luck with your demons, Harry."

"Yeah."

"If you ever change your mind about things, I'm here. We're here."

I nodded.

"She's going to change *your* mind, Eleanor. You wait and see."

She smiled but in a sad way and gently caressed my chin with her hand.

"Will you make sure the door is locked when you leave?"

"Always."

I let go of her and watched her walk out of the kitchen. I then looked down at the drawing of the man fighting his demon. In the picture my daughter had put a smile on my face.

36

BEFORE GOING UP TO my efficiency at the Double X, I stopped by the office and told Mr. Gupta, the night man, that I would be checking out. He told me that because I had been keeping the place on a weekly basis, my credit card had already been dinged for the entire week and I told him that was fine, I was still leaving. I told him I would leave the key on the dinette table after I gathered up my belongings. I was about to leave the office when I hesitated and then asked him about my neighbor Jane.

"Yes, she is gone, too. Same thing."

"What do you mean, same thing?"

"We charge her for a week but she not stay a week."

"Hey, do you mind me asking, what was her full name? I never got it."

"She is Jane Davis. You like?"

"Yeah, she was nice. We talked on the balconies. I didn't get to say good-bye. She didn't leave a forwarding address or anything like that, did she?"

Gupta smiled at the prospect of this. He had very pink gums for someone with such dark skin.

"No address," he said. "Not that one."

I nodded my thanks for the information he had given me. I left the office and went up the stairs and then down the walkway to my room.

It took me less than five minutes to gather my things. I had some shirts and pants on hangers. I then took out of the closet the same box in which I had brought everything and filled it with the rest of my belongings and a couple of toys I kept in the place for Maddie. Buddy Lockridge had been close, calling me Suitcase Harry. But Beer Box Harry would have been better.

Before leaving I checked the refrigerator and saw I had one bottle of beer left. I took it out and cranked it open. I figured one beer for the road wouldn't hurt me. I had done worse in the past before a drive. I thought about making another cheese sandwich but skipped it when the thought reminded me of Backus's routine of eating grilled cheese sandwiches each day at Quantico. I went out onto the balcony with the beer for one last look at the rich men's jets. It was a cool and crisp evening. The blue lights on the far runway twinkled like sapphires.

The two black jets were gone, their owners either quick winners or losers. The big Gulfstream remained in place, red dust caps over the intakes on its jet engines. It was settled in. I wondered what the jets might have had to do with Jane Davis and her stay at the Double X.

I looked over at Jane's empty balcony, just four feet from my own. The ashtray was sitting on the railing and I could see it was still filled with half-smoked butts. Her unit had not been cleaned yet.

And that gave me an idea. I looked around and down at the parking lot. I saw no human movement except for out on Koval, where the traffic was stalled at a traffic light. I saw no sign of the night security man or anyone else in the parking lot. I quickly hoisted myself up onto the railing and was about to climb across to the next balcony when I heard a knock on my door. I quickly dropped back down and went in and answered the door.

It was Rachel Walling.

"Rachel? Hello. Is something wrong?"

"No, nothing that catching Backus couldn't cure. Can I come in?"

"Sure."

I stepped back to let her enter. She saw the box with my belongings piled into it. I spoke first.

"How did it go today when you got back into town?"

"Well, I got the usual tongue-lashing from the SAC."

"Did you lay it all on me?"

"As planned. He fumed and fussed but what's he going to do? I don't want to talk about him right now."

"Then what?"

"Well, for starters, do you have another one of those?"

She meant the beer.

"Actually, no. I was just finishing this one and was going to take off."

"Then I'm glad I caught you."

"You want to split it? I'll get you a glass."

"You said you wouldn't trust the glasses here."

"Well, I could wash—"

She reached over for the bottle and took a sip from it. She handed it back, her eyes staying on mine. She then turned and pointed to the box.

"So you're leaving."

"Yeah, back to L.A. for a while."

"You'll miss your daughter, I guess."

"A lot."

"You'll come back to see her?"

"As often as I can."

"That's nice. Anything else?"

"What do you mean?" I asked, though I thought I knew what she meant.

"Will you be coming back for anything else?"

"No, just my daughter."

We stood there looking at each other for a long moment. I held the beer out to her but when she came forward it was for me. She kissed me on the lips and then quickly we put our arms around each other.

I know it had something to do with the trailer, our nearly dying together out there in the desert, that made us press so hard against each other and move toward the bed, that made me reach over and put the beer bottle on the table so I could use both my hands as we pulled at each other's clothes.

We fell onto the bed and made survivors' love. It was quick and maybe to some degree even brutal—on both our parts. But most of all it satisfied the primal urge in both of us to fight death with life.

When it was over we were entwined on top of the bed covers, she on top of me, my fists still tangled in her hair.

She leaned to her left and reached for the beer bottle, knocking it over first and spilling most of what was left on the bed table and floor.

"There goes my security deposit," I said.

There was enough left in the bottle for her to take a draw and then pass it to me.

"That was for today," she said as I drank.

I gave her the rest.

"What do you mean?"

"After what happened out there, we had to do this."

"Yeah."

"Gladiator love. That's why I came here. To catch you."

I smiled, thinking of a gladiator joke from an old movie I liked. But I didn't tell her and she probably thought I was smiling at her words. She leaned down and put her head on my chest. I held up some of her hair, more gently this time, to look at the singed ends. I then moved my hands down and rubbed her back, thinking it was strange that we were being so gentle with each other now, just moments after being gladiators.

"I don't suppose you'd be interested in opening a branch of your private investigations office in South Dakota, would you?"

I smiled and stifled a laugh in my chest.

"How about North Dakota?" she asked. "I could be going back there, too."

"You have to have a tree to have a branch."

She hit me with a gentle fist on the chest.

"I didn't think so."

I shifted my body so that I came out of her. She groaned but stayed on top of me.

"Does that mean you want me to get up and get off and get out of here?"

"No, Rachel. Not at all."

I looked over her shoulder and saw that the door was unlocked. I had a vision of Mr. Gupta coming up to see if I had left yet and finding the two-backed monster on the bed in the supposedly empty unit. I smiled. I didn't care.

She raised her face up to look at me.

"What?"

"Nothing. We left the door unlocked. Somebody could come in."

"*You* left it unlocked. This is your place."

I kissed her, realizing I had not kissed her lips during the entire time we had made love. Another strange thing.

"You know what, Bosch?"

"What?"

"You're good at this."

I smiled and told her thanks. A woman can play that card anytime and every time and always get the same response.

"I mean it."

She dug her nails into my chest to underline her point. With one arm I held her tightly to me and we rolled over. I figured I had at least ten years on her but I wasn't worried about it. I kissed her again and got up, gathering my clothes off the floor and walking over to the door to lock it.

"I think there's one last clean towel in there," I said. "You can use it."

She insisted I take the first shower and I did. Then while she showered I left the unit and walked across Koval to a convenience store to pick up two more beers. I was going to limit it to that because I was driving that night and didn't want alcohol to slow me down getting to the road or while on it. I was sitting at the dinette when she came out of the bathroom fully dressed and smiling when she saw the two bottles.

"I knew you'd make yourself useful."

She sat down and we clicked bottles.

"To gladiator love," she said.

We drank and just were quiet for a few moments. I was trying to figure out what the last hour now meant to me and to us.

"What are you thinking about?" she asked.

"About how this could get complicated."

"It doesn't have to. We can just see what happens."

That didn't sound the same to me as being asked to move to the Dakotas.

"Okay."

"I better get going."

"Where to?"

"Back to the FO, I guess. See what's shaking."

"Did you hear what happened to the fire barrel out there after the blast? I forgot to look."

"No, why?"

"I looked in it when we were out there. For just a minute. It looked like he had been burning credit cards, maybe IDs."

"The victims'?"

"Probably. He burned books in it, too."

"Books? Why do you think he did that?"

"I don't know but it's strange. Inside the trailer he had books all over the place. So he burned some and some he didn't burn. Seems strange."

"Well, if there is anything left of the barrel the ERT will get to it. Why didn't you mention it before, when you were interviewed out there?"

"Because my head was ringing and I sort of forgot, I guess."

"Short-term memory loss associated with concussion."

"I don't have a concussion."

"I meant the blast. Could you tell what books they were?"

"Not really. I didn't have time. There was one I picked out. It was the least burned of what I could see. It looked like it was poetry. I think."

She looked at me and nodded but didn't say anything.

"What I don't get is why he burned the books. He set the whole trailer to go up but he takes the time to go out to the barrel and burn some books. Almost like . . ."

I stopped talking and tried to put the pieces together.

"Almost like what, Harry?"

"I don't know. Like he didn't want to leave the trailer thing to chance. He wanted to make sure those books were destroyed."

"You are assuming that both things are together. Who knows, maybe he burned the books six months ago or something. You can't just connect the two things."

I nodded. She was right about that but still the incongruity bothered me.

"The book I found was near the top of the barrel," I said. "It was burned the last time the barrel was used. There was also a receipt in it. Half burned. But maybe they can trace it."

"When I get back I'll check it out. But I don't remember seeing that barrel after the blast."

I shrugged.

"Neither do I."

She stood up and so did I.

"There's one other thing," I said as I reached into the inside pocket of my jacket. I pulled out the photo and handed it to her.

"I must've grabbed it while I was in the trailer and then sort of forgot about it. I found it in my pocket."

It was the photo taken from the printer tray. The two-story house with the old man out front next to the station wagon.

"Great, Harry. How am I going to explain this?"

"I don't know but I figured you'd want to try to ID the place or the old man."

"What's the difference now?"

"Come on, Rachel, you know it's not over."

"No, I don't know that."

It bothered me that she could not talk to me after we had been so intimate just a few minutes before.

"Okay."

I picked up my box and the clothing I had on hangers.

"Wait a minute, Harry. You're just going to leave it like that? What do you mean it's not over?"

"I mean we both know that wasn't Backus in there. If you and the bureau aren't interested in it, that's fine. But don't bullshit me, Rachel. Not after what we went through today, and not after what we just did."

She relented.

"Look, Harry, it's out of my hands, okay? Right now we are waiting on forensics to make a call on it. The bureau's official position probably won't be formulated until tomorrow when the director holds a press conference."

"I'm not interested in the official position of the bureau. I was talking to you."

"Harry, what do you want me to say?"

"I want you to say you are going to get this guy, no matter what the director says tomorrow."

I headed to the door and she followed. We left the efficiency and she pulled the door closed for me.

"Where's your car?" I asked. "I'll walk you over."

She pointed the way and we went down the steps and to her car, parked near the office. After she opened the door we turned and faced each other.

"I want to get this guy," she said. "More than you could know."

"Okay, good. I'll be in touch."

"Well, what are you going to do?"

"I don't know. When I do, I'll let you know."

"Okay. See you, Bosch."

"Good-bye, Rachel."

She kissed me and then she got in the car. I walked to my car, ducking between the two buildings that made up the Double X to get to the other parking lot. I was pretty sure it was not the last time I would see Rachel Walling.

37

ON THE WAY OUT of town I could have avoided the traffic of the strip but I decided not to. I thought all the lights might cheer me up. I knew I was leaving my daughter behind. I was going to Los Angeles to rejoin the department. I would see my daughter again but I wouldn't be able to spend the kind of time with her I needed and wanted to. I was leaving to join the depressing legions of weekend fathers, the men who have to compress their love and duty into twenty-four-hour stands with their children. The thought of it raised a dark dread in my chest that a billion kilowatts of light could not cut through. There was no doubt I was leaving Las Vegas as a loser.

Once I cleared the lights and the city limits the traffic grew sparse and the skies dark. I tried to ignore the depression my choice had put upon me. Instead, I worked the case as I drove, following the logic of the moves from the perspective of Backus, grinding it down until the story was smooth powder and I had only unanswered questions left. I saw it the same way the bureau did. Backus, having adopted the name Tom Walling, was living in Clear and preying on the customers he drove from the brothels. He operated with impunity for years because he chose the perfect victims. That is until the numbers went against him and investigators from Vegas started to see a pattern and put together their list of six missing men. Backus probably knew that it was only a matter of time before the connection might be made to Clear. He probably knew that that time would be even shorter once he saw Terry McCaleb's name in the newspaper. Maybe he even got wind that McCaleb had gone to Vegas. Maybe McCaleb had even gone up to Clear. Who knows? Most of the answers died with McCaleb and then in that trailer in the desert.

There were so many unknowns in this story. But what did seem obvious from this point was that Backus had closed up shop. He made plans to end his desert run in a blaze of glory—to take out his two protégés, McCaleb and Rachel, in a pathological display of mastery, and to leave behind in his trailer a burned and destroyed body that would beg the question of whether he was alive or dead. In recent years Saddam Hussein and Osama bin Laden had gotten good mileage by leaving behind the same question. Maybe Backus saw himself on the same stage.

The books in the fire barrel bothered me the most. Despite Rachel's dismissing them because the circumstances of their burning were unknown, it still seemed like an important piece of the investigation to me. I wished I had spent more time studying the book I had pulled out, maybe even identifying it. The burned book gave an indication of a part of the Poet's plan nobody knew about yet.

Remembering the partial receipt I had seen in the book, I opened my cell phone, checked to make sure I had service and called information for Las Vegas. I asked if there was a listing for a business called Book Car and the operator told me there was not. I was about to hang up when she told me there was, however, a listing for a store called Book Caravan on Industry Road. I told her I would try it and she connected me.

I guessed that the store would be closed because it was late. I was hoping for a message machine on which I could ask the owner to call me in the morning. But the call was answered after two rings by a gruff voice.

"You're open?"

"Twenty-four hours. How can I help you?"

I got an idea what kind of store it was by the hours. I took a shot anyway.

"You don't sell any books of poetry there, do you?"

The gruff man laughed.

"Very funny," he said. "There once was a man from Timbuktu. As far as poetry goes, fuck you."

He laughed again and hung up on me. I closed the phone and had to smile at his on-the-spot rhyming skill.

Book Caravan seemed like a dead end but I would call Rachel in the morning and tell her it might be worth checking for connections to Backus.

A green highway sign came out of the darkness and into the spray of my headlights.

ZZYZX ROAD
I MILE

I thought about pulling off and driving down the bouncing desert road into the darkness. I wondered if there was still a forensic crew on duty at the burial site. But what would the point of going down that road be other than to engage with the ghosts of the dead? The mile came and went and I drove on by the exit, leaving the ghosts alone.

The beer and a half I'd had with Rachel proved to be a mistake. By Victorville I was growing fatigued. Too much thinking with the added mix of alcohol. I pulled off for coffee in a McDonald's that was open late and designed to look like a train depot. I bought two coffees and two sugar cookies and sat in a booth in an old train car reading through Terry McCaleb's file on the Poet investigation. I was getting to know the order of reports and their summaries just about by heart.

After one cup of coffee I had nothing going and closed the file. I needed something new. I needed to either let it go and hope and believe the bureau would get the job done or find a new angle to pursue.

I'm not against the bureau. My take is that it's the most thorough, well-equipped and relentless law enforcement agency in the world. Its problems lie in its size and the many cracks in communication between offices, squads and so on down the line to the agents themselves. It only takes a debacle like 9/11 to make clear to the world what most people in the law enforcement world, including the FBI agents, already know.

As an institution it cares too much about its reputation and it carries too much weight in politics, going all the way back to J. Edgar Hoover himself. Eleanor Wish once knew an agent who had been assigned to Washington headquarters back during the time J. Edgar ruled the place. He said the unspoken law was that if an agent was in an elevator and the director got on, the agent was not allowed to address him, even to say hello, and was required to immediately step off so the big man could ride alone and ponder his great responsibilities. That story always stuck with me for some reason. I think because it carries the perfect arrogance of the FBI.

The bottom line was I didn't want to call Graciela McCaleb and tell her that her husband's killer was still out there and that the FBI would handle it. I still wanted to handle it. I owed that to her and to Terry and I always paid what I owed.

Back on the road the coffee and sugar got me going again and I pressed on toward the City of Angels. When I hit the 10 freeway I also hit the rain and traffic slowed to a crawl. I flipped on the radio to KFWB and learned it had rained all day and wasn't expected to stop until the end of the week. There was a live report from Topanga Canyon where residents were sandbagging their doors and garages, expecting the worst. Mud slides and flooding were the dangers. The catastrophic fires that swept through the hills the year before had left little ground cover to hold the rain or soil. It was all coming down.

I knew the weather would cost me an extra hour getting home. I checked my watch. It was just past midnight. I had planned to wait until getting home to call Kiz Rider but decided it might be too late to call by then.

I opened my phone and called her at home. She picked up right away.

"Kiz, it's Harry. You up?"

"Sure, Harry. I can't sleep when it rains."

"I know what you mean."

"So what's the good word?"

"Everybody counts or nobody counts."

"Which means?"

"I'm in if you're in."

"Come on, Harry, don't put that on me."

"I'm in if you're in."

"Come on, man, I'm already in."

"You know what I mean. This is your salvation, Kiz. We got sidetracked. We both did. You and I know what we should be doing. It's time we both went back to it."

I waited. There was a long period of silence from her, then finally she spoke.

"This is going to upset the man. He's got me on a lot of things."

"If he's the man you say he is he'll understand. He'll get it. You'll be able to make him get it."

More silence.

"Okay, Harry, okay. I'm in."

"All right then, I'll come down tomorrow and sign up."

"All right, Harry. I'll see you then."

"You knew I'd call, didn't you?"

"Put it this way, I have the papers you have to fill out sitting on my desk."

"You were always too smart for me."

"I meant what I said about us needing you. That's the bottom line. But I also didn't think you'd last long out there on your own. I know guys who have pulled the pin and gone the PI route, sold real estate, cars, appliances, even books. It worked fine for most of them, but not you, Harry. I figured you knew that, too."

I didn't say anything. I was staring into the darkness beyond the reach of my lights. Something Kiz had just said triggered the avalanche.

"Harry, you still there?"

"Yeah, listen, Kiz, you just said *books*. You knew a guy who retired and sold books. Is that Ed Thomas?"

"Yeah, I came to Hollywood about six months before he put in his papers. He left and opened a bookstore down in Orange."

"I know. You ever been there?"

"Yeah, one time he had Dean Koontz signing one of his books there. I saw it in the paper. He's my favorite and he doesn't sign books too many places. So I went down. There was a line out the door and down the sidewalk but as soon as Ed saw me he ushered me right on up to the front and he introduced me and I got my book signed. It was embarrassing, actually."

"What's the name of it?"

"Um . . . I think it was *Strange Highways*."

That deflated me. I thought I was about to make a leap in logic and a connection.

"No, actually, it was after that," Kiz said. "It was *Sole Survivor*—the plane crash story."

I realized what she was saying and how we'd gotten confused.

"No, Kiz, what's the name of Ed's bookstore?"

"Oh, it's called Book Carnival. I think that was what it was called when he bought the business. Otherwise I think he'd have called it something else, something mysterious, since he sells mostly mystery books there."

Book Car as in Book Carnival. I involuntarily pressed the accelerator down harder.

"Kiz, I gotta go. I'll talk to you later."

I closed the phone without waiting for a good-bye from her. Glancing between the road and the phone's display I scrolled through my recent calls list and pressed the connect button after highlighting Rachel Walling's cell number. She answered before I even heard it ring.

"Rachel, it's Harry. Sorry to call so late but it's important."

"I'm in the middle of something," she whispered.

"You're at the field office still?"

"That's right."

I tried to think of what would keep her there after midnight on a day that had started so early.

"Is it the trash barrel? The burned book?"

"No, we haven't gotten there yet. It's something else. I have to go."

Her voice was somber and because she had not used my name I got the idea there were other agents present and that whatever she was in the middle of was not good.

"Rachel, listen, I have something. You have to come to L.A."

Her tone changed. I think she could tell by the urgency in my voice that this was serious.

"What is it?"

"I know the Poet's next move."

38

I'LL HAVE TO CALL you back."

Rachel closed her phone and slid it into the pocket of her blazer. Bosch's last words echoed in her heart.

"Agent Walling, I'd appreciate it if you could stay in our conversation."

She looked up at Alpert.

"Sorry."

She looked past him at the telecommunication screen where Brass Doran's face was larger than life. She was smiling.

"Agent Doran, continue," Alpert said.

"Actually, I'm finished. That's all we have at this time. We can confirm through the latents that Robert Backus was at that trailer. We cannot confirm that he was in it when it exploded."

"What about the DNA?"

"The DNA evidence gathered by Agent Walling, at great danger, I might add, and later by the ERT will only be useful if we have something to compare it with. That is, if we somehow find a source of Robert Backus's DNA. Or we use it to identify the body that was in the trailer as someone else."

"What about Backus's parents? Can't we extract his DNA from—"

"We went that route before. His father was dead and cremated before we thought of it—the science wasn't really there back then—and his mother has never been located. There is some thought that she might have been his first victim. She disappeared some years ago without the proverbial trace."

"This guy thought of everything."

"In the case of the mother it was more likely a revenge thing for her abandonment. It is hard to believe that he did something back then in order to prevent later DNA extraction."

"All I meant was that we are genuinely fucked."

"I am sorry, Randal, but the science can only go so far."

"I know that, Agent Doran. Can you tell me anything else? Anything new?"

"I guess not."

"Terrific. Okay, so then I will tell the director just that. That we know Backus was in that trailer—we have forensics and witness accounts to that effect. But as of this time we cannot take the next step and say he is dead and good riddance."

"Is there no way we can convince the director to sit tight and give us more time to sew it all up? For the good of the investigation."

Rachel almost laughed. She knew the good of the investigation would always take second place to political considerations in the Hoover Building in D.C.

"I have already tried," Alpert said. "The answer is no. There is too much at stake. The cat is out of the bag on this—thanks to the explosion in the desert. If that was Backus blown to bits out there, then fine, we'll eventually confirm it and everything will be fine. If that was not Backus and he has some other play in mind, the director has to get on record with this now or the consequences of the blowback could be fatal. So he is going on record with what we know now: Backus was there, Backus is the suspect in the killings in the desert, Backus may or may not be dead. There is no dissuading him at this point."

Alpert had thrown Rachel a look when he said the cat was out of the bag, as if he held her responsible for everything. She thought about revealing what Bosch had just told her but in that instant decided against it. Not yet. Not until she knew more.

"Okay, people, that's it," Alpert announced abruptly. "Brass, we'll see you on the big screen tomorrow morning. Agent Walling, can you stay behind for a moment?"

Rachel watched Brass leave the screen and then it went black, the transmission ended. Alpert then walked up close to the table where Rachel sat.

"Agent Walling?"

"Yes?"

"Your work is done here."

"Excuse me?"

"You're finished. Go back to your hotel and pack your bags."

"There's still a lot to do here. I want to—"

"I don't care what you want. I want you out of here. You have undermined this investigation since you arrived. Tomorrow morning I want you on the first plane back to wherever it is you come from. Understand?"

"You are making a mistake. I should be a part of—"

"You are making a mistake arguing with me about it. I can't make it any clearer for you. I want you out of here. Turn in your paperwork and get on a plane."

She stared at him, trying to communicate all the anger that was behind her eyes. He held a hand up as if to ward something off.

"Be careful what you say. It could come back to bite you on the ass."

Rachel swallowed back her anger. She spoke in a controlled and calm voice.

"I'm not going anywhere."

Alpert looked like his eyes might pop out of his head. He turned and waved Dei out of the room. He then turned back to Rachel and waited for the sound of the door closing.

"Excuse me? What did you just say?"

"I said I am not going anywhere. I am staying on this case. Because if you put me on a plane, I won't go back to South Dakota. I'll go to D.C. headquarters and right into the Office of Professional Responsibility to file on you."

"For what? What are you going to file?"

"You've used me as bait since the beginning. Without my knowledge or consent."

"You don't know what you are talking about. Go ahead. Go to the OPR. They'll laugh you back to the Badlands and put you down for another ten years out there."

"Cherie made a mistake and then you did, too. When

I called in from Clear she asked me why we took Bosch's car. Then in the hangar you did the same thing. You knew I had gone up there in Bosch's car. I started thinking about that and then I figured out why. You put a GPS tag on my car. I went underneath it tonight and found it. Standard bureau issue, even has the code label still on it. There will be a record of who checked it out."

"I have no idea what you are talking about."

"Well, I'm sure the OPR will be able to figure it out. My guess is Cherie will help them. I mean if I were her I wouldn't tie my career to you. I'd tell the truth. That you brought me out here as bait, that you thought I would draw Backus out. I bet you had a shadow team on me the whole time. There will be a record of that, too. What about my phone and my hotel room? Did you bug them?"

Rachel saw Alpert's eyes change. He went inward, his mind no longer consumed by her accusations but by the future consequences of an ethics complaint and investigation. She saw him recognize his own doom. One agent bugging and following another agent, using her as unwitting bait in a high-stakes gamble. Under the current climate of media scrutiny and bureau-wide avoidance of any controversy, his actions wouldn't hold up. It would be he who would go down, not her. Quickly and quietly he would be dealt with. Maybe, if he was lucky, he'd end up working side by side with Rachel in the Rapid City office.

"The Badlands are really quite beautiful in the summer," she said.

She stood up and headed to the door.

"Agent Walling?" Alpert said to her back. "Hold on a second."

39

RACHEL'S PLANE LANDED A half hour late at Burbank because of the rain and wind. It had not let up through the night and the city was cast in a shroud of gray. It was the kind of rain that paralyzed the city. Traffic moved at a crawl on every street and every freeway. The roads weren't built for it. The city wasn't either. By dawn the storm water culverts were overflowing, the tunnels were at capacity and the runoff to the Los Angeles River had turned the concrete-lined canal that snaked through the city to the sea into a roaring rapids. It was black water, carrying with it the ash of the fires that had blackened the hills the year before. There was an end-of-the-world gloom about it all. The city had been tested by fire first and now rain. Living in L.A. sometimes felt like you were riding shotgun with the devil to the apocalypse. People I saw that morning carried a what's-next look in their eyes. Earthquake? Tsunami? Or maybe a disaster of our own making? A dozen years earlier fire and rain had been the harbingers of both tectonic and social upheaval in the City of Angels. I didn't think there was anybody here who doubted it could happen again. If we are doomed to repeat ourselves in our follies and mistakes, then it is easy to see nature and balance operating on the same cycle.

I thought about this as I waited for Rachel at the curb outside the terminal. The rain pounded the windshield, turning it translucent and murky. The wind rocked the car on its springs. I thought about rejoining the cops, already second-guessing my decision and wondering if I would be repeating myself in folly or if I had a chance this time at grace.

I didn't see Rachel in the rain until she knocked on the passenger-side window. She then opened the back hatch and threw in her bag. She was wearing a green parka with the hood up. It must have done her well facing the elements in the Dakotas but it looked too large and bulky on her in L.A.

"This better be good, Bosch," she said as she climbed in and dropped wetly onto the passenger seat. She showed no outward sign of affection and neither did I. It was one of the agreements we'd made on the phone. We were to act as professionals until we played my hunch out.

"Why, you got alternatives?"

"No, it's just that I put everything on the line last night with Alpert. I'm one fuckup short of a permanent posting in South Dakota, where, by the way, the weather might actually be nicer than this."

"Well, welcome to L.A."

"I thought this was Burbank."

"Technically."

After we cleared the airport I dropped down to the

134 and took that east to the 5. Between the rain and the morning rush hour our progress was slow as we skirted around Griffith Park and pointed south. I wasn't ready to begin worrying about time yet but I was getting close.

For a long time we rode silently because the mix of rain and traffic made the drive intense, probably more so for Rachel who had to sit and do nothing while I had control of the wheel. Finally she spoke, if only to siphon off some of the tension in the car.

"So are you going to tell me this grand plan of yours?"

"No plan, just a hunch."

"No, you said you *knew* his next move, Bosch."

I noticed that since we had made love on the bed of my efficiency unit she had started calling me by my last name. I wondered if this was part of the agreement to act as professionals or some form of reverse endearment, calling someone you had been most intimate with by his least intimate name.

"I had to get you here, Rachel."

"Well, all right then, I'm here. Tell it to me."

"It's the Poet who has the grand plan. Backus."

"What's he going to do?"

"Remember the books I told you about yesterday, the books in the barrel and the one I pulled out?"

"Yes."

"I think I figured out what it all means."

I told her about the partially burned receipt I had seen and how I thought Book Car was actually Book Carnival, the bookstore operated by retired police detective Ed Thomas, the last intended target of the Poet eight years before.

"You think because of this book in the fire barrel that

he's here and is going to make good on the killing we took away from him eight years ago."

"Exactly."

"That's a stretch, Bosch. I wish you had told me all of this before I risked my ass flying over here."

"There's no such thing as coincidence, especially like this."

"Okay, run the story out for me, then. Give me the profile. Tell me the Poet's grand plan."

"Well, that's the bureau's job, to profile crimes. I'm not going to do that. But this is what I think he's doing. I think the trailer and the explosion were all set up to look like the grand finale. And then, as soon as the director steps in front of the television cameras and says I think we've got him, he's going to take out Ed Thomas. The symbolism would be perfect. It's the grand gesture, the ultimate fuck-you. It's checkmate, Rachel. While the bureau is bragging about itself he moves in right under their noses and takes out the guy the bureau was all puffed up about saving the last time."

"And why the books in the barrel? How does all of that fit in?"

"I think they were books he bought from Ed Thomas. From Book Carnival by mail order or maybe even in person. Maybe they were marked in some way and could be traced back to the store. He didn't want that so he burned them. He couldn't risk that they might survive the trailer blast.

"But then on the other end, after Ed Thomas is gone and Backus has split, the agents would find his connection to the store and would begin to see how long and how hard Backus was planning this. It would help show his genius. That's what he wants, right? I mean, you are the profiler. Tell me if I'm wrong."

"I *was* the profiler. Right now I handle reservation crimes in the Dakotas."

The traffic was starting to open up as we passed by downtown, the spires of the financial district disappearing in the upper mist of the storm. The city always looked haunting in the rain to me. There was a foreboding sense about it that always depressed me, that always made me feel like something had broken loose in the world and was wrong.

"There is only one thing wrong with all of that, Bosch."

"What?"

"The director is holding a press conference today but he isn't going to say we caught the Poet. Just like you, we don't think that was Backus in that trailer."

"So, Backus doesn't know that. He'll watch it on CNN like everybody else. But it won't change his plan. Either way, I say he hits Ed Thomas today. Either way, he makes his point. '*I am better and smarter than you.*'"

She nodded and thought about that for a long moment.

"Okay," she finally said. "What if I'm buying it? What is our play? Have you called Ed Thomas?"

"I don't know what our play is yet and I haven't called Ed Thomas. We're heading toward his store now. It's down in Orange and he opens up at eleven. I called and got his hours off the answering machine."

"Why his store? All the other cops Backus killed were in their homes, one in his car."

"Because at the moment I don't know where Ed Thomas lives and because of the book. My guess is

Backus will make his move at the bookstore. If I'm wrong and Ed doesn't show up at the store, then we find out where he lives and go there."

Rachel nodded in agreement with the plan.

"There were three different books written on the Poet case. I read them all and they all had postscripts on the players. They said Thomas retired and opened a bookstore. I think one even named the store."

"There you go."

She looked at her watch.

"Are we going to make it there before he opens?"

"We'll make it. Did they set a time for the director's press conference?"

"Three o'clock D.C. time."

I checked the dash clock. It was ten a.m. We had an hour before Ed Thomas opened for business and two hours before the press conference. If my theory and hunch were correct we would be in the presence of the Poet very soon. I was ready and I was juiced. I felt the high octane moving in my blood. By old habit I dropped my hand off the wheel and checked my hip. I had a Glock 27 holstered there. It was illegal for me to be carrying a weapon and if I ended up using it, there could be trouble—the kind that could prevent me from rejoining the police department.

But sometimes the risks you face dictate the other risks you must take. And my guess was that this was going to be one of those times.

40

T HE RAIN MADE IT hard to watch the store. If we had left the windshield wipers on, it would have been a dead giveaway. So we watched at first through the murk of water on glass.

We were parked in the lot of a strip shopping center on Tustin Boulevard in the city of Orange. Book Carnival was a small business between a rock shop and what looked like a vacant slot. Three doors down was a gun store.

There was a single public entrance. Before taking our position in the front lot we had driven behind the shopping center and seen a rear door with the store's name on it. There was a doorbell and a sign that said RING BELL FOR DELIVERIES.

In a perfect world we'd have been on the front and back of the store with a minimum of four sets of eyes. Backus could come in either way, posing as a customer through the front or as a deliveryman through the back. But nothing was perfect about the world on this day. It was raining and it was just the two of us. We parked the Mercedes at a distance from the front of the store but still close enough to see and act if necessary.

The front counter and cash register were just behind the front window of Book Carnival. This worked in our favor. Shortly after we watched him open the store for business, we watched Ed Thomas take a position behind the counter. He put a cash drawer into the register and made some phone calls. Even with the rain and the blurring of the windshield we could keep him in view as long as he stayed at the register. It was the recesses of the store behind him that disappeared in the gloom. On the occasions that he left his post and walked back toward the shelves and displays in the rear, we lost sight of him and the tingling sense of panic took hold.

On the way down Rachel had told me about the discovery of the GPS tag on her car and the confirmation that she had been used by fellow agents as bait for Backus. And now here we sat watching a former colleague of mine, in a way using him as the new bait. It didn't sit well with me. I wanted to go in and tell Ed the crosshairs were on him, that he should take a vacation, get out of town. But I didn't because I knew if Backus was watching Thomas and saw any deviation in the norm, then we might lose our only chance at him. So Rachel and I got selfish with Ed Thomas's life and I knew in the days ahead I would deal with the guilt from that. The only question was, depending on how things turned out, how much guilt there would be.

The first two customers of the day were women. They arrived shortly after Thomas had unlocked the front door. And while they were browsing in the store a man pulled up, parked in front and went in as well. He was too young to be Backus so we didn't go to full alert. He left in a hurry and without purchasing a book. Then, when the two women left, clutching their bags of books, I got out of the Mercedes and ran across the lot to the overhang in front of the gun shop.

Rachel and I had decided not to bring Thomas into our investigation, but that wasn't going to stop me from going into the store on a reconnaissance mission. We decided that I would go into the store with a cover story, nonchalantly reacquaint myself with Thomas and see if he might already be alert to the idea that he was being watched. So once the first customers of the day had come and gone, I made the move.

I first ducked into the gun store since it was the store closest to where we had parked and it would have looked odd to anyone watching the shopping plaza for me to park on one end and go directly to the bookstore at the other end. I took a cursory look at the gleaming firearms displayed in the glass counter and then up at the paper shooting targets on the back wall. They had the usual silhouettes but they also had versions featuring the faces of Osama bin Laden and Saddam Hussein. I guessed that these were the big sellers.

When a man behind the counter asked if I needed help I told him I was just browsing and then walked out of the store. I walked down toward Book Carnival, stopping first to check out the empty storefront next door. Through the soaped glass I could see boxes marked with what I guessed were the titles of books. I realized Thomas was using the slot for storing books. There was a FOR LEASE sign and a phone number, which I committed to memory in case it played into an angle we would work later.

I entered Book Carnival and Ed Thomas was behind the counter. I smiled and he smiled in recognition but I could tell that it took a few seconds for him to place the face he recognized.

"Harry Bosch," he said once he had it.

"Hey, Ed, how are you doing?"

We shook hands and his eyes behind the glasses had a warmth to them I liked. I was pretty sure I hadn't seen him since his retirement dinner at the Sportsman's Lodge up in the Valley six or seven years before. There was more white than not in his hair. But he was still tall and thin like I remembered him from the job. He had a tendency at crime scenes to hold his notebook up high and close to his face when he was writing. This was because his glasses were always a prescription or two behind his eyes. The arms-high pose got him the nickname of the Praying Mantis around the homicide table. I suddenly remembered that now. I remembered the flyer for his retirement party showed a caricature of Ed as a superhero with a cape and a mask and a large P on his chest.

"How's the book business doing?"

"It's doing good, Harry. What brings you down here from the big bad city? I heard you retired a couple years ago."

"Yeah, I did. But I'm thinking about going back."

"You miss it?"

"Yeah, I sort of do. We'll see what happens."

He seemed surprised and I knew then that he didn't miss a thing about the job. He'd always been a reader, always had a box of paperbacks in the trunk for surveillances and while sitting on wiretaps. Now he had his pension and his bookstore. He was doing well without all of the nastiness of the job.

"You just passing by?"

"No, actually, I came here for a real reason. You remember my old partner, Kiz Rider?"

"Yeah, sure, she's been in here before."

"That's what I mean. She's been helping me with something and I want to get her a little gift. I remember she told me once that your store was like the only place around where you could get a book signed by a writer named Dean Koontz. So I was wondering if you got any of those around. I'd like to get her one."

"I think I might have something left in the back. Let me go check. Those things go fast but I usually keep a stash."

He left me at the counter and walked through the store to a door at the back that appeared to lead to a stockroom. I assumed the rear delivery door was back there. When he was out of sight I leaned over the counter and looked at the shelves beneath. I saw a small video display tube with its screen cut into four segments. There were four interior camera angles showing the cash register area, with me leaning over the counter; a long view of the entire store; a tighter view of a group of shelves; and the rear stockroom, where I could see Thomas looking at a similar VDT tube on a shelf.

I realized he was looking at me leaning over his counter. I straightened up, my mind quickly trying to come up with an explanation. A few moments later Thomas came back to the counter carrying a book.

"Find what you were looking for, Harry?"

"What? Oh, you mean me looking over the counter? I was just sort of wondering if you, you know, had any protection back there. You being a former cop and all. You ever worry about somebody coming in here who you knew from back when?"

"I take precautions, Harry. Don't worry about that."

I nodded.

"Good to hear. Is that the book?"

"Yeah, does she have this one? It came out last year."

He showed me a book called *The Face*. I didn't know if Kiz had it or not but I was going to buy it.

"I don't know. Did he sign it?"

"Yeah, signed and dated."

"Okay, I'll take it."

While he rang up the sale I tried some small talk which really wasn't small talk.

"I saw you have the camera set up underneath there. Seems like a little much for a bookstore."

"You'd be surprised. People like to steal books. I got a collectibles section back there—expensive stuff from the collections I buy and sell. I keep a camera right on it and I caught a kid in there just this morning trying to shove a copy of *Nick's Trip* down his pants. Early Pelecanos is tough to find. That would've been about a seven-hundred-dollar loss for me."

That seemed like an inordinate amount of money for a single book. I had never heard of the book but guessed that it must have been fifty or a hundred years old.

"You call the cops?"

"No, I just kicked him in the pants and told him if he came back again I would call the law."

"You're a nice guy, Ed. You must have mellowed out since you left. I don't think the Praying Mantis would've just let the kid slide."

I handed him two twenties and he gave me the change.

"The Praying Mantis was a long time ago. And my wife doesn't think I'm so mellow. Thanks, Harry. And tell Kiz I said hello."

"Yeah, I will. You ever run into anybody else from the table?"

I didn't want to leave yet. I wanted more information so I continued the banter. I looked up over his head and spotted a small two-camera dome. It was mounted up near the ceiling, one lens angled down on the register and one taking in the long view of the store. There was a small red light glowing and I could see a small black cable snaking from the camera housing and up into the drop ceiling. While Thomas answered my question I was thinking about the possibility that Backus had been in the store and was captured on a surveillance tape.

"Not really," Thomas said. "I sort of left all of that behind. You say you miss it, Harry, but I don't miss a thing about it. Not really."

I nodded like I understood but I didn't. Thomas had been a good cop and a good detective. He took the work to heart. That was one reason why the Poet had put him in the sights. He was paying lip service to something I didn't think he really believed.

"That's good," I said. "Hey, do you have that kid you

kicked out of here on tape from this morning? I'd like to see how he tried to rip you off."

"Nah, I just have live feeds. I got the cameras out in the open and a sticker on the door. It's supposed to be a deterrent but some people are dumb. A setup with a recorder would be too expensive and a pain in the ass in maintenance. I just have the live setup."

"I see."

"Listen, if Kiz already has that book I'll take it back. I can sell it."

"No, that's cool. If she already has it I'll keep it and read it myself."

"Harry, when's the last time you read a book?"

"I read a book about Art Pepper a couple months ago," I said indignantly. "He and his wife wrote it before he died."

"Nonfiction?"

"Yeah, it was real stuff."

"I'm talking about a novel. When was the last time you read one?"

I shrugged. I didn't remember.

"That's what I thought," Thomas said. "If she doesn't want the book bring it back and I'll get it to somebody who'll read it."

"Okay, Ed. Thanks."

"Be careful out there, Harry."

"I will be. You, too."

I was heading to the door when things came together—what Thomas had told me and what I knew about the case. I snapped my fingers and acted like I just remembered something. I turned back to Thomas.

"Hey, I got a friend lives all the way in Nevada but he

says he's a customer of yours. Mail order probably. You do mail order?"

"Sure. What's his name?"

"Tom Walling. Lives all the way up in Clear."

Thomas nodded but not in any happy sort of way.

"He's your friend?"

I realized I might have stepped in it.

"Well, an acquaintance, you could say."

"Well, he owes me some money."

"Really? What happened?"

"It's a long story. But I sold him some books out of a collection I was handling and he paid very promptly. Paid with a money order and everything was fine. So when he wanted more books I sent them before I got his money order. Big mistake. That was three months ago and I haven't gotten a dime from him. If you see this acquaintance of yours again, tell him I want my money."

"I will, Ed. That's too bad. I didn't know the guy was a rip-off artist. What books did he buy?"

"He's into Poe, so I sold him some books out of the Rodway collection. Some old ones. Pretty nice books. Then he ordered more when I got another collection in. He didn't pay for them."

My heart rate was kicking into an upper gear. What Thomas was telling me was confirmation that Backus was somehow in play here. I wanted to stop the charade at that moment and tell Thomas what was happening and that he was in danger. But I held back. I needed to talk to Rachel first and form the right plan.

"I think I saw those books in his place," I said. "Was it poetry?"

"Mostly, yeah. He didn't really care for the short stories."

"Did these books have the original collector's name in them? Rodman?"

"No, Rodway. And yes, they had his library seal embossed in them. That hurt the price but your friend wanted the books."

I nodded. I saw my theory coming together. It was more than theory now.

"Harry, what are you really up to?"

I looked at Thomas.

"What do you mean?"

"I don't know. You're asking a lot of—"

A loud ring sounded from the back of the store, cutting Thomas off.

"Never mind, Harry," he said. "It's more books. I need to go take a delivery."

"Oh."

"I'll see you later."

"Yeah."

I watched him leave the counter area and head to the back. I checked my watch. It was noon. The director was stepping before the cameras to talk about the explosion in the desert and say that it was the work of the killer known as the Poet. Could this be the moment Backus chose to strike Thomas? My throat and chest tightened as though the air had been sucked out of the room. As soon as Thomas slipped through the doorway to the stockroom, I moved back to the counter and leaned over to look at the security monitor. I knew if Thomas checked the backroom monitor he would see that I hadn't left the store, but I was counting on him going right to the door.

On the corner of the screen showing the stockroom I saw Thomas lean his face up to the rear door and look through a peephole. Apparently unalarmed by what he saw, he proceeded to turn the dead bolt and open the door. I stared intently at the screen, even though the image was small and I was viewing it upside down.

Thomas stepped back from the door and a man entered. He was wearing a dark shirt and matching shorts. He was carrying two boxes, one stacked on top of the other, and Thomas directed him to a nearby worktable. The deliveryman put the boxes down and then took an electronic clipboard off the top box and turned back to Thomas for a delivery confirmation signature.

Everything seemed all right. It was a routine delivery. I quickly got off the counter and went to the door. As I opened it I heard an electronic chime sound but I didn't worry about that. I headed back to the Mercedes, running through the rain after putting the autographed book under my raincoat.

"What was all of that, with you leaning over the counter like that?" Rachel asked once I was behind the wheel again.

"He's got a security box. There was a delivery and I wanted to make sure it was legit before I left. It's after three o'clock in D.C."

"I know. So what did you learn from him or were you just in there buying a book?"

"I learned a lot. Tom Walling is a customer. Or was, until he stiffed him for an order of Edgar Allan Poe books. It was mail order like we thought. He never saw him, just sent the books out to Nevada."

Rachel sat up straight.

"Are you kidding me?"

"No. The books were out of some guy's collection that Ed was selling. So they were marked and therefore traceable. That was why Backus burned them all in the fire barrel. He couldn't risk that they'd survive the blast intact and be traced back to Thomas."

"Why?"

"Because he is definitely in play here. He's got to be setting up on Thomas."

I started the car.

"Where are you going?"

"Around back to make sure about the delivery. Besides, it's good to change locations every now and then."

"Oh, you're giving me surveillance one-oh-one lessons now."

Without responding I drove around to the back of the plaza and saw the brown UPS van parked by the open rear door of Book Carnival. We drove on by and during the brief glimpse I had of the back of the truck and the open door of the stockroom, I saw the deliveryman struggling to carry several boxes up a ramp to the back of his truck. The returns, I guessed. I kept driving without hesitation.

"He's legit," Rachel said.

"Yeah."

"You didn't give yourself away with Thomas, did you?"

"No. He was suspicious but then I was sort of saved by the bell. I wanted to talk to you first. I think we need to bring him in on it."

"Harry, we talked about this. If we bring him into it he may change his routine and demeanor. It might be a giveaway. If Backus has been watching him, any little change could be a tell."

"And if we don't warn him and this thing goes wrong, then we . . ."

I didn't finish. We had been over this argument twice before, each of us alternately taking the other side. It was a classic contradiction of intentions. Do we ensure Thomas's safety at the risk of losing Backus? Or do we risk Thomas's safety to ensure getting close to Backus? It was all about the means to an end and neither of us would be happy no matter which way we went.

"I guess that means we can't let anything go wrong," she said.

"Right. What about backup?"

"I also think it's too risky. The more people we bring into this, the greater the chance of tipping our hand."

I nodded. She was right. I found a spot on the opposite end of the parking lot from where we had parked and watched before. I wasn't kidding myself, though. There were only so many cars in the lot in the middle of a rainy weekday and we were noticeable. I started to think that maybe we were like Ed Thomas's cameras. Strictly a deterrent. Maybe Backus had seen us and it had stopped him from moving forward with his plan. For now.

"Customer," Rachel said.

I looked across the lot and saw a woman heading toward the store. She looked familiar to me and then I remembered her from the Sportsman's Lodge.

"That's his wife. I met her once. I think her name is Pat."

"She bringing him lunch, you think?"

"Maybe. Or maybe she works there."

We watched for a while but there was no sign of Thomas or his wife in the front of the store. I grew concerned and took out my cell phone and called the store, hoping the call would bring them to the front counter, where the phone was.

But a woman answered right away and there was still no one at the counter. I quickly hung up.

"There must be a phone in the stockroom."

"Who answered?"

"The wife."

"Should I take a walk and go in?"

"No. If Backus is watching he'll recognize you. You can't be seen."

"All right, then what?"

"Then nothing. They're probably at the table I saw in the back room having lunch. Be patient."

"I don't want to be patient. I don't like just sitting—"

She stopped when we saw Ed Thomas walk out the front of the store. He was wearing a raincoat and carrying an umbrella and a briefcase. He got into the car we had seen him arrive at the store in that morning, a green Ford Explorer. Through the store's front window I saw his wife take a seat on a stool behind the front counter.

"Here we go," I said.

"Where's he going?"

"Maybe he's going to get lunch."

"Not with a briefcase. We stay on him, right?"

I restarted the car.

"Right."

We watched as Thomas pulled out of a parking space in his Ford SUV. He headed toward the exit and turned right on Tustin Boulevard. After his car was absorbed into the passing traffic I pulled up to the exit and followed him into the rain. I pulled out my phone and called the store. Ed Thomas's wife answered.

"Hi, is Ed there?"

"No, he's not. Can I help you?"

"Is this Pat?"

"Yes, it is. Who's this?"

"It's Bill Gilbert. I think we met at the Sportsman's Lodge a while back. I used to work with Ed in the department. I was going to be in the area and thought I'd drop by the store today to say hello. Will he be back later?"

"That's hard to say. He went to do an appraisal and who knows, it might take the rest of the day. With this rain and the distance he had to go."

"An appraisal? What do you mean?"

"A book collection. Someone wants to sell his collection and Ed just left to go see what it is worth. It's all the way up in the San Fernando Valley and from what I understand it's a big collection. He told me I'd probably be closing the store tonight."

"Is it more of the Rodway collection? He told me about that the last time we talked."

"No, that's just about all been sold. This is a man named Charles Turrentine and he has over six thousand books."

"Wow, that's a lot."

"He's a well-known collector but I guess he needs the money because he told Ed he wants to sell everything."

"Strange. A guy spends all that time collecting and then he sells it all."

"We see it happen."

"Well, Pat, I'll let you go. And I'll catch Ed next time. Tell him I said hello."

"What was your name again?"

"Tom Gilbert. Bye now."

I closed the phone.

"You were Bill Gilbert at the start of the conversation."

"Whoops."

I recounted the conversation for Rachel. I then called information in the 818 area code but there was no listing for a Charles Turrentine. I asked Rachel if she had a connection in the bureau's Los Angeles field office who could get an address for Turrentine and maybe an unlisted number.

"Don't you have somebody in the LAPD you can use?"

"At the moment I think I've used up all the favors owed me. Besides, I'm an outsider. You're not."

"I don't know about that."

She pulled out her phone and went to work on it and I concentrated on the taillights of Thomas's SUV, just fifty yards ahead of me on the 22 freeway. I knew Thomas had a choice up ahead. He could turn north on the 5 and go through downtown L.A., or he could keep on going and take the 405 north. Both routes would lead him to the Valley.

Rachel got a call back in five minutes with the information she had asked for.

"He lives on Valerio Street in Canoga Park. Do you know where that is?"

"I know where Canoga Park is. Valerio runs east-west across the whole Valley. Did you get a phone number?"

She answered by punching in a number on her cell phone. She then held it to her ear and waited. After thirty seconds she closed the phone.

"There was no answer. I got the tape."

We drove in silence as we thought about that.

Thomas passed by the exit to the 5 north and proceeded on toward the 405. I knew he would turn north there and take the Sepulveda Pass into the Valley. Canoga Park was on the west side. With the weather we were talking about at least an hour's drive. If we were lucky.

"Don't lose him, Bosch," Rachel said quietly.

I knew what she meant. She was telling me she had the vibe, that she thought this was it. That she believed Ed Thomas might be leading us to the Poet. I nodded because I had it, too, almost like a humming coming from the center of my chest. I knew without really knowing that we were there.

"Don't worry," I said. "I won't."

41

THE RAIN WAS GETTING to Rachel. The relentlessness of it. It never let up, never paused. It just came down and hit the windshield in a nonstop torrent that overpowered the wipers. Everything was a blur. There were cars pulled off on the shoulders of the freeway. Lightning cracked the sky to the west, somewhere out over the ocean. They passed accident after accident and these just made Rachel all the more nervous. If they got into an accident and lost Thomas, they would carry an awful burden of responsibility for what happened to him.

She was afraid that if she looked away from the red glow of the taillights on Thomas's car, they would lose him in the sea of blurred red. Bosch seemed to know what she was thinking.

"Relax," he said. "I'm not going to lose him. And even if I do, we know where he is going now."

"No, we don't. We only know where Turrentine lives. That doesn't mean his books are there. Six thousand books? Who keeps six thousand books in their house? He probably has them in a warehouse somewhere."

Rachel watched Bosch adjust his grip on the steering wheel and add a few more miles to his speed, drawing them closer to Thomas.

"Didn't think about that, did you?"

"No, not really."

"So don't lose him."

"I told you, I won't."

"I know. It just helps me to say it."

She gestured toward the windshield.

"How often does it get like this?"

"Almost never," Bosch said. "They said on the news that it's a hundred-year storm. It's like something's wrong, something's broken. The canyons are probably washing out in Malibu. Landslides in the Palisades. And the river's probably over its sides. Last year we had the fires. This year maybe it's going to be rain. One way or another it's always something. It's like you always have to pass a test or something."

He turned on the radio to pick up a weather report. But Rachel immediately reached over and turned it off and pointed ahead through the windshield.

"Concentrate on this," she ordered. "I don't care about the weather report."

"Right."

"Get closer. I don't care if you're right behind him. He won't be able to see you in this mess."

"I get behind him I might hit him, then what do we say?"

"Just don't—"

"Lose him. Yeah, I know."

They drove for the next half hour without a word. The freeway rose and crossed over the mountains. Rachel saw a large stone structure on the top of the mountain. It looked like some sort of postmodern castle in the gray and gloom and Bosch told her it was the Getty Museum.

As they descended into the Valley she saw the turn signal flare from the back of Thomas's car. Bosch moved into the turning lane three cars back.

"He's taking the one-oh-one. We're almost there."

"You mean to Canoga Park?"

"That's right. He'll take this out west and then go north again on surface streets."

Bosch grew quiet again as he concentrated on the driving and following. In another fifteen minutes the turn signal on the Explorer flared again and Thomas exited on DeSoto Avenue and headed north. Bosch and Walling trailed behind on the exit ramp, but this time without the cover of other traffic.

On DeSoto, Thomas almost immediately pulled to the curb in a no parking area and Bosch had to drive by him or the surveillance would have been obvious.

"I think he's looking at a map or directions," Rachel said. "He had the light on and his head was down."

"Okay."

Bosch pulled into a service station, circled around the pumps and then drove back out to the street. He paused before pulling out, looking left down the street at Thomas's Explorer. He waited and after a half minute Thomas pulled his Explorer back into traffic. Bosch waited for him to go by, holding his cell phone up to his left ear to block any view of his face in case Thomas was looking and could see in the rain. He let another car go by and then pulled out.

"He must be close," Rachel said.

"Yeah."

But Thomas drove several more blocks before turning right. Bosch slowed before doing the same.

"Valerio," Rachel said, seeing the street sign in the murk. "This is it."

When Bosch made the turn she saw the brake lights on Thomas's car. He was stopped in the middle of the road three blocks ahead. He was at a dead end.

Bosch quickly pulled to the curb behind a parked car.

"The dome light's on," Rachel said. "I think he's looking at his map again."

"The river," Bosch said.

"What?"

"I told you, Valerio cuts across the whole Valley. But so does the river. So he's probably figuring out a way to get around it. The river cuts off all these streets in here. He probably has to get to Valerio on the other side."

"I don't see any river up there. I see a fence and concrete."

"It's not what you would consider a river. In fact, technically that isn't the river. It's probably either the Aliso or Brown's Canyon wash. It goes to the river."

They waited. Thomas didn't move.

"The river used to flood in storms like this. It would wipe out a third of the city. So they tried to control it. Contain it. Somebody had the idea to capture it in stone, put it in concrete. So that's what they did and everybody's house and home was supposedly safe after that."

"I guess that's called progress."

Bosch nodded and then re-gripped his hands on the wheel.

"He's moving."

Thomas turned left and once his car was out of sight Bosch pulled away from the curb and followed. Thomas drove north to Saticoy and then took a right. He went over a bridge crossing the wash below. As they followed, Rachel looked down and saw the torrent of water in the concrete channel.

"Wow. I thought I lived in Rapid City."

Bosch didn't answer. Thomas turned south on Mason and came back down to Valerio. But now he was on the other side of the concrete channel. He turned right again on Valerio.

"That'll be another dead end," Bosch said.

He stayed on Mason and drove on by Valerio. Rachel looked through the rain and saw that Thomas had pulled into a driveway in front of a large two-story home that was one of five homes on the dead-end street.

"He pulled into a driveway," she said. "He's there. Jesus, it's the house!"

"What house?"

"The one from the photo in the trailer. Backus was so sure of himself he left us a goddamn picture."

Bosch pulled to the curb. They were out of sight of the homes on Valerio. Rachel turned and looked out all of the windows. Every home around them was dark.

"There must be a power outage around here."

"Under your seat there's a flashlight. Take it."

Rachel reached down and got it.

"What about you?"

"I'll be all right. Let's go."

Rachel started to open her door but then looked back at Bosch. She wanted to say something but hesitated.

"What?" he asked. "Be careful? Don't worry, I will."

"Actually, yes, be careful. But what I was going to say is that I have my second gun in my bag. Do you—"

"Thanks, Rachel, but this time I brought my own."

She nodded.

"I should have figured that. And what are your views on backup now?"

"Call it in if you want. But I'm not waiting. I'm going down there."

THE RAIN FELT COLD on my face and neck as I got out of the Mercedes. I pulled the collar on my jacket up and started heading back toward Valerio. Rachel came over and walked next to me without saying a word. When we got to the corner we used the wall surrounding the corner property as cover and looked down into the cul-de-sac and the dark house where Ed Thomas had parked his car. There was no sign of Thomas or anyone else. Every window at the front of the house was dark. But even in the grayness I could tell that Rachel was right. It was the house from the photo Backus had left for us.

I could hear the river but not see it. It was hidden behind the homes. But its furious power was almost palpable, even from this distance. In storms like this the whole city washed itself out over its smoothed concrete surfaces. It snaked through the Valley and around the mountains to downtown. And from there west to the ocean.

It was a mere trickle most of the year. A municipal

joke even. But a rainstorm would awaken the snake and give it power. It became the city's gutter, millions and millions of gallons banging against its thick stone walls, tons of water raging to get out, moving with a terrible force and momentum. I remembered a boy who was taken when I was a kid. I didn't know him. I knew of him. Four decades later I even remembered his name. Billy Kinsey was playing on the river's shoulder. He slipped in and in a moment he was gone. They found his body hung up in a viaduct 12 miles away.

My mother had taught me early and often, when it rains . . .

"Stay out of the narrows."

"What?" Rachel whispered.

"I was thinking about the river. Trapped between those walls. When I was a kid we called it 'the narrows.' When it rains like this the water moves fast. It's deadly. When it rains you stay away from the narrows."

"But we're going to the house."

"Same thing, Rachel. Be careful. Stay out of the narrows."

She looked at me. She seemed to understand what I meant.

"Okay, Bosch."

"How about you take the front and I take the back?"

"Fine."

"Be ready for anything."

"You, too."

The target house was three properties away. We walked quickly along the wall surrounding the first property and then cut up the driveway of the next. We skirted the fronts of two houses until we came to the home where Thomas's car was parked. Rachel gave me a last nod and we separated then, both of us pulling our weapons in unison. Rachel moved to the front while I started down the driveway toward the rear. The gloom and the sound of the rain and the river channel gave me visual and sound cover. The driveway was also lined with squat bougainvillea trees that had been let go for some time without training or trimming. But the house behind the windows was dark. Someone could be behind any glass watching me and I wouldn't know it.

The rear yard was flooded. In the middle of the big puddle stood the rusted twin A-frames of a swing set with no swings left on it. Behind it was a six-foot fence that separated the property from the river channel. I could see the water was near the top of its concrete siding and was rushing by in a mad torrent. It would flood by day's end. Further upstream, where the channels were shallower, it probably already had stemmed its sides.

I turned my attention back to the house. There was a full porch off the rear. There were no gutters on the roof here and the rain was coming off in sheets, so heavy that it obscured everything within. Backus could've been sitting in a rocker on the porch and I wouldn't have seen him. The line of bougainvilleas carried along the porch railing. I ducked below the sight line and moved quickly to the steps. I took the three steps up in one stride and was in out of the rain. My eyes and ears took a moment to adjust and that was when I saw it. There was a white rattan couch on the right side of the porch. On it a blanket covered the unmistakable shape of a human form sitting upright but slumped against the left arm. Dropping to a crouch I moved closer and reached for a corner of the blanket on the floor. I slowly pulled it off the form.

It was an old man. He looked like he had been dead at least a day. The odor was just starting. His eyes were open and bugged, his skin was the color of white paint in a smoker's bedroom. A snap-cuff had been pulled tight—too tight—around his neck. Charles Turrentine, I presumed. I also presumed he was the old man in the photo Backus had taken. He had been killed and then left there on the porch like a stack of old newspapers. He'd had no business with the Poet. He'd just been a means to an end.

I raised my Glock and went to the house's back door. I wanted to get a warning to Rachel but there was no way to do it without revealing my own position and possibly compromising hers. I just had to keep moving, going further into the darkness of this place until I came across her or Backus.

The door was locked. I decided I would go around, catch up to Rachel from the front. But as I turned, my eyes fell back on the body and I was struck with a possibility. I moved to the couch and patted down the old man's pants. And I was rewarded. I heard the jingle of keys.

RACHEL WAS SURROUNDED. STACKS and stacks of books lined every wall in the front hallway. She stood there, gun in one hand and flashlight in the other, and looked into the living room to her right. More books. Shelves lined every wall and every shelf was filled to capacity. Books stacked on the coffee table and the end tables and every horizontal surface. Somehow it made the place seem haunted. It was not a place of life but a place of doom and gloom where bookworms ate through the words of all the authors.

She tried to keep moving without dwelling on her rising fears. She wavered and thought about turning back to the door and leaving before she was discovered. But then she heard the voices and knew she must press on.

"Where is Charles?"

"I said *sit down.*"

The words came to her from an unknown direction. The pounding of the rain outside, the rage of the nearby river, and the books stacked everywhere combined to obliquely camouflage the origin of sounds. She heard the voices but could not tell where they came from.

More sounds and voices came to her. Murmurs mostly and every few moments a recognizable word, sculpted in anger or fear.

"You thought . . ."

She bent down and left the flashlight on the floor. She had not used it yet and couldn't risk it now. She moved into the deeper gloom of the hallway. She had already checked the front rooms and knew the voices were coming from somewhere further into the house.

The hallway led to a foyer from which doors opened in three different directions. As she got there she heard the voices of two men and thought for sure that they came from somewhere to the right.

"Write it!"

"I can't see!"

Then a popping sound. A ripping sound. Curtains being pulled off a window.

"There, you see now? Write it or I'll end it right now!"

"All right! All right!"

"Exactly as I say it. Once upon a midnight dreary . . ."

She knew what it was. She recognized the words of Edgar Allan Poe. And she knew it was Backus, though the voice was different. He was using the poetry again, re-creating the crime taken from him so long ago. Bosch had been right.

She moved into the room to the right and found it empty. A billiard table stood in the middle of the room, every inch of its surface taken up by stacks of more books. She understood what Backus had done. He had lured Ed Thomas here because the man who lived here—Charles Turrentine—was a collector. He knew Thomas would come for this collection.

She started to turn in order to retreat, to check the next room off the foyer. But before she had moved more than a few inches she felt the cold muzzle of a gun pressed against her neck.

"Hello, Rachel," Robert Backus said with his surgically changed voice. "What a surprise to see you here."

She froze and in that moment knew that he could not be played in any way, that he knew all the plays and all the angles. She knew she only had one chance. That was Bosch.

"Hello, Bob. It's been a long time."

"Yes, it has. Would you like to leave your weapon here and join me in the library?"

Rachel put her Sig down on one of the stacks on the billiard table.

"I sort of thought the whole place was a library, Bob."

Backus didn't respond. She felt him grab the back of her collar, press his gun against her spine and then push her in the direction he wanted her to go. They left the room and went into the next, which was a small room with two high-backed wooden chairs arranged to face a large stone fireplace. There was no fire and Rachel could hear rain dripping down the chimney into the hearth. She saw that it was creating a puddle there. Windows on either side of the fireplace had rain washing down them, turning them translucent.

"We happen to have just enough chairs," Backus said. "Have a seat, won't you?"

He roughly brought her around one of the chairs and pushed her down into it. He made a quick check of her body for other weapons and then stepped back and dropped something onto her lap. Rachel looked into the other chair and saw Ed Thomas. He was still alive. His wrists were held to the arms of the chair by plastic snap-cuffs. Two more cuffs had been joined and then used to hold him by his neck to the back of the chair. He had been gagged with a cloth napkin and his face was overly red with exertion and lack of oxygen.

"Bob, you can stop this," Rachel said. "You've made your point. You don't—"

"Put the cuff around your right wrist and lock it to the chair's arm."

"Bob, please. Let—"

"Do it!"

She wrapped the plastic cuff around the arm of the chair and her wrist. She then pulled the tab through the slide lock.

"Tight, but not too tight. I don't want to leave a mark."

When she was done he told her to put her free arm on the other arm of the chair. He then moved in and grabbed the arm to keep it in place while he looped another snap-cuff around it and locked it. He stepped back to admire his work.

"There."

"Bob, we did a lot of good work together. Why are you doing this?"

He looked down at her and smiled.

"I don't know. But let's talk about it later. I have to finish with Detective Thomas. It's been a long time coming for him and me. And just think, Rachel, you get to watch. What a rare opportunity for you."

Backus turned to Thomas. He stepped over and yanked the gag out of his mouth. He then reached into his pocket and pulled out a folding knife. He opened it and in one swift movement sliced through the cuff holding Thomas's right arm to the chair.

"Now, where were we, Detective Thomas? Line three, I believe."

"More like the end of the line."

Rachel recognized Bosch's voice from behind her. But when she turned to look for him the chair back was too high.

I HELD THE GUN steady, trying to figure out the best way to handle him.

"Harry," Rachel called out calmly. "He's got a gun in his left and a knife in his right. He's right-handed."

I steadied my aim and told him to put the weapons down. He complied without hesitation. This gave me pause, as if he was moving too quickly to plan B. Was there another weapon? Another killer in the house?

"Rachel, Ed, you all right?"

"We're fine," Rachel said. "Put him on the ground, Harry. He's got snap-cuffs in his pocket."

"Rachel, where's your gun?"

"In the other room. Put him down on the ground, Harry."

I took a step further into the room but then paused to study Backus. He had changed again. He no longer looked like the man who had called himself Shandy. No beard, no hat over gray hair. His face and head were shaved. He looked completely different.

I took another step but stopped again. I suddenly thought about Terry McCaleb and his wife and his daughter and his stepson. I thought about the shared mission and what had been lost. How many bad men would roam the world free because Terry was taken away? A rage as strong as the river built inside me. I didn't want to put Backus on the ground, cuff him and watch him driven away in a patrol car to a life behind bars of celebrity attention and fascination. I wanted to take from him everything he had taken from my friend and all of the others.

"You killed my friend," I said. "For that you—"

"Harry, don't," Rachel said.

"I'm sorry," Backus said. "But I've been kind of busy. Who might your friend be?"

"Terry McCaleb. He was your friend, too, and you—"

"Actually, I wanted to take care of Terry. Yes, he had the potential of becoming a stone in my shoe. But I—"

"Shut up, Bob!" Rachel yelled. "You couldn't carry Terry's lunch. Harry, this is too dangerous. Put him down! Do it now!"

I broke off my rage and focused on the moment at hand. Terry McCaleb retreated in the gloom. I stepped toward Backus, wondering what Rachel was telling me. Put him down? Did she want me to shoot him?

I took two more steps.

"Get on the ground," I ordered. "Away from the weapons."

"Whatever you say."

He turned as if to move away from where he had dropped his weapons and to choose a spot to get down.

"Do you mind, there's a puddle here. Leaky fireplace."

Without waiting for an answer from me he took a step toward the window. And I suddenly saw it. I knew what he was going to do.

"Backus, no!"

But my words did not stop him. He planted his foot and dove headfirst into the window. Its framework softened by years of sunlight and rains like this day's, the window gave way as easily as a Hollywood prop. Wood splintered and glass shattered as his body went through. I quickly ran to the opening and saw the immediate muzzle flash from Backus's second gun. Plan B.

Two quick pops and I heard the bullets zing by and hit the ceiling above and behind me. I ducked back behind the wall and fired off two quick returns without looking. I then dropped to the floor, crawled beneath the window and came up on the other side. I looked out and Backus was gone. On the ground I saw a little two-shot derringer. His second had been a little vest gun and he was now unarmed, unless there was a plan C.

"Harry, the knife," Rachel called from behind me. "Cut me loose!"

I grabbed the knife from the floor and quickly sliced through her bonds. The plastic cut easily. I then turned to Thomas and put the knife in his right hand so he could free himself.

"I'm sorry, Ed," I said.

I could give him the rest of the apology later. I turned back to Rachel, who was at the window, looking through the gloom. She had picked up Backus's gun.

"See him?"

I joined her there. Thirty yards to the left was the river wash. Just as I looked I saw the overflowing torrent carrying a whole oak tree on its surface. Then there was movement. We saw Backus jump from the cover of a bougainvillea and start to scale the fence that kept people away from the river. Just as he was going over the top Rachel raised a gun and fired two quick shots. Backus dropped down onto the gravel shoulder next to the channel. But he then jumped up and started running. Rachel had missed.

"He can't get across the river," I said. "He's hemmed in. He's heading up to the bridge at Saticoy."

I knew if Backus made it to the bridge we would lose him. He could cross and disappear in the neighborhood on the west side of the channel or the business district near DeSoto.

"I'll go from here," Rachel said. "You get the car and get there faster. We'll trap him at the bridge."

"Got it."

I headed for the door, getting ready to run through the rain. I pulled my cell phone from my pocket and threw it to Thomas as I went.

"Ed," I called over my shoulder. "Call the cops. Get us some backup."

42

RACHEL EJECTED THE MAGAZINE from Backus's gun and found it had been fully loaded until she took the two shots at him. She slapped it back into place and went to the window.

"You want me to go with you?" Ed Thomas asked from behind.

She turned. He had cut himself free. He was standing, holding the knife up and ready.

"Do what Harry said. Get us backup."

She stepped onto the sill and jumped out into the rain. She quickly moved along the bougainvillea until she found an opening and pushed through to the river fence. She put Backus's gun in her holster and climbed up and over, snagging her jacket sleeve on the top and tearing it. She dropped onto the gravel shoulder two feet from the edge. She looked over the side and saw the water was only three feet from the overflow. It was cascading against the concrete, creating the roaring sound of death. She looked away and then further down the track. She saw Backus running. He was halfway to the bridge at Saticoy. Rachel got up and started running. She fired a shot into the air so he would think about what was coming behind him, not what might be waiting for him at the bridge.

THE MERCEDES SKIDDED INTO the curb on the top of the bridge. I jumped out, not bothering to kill the engine, and ran to the railing. I saw Rachel running toward me, gun up, on the shoulder of the canal. But I didn't see Backus.

I stepped back and looked in all directions but still didn't see him. I thought that it would have been impossible for him to have reached the bridge ahead of me. I ran down to the gate that sided the bridge and offered entrance to the channel's shoulder. It was locked but I could see that the shoulder continued under the bridge. It was the only alternative. I knew Backus had to be hiding under there.

Quickly I climbed over the gate and dropped down to the gravel. I came up, gun pointed in both hands at the dark opening beneath the bridge. I ducked and moved into the darkness.

The noise of the rushing water echoed loudly beneath the bridge. The underside of the bridge was segmented by four large concrete supports. Backus could easily be hidden behind any one of them.

"Backus!" I called out. "You want to live, come out! Now!"

Nothing. Only the sound of the water. Then I heard the far-off sound of a voice and I turned back to see

Rachel. She was still a hundred yards away. She was yelling but her words were lost in the water noise.

BACKUS HUDDLED IN THE darkness. He tried to stave off all the emotions and concentrate on the moment. He had been here before. Cornered in the dark. He had survived before and he would survive now. What was important now was to concentrate on the moment, draw his strength from the darkness.

He heard his pursuer call out to him. He was close now. He had the weapon but Backus had the darkness. Darkness had always been on his side. He pressed back against the concrete and willed himself to disappear in the shadows. He would be patient and make his move when the time was right.

I TURNED AWAY FROM the distant figure of Rachel and focused back on clearing the bridge. I moved forward, staying as far back from the concrete shelters as I could without falling into the channel. I cleared the first two and glanced back at Rachel again. She was fifty yards away now. She started signaling with her left arm but I didn't understand the hooked movement she was repeating.

I suddenly realized my mistake. I had left the keys in the car. Backus could come up on the other side of the bridge and get to the car.

I started to run, hoping to get there in time to take a shot at the tires. But I was wrong about the car. As I passed the third concrete support Backus suddenly leaped out at me, hitting me solidly with his shoulder. I went sprawling backward with him on top of me, sliding on the gravel to the edge of the concrete channel.

He was going for my gun, using both hands to tear it from my grip. I knew in an instant that if he got the gun everything was over, that he'd kill me and then Rachel. He couldn't get the gun.

He slammed his left elbow into my jaw and I felt my grip weaken. I fired the gun twice, hoping I might catch a finger or a palm. He yelped in pain but then I felt the pressure even more as he redoubled his effort, now fueled by pain and red anger.

His blood worked its way into my grip and helped loosen it. I was going to lose the gun. I could tell. He had position on me and an animal strength. My grip was slipping. I could try to hang on a few more seconds until Rachel got there but by then she could also be running into a death trap.

Instead I took the only alternative I had left. I dug my heels into the gravel and flexed my whole body upward. My shoulders slid over the concrete edge. I replanted my heels and did it again. This time it was enough. Backus seemed to suddenly realize his situation. He let go of the gun and reached back to the edge. But it was too late for him, too.

Together we went over the edge and into the black water.

RACHEL SAW THEM FALL from just a few yards away. She yelled *"No!"* as if that might stop them. She got to the spot and looked down and saw nothing. She then ran along the edge and out from beneath the bridge. She saw nothing. She looked downriver for any sign of them in the cascading current.

Then she saw Bosch come up and whip his head around as if to check his position. He was struggling with something under the water and then she realized it was his raincoat. He was trying to take it off.

She scanned the river but didn't see the bald head of Backus anywhere. She looked back at Bosch as he was carried away from her. She saw him looking back at her. He raised an arm out of the water and pointed. She followed and saw the Mercedes parked on top of the bridge. She saw its windshield wipers moving back and forth and she knew the keys were still there.

She started running.

THE WATER WAS COLD, more so than I would have imagined. And I was already weak from the struggle with Backus. I felt heavy in the water and found it difficult to keep my face up and clear. The water seemed to be alive, as if it was gripping me and pulling me down.

My gun was gone and there was no sign of Backus. I spread my arms and tried to maneuver my body so that I could simply ride the rapids until I had some strength back and could make a move or Rachel got help.

I remembered the boy who had gone into the river so many years before. Firemen, cops, even passersby tried to save him, hanging down hoses and ladders and ropes. But they all missed and he went down. Eventually, they all go down in the narrows.

I tried not to think about that. I tried not to panic. I

turned my palms down and I seemed to be able to keep my face up out of the water better. It increased my speed in the current but it kept my head up out of the water. It gave me confidence. I started to think that I could make it. For a while. It all depended on when help got to me. I looked up into the sky. No helicopters. No fire department. No help yet. Just the gray void of emptiness up there and rain coming down.

THE 911 OPERATOR TOLD Rachel to stay on the line but she couldn't drive fast and well and safely with the phone to her ear. She dropped it on the passenger seat without disconnecting. When she came to the next stop sign she stopped so short that the phone was hurled into the foot well and out of her reach. She didn't care. She was speeding down the street checking to her left at every intersection for the next bridge crossing the channel. When she finally saw one she sped to it and stopped the Mercedes right on top of it in a traffic lane. She jumped out and went to the railing.

Neither Bosch nor Backus was in sight. She thought she might have gotten ahead of them. She ran across the street, drawing a horn blast from a motorist but not caring, and went to the opposite rail.

She studied the roiling surface for a long moment and then saw Bosch. His head was above the surface and canted back, his face to the sky. She panicked. Was he still alive? Or was he drowned and his body just moving in the current? Then almost as quickly as the fear had grabbed her she saw movement as Bosch whipped his head, as swimmers often do to get hair and water out of their eyes.

He was alive and maybe a hundred yards from the bridge. She could see him struggling to move his position in the stream. She leaned forward and looked down. She knew what he was doing. He was going to try to catch one of the bridge's support beams. If he could grab it and hold on, he could be extracted and saved right here.

Rachel ran back to the car and threw open the rear hatch. She looked in the back for anything that might help. Her bag was there and almost nothing else. She yanked it out to the ground without caring and lifted the carpeted floor panel. Someone stuck behind the Mercedes on the street started honking. She didn't even turn to look.

I HIT THE MIDDLE pier of the bridge so hard that I lost all of my breath and thought I'd broken four or five ribs. But I held on. I knew this was my shot. I held on with everything I had left.

The water had claws. I could feel them as it rushed by me. Thousands of claws pulling at me, grabbing me, trying to take me back into the dark torrent. The water backed up on me and rose into my face. Arms on either side of the pier, I tried to shimmy up the slippery concrete but every time I gained a few inches, the claws would grab me and pull me back down. I quickly learned that the best I could do was hold on. And wait.

As I hugged the concrete I thought of my daughter. I thought of her urging me to hold on, telling me I had to make it for her. She told me no matter where I was or what I did, she still needed me. Even in the moment, I knew it was illusion but I found comfort in it. I found the strength to hold on.

THERE WERE TOOLS AND a spare tire in the compartment, nothing that would work. Then, beneath the tire, through the design holes in the wheel, she saw black and red cables. Jumper cables.

She put her fingers through the holes in the wheel and yanked it upward. It was large, heavy and awkward but she was not deterred. She pulled the wheel up and out and just dropped it on the road. She grabbed the cables and ran back across the road, causing a car to slide sideways as its driver hit the brakes.

At the railing she looked into the river but didn't see Bosch at first. Then she looked down and saw him clinging to the support beam, the water backing up against him as it grabbed and pulled at him. His hands and fingers were scratched and bloody. He was looking up at her and had what she thought might have been a small smile on his face, almost like he was telling her that he was going to be all right.

Not sure how she was going to complete the rescue, she dropped one end of the cables over the side. They were far too short.

"Shit!"

She knew she had to go over. There was a utility pipe running along the side of the bridge. She knew if she could get down to that she could lower the cables another five feet down. It might be enough.

"Lady, are you all right?"

She turned. There was a man standing there. He was under an umbrella. He had been crossing the bridge.

"There's a man down there in the river. Call nine-one-one. Do you have a cell? Call nine-one-one."

The man began pulling a cell phone from his jacket pocket. Rachel turned back to the railing and started to climb up on it.

That was the easy part. Going over the railing and climbing down to the pipe was the risky maneuver. She put the cables around her neck and slowly reached one foot down to the pipe, then the other. She slid down with one leg on either side of the pipe like she was riding a horse.

This time she knew the cable would reach Bosch. She started lowering it to him and he reached for it. But just as his hand grabbed it, there was a blur of color in the water and Bosch was struck by something and knocked loose from the support beam. In that moment Rachel realized it was Backus, either alive or dead, that had knocked him loose.

She hadn't been ready. When Bosch was knocked loose he kept his grip on the cable line. But his weight and Backus's weight and the current were too much for Rachel. The other end of the cable was jerked out of her grasp and it went down into the water and under the bridge.

"They're coming! They're coming!"

She looked up at the man under the umbrella at the top of the railing.

"It's too late," she said. "He's gone."

* * *

I WAS WEAK BUT Backus was weaker. I could tell he
didn't have the same strength he'd brought to the con-
frontation on the river's edge. He had pulled me loose
from the bridge because I hadn't seen him coming and
he'd hit me with all his weight. But now he was grabbing at me like a drowning man, just trying to hold on.

We tumbled through the water, drawing down to the
bottom. I tried to open my eyes but the water was too
dark to see through. I drove him down hard into the concrete floor and then shifted behind him. I wrapped the
cable I still gripped around his neck. I did it again and
again until his hands let go of me and went to his own
neck. My lungs were burning. I needed air. I pushed off
him to move toward the surface. As we separated he
made a last grab for my ankles but I was able to kick
away and break his grasp.

IN THE LAST MOMENTS Backus saw his father. Long
dead and burned, he appeared alive. He had the stern set
of eyes that Backus always remembered. He had one
hand behind his back, as if he was hiding something. His
other hand beckoned his son to come forward. To come
home.

Backus smiled and then he laughed. Water rushed
into his mouth and lungs. He didn't panic. He welcomed
it. He knew he would be reborn. He would return. He
knew evil could never be vanquished. It just moved
from one place to another and waited.

* * *

I SURFACED AND GULPED down air. I spun in the water to look for Backus but he was gone. I was safe from him but not from the water. I was exhausted. My arms felt so heavy in the water that I could barely bring them to the surface. I thought about the boy again, about how scared he must have been, all alone and the claws grabbing at him.

Up ahead I could see where the wash emptied into the main river channel. I was fifty yards away and I knew the river would be wider and shallower and more violent there. But the concrete walls were sloped in the main channel and I knew I might have a shot at pulling myself out if I could somehow slow my speed and find purchase.

I lowered my eyes and decided to move as close to the wall as I could without getting pushed hard into it. Then I saw a more immediate salvation. The tree I had seen in the channel from the window of Turrentine's house was a hundred yards ahead of me in the river. It must have gotten hung up at the bridge or in the shallows and I had caught up to it.

Using my last reserve of strength I started swimming with the current, picking up speed and heading to the tree. I knew it would be my boat. I'd be able to ride it all the way to the Pacific if I needed to.

RACHEL LOST THE RIVER. The streets took her further away from it and soon she had lost it. She couldn't get back to it. There was a GPS screen in the car but she didn't know how to work it and doubted she'd be able to get a satellite fix in this weather anyway. She pulled over and banged the wheel angrily with the heel of her palm. She felt like she was deserting Harry, that it was going to be her fault if he drowned.

Then she heard the helicopter. It was low flying and moving fast. She leaned forward to see up through the windshield. She didn't see anything. She got out in the rain and turned circles on the street looking. She could still hear it but she couldn't see it.

It had to be the rescue, she thought. In this weather, who else would be flying? She got a bead on the sound and jumped back into the Mercedes. She took the first right she came to and started heading to the sound. She drove with the window down, with the rain coming in but her not caring. She listened to the sound of the helicopter in the distance.

Soon she saw it. It was circling ahead and to the right. She kept going and when she came to Reseda Boulevard she turned right again and could see there were actually two helicopters, one low and the other above it. Both were red with white lettering on the side. Not television or radio call letters. The helicopters were marked LAFD.

There was a bridge ahead and Rachel could see cars stopped and people getting out in the rain to rush to the railing. They were looking down into the river.

She pulled up, stopped in a traffic lane and did the same. She rushed to the railing in time to see the rescue. Bosch was in a yellow safety harness being lifted on a wire out of a fallen tree that was stalled in the shallows where the river widened to fifty yards across.

As he was raised to the helicopter Bosch looked down into the raging current below him. Soon the tree broke free of its catch and tumbled over and over in the cascades. It picked up speed and washed beneath the bridge, its branches crashing into the support pylons and shearing off.

Rachel watched the rescuers bring Bosch into the helicopter. Not until he was inside and safe and the helicopter started to bank away did she look away. And that was only when some of the others on the bridge had started to yell and point down into the river. She looked down and saw what it was. Another man in the water. But for this man there would be no rescue. He floated facedown, his arms loose and his body limp. Red and black jumper cables were tangled around his body and neck. His shaven skull looked like a child's lost ball bobbing in the current.

The second helicopter followed the body from above, waiting for it to get hung up like the tree had before any extraction was risked. There was no hurry this time.

As the current thickened to move between the pylons of the bridge, the body's fluid travel was disturbed and it turned over in the water. Just before it went under the bridge Rachel caught a glimpse of Backus's face. His eyes were open beneath the glaze of water. But it seemed to her that he was looking right at her before he disappeared under the bridge.

MANY YEARS AGO, WHEN I served in the army in Vietnam, I was wounded in a tunnel. I was extracted by my comrades and put on a helicopter back to base camp. I remember that as the chopper rose and took me from harm's way, I felt an elation that far obscured the pain of my wound and the exhaustion I had felt.

I felt the same way that day on the river. Déjà vu all over again, as they say. I had made it. I had survived. I was out of harm's way. I was smiling as a fireman in a safety helmet wrapped a blanket around me.

"We're taking you to USC to get checked out," he yelled over the roar of the rotor and the rain. "ETA in ten minutes."

He gave me the okay sign and I gave it back to him, noticing that my fingers were a bluish white and that I was shaking with something more than cold.

"I'm sorry about your friend," the fireman yelled.

I saw he was looking down through a glass panel on the lower part of the door he had just slid closed. I leaned over and looked and I could see Backus in the water below. He was faceup and moving languidly in the current.

"I'm not sorry," I said, but not loud enough to be heard.

I leaned back on the jump seat they had put me on. I closed my eyes and nodded to the conjured image of my silent partner, Terry McCaleb, smiling and standing in the stern of his boat.

43

THE SKIES CLEARED A couple days later and the city started to dry out and dig out. There had been landslides in Malibu and Topanga. The coast highway was down to two lanes for the foreseeable future. In the Hollywood Hills there had been flooding in the lower streets. One house on Fareholm Drive had broken free and was washed into the street, leaving an aging movie star homeless. Two deaths were attributed to the storm—a golfer who had inexplicably decided to get in a few holes between bands of the storm and was hit on a backswing by a bolt of lightning, and Robert Backus, the fugitive serial killer. The Poet was dead, the headlines and news anchors said. Backus's body was fished out of the river at the Sepulveda Dam. Cause of death: drowning.

The seas calmed, too, and I took a morning ferry out to Catalina to see Graciela McCaleb. I rented a golf cart and drove up to the house, where she answered the door and received me with her family. I met Raymond, the adopted son, and Cielo, the girl Terry had told me about. Meeting her made me miss my own daughter and reminded me of the new vulnerability I would soon have in my life.

The house was filled with boxes and Graciela explained that the storm had delayed their move back to the mainland. In another day their belongings would be shuttled down to a barge and then taken across to the port, where a moving truck would be waiting. It was complicated and expensive but she had no regrets. She wanted to leave the island and the memories it held.

We went out to the table on the porch so we could talk without the children hearing. It was a nice spot with a view of all of Avalon Harbor. It made it hard to believe she wanted to leave. I could see *The Following Sea* down there and I noticed there was someone in the stern and that one of the deck hatches was open.

"Is that Buddy down there?"

"Yes, he's getting ready to move the boat. The FBI brought it back yesterday without calling ahead. I would have told them to take it to Cabrillo. Now Buddy has to do it."

"What's he going to do with it?"

"He's going to continue the business. He'll run the charters from over there and pay me rent on the boat."

I nodded. It sounded like a decent plan.

"Selling the boat wouldn't bring that much in. And, I don't know, Terry worked so hard on that boat. It feels wrong to just sell it to a stranger."

"I understand."

"You know, you could probably get a ride back with

Buddy instead of waiting for the ferry. If you want. If you're not sick of Buddy."

"No, Buddy's fine. I like Buddy."

We sat in silence for a long moment. I didn't feel I needed to explain anything about the case to her. We had talked on the phone—because I wanted to explain things before it hit the media—and the story had been all over the papers and television. She knew the details, large and small. There was little left to say but I thought I needed to visit with her in person one last time. It had all started with her. I figured it should end with her as well.

"Thank you for what you did," Graciela said. "Are you all right?"

"I'm fine. Just a few scratches and bruises from the river. It was a wild ride."

I smiled. The only visible injuries I had were scrapes on my hands and one above my left eyebrow.

"But thank you for calling me. I'm glad I got the chance. That's why I came, just to say thanks and to say good luck with everything."

The sliding door opened and the little girl came out carrying a book.

"Mommy, will you read this to me now?"

"I'm visiting with Mr. Bosch right now. In a little while, okay?"

"No, I want you to read it now."

The girl looked like it was a life-or-death request and her face knotted up, ready for a cry.

"It's okay," I said. "Mine's like that, too. You can read it."

"It's her favorite book. Terry used to read it to her just about every night."

She pulled the girl up onto her lap and brought the book up to read. I saw that it was the same book Eleanor had just gotten for my daughter. *Billy's Big Day,* with the monkey receiving the gold medal on the cover. Cielo's copy was worn around the edges from reading and rereading. The cover had been ripped in two places and then taped.

Graciela opened it and started to read.

"One bright summer day the circus animal Olympics were held under the big top in Ringlingville. All the animals had the day off from all of the circuses and were allowed to compete in the many different events."

I noticed that Graciela had changed her voice and was reading the story with an inflection of excitement and anticipation.

"All the animals lined up at the bulletin board outside Mr. Farnsworth's office. The list of events was posted on the board. There were races and relays and many other contests. The big animals got closest to the board and were crowding it, so the others couldn't see. A little monkey squeezed between the legs of an elephant and then climbed the pachyderm's trunk so that he could see the list. Billy Bing smiled when he finally saw it. There was one race called the hundred-yard dash and he knew he was very good at dashing."

I didn't hear the rest of the story after that. I got up and went to the railing and looked down into the harbor. But I didn't see anything down there either. My mind was too busy for the external world. I was flooded with ideas

and emotions. I suddenly knew that the name William
Bing, the name Terry McCaleb had scrawled on the flap
of his file, belonged to a monkey. And I suddenly knew
that the story wasn't finished, not by a long shot.

44

RACHEL CAME TO SEE me at my house later that day. I had just gotten in after filing my paperwork with Kiz Rider at Parker Center and was listening to a phone message from Ed Thomas. He was thanking me for saving his life when all along it was I who owed him an apology for not warning him in the first place. I was feeling guilty about that and thinking about calling the bookstore when Rachel knocked. I invited her in and we went out to the back deck.

"Wow, nice view."

"Yeah, I like it."

I pointed down to the left, where a small cut of the river was in the view behind the soundstages on the Warner Brothers lot.

"There it is, the mighty Los Angeles River."

She squinted and looked and then found it.

"The narrows. Looks pretty weak right now."

"It's resting. Next storm, it will be back."

"How are you feeling, Harry?"

"Good. Better. I've been sleeping a lot. I'm surprised you're still in town."

"Well, I took a few days. I'm actually looking at apartments."

"Really?"

I turned with my back to the railing so I could just look at her.

"I'm pretty sure this whole thing will be my ticket out of South Dakota. I don't know what squad they'll put me on but I'm going to ask for L.A. Or I was, until I saw what some of these apartments go for. In Rapid City I pay five-fifty a month for a really nice and secure place."

"I could find you five-fifty here but you probably won't like the location. You'd probably have to learn another language, too."

"No, thanks. I'm working on it. So what have you been doing?"

"I just came back from Parker Center. I put in my papers. I'm going back on the job."

"Then I guess this is it for us. I heard the FBI and the LAPD don't talk."

"Yeah, there is a wall there. But it's been known to come down from time to time. I have some friends with the bureau. Believe it or not."

"I believe it, Harry."

I noticed that she was back to calling me by my first name. I wondered if that meant the relationship was over.

"So," I said, "when did you know about McCaleb?"

"What do you mean? Know what?"

"I mean when did you know that Backus didn't kill him? That he killed himself."

She put both hands on the railing and looked down into the arroyo. But she wasn't really looking at anything down there.

"Harry, what are you talking about?"

"I found out who William Bing is. He's a monkey from the pages of his daughter's favorite book."

"So? What's that mean?"

"It means he checked himself into the hospital in Vegas under a phony name. He had something wrong with him, Rachel. Something inside."

I touched the center of my chest.

"Maybe he was chasing the case, maybe not. But he knew something was wrong and he went over there to that hospital to have it checked and to keep it quiet. He didn't want his wife and his family to know. And so they checked him out and gave him the bad news. His second heart was going the way his first one went. Cardio . . . myo . . . whatever it's called. Bottom line was he was dying. He needed another heart or he was going to die."

Rachel shook her head like I was a fool.

"I don't know how you think you know all of this but you can't possib—"

"Look, I know what I know. And I know he had already burned through his medical insurance and if he was going to get in line for another heart, they would lose everything, the house, the boat, everything. Everything for another heart."

I paused and then continued in a quiet and calm voice.

"He didn't want that. He also didn't want his family to see him waste away and die, on the public dole. And he didn't like the idea of another person dying so he could live. He had already been through that, too."

I stopped there to see if she would protest again and try to dissuade me. She remained silent this time.

"The only things he had left were his life insurance and his pension. He wanted them to have that. So he was the one who changed out his pills. There's a receipt for a health food store under the seat of his car. I called there this morning to see if they sell powdered shark cartilage. They do.

"He changed out his pills and just kept on taking them. He figured as long as he made a show of taking them there'd be no autopsy and everything would work out fine."

"But it didn't, did it?"

"No, but he had a backup plan for that, too. That's why he waited for the long charter. He wanted to die out there on the boat. He wanted it to be in waters that would come under federal jurisdiction. His hope was that if anything came of it, his friends in the bureau would take care of everything for him.

"The only problem with his whole big plan was that he had no idea about the Poet. He had no idea his wife would come to me or that a few lines scribbled in a file would lead to all that happened."

I shook my head.

"I should have seen it. The med switch wasn't Backus's style. Too complicated. The complicated ones are usually inside jobs."

"What about the threat to his family? Whether or not he knew it was Backus, he knew somebody had threatened his family. He got those photographs—somebody stalking his family. You are saying he checked out and left his family at risk? That's not the Terry McCaleb I knew."

"Maybe he thought he was ending the risk. The threat to his family was aimed at him. If he was gone, then so, too, was the threat."

Rachel nodded, but it wasn't in any sort of confirmation.

"If nothing else, your fact chain is interesting, Harry. I'll give you that. But what makes you think we know about this, that I know about it?"

"Oh, you know. The way you dismissed my questions about William Bing for one thing. But the other is what you did in that house the other day. When I had the gun on Backus, he was about to say something about Terry and you cut him off. You jumped all over what he was about to say. I think he was about to say he didn't kill Terry."

"Oh, yeah, a killer denying one of his victims. Isn't that unusual."

Her sarcasm sounded defensive to me.

"This time it would have been. He was no longer hiding. He was out in the open and he would have taken credit if credit was due him. You knew that and that's why you cut him off. You knew he was going to deny it."

She came away from the railing and stood in front of me.

"Okay, Harry, you think you've got it all figured out. You found a sad little suicide hidden in all the murders. What are you going to do with it? You going to go out there and announce it to the world? The only thing that might do is take the money away from the family. Is that what you want? Maybe you can get a piece of it as the whistleblower reward."

Now I turned away from her and leaned down on the railing.

"No, I don't want that. I just don't like being lied to."

"Oh, I get it. This really isn't about Terry. It's about you and me, isn't it?"

"I don't know what it's about, Rachel."

"Well, when you do, when you figure it all out, let me know, okay?"

She suddenly came up next to me and kissed me hard on the cheek.

"Good-bye, Bosch. Maybe I'll see you around once the transfer comes through."

I didn't turn around to watch her go. I listened as her angry footsteps crossed the deck and then the maple floor inside. I heard the front door slam with a finality that reverberated right through me. It was that tumbling bullet again.

45

I STOOD ON THE porch, elbows on the railing, for a
long time after Rachel left. My guess was that I
would never see her again, whether or not she took a
transfer to Los Angeles. I felt a loss. I felt like something
good had been taken from me before I really knew how
good it could be.

I tried to put her out of my mind for a little while.
Terry McCaleb, too. I looked out at the city and thought
it was beautiful. The rain had cleaned the sky out and I
could see all the way to the San Gabriels and the snow-
covered peaks beyond. The air seemed to be as clean
and as pure as the air breathed by the Gabrieleños and
the padres so many years before. I saw what they had
seen in the place. It was the kind of day you felt you
could build a future on.

Acknowledgments

THE AUTHOR WOULD LIKE to thank many individuals who helped with the writing of this book. They include Michael Pietsch, Jane Wood, Pamela Marshall, Perdita Burlingame, Jane Davis, Terry Hansen, Terrill Lee Lankford, Ed Thomas, Frederike Leffelaar, Jerry Hooten, and researcher Carolyn Chriss. Also of great help to the author were Philip Spitzer, Joel Gotler, Shannon Byrne, Sophie Cottrell, John Houghton, Mario Pulice, Mary Capps, Ken Delavigne, Patricia and George Companioni, and the entire staff at Little, Brown and Company as well as the Time Warner Book Group.

Two books that were very helpful to the author were *Zzyzx: History of an Oasis,* by Anne Q. Duffield-Stoll, and *Rio L.A.: Tales from the Los Angeles River,* by Patt Morrison with photographs by Mark Lamonica.

Special thanks go to Chief William Bratton and Detective Tim Marcia of the Los Angeles Police Department and special agents Gayle Jacobs and Nina Roesberry of the FBI's Las Vegas field office.

MICHAEL CONNELLY is a former journalist and author of the bestselling series of Harry Bosch novels, along with the bestselling novels *Chasing the Dime, Void Moon, Blood Work,* and *The Poet.* Connelly has won numerous awards for his journalism and novels, including an Edgar Award. He is currently the president of the Mystery Writers of America.

I

WITHIN THE PRACTICE and protocol of the Los Angeles Police Department a two-six call is the one that draws the most immediate response while striking the most fear behind the bulletproof vest. For it is a call that often has a career riding on it. The designation is derived from the combination of the code two radio call out, meaning *Respond as soon as possible*, and the sixth floor of Parker Center from which the chief of police commands the department. A two-six is a forthwith from the chief's office and any officer who knows and enjoys his position in the department will not delay.

Detective Harry Bosch spent over twenty-five years with the department in his first tour and never once received a forthwith from the chief of police. In fact, other than receiving his badge at the academy in 1972, he never shook hands or spoke personally with a chief again. He had outlasted several of them—and, of course, seen them at police functions and funerals—but simply never met them along the way. On the morning of his return to duty after a three-year retirement he received his first two-six while knotting his tie in the bathroom mirror. It was an adjutant to the chief calling Bosch's private cell phone. Bosch didn't bother asking how they had come up with the number in the chief's office. It was simply understood that the chief's office had the power to reach out in such a way. Bosch just said he was on the way. He finished knotting his tie in his car while driving as fast as traffic allowed on the 101 Freeway toward downtown.

It took Bosch exactly twenty-four minutes from the moment he closed the phone on the adjutant until he walked through the double doors of the chief's suite on the sixth floor at Parker Center. He thought it had to have been some kind of record, notwithstanding the fact that he had illegally parked on Los Angeles Street in front of the police headquarters. If they knew his private cell number, then surely they knew what a feat it had been to make it from the Hollywood Hills to the chief's office in under a half hour.

But the adjutant, a lieutenant named Hohman, stared him down with disinterested eyes and pointed to a plastic-sealed couch that already had two other people sitting on it.

"You're late," he said. "Take a seat."

Bosch decided not to protest, not to make matters possibly worse. He stepped over to the couch and sat between the two uniformed men who had staked out the armrests. They sat bolt upright and did not make small talk. He figured they had been two-sixed as well.

Ten minutes went by. The men on either side of him were called in ahead of Bosch, each dispensed with by the chief in five minutes flat. While the second man was in with the chief, Bosch thought he heard loud voices from the inner sanctum and when the officer came out his face was ashen. He had somehow fucked up in the eyes of the chief and the word——which had even filtered to Bosch in retirement——was that this new man did not suffer fuckups lightly. Bosch had read a story in the *Times* about a command staffer who was demoted for failing to inform the chief that the son of a city councilman usually allied against the department had been picked up on a deuce. The chief only found out about it when the councilman called to complain about harassment, as if the department had forced his son to drink six vodka martinis at Bar Marmount and drive home via the trunk of a tree on Mulholland.

Finally Hohman put down the phone and pointed his finger at Bosch. He was up. He was quickly shuttled into a corner office with a view of the Union Station and the surrounding train yards. It was a decent view but not a great one. It didn't matter because the place was coming down soon. The department would move into temporary offices while a new and modern police headquarters was rebuilt on the same spot. The current headquarters was known as the Glass House by the rank and file, supposedly because there were no secrets kept inside. Bosch wondered what the next place would become known as.

The chief of police was behind a large desk, signing papers. Without looking up from this work he told Bosch to have a seat in front of the desk. Within thirty seconds the chief signed his last document and looked up at Bosch. He smiled.

"I wanted to meet you and welcome you back to the department."

His voice was marked by an eastern accent. *De-pahtment.* This was fine with Bosch. In L.A. everybody was from somewhere else. Or so it seemed. It was both the strength and the weakness of the city.

"It is good to be back," Bosch said.

"You understand that you are here at my pleasure."

It wasn't a question. "Yes, sir, I do."

"Obviously, I checked you out extensively before approving your return. I had concerns about your . . . shall we say *style,* but ultimately your talent won the day. You can also thank your partner, Kizmin Rider, for her lobbying effort. She's a good officer and I trust her. She trusts you."

"I have already thanked her but I will do it again."

"I know it has been less than three years since you retired but let me assure you, Detective Bosch, that the department you have rejoined is not the department you left."

"I understand that."

"I hope so. You know about the consent decree?"

Just after Bosch had left the department the previous chief had been forced to agree to a series of reforms in order to head off a federal takeover of the LAPD following an FBI investigation into wholesale corruption, violence, and civil rights violations within the ranks. The current chief had to carry out the agreement or he would end up taking orders from the FBI. From the chief down to the lowliest boot, nobody wanted that.

"Yes," Bosch said. "I've read about it."

"Good. I'm glad you have kept yourself informed. And I am happy to report that despite what you may read in the *Times*, we are making great strides and we want to keep that momentum. We are also trying to update the department in terms of technology. We are pushing forward in community policing. We are doing a lot of good things, Detective Bosch, much of which can be undone in the eyes of the community if we resort to old ways. Do you understand what I am telling you?"

"I think so."

"Your return here is not guaranteed. You are on probation for a year, so consider yourself a rookie again. A boot—the oldest living boot at that. I approved your return—I can also wash you out without so much as a reason anytime in the course of the year. Don't give me a reason."

Bosch didn't answer. He didn't think he was supposed to.

"On Friday we graduate a new class of cadets at the academy. I would like you to be there."

"Sir?"

"I want you to be there. I want you to see the dedication in our young people's faces. I want to reacquaint you with the traditions of this department. I think it could help you, help you rededicate yourself."

"If you want me to be there I will be there."

"Good. I will see you there. You will sit under the VIP tent as my guest."

He made a note about the invite on a pad of paper next to the blotter. He then put the pen down and raised his hand to point a finger at Bosch. His eyes took on a fierceness.

"Listen to me, Bosch. Don't ever break the law to enforce the law. At all times you do your job constitutionally and compassionately. I will accept no other way. This *city* will accept no other way. Are we okay on that?"

"We are okay."

"Then we are good to go."

Bosch took his cue and stood up. The chief surprised him by also standing and extending his hand. Bosch thought he wanted to shake hands and extended his own. The chief put something in his hand and Bosch looked down to see a gold detective's shield. He had his old number back; it had not been given away. He almost smiled.

"Wear it well," the police chief said. "And proudly."

"I will."

Now they shook hands but as they did so the chief didn't smile.

"The chorus of forgotten voices," he said.

"Excuse me, Chief?"

"That's what I think about when I think of the cases down there in Open-Unsolved. It's a house of horrors. Our greatest shame. All those cases. All those voices. Every one of them is like a stone thrown into a lake. The ripples move out through time and people. Families, friends, neighbors. How can we call ourselves a city when there are so many ripples, when so many voices have been forgotten by this department?"

Bosch let go of his hand and didn't say anything. There was no answer for the chief's question.

"I changed the name of the unit when I came into the department. Those aren't cold cases, Detective. They never go cold. Not for some people."

"I understand that."

"Then go down there and clear cases. That's what your art is. That's why we need you and why you are here. That's why I am taking a chance with you. Show them we do not forget. Show them that in Los Angeles cases don't go cold."

"I will."

Bosch left him there, still standing, maybe a little haunted by the voices. Like himself. Bosch thought that maybe for the first time he had actually connected on some level with the man at the top. In the military it is said that when you go into battle you are willing to die for the men who sent you. Bosch had never felt that when he was moving through the darkness of the tunnels in Vietnam. He had felt alone and that he was fighting for himself, fighting to stay alive. That feeling had come with him into the department and he had, at times, adopted the view that he was fighting *in spite* of the men at the top. Now maybe things would be different.

In the hallway he punched the elevator button harder than he needed to. He had too much excitement and energy and he understood this. *The chorus of forgotten voices.* The chief seemed to know the song they were singing. And Bosch certainly did, too. Most of his life had been spent listening to that song.

2

B OSCH RODE THE elevator just one flight down to five.
This, too, was new territory for him. Five had always
been a civilian floor. It primarily housed many of the department's mid- and low-level administrative offices, most
of them filled with non-sworn employees, budgeters, ana-
lysts, pencil pushers. Civilians. Before now there had been
no reason to come to the fifth.

There were no placards in the elevator lobby that
pointed the way to specific offices. It was the kind of floor
where you knew where you were going before you stepped
off the elevator. But not Bosch. The hallways on the floor
formed the letter *H* and he went the wrong way twice before finally finding the door marked 503. There was nothing else on the door. He paused before opening it and
thought about what he was doing and what he was starting.
He knew it was the right thing. It was almost as if he could
hear the voices coming through the door. All eight thousand of them.

Kiz Rider was sitting on a desk just inside, sipping a cup
of steaming coffee. The desk looked like a place for a

receptionist but Bosch knew from his frequent calls in the prior weeks that there was no receptionist in this squad. There was no money for such a luxury. Rider raised her wrist and shook her head as she checked her watch.

"I thought we agreed on eight o'clock," she said. "Is that how it's going to be, partner? You waltzing in every morning whenever you feel like it?"

Bosch looked at his watch. It was five minutes after eight. He looked back at her and smiled.

Rider smiled back and said, "We're over here."

She was a short woman who carried a few extra pounds. Her hair was short and now had some gray in it. She was very dark complected, which made her smile all the more brilliant. She slipped off the desk and raised a second cup of coffee to him.

"See if I remembered that right."

He checked and nodded.

"Black, just like I like my partners."

"Funny. I'll have to write you up for that."

She led the way. The office seemed to be empty. It was large, even for a squad room serving nine investigators—four teams and an OIC. The walls were painted a light shade of blue, like Bosch often saw on the screens of computers. The floors were carpeted in gray. There were no windows; where they should have been were bulletin boards or nicely framed crime scene photos from many years back. Bosch could tell that in these black-and-whites the photographers had often put their artistic skills ahead of their clinical duties. The shots were heavy on mood and shadows. Not many of the crimes scene details were apparent. Rider must have known he was looking at the photos.

"They told me that the writer James Ellroy picked these out and had them framed for the office," she said.

She led him around a partial wall that broke the room in two and into an alcove where two gray steel desks were pushed together so the detectives who sat at them would face each other. Rider put her coffee down on one. There were already files stacked on it and personal things like a coffee mug full of pens and a picture frame at an angle that hid the photo it held. A laptop computer was open and humming on the desk. She had moved into the squad the week before while Bosch was still clearing customs—customs being the medical exam and final paperwork that brought him back onto the job.

The other desk was clean, empty, and waiting for him. He moved behind it and put his coffee down. He suppressed a smile as well as he could.

"Welcome back, Roy," Rider said.

That made the smile break through. It made Bosch feel good to be called Roy again. It was a tradition carried by many of the city's homicide detectives. There was a legendary homicide man named Russell Kuster who worked out of Hollywood Division many years back. He was the ultimate professional and many of the detectives working murders in the city today had come under his tutelage at one point or another. He was killed in an off-duty shoot-out in 1990. But his habit of calling people Roy—no matter their real name—was carried on. Its origin had become obscure. Some said it was because Kuster once had a partner who loved Roy Acuff and it had started with him. Others said it was because Kuster liked the idea of the homicide cop being the Roy Rogers type, wearing the white hat and riding to the rescue, making things right. It didn't matter anymore. Bosch knew it was an honor just to be called Roy again.

He sat down. The chair was old and lumpy, guaranteed

to give him a backache if he spent too much time on it. But he hoped that would not be the case. In his first run as a homicide detective he had lived by the adage *Get off your ass and knock on doors.* He didn't see any reason that should change this time around.

"Where is everybody?" he asked.

"Having breakfast. I forgot. They told me last week that the routine is that on Monday mornings everybody meets early for breakfast. They usually go over to the Pacific. I didn't remember until I got in here this morning and found the place dead, but they should be back here soon."

Bosch knew the Pacific Dining Car was a longtime favorite with LAPD brass and the Robbery-Homicide Division. He also knew something else.

"Twelve bucks for a plate of eggs. I guess that means this is an overtime approved squad."

Rider smiled in confirmation.

"You got that right. But you wouldn't have been able to finish your fancy eggs anyway, once you got the forthwith from the chief."

"You heard about that, huh?"

"I still have an ear out on six. Did you get your badge?"

"Yeah, he gave it to me."

"I told him what number you'd want. Did you get it?"

"Yeah, Kiz, thanks. Thanks for everything."

"You already told me that, partner. You don't need to keep saying that."

He nodded and looked around their space. He noticed that on the wall behind Rider was a photo of two detectives huddled beside a body lying in the dry concrete bed of the Los Angeles River. It looked like a shot from the early fifties, judging by the hats the detectives wore.

"So, where do we start?" he asked.

"The squad breaks the cases up in three-year incre-
ments. It provides some continuity. They say you get to
know the era and some of the players in the department. It
overlaps. It also helps with identifying serials. In two years
they've already come up with four serials nobody ever
knew about."

Bosch nodded. He was impressed.

"What years did we get?" he asked.

"Each team has four or five blocks. Since we're the new
team we got four."

She opened the middle drawer of her desk and took out
a piece of paper and handed it across to him.

Bosch / Rider—Case Assignments

1966	1972	1987	1996
1967	1973	1988	1997
1968	1974	1989	1998

Bosch studied the listing of years for which they would
be responsible. He had been out of the city and in Vietnam
for most of the first block.

"The summer of love," he said. "I missed it. Maybe
that's what's wrong with me."

He said it just to be saying something. He noticed that
the second block included 1972, the year he had come onto
the force. He remembered a call out to a house off Vermont
on his second day on the job in patrol. A woman back east
asked police to check on her mother who was not answering the phone. Bosch found her drowned in a bathtub, her
hands and feet bound with dog leashes. Her dead dog was
in the tub with her. Bosch wondered if the old woman's

murder was one of the open cases he would now be charged with solving.

"How was this arrived at? I mean, why did we get these years?"

"They came from the other teams. We lightened their caseload. In fact, they already started the ball rolling on cases from a lot of those years. And I heard on Friday that a cold hit came in from eighty-eight. We're supposed to run with it starting today. I guess you could say it's your welcome back present."